What's Mine and Yours

WHAT'S MINE
AND YOURS

A NOVEL

NAIMA COSTER

THORNDIKE PRESS
A part of Gale, a Cengage Company

LIBRARY OF CONGRESS CIP DATA ON FILE.
CATALOGUING IN PUBLICATION FOR THIS BOOK
IS AVAILABLE FROM THE LIBRARY OF CONGRESS.

ISBN-13: 978-1-4328-8978-4 (hardcover alk. paper)

Published in 2021 by arrangement with Grand Central Publishing, division of Hachette Book Group, Inc.

Printed in Mexico
Print Number: 01   Print Year: 2022

What's Mine and Yours

1

The street was dark when Ray pulled up behind the bakery. The birds sang wild in the trees, the only things astir so early in the morning, the sky a deep and cloudless blue. His little boy, Gee, was asleep in the backseat, neat in his school clothes and fogging up the window with his breath. Ray lifted him out quietly, the keys to the shop jangling in his free hand. They walked around to the front, and the boy was already drooling on him, on his pressed collared shirt, red-and-pink plaid.

"My good luck charm," Ray whispered as he unlocked the gate, holding the boy close.

Superfine stood near the corner of Beard Street, about a mile north of the city square. A neon sign hung out front, the window boxes planted with yellow mums. This part of town used to be where people would fuel up before driving out of the city, or if they were passing through downtown. There was a garage at the end of the block and a gas station where you could pay only in cash. Otherwise, the neighborhood was empty lots, one-story houses, a ballfield the minor league used in the summer. Wildflowers and busted tires swelled out of the plots of land where the old factories were boarded up. But in the past year, a brewing company had opened in one of the old buildings. They gave tours and served beer in tiny glasses. A lunch window had opened to serve chopped barbecue and hot dogs for a few hours every day. And there was Super-fine, which was open from dawn until dusk. They served biscuits and breakfast pastries, coffee, in the morning. At lunch, they sold sandwiches and fresh-baked bread. In the afternoon, they added cookies and lemon bars, slices of chocolate cake. Customers trickled in on their way to work downtown or stopped by to sober up after drunk tours at the brewery across the street. Superfine was cheaper than the coffee stand down-town, and it was the only place this close to get a fresh ham sandwich, a biscuit and peach jam, coffee that didn't taste like hot water and tar mixed together.

It had been Ray's idea to open the shop, although Linette was the one who bank-rolled it with the money she got from her husband's life insurance. They knew each other from a job at a coffeehouse an hour away where she had been the manager and he a barista. He'd worked three jobs then, but now Superfine was his everything.

Ray set the boy down on the bench by the windowsill. He ran behind the counter to fetch a bottle of cold coffee from the refrigerator. He dribbled an ounce or two into a glass of milk, stirred it with his finger, and then took it to Gee. He was spread out on the cushions by the window, one arm flung behind his head, the other across his chest, palm flat, as if he were trying to protect himself, to cover up his heart while he slept.

"Morning, my man," Ray whispered. "Drink this," he said, holding the glass to the boy's mouth. Gee would have a longer day than Ray wanted him to. A little caffeine wouldn't hurt him.

"Daddy, why'd you bring me here?"

"Well, it's a big day for me. I thought you could be my helper."

Gee shone at the prospect, sat a little taller in the window.

"Am I still going to school today?"

"We go to school every day," Ray said. "I'll run you over when it's time. Come on now, let's get you an apron."

They had to fold the apron over twice so it would fit Gee, who was small even for a six-year-old. Gee laughed at the sight of himself in the mirror. He was missing one of his front teeth, a baby tooth he'd chipped so badly they'd needed to get it pulled, but he was still a beautiful boy: brown skinned and brown haired with big hands and feet for his stature. He had a cleft in his chin, and dimples, eyes that watered when he smiled. He had a hoarse whisper of a voice that Ray liked to joke was from talking too much. Gee was a truth teller: he liked to tell about what he saw, and he saw everything. It made Ray nervous that one day the boy would tell the truth about the wrong thing.

They rolled up their sleeves and washed their hands in the sink. Then Ray sat Gee on a stool in the kitchen and told him to turn on the radio. Ray started folding up croissants and sliding them into the proof box. He made pretty knots of dough for the morning buns, sprinkled them with sugar. He explained what he was doing and sometimes asked Gee how much butter he thought he should brush on top of the biscuits, whether the dough had come out of the sheeter smooth. It was the only way he could let Gee help this morning. This

10

was a day that could change their lives — for the shop, for Linette, but most of all for him and Gee and Jade. If business picked up after the story came out, like they hoped it would, Ray had a list of things he'd do — he'd buy Jade a ruby ring and ask her to marry him; he'd buy Gee a set of drawers to keep his things; they'd go on a trip somewhere, like Washington, DC, or Florida. He'd take pictures of Gee in front of the Lincoln Memorial, Jade in front of the cherry blossoms, all of them in front of the castle at the Magic Kingdom — they'd ask a stranger to take the shot, and put Gee in those funny ears.

But first, the reporter, and the feature on Beard Street, the way it was coming back to life. *We've got to steal the show,* Linette had said, and Ray knew she was right. He was making a special just for the day — a devil's food cake doughnut. He'd spent the weekend perfecting the recipe with Gee. What Ray loved about doughnuts was that nobody really needed them. Coffee, you could get hooked on to the point where you couldn't live without it. But doughnuts — soft, rolled in cinnamon sugar, glazed, dripping with caramel, fat with fruit at the center — had no reason for being. They were his secret power, his mark on Superfine.

11

Linette arrived at seven a.m., just before they were set to open. Gee was counting out quarters into the register, Ray listing the day's pastries on the chalkboard menu. He had named his doughnut Gee's Devil's Food, which had given the child a thrill.

Linette came in carrying an armload of gardenias in waxed paper. She looked ready for battle. Ray liked to tease her that he'd be an old man before she retired and left him the shop. She drank, on average, six cups of coffee a day, and she never stopped moving. She was all muscle and fat, gray haired, her face painted in a different palette of bright colors every morning. She brought in with her the scent of perfume and hair oil, a pair of shears sticking out of her purse.

"You look tired, Raymond. Didn't you know they were going to take our picture? I was counting on your face to bring in the ladies."

Linette laughed at her own joke, and Gee went running to meet her. He stopped short, waiting for her to react to him, to put her arms around him or pick him up. He could be like this — hesitant — as if he didn't expect to get the things he wanted.

Ray didn't like to see him that way.

"Go on and give Ms. Linette a hug," he said. "Say good morning." He measured coffee into the grinder and started the machine.

"What's my big boy Gee doing here?"

"Daddy needed my help." Gee pointed proudly to the sign with the name of his doughnut.

"Devil's food? But you're too sweet. Does that mean this doughnut is going to be too sweet?" Linette sent the boy, laughing, off to wash his hands. When he was out of earshot, she turned to Ray. "Today of all days?"

"He didn't slow me down, I promise."

Linette shook her head and started putting the gardenias in tiny bloom vases she'd brought along in her purse.

"Doesn't that boy have school today?"

"I won't be gone more than five minutes when I run him there."

"I thought that was his mama's job."

"He's my son, too."

"What are his mama's responsibilities exactly? Or were they done the day she pushed him out and handed him over to you?"

Ray didn't contradict her. He didn't want to fight about Jade this morning.

"That's why I never had children, you know," Linette said. "I didn't want to take care of anyone but myself. I got enough of that when I was young. My mother —"

"Birthed five children, and you raised them all. I know."

Linette liked to tell this story, as if everything there was to know about her had been decided when she was a girl, missing days of school to take care of her siblings and ferry them to the doctor. "Did you ever think that with all the things you do for the two of them all the time, you could be doing something for yourself? You could be taking a class. Getting your degree."

"Why do I need my degree? You're still leaving me Superfine, right? Or are you going to cut me loose, Linette?"

Linette polished the tables in the front room, somber now. "You can't count so much on other people, Ray. Not even me. One day I'm going to die. Everybody dies."

"Well, hold off on dying until after that reporter comes."

Linette smiled and snapped her cleaning rag in Ray's direction. He kissed her on the cheek, triumphant, and started setting the table for just the three of them.

They sat by the window, drinking the fresh coffee, devouring biscuits. The whole shop

14

smelled of devil's food: thick chocolate, sugar, and starch. By seven thirty, the two front girls, Michelle and Michaela, arrived. They fawned over Gee, put on their hairnets, and a feud ensued over what to play on the radio. Linette settled it by putting on the gospel station, although she wasn't religious. She did it to bring a blessing down on the shop, and all of them. They were all humming along by the time Ray withdrew to the kitchen and left Gee in the window seat, looking forlorn. The boy was one child with him — easy, bright — and another without him.

The shop was full when Jade burst into Superfine, her sunglasses on, her hair folded into a side braid already coming apart at the ends. She was still wearing the gray leggings and Bad Brains T-shirt she'd slept in, underneath a tan trench coat. Gee leapt up to kiss her, and Jade let him and then held him away and asked where she could find Ray.

"Why'd you take him?" she asked as Ray emerged from behind the counter. Her voice was high and thin, and the customers turned in their seats to look at them. "I know how to take care of my son."

Ray took her by the arm and steered her

15

out to the street.

"You all right?"

"My head," Jade said, pressing her fingers to her temples. She didn't explain where she'd been last night, but Ray could figure. There was a restaurant off the freeway that she liked to go to with the girls from her class. They served frozen jack and cokes.

"I had an alarm set. I was ready to take him. But I woke up, and everybody was gone."

"I didn't want him to miss another day of school."

"I would have done it," she said.

Jade pushed her sunglasses up, and he saw last night's eyeliner thick around her down-turned eyes. Her nails were painted black, and she was wearing her lace-up boots. How pretty she was, how small, was all the more obvious in her dark, clunky clothes. He'd seen the pictures of her from high school right before she got pregnant with Gee — a black-girl goth who read comic books and hung out with nerds, dreamed about going to punk shows out of town if she could ever find a ride. It was a much older boy who'd gotten her pregnant, someone at the community college where she was taking a math class. He'd wanted nothing to do with Gee, so Jade lived with her mother until she met

16

Ray and he said to her, *Let's find a place, the three of us.*

Jade stared at him, as if she were thinking of apologizing.

"Did that reporter come by yet?"

Ray could sense her mood shifting. She was penitent, maybe because she wanted him to bake the best he ever had and impress that reporter, or maybe there was no reason at all. Sometimes, Jade was tender, gathering up Ray and Gee in her arms, declaring how lucky she was to have a family that loved her. Other times, she tore through the house, kicking things that were out of place and going on about how she hated living all cooped up, and she hated her dinged-up car, and she hated that Gee was never quiet when she had to study, when she had two hours to sleep before her shift.

"We're just watching the door," Ray said. "He's supposed to come by before three."

"I've got an exam today, too. Drawing blood. I was going to practice on you last night, but I lost track of time."

"You were gonna come home and stick a needle in me even if you couldn't see straight?"

Jade laughed and covered half of her face with her hand. "No, I was going to find your

17

vein. Pretend to stick you."

"You can pretend later. Tonight. You can show me how after you've aced it."

"Why are you so sweet to me, Raymond?"

Ray leaned toward Jade and kissed her. She smelled of the musty couch where she'd fallen asleep, her rose perfume, the cream she rubbed on after a shower, naked in the bathroom, her limbs spread wide. She was all ribs and small breasts, a brush of hair between her legs. Ray groaned a little, without meaning to, thinking of her. They had been missing their time together lately, Jade hard asleep in the mornings before he left for the shop.

Linette could say what she wanted about Jade, but she deserved, at least, some respect. None of her people had gone to school, and here she was, pushing, making a way. Who could blame her if sometimes she needed a break, to go out and have a few drinks?

Ray kissed her again. "You deserve all the sweet things in life," he said, and went inside to collect Gee. When they returned, Jade had her headphones on, a song roaring in her ears. Ray handed her coffee and a devil's food doughnut, then kissed his boy two, three, four times.

"Come and meet us after your shift. We'll

be at Wilson's house. He called for a favor."

"What's he want?" Ray asked.

"Help moving furniture or something."

"He can't ask one of his boys to do that?"

Jade shrugged. "I never ask Wilson questions."

"I don't like you going over there alone."

Wilson lived in a rough corner of the east side, but it wasn't just the neighborhood that bothered Ray. Wilson was the sort of man who lied about the plainest things: how much he'd paid for a microwave, why he'd been fired from his last job. He teased Gee for his missing tooth, slapped Jade's behind to say hello and good-bye. More than once, Ray had run interference for Wilson after he started an argument at a bar. More than once, they'd lent him cash they'd needed themselves. But Jade tolerated him because he was her cousin, and he'd been good to her. He'd bought her beers when she was sixteen, taken her to her appointments when she was pregnant with Gee.

"Did he ask you to bring money? Who else is going to be over there?"

"You worry too much," Jade said, and kissed Ray good-bye. She pulled Gee along by the hand, and the boy leaned into his mother, content to finally have her eyes on him.

Ray watched them walk to the corner. He felt distinctly that he was watching his whole life move away from him: the slender shape of Jade and her mussed hair, Gee's backpack immense on his little body. He wanted to run after them and draw them back, keep them in the shop, where he could protect them. From what? From Wilson? Ray knew it didn't make sense, these urges he got sometimes to hold everything he loved close, the occasional shock of how much he had to lose. Maybe he was nervous the reporter wouldn't like his doughnuts. Maybe he'd poured himself too many cups of coffee. He moved to follow them, to give Jade another kiss, his boy another squeeze, but he knew it was just nerves. He stayed put. By sundown, they'd all be back at home.

At noon, the reporter still hadn't arrived, and Michaela and Michelle gave up their waiting and left for lunch. Linette sat in her office, a supply closet where she'd installed a fan, a hanging bulb. Ray was alone at the register, watching Beard Street out the windows. The passing traffic was sparse: a truck headed for the highway, the sleek cars pulling up to the lunch window. They wore suits, the people who came from downtown, and Ray had no idea what kinds of jobs they had. A pair of police officers came into the bakery for sandwiches, and a crew of construction workers, Latin American, for coffees. They were tearing down one of the old tobacco factories nearby. Eventually, the mechanic from the garage came in for his weekly sandwich, on the house.

He was close to Ray in age, but he looked much older, a lean man with the beginnings of a paunch at his hips. He had a sunburned brow, a dark mustache, and no beard, and he wore his wavy hair hardened to his head with gel. He came into the shop, wearing aviators and a white polo shirt that somehow wasn't stained with grease.

"White, man? How you going to wear white to work on cars?"

The mechanic laughed. Ray could hardly ever remember his first name, but he usually wore his last name embroidered on the pocket of his uniform: *Ventura.*

"You just got to be careful, man. You need to do it like I do."

He was cocky, which was one of the things Ray liked about him. At first, he'd wondered if Ventura was gay, if he was flirting at him when he winked and bragged and pooched out his lips at him. But he'd learned it was just the way he talked, although Ray wasn't sure how much of it was because he was

Latin and how much of it was because he was from New York.

Once, after work, Ray's car wouldn't start, and he'd walked up the street to the garage to ask if someone could take a look. They told him it would cost fifty bucks to tow the car, even if it was going just to the end of the block. One of the mechanics had agreed to help him push, off the clock, since his shift was over. "It's all right," the mechanic had said, "he's my neighbor," although they'd never seen each other before. He helped Ray get the car in, and the next day, Ray brought him a coffee and a sandwich. After that, the mechanic came by once a week for his lunch.

He handed Ventura his sandwich, a cup of coffee. "The secret is I wear my work shirt over the white," he said. "That way, when I leave the garage, I'm looking nice."

Ray shook his head. "Out here? For what? There ain't nobody out here."

Ventura laughed and gestured at the two of them, as if they were enough of a reason. He pulled a pack of cigarettes from his jeans and waved them in the air.

Linette surfaced from the back, as if she had read their minds. "You're due for a break, Ray. Go on and take your lunch, just don't go too far."

22

"Yes, ma'am," Ray said, and he and Ventura hurried out like boys given leave to go and play.

They went around to the back of Superfine and lit up.

"I'm buying a house. I told you?" Ventura said. "Out by the forest. We're going to be living in the trees." He smiled, all his good teeth gleaming, a gold chain visible underneath the collar of his shirt. Ventura always looked sharp. "My wife is packing us up right now."

"You've got two girls, right?"

"Three. My youngest had her first birthday a few months ago. You only got the one, right?"

Ray hadn't bothered to explain about Gee, so he nodded.

"It's crazy, man. I thought I loved my wife — I do. But you'd do anything for your kids. It's like something changes in your brain. They climb in there and take over. They're the ones in charge. They don't know it, but they are."

Ray figured there was no point in saying it wasn't automatic. Something in him had been reordered when he met Gee because he'd let the boy come in and rearrange everything. But it hadn't happened with his own parents: his father, who'd left him with

23

his mother, or his mother, who left him to watch the kids she babysat, returning once in a while to drop off juice and chips and hot cereal, until she didn't return at all, and Ray went to live with his grandmother until she died. He was twenty by then, and he met Jade waiting in line at the DMV. She was getting her first driver's license, Gee nodding off on her chest, and she looked too skinny to be someone's mother, her teeth pretty and wide and set apart, and Ray was there to change his last name. He figured he didn't want anything in common with his mother, his father, so he took on his grandmother's first name as his last, Gilbert, from Gilberta, and Jade thought it was funny. If he wanted to honor his grandmother, why change her name into a man's name? "If you're going to do it, you might as well do it all the way," she'd said, and he'd known then that was how she lived her life, whether she was drinking or studying or screwing a college boy, or giving her opinion on a band or an election or how much sugar Ray put in her coffee. He'd seen quickly that he wanted to live just like that, *all the way*, with her.

Ventura went on about the house. "It's on the north side of the county. Feels like the country. There's too much crime around

24

here. I thought New York was bad. But every time you read the paper, there's some kid who moved down here from the Bronx because his moms thought it would be safer, and he winds up dead." Ventura fired an imaginary gun with his hand.

Ray nodded. He had heard more than one story like that.

"You get a good deal on the house?"

"Almost nothing down, can you believe it? It's not like I thought. They only care if you can make the payments on time." Ventura squinted at the sun, running his tongue over his bottom lip. "You know, nobody in my family has ever owned anything. Not in Colombia, not here. But now I have something to leave for my kids."

Ray laughed. "Everybody's talking about dying today. You got a disease I don't know about or something?"

"You think about it, man," Ventura said. "You see the next generation, and you remember we're on the way out. We got to leave them something to hold on to when we're gone."

"Yeah." Ray nodded. "Memories. Good times."

Ventura dragged on his cigarette, shook his head. "You can't live in good times, man. You can't live inside a memory. You

25

need a deed with your name on it."

They could see downtown from the back of the shop, the compact cluster of brick buildings, the water tanks, a few newer towers made of glass. Beyond the city, to the north, rose a bank of longleaf pines. Even farther, the state park surged with trees blushing rose and yellow.

Ray told Ventura about the reporter.

"Then you should be thinking about a house. Start saving. Don't you live on the east side?"

"My whole life," Ray said.

Ventura shook his head. "You got to be thinking about schools. If your boy stays on the east side, his future will be over before it starts."

Ray shrugged. School was the least of his worries for Gee. The boy was quick. He'd be fine anywhere, as long as he got what both Ray and Jade had been missing: two parents, a peaceful home. That's why Ray was always working on Jade. More than once, in a rage, she'd told him she was too smart for her life. What haunted Ray wasn't the meanness of it, but the truth.

"I'm telling you," Ventura said. "If there's something I've learned in this country, it's that your address decides everything. You've got to get out."

26

"Maybe," Ray said. Ventura had made the long journey from the country where he was born to New York to North Carolina. Why shouldn't he be able to get to the other side of town, if he set his mind to it?

Ventura drained his cup. "Life is funny. One day, you're in the mountains picking coffee beans. Another day, you're here, drinking coffee, with an American wife and a house."

"I know what you mean," Ray said. He didn't own a home, but he knew how he felt. One day, you're a boy, home alone, giving a stranger's baby your finger to suck on, and the next, you're a man, with a boy of your own, waiting for a reporter to come and put your picture in the paper.

"If we ever get a house, maybe we can have you all over," Ray said. "For dinner or something."

It surprised Ray to say it — he and Jade weren't the entertaining type, but maybe they would be, if they lived in a house. Ventura picked up the idea quickly. He smiled and snuffed out his cigarette on the concrete, working his way up to whatever slick line he was planning to deliver to send Ray laughing and seal their fifteen minutes of smoking and standing together, before they both went back to work.

"All right, Ray," he said. "But I want some real food. Don't make us no sandwiches."

By two thirty, the reporter hadn't arrived, and Ray was getting listless. He had been working nearly ten hours, Michaela and Michelle had left to pick up their kids, and Linette called the paper but couldn't get through.

"Maybe they got backed up," she said.

The shop was empty, in the lull before the after-work crowd came by. Linette said one day this would be their busiest time: when people came in for afternoon coffee and lingered. Women who stayed home with their kids, people who got days off, the university students. They just didn't know about Superfine yet, but they would. They'd be better than Starbucks, and there was no Starbucks opening in town anytime soon. If there was something Ray admired about Linette, it was that she wasn't afraid to dream, once you showed her she wouldn't be doing all the dreaming alone.

Ray called Jade from the phone in the back to ask about her test.

"I got a one hundred at least," she said.

"That's my girl. How's that headache?"

"I helped Wilson put everything out in the yard — he's selling all his furniture. I want to lie down, but I'm fixing to get Gee."

"Let me get him. Nothing's going on over here."

"You sure?"

"I'll bring you another doughnut. There's a lot left over."

Jade softened, as if she knew it hurt his feelings to say out loud that his doughnuts hadn't sold like he hoped they would. "Bring me two," she said, and hung up.

He was waiting for the engine to warm up when Linette came bounding out the back door.

"He's coming!" she called. "A reporter and a photographer. They'll be here in half an hour."

"They starting with us?"

"I don't know."

Ray made to turn off the car, but then he thought of Jade and her headache. The truth was he didn't need his picture in the paper, as long as the bakery made it in, some line about the goodness of everything he'd made. He told Linette that Jade and Gee were waiting on him.

"But I need you here."

"I'll be quick," Ray said. Wilson's house was no more than five minutes from Gee's school, which was ten minutes from Superfine on the highway. Fewer, if he hustled.

"I'll be right back, Linette — you'll see."

Ray yanked out of the lot and sped toward the highway.

Gee was waiting in front of the school with his teacher. Ray signed the checkout clipboard and caught the boy up in his arms. He settled into the backseat, and Ray told him to buckle up, the reporter was coming, and they had to rush.

Wilson lived in a neighborhood of battered brick ranch houses with empty, overgrown lawns. At least where he and Jade lived had signs of life: bicycles underneath the porches, plastic slides in the yard. And, still, it was nothing like the west side, where the houses had deep porches, ivory-white pillars, flower gardens. The apartment Jade and Ray lived in was an old millhouse that had belonged to tobacco workers. He had been told the east side was once a nice place to live before the factories closed and the city hollowed out, only the west side left intact. Maybe Ventura had the right idea, buying a house along the edge of the county. Maybe a house would satisfy Jade more than a ruby ring, a trip to Florida.

Ray looked at Gee in the rearview mirror. "What do you think about living in a house one day? One that's really ours?"

"Our house isn't ours?"

Ray didn't want to explain about rent and mortgages, and he wasn't sure he knew how it all worked himself. But he wanted his boy to understand.

"When a house is yours, nobody can take it away. It's mine, and then one day, it passes on to you. It has your name on it. You know what a legacy is?"

Ray turned onto Wilson's street and put the car in park. He wanted to go on talking to Gee, but he knew he had no time. He turned to tell his boy to run up to the house, when he saw Jade and Wilson in the yard, talking to a man in a dark blue sweatshirt. His back was to the street, so Ray couldn't see his face. He was hardly moving but Ray could tell something was wrong. Jade had her finger pointing at the man and she was yelling. Wilson had his hands stuffed in his pockets, and his face too nonchalant, like he was doing his best not to explode.

"You stay in the car," Ray said and unlocked the door.

"Daddy?"

Ray turned to face his boy. "You pay me mind," he said more sternly. Gee nodded. He sat up taller in his seat, strained to peer out the window.

Ray handed him the box of doughnuts. "I'll be right back," he said more softly, and

31

scaled fast up the lawn.

Jade said his name as soon as she saw him, and the man in blue turned around. He had a pale face, a toothpick dangling out the side of his mouth. He slit his eyes at Ray and said, "Who the fuck is this? Did you call somebody?" He pointed his finger at Wilson, who was tapping his foot against the ground. He was either agitated or scared. Jade was both, Ray could see. He went and stood beside her.

"What's going on?" he said. He was still wearing his apron, but he made himself look broad, his voice low.

"Your cousin owes me money. Selling all this furniture isn't going to make you enough to pay me back. And I'm tired of waiting."

"I already told you, I don't have it on me," Wilson said.

The man in blue shook his head. "Then I'm here to take you to the bank where you can get it. Or I'm taking *her* to the bank —" He nodded at Jade. "I don't care who it is. Somebody is going to pay me my money today."

He was shouting, and Ray wanted to take Jade, put her in the car, drive her and Gee back to Superfine, but he knew he couldn't. This man wouldn't let them off, he could see, and, if they weren't careful, it would come to a fight. He didn't want to fight him, not with Gee in the car. The little boy had his face to the window, his hand on the glass.

"How much does he owe you?" Ray asked. The man said the number, and Ray shook his head. "I can't help you with that."

"Then maybe she can," the man in blue said, and he took a step toward Jade.

Ray put his arm around her, even if it didn't make sense, even if he should keep his hands free. She was looking away from the three of them, toward the car, watching their son.

"That's enough," Wilson said finally. "Let's go to the bank. Just leave my cousin out of this." He inched his hand around his back.

"What are you doing?" the man in blue shouted at him. "Hey, man, what you doing?"

Before Wilson could answer, the man pulled out a gun, held it straight up to his face. Jade gasped, and Ray took her by the shoulders, pushed her hard behind him, but all the man in blue saw was Ray moving. He turned the gun toward him and shot.

His daddy had told him not to move from the car, and Gee didn't mean to disobey, but his body started going all on its own. He was running up the lawn. His mother was slumped over, like she'd been knocked down, too, and she was screaming. There were doors opening down the street, but Gee couldn't turn to look — his eyes were set on his father, fallen down, like he had been playing a game where one moment he was up, and the next, he was splayed out. Gee wedged himself between the grown-up bodies to kneel next to his daddy. He felt his mother lifting him away. He fought and kicked to stay close. She lost her grip on him, and he sank nearer to him, the one he loved. He used his hands to pinch his father's shoulders, his pretty ironed shirt, his favorite, red-and-pink plaid. Gee shook him, called out to him, but he stayed still. He stuck his hand underneath his daddy's body, to prop him up, so he could hear. *Daddy,* he said. *Daddy.* When his hand came back to him, it was shining with blood.

34

2

It was a Wednesday, newly November, and Lacey May Ventura was raking the leaves in the yard. Her fingers were red and sore, and it occurred to her to check the gas tank behind the house. In the Piedmont, winter never announces itself; the days turn toward the cold and away from it, the first dusting of snow arriving gently, without warning.

Lacey May pulled up the metal lid and saw the needle on the gauge pointing down to 15 percent. She ran inside, still holding the rake, and dropped the heat down as low as she could stand.

She passed the rest of the day in her good coat, a kettle boiling on the stove. She drank cup after cup of coffee to keep her hands warm, and by noon, she was shaking from all the caffeine, her fingernails tinged with blue. She wanted Robbie to call so she could ask how long 15 percent would last, but he didn't. She called the agency instead

35

to ask if they'd found anything for her yet.

"It's kinda hard when you haven't worked in ten years. And all you've ever done is fry fries." The receptionist spoke slowly, as if she didn't expect Lacey to understand.

"I've been raising my girls," Lacey said.

"I mean real work, out of the house. Employment."

"I'm pretty sure I could answer the phone."

"You don't have any qualifications."

Lacey wanted to hang up on her, or to insult her again, but she couldn't risk ticking off the woman who could move her folder down to the bottom of the pile. So Lacey mentioned how she had earned decent grades in high school, was quick in the kitchen, better behind the wheel than most. The receptionist was quiet for a while, then said she'd add a note to Lacey's file and hung up.

Later on, when she heard the school bus turn up the road, Lacey stationed herself at the door, her arms loaded with woolen things. The girls blazed in, chattering, their cheeks windblown, and Lacey handed them each a sweater and a pair of mittens, a scarf for Diane.

"It's winter in our house!" she said, and the girls caught on quickly. They dropped

36

their bags and swathed themselves in the new layers, made a big noise stomping around the living room. Soon they were all explorers, sliding across a stretch of ice in Alaska. Somehow, Lacey became a sled, and the girls scrambled on top of her. Margarita pretended to be one of those racing dogs, so she got down on all fours and howled, which made the real dog Jenkins dart behind the couch to hide.

They kept on their sweaters and scarves while they cooked grilled cheese, the yellow squares gobbled up faster than Lacey could set them in the pan. They were pleased when they were all allowed to lie down in bed with Lacey, and she didn't make them crawl out from under the blankets to wash their hands. Jenkins dozed beneath them, and the girls watched their breath puff overhead.

"That's oxygen," Lacey said. "It's what we breathe. You spell it O-X-Y —"

Her oldest, Noelle, was bright as a lamp, almost ten. She liked books about outer space and the ocean; she could be a scientist one day. Lacey considered her the one of her girls who could go the furthest. She was doing the spelling for her.

Noelle repeated after her mother: *"G-E-N."* Diane and Margarita burst into applause.

The next morning the girls went off to school, all of them with pink noses and runny eyes. Lacey saw them down the hill, and she was jealous they were off to somewhere the thermostat was set much higher than fifty-five.

She took a shower to beat the cold, and it was the most pleasure she had felt since Robbie went away. Had water always been this warm and good? Her hands set to work on every inch of her, and the heat seemed to sink in deep, underneath the top layer of skin — what was it called? The epidermis? She had learned the name in high school. It was only these last few weeks, since the nurse moved in next door, that Lacey started remembering she hadn't been half-bad at biology. She had seen the nurse driving down the road to her shift at the hospital and thought, *I could have been you.* Sure, the nurse was fat and had no husband and left her boy with a babysitter overnight, didn't even bother with the leaves in the yard, but it was probably seventy, seventy-five degrees over in her bungalow, and wasn't that worth something?

Lacey shivered, and wrapped her head in

towels. She felt the sin of her wet hair. How much gas was she using now? How many percents did it take to heat the house every day?

She opened all the curtains to let in the sunshine, thinking some light might warm the place. Half an hour later, she went around drawing them all closed because maybe she was letting in a draft. She had lived in the house for four years, ever since Robbie moved them all up to the north of the county, and still she didn't know how it all worked. When she went to get dressed, she had a sudden, terrible thought: How did the water get heated? Did that use up the gas, too?

She didn't want to call Robbie's old boss, but she did. There was nothing else to do.

"I'm worried it might be bad for the girls. All this cold."

"Can't you sell your food stamps?"

"We've got to eat, Annette."

"Well, the cold never killed anybody. Take Robbie. He grew up in a tropical place, where it's hot all the time, and look at how he turned out —"

"Annette, I've told you, it's not his fault. He's got . . ." Lacey searched for the words, tried to remember the lawyer's exact phrase. "A chemical unbalanced."

39

Annette sighed. "You played dumb for too long, Lacey May."

"All we need is a little loan."

"No, ma'am. Robbie already cleaned me out, remember?"

Lacey May didn't like when Annette brought up the garage. After all his years of working for her so faithfully, Annette had nearly turned him in until Lacey May showed up at Beard Street and begged for her to look the other way, just this once. All he'd done was sell off a few spare parts.

"Anyway, aren't you still getting those government checks?" Annette said. "How'd you burn through the money so quick?"

When Lacey said nothing, Annette cursed. "You're as shit-rotten as he is," she said. "You don't love those little girls half as much as they deserve."

Lacey put herself to bed, her hair leaking all over the pillows. The dog followed her into the room, whimpering. She drew three blankets up over herself and started talking out loud. *Why'd you buy me this house if it was going to be so cold? Why'd you buy me this house if you were going to leave me alone?*

It had been good for a long time. They had bought this little wooden house, blue with white shutters, because it sat on a large patch of land at the bottom of a hill. Robbie had built the wraparound porch himself, and they used to sit out back and drink beers after the girls had gone to sleep. If they drank too much, he would take her right there on the porch. *This is freedom,* he would say. *I can fuck my wife under a sky full of stars, if I want.* He could slap her rump and pull her hair, and she could bite down on his finger, and Lacey wanted it all, how he handled her, how it could feel like they didn't just own the house, but the whole hill, the woods, their own skin, one another.

Those were the only times he was rough. He never hit her, or the girls, not even after he got real bad. He would scream and he would cry, but he raised his hand only if she asked him, and it was just a part of their way, as good a feeling as his cock prodding at the inside parts that made her sing.

It had comforted her when the lawyer told her about the trouble in Robbie's brain. It was why he needed the drugs, why he would disappear and get up to no good. It wasn't that he had stopped loving her or the girls. It was like being sick, the lawyer had said, but it hadn't made much difference to the judge.

There was likely an event that had set him off — a catastrophic event, a tragedy. A trigger. Lacey May had tried to think of what it could be, but all the big things had happened long before. Robbie coming to this country, Robbie moving down from New York, Robbie's mother dying in Colombia. There was the man he'd known from work, the one who left a little boy behind. Lacey had never even heard of the man until Robbie came home, turned on the news, and pointed at the awful picture on the screen, all the yellow caution tape spread over the lawn of a house on the east side of town. "They killed my friend," Robbie had said, but, surely, it couldn't have been that. No matter how she searched their past, Lacey May couldn't find a reason.

When she was all out of tears, Lacey May got the coin jar out from under the sink, patted Jenkins good-bye, and drove along the service road to the store. Inside she found a clerk and asked for Hank, and she waited for him by the coin machine, trading in all her pennies for a flimsy receipt that said she had earned nine dollars. Hank surfaced from one of the aisles in jeans and a neon-yellow worker's vest. His hair was long, combed over so it hung down one side of his face. He waved her out the sliding doors and into the parking lot, where he kissed her behind the ear and lit a cigarette.

"God, Lacey, you're as pretty as you ever were. Do you know that? Your teeth are fit to eat."

Lacey hardly felt beautiful at all these days. Her eyes were red from too little sleep; she hadn't been able to afford her good shampoo in weeks. But she did still have her smile, at least. She looked at Hank and turned it on, explained about the 15 percent. She had been careful and budgeted for everything except the gas. It hadn't gotten cold yet since Robbie went away. She didn't know.

"You ever think about selling that house?"

"Robbie wouldn't like that. It's the only thing we got to pass down to the girls."

"What good is the house if they freeze to death?"

"Can you bring me on to work or not?"

Hank tapped a cigarette out of the pack and handed it to her. She bent over his lighter, and when she straightened up, she saw he was staring at her. They had been teenagers together, all three of them, her and Hank and Robbie, when they were in high school and working at the Hot Wing. Hank had a face full of acne then, but it had cleared now to nothing but scars, dark shadows along his cheeks. He had always wanted her, she knew, and she had liked having him get things off a high shelf for her, or rush over with a washcloth if she burned herself with the oil. But Robbie was the one who had won her, and they forgot all about Hank until they came in to do their shopping with the girls, and saw him patrolling the aisles with his walkie-talkie and neon vest.

"You know I got a place?" Hank sucked on the tip of his cigarette and let it dance between his lips. "I've got a yard and everything. You and your girls would fill it right up."

"You would do that for us? You've got an extra room?"

"I've got a pullout in the basement."

"It would be tight, all four of us on the couch, but it's better than letting the girls freeze —"

Hank laughed and shook his head. "Lacey May, you never could take a hint."

Lacey looked at him, confused.

"Let's put it this way — if you stayed with me, it wouldn't cost you nothing, but it wouldn't be free neither."

The wind blew hard and kicked up the smell of gasoline from the pump at the edge of the lot. Lacey pulled her coat around her.

"How would I explain that to the girls? They think their father's on the coast working a fishing job."

Hank shrugged. "I'm a man, not a saint, Lacey."

She stared at the white button on his vest: TEAM LEADER. Until now she had never believed the stories she had heard about him. The rumor was that he gave the high school girls who stocked the aisles overtime and whatever shifts they wanted if they let him fondle their tits in the back lot during their breaks. It wasn't the worst thing she'd ever known a man to do, but she wouldn't have pinned it on a man like Hank.

"I think I'll go inside and get a few things for the girls," Lacey said. She stepped around him and walked toward the store. Hank called after her.

"You were always too proud, Lacey May."

With her nine dollars, Lacey bought a tin of coffee, another block of cheese, a magazine about TV stars and their weddings, and a fistful of bubblegum lollipops for the girls. She drove back with the heat on low so she could idle in the driveway for a few extra minutes with the engine on.

When the girls clattered in after school, Lacey gave them each a lollipop, and Diane, who had lost three baby teeth to cavities, looked at her mother, as if to see if she were sure. Lacey nodded at her and said, "That's right, sweetheart. Go ahead, let it rot your teeth."

She asked the girls to tell her what they had learned in school while she made their sandwiches and mixed chocolate powder into hot milk. Noelle sliced the cheese into perfect thin squares. "You could perform surgery with those hands," Lacey said. "Gifted hands!" She'd heard the phrase before, but she couldn't remember where. Noelle didn't seem touched by the compliment.

"How come Daddy doesn't come back on the weekends? We've been to the beach — it's not too far to drive."

Lacey gave her a little tap on the nose. "Cause that's when they catch the biggest fish — something about the tide. When he calls, I'll have him explain it."

"Is it still winter in our house?" Margarita asked, and Lacey kissed the top of her head.

"Yes, ma'am. Isn't it fun?" She turned on the TV.

They watched a cop show, and the girls didn't mention their father. They didn't notice Lacey look away when the officers caught a burglar, wrestled him onto the shoulder of the highway.

The phone rang, and Lacey leapt up. It

46

was Robbie! He'd received the money she put in his commissary, and soon it would all be worth it. The girls would hear their father's voice, know he hadn't wanted to leave them.

"Miss Ventura," said a bland voice. It was the receptionist from yesterday.

"Yes, this is Mrs. Ventura."

She waited to hear they'd found her a job, maybe in a laundromat, selling tiny bottles of detergent to people who had forgotten theirs, or a doctor's office where she could label the samples of pee, point people to the bathroom. She had a good manner — her boss at the Hot Wing had told her so. She had her smile. Most of all, she wasn't stupid. There was plenty she could learn to do.

"Mrs. Ventura, the check you gave us with your application bounced. We can't process any paperwork until you write another and refund the thirty dollars we got charged for your bad check."

"I had the money when I first wrote the check. Why'd you wait so long to cash it?"

Lacey didn't hear the receptionist's answer because Margarita had started to cry.

"Mama, I'm so cold. Why is it so cold?"

"Cause Daddy left us," Noelle said. "He doesn't want us anymore."

Lacey dropped the phone and slapped her child. Diane tried to defend her sister and say they shouldn't fight, so Lacey slapped her, too, and then Margarita for good measure, and sent them all to bed.

She knew they would be warmer if they all gathered in her bed, but she let them cry softly into the dark. They were carrying on as if the heat weren't on at all, as if she weren't trying to do what was right. She hadn't wanted to send the last of her cash to Robbie, but he needed all kinds of things in there: underwear and cups of instant soup. He needed money to place a call.

In the night, Lacey went to check on her daughters. She sealed the covers around their skinny bodies like cocoons. They slept heavy. How lucky they were. How little they knew. They sensed his absence only in the few hours before bed — Lacey never got away from it.

Diane woke with a fever. She was eating her cereal too slowly, and when Lacey touched her hand to the girl's forehead, her skin was burning up.

Noelle stood up from the table, hand on her hip. "You did this. This is all your fault."

"It's sixty degrees in here!" Lacey screamed. "That's the temperature right

48

now in California!" She had made up the fact, but it sounded true. She started yelling that they were spoiled, ungrateful children. They'd be off to school soon where it was warm, while she was stuck here.

"Well it's Friday now!" Noelle shouted. "What's going to happen on the weekend?"

And while Noelle yelled at her, and Margarita started moaning about her daddy, Diane vomited on the kitchen floor. Jenkins started to lap it up, and Lacey kicked him hard.

The girls nearly missed the bus, and Lacey had to chase it down in her slippers and her robe. The only girl who kissed her good-bye was sick little Diane, her face crimson, her hair sticking to her face with sweat. She knew she had to have the heat on by the time the girls came back.

Lacey went to the shed for her rake and shears, then she walked across a quarter acre of woods to knock on the door of the fat, unmarried nurse. Lacey read the name on the mailbox — RUTH GREEN. She started rehearsing the lines in her head.

It was a while before the door opened, and Ruth, fleshy and tall, stood in checkered pajamas, her hair in a big wet knot on top of her head. Lacey could feel the heat streaming out the open door. It licked her fingertips, her cracked lips.

"Morning. I wanted to see if I could help clear out your yard."

Ruth Green stared at her as if she had no teeth at all.

"You know, prune back the bushes, rake the leaves. Clear the gutters if you've got a ladder."

She realized then she should have changed out of her robe and slippers, put on her good blue blouse, her boots, dressed herself like a woman who worked.

Ruth Green clucked her tongue.

"Why would I pay you to clean up this yard when it'll be covered up in ice in a few weeks?"

Lacey wondered whether this nurse, whose lights were always on, whose house was warm, who had a babysitter watch her boy when she left, could ever understand what it was to have a husband, to love him with your bones.

"My propane is down to fifteen percent. Probably ten now."

"That'll last you till Monday when the truck comes around. You need their number?"

Lacey explained her youngest had a fever; she was only five. They were making do with Robbie gone — it was just the heat.

Ruth crossed her arms. "You see, the rest of us, we work. We don't depend on the government or no husband."

"Maybe you could just lend me a few gallons out of your tank to hold us over."

"If you expect me to pity you, I don't. You're not the only one who married some son of a bitch who can't take care of his own kids."

"It's not his fault. He's got a chemical unbalanced —"

"They all do," Ruth said, and she went to close the door.

Lacey pushed her hand against the door. "My babies are freezing."

"This is real life, sweetheart. What did you think would happen?"

"Please."

"You'll find a way — that's what women do."

"You fat cunt."

The nurse slammed the door.

Lacey stomped through the woods, smashing down fallen branches under her slippers. As she neared the house, she heard the phone ringing. She ran to make it in time.

"Robbie?"

It was the school nurse. Diane had vomited again on the bus, and she needed to go

51

home. Could Lacey come and pick her up? On the long drive to the school, Lacey found herself shaking.

Margarita was the one who had spilled the beans. When her teacher asked her why she kept putting her head down on her desk, she said she hadn't slept right because it was winter in her house. And since Diane threw up on the bus, it wasn't hard to put two and two together.

"I'm working on a solution," Lacey said in the principal's office.

The principal shook her head and asked what was going on. It hadn't occurred to Lacey that they didn't know. Shouldn't there have been a letter from court to the school? Wasn't there something the government had done to spare her this moment?

"My husband got high and stole a cop car. Not a black-and-white sheriff's one, a regular one. It just belonged to a cop. It was parked in front of a bar downtown. He didn't know."

"I'm sorry, Mrs. Ventura," the principal said. "But after Monday, I'll have to make a call. You've got the weekend."

Lacey went around to the classrooms and got all her girls. They drove home in silence, past the rows of houses in town, then fields and forgotten barns, the railroad tracks where they had to stop and wait for a train to pass.

"Woo-woo!" sang Margarita, and it made Diane smile weakly, her cheeks pink.

Back at home, she boiled cans of broth for the girls, peeled and dropped in potatoes, a tin of shredded chicken. And then she made grilled cheeses, too, and chocolate milk, and they carried it all into Lacey's bed, where she piled blankets on top of the girls and then crawled in herself.

"If one of us is going to be sick, we might as well all be sick together," she said, and she kissed her girls on the nose. It was still light out, hardly past midday.

"Aren't you going to turn up the heat? You heard what the principal said."

Noelle still wasn't looking at her, her ears flushed bright, and Lacey wondered whether she was catching a fever, too, or if she was just ashamed.

"Hush," Lacey said. "I'm going to tell y'all a story."

The girls squeezed in closer to their mother, even Noelle, although she probably only wanted to get warm.

"Once upon a time, there was a princess, and she lived in a castle deep in a forest, with just her sisters. All the men were at war, and it was a kingdom with no old people, you see, so there was no one to show them how to live. How to fill the moat, how to feed the horses, how to keep the torches lit, and the dungeons clean —"

"What's a moat?" Diane asked, sucking on a Tylenol and making a face. Lacey told her to swallow.

"So they saddled up the horses, and they went riding, far and far, over valleys and streams to a kingdom where they had heard the men went to war and never came back. The princesses there showed them how to do all the things they were afraid of — how to clean the stables and grow wheat, how to cast spells, and burn the dead —"

"How to fill the moat?"

"Mm-hmm — and when they knew everything they needed to know, they went riding back to their kingdom, all day, and all night, and they weren't afraid anymore. They were all ready to rule. But they didn't have to, after all, cause while they were gone, the princes had come home. They had won the war."

Noelle rolled her eyes. "Short war," she said. "What a stupid story. They rode all that way and learned all those things, and then it doesn't even matter."

Lacey wanted to explain that you should never give up a prince if the prince really loves you, but Noelle plugged her ears, and Margarita shouted that she wanted to be a princess, and Diane stood solemnly and asked for someone to go with her to the bathroom because she had to throw up.

After the girls nodded off, Lacey slipped out from under the blankets. She shut off the light and went out to the back porch with one of the leftover lollipops from the supermarket. She cracked the hard candy between her front teeth and counted the days on her fingers since she had sent Robbie the money — five, and he still hadn't called. *Goddamn you, Robbie,* she thought. Goddamn.

She went back in the house, and she didn't feel a difference anymore between inside and out. Lacey found her old address book in a drawer, and she went flipping through the pages until she found him there, alphabetized by last name. *Gibbs, Hank.* She carried the address book and the phone out to the living room. She muted the TV and dialed, waited for the ringing to stop.

"I knew you'd change your mind," he said, and Lacey, with her free hand, turned up the thermostat a full ten degrees.

The sun wasn't up yet when Noelle went out to the porch to decide what to do about the party invite. The Suttons threw this party every year, and she'd gone to the first with Nelson when they moved into Golden Brook. It had been exciting, all their neighbors' German cars, the crystal wineglasses, the women and men in crisp, creamy-colored clothes. They talked about local government, the community initiative to build a bigger dog park. It was like being cast in a minor role in a dull but pleasant movie.

The shimmer was gone now — from the Suttons, their gabled house, and all of Golden Brook. Even the cottage she and Nelson had bought looked too small to her now when she drove up. The lawn, where she'd said she wanted to plant a garden, was bare except for the signs they'd driven into the grass to announce they leaned left,

56

voted blue.

It was warm, even in the early dark, and Noelle went out with her coffee, bottle of vitamins, a nail file, the invitation. She laid it on her lap while she scraped her nails into shape. How many things about herself did she no longer tend to? She hardly exercised; she drank too much; her hair was thinning at the ends. She took the vitamins, still, at least. She couldn't remember the last time she'd read a play.

This curve of Golden Brook was shaded by oaks so tall they must have been older than seemed possible. "From slavery times," Nelson had said when they moved in. It was the kind of joke she had learned to laugh at over the years but would never make herself.

If she went to the Sutton house tonight, at least she'd look the part. She'd put yogurt in her hair, shave her legs, smear on one of those citrus-smelling serums that promised to lift and tighten and erase. When she looked at Nelson, she could see the old adage was true — black don't crack. She, on the other hand, had a fan of lines around her smile, her eyes. It didn't bother her, really, to look older. It was more what the wrinkles signified: time was running out.

It was noon in France, too early for a lunch meeting, too late for a morning shoot, so Noelle called Nelson. The phone rang and rang.

"Sweetheart," she said when she got his voicemail. "I'm almost happy you're not here. If you were, you'd be stuck going to the Suttons'. You're the lucky one, yeah? Love you."

She'd expected him to call more, even with the time difference, his work. But the way they'd left things — she couldn't blame him. She dialed again. "I guess you're working. I missed your voice yesterday. Call me soon."

Noelle felt her chest draw inward, as if she were getting narrower, shrinking. It was a sick feeling. She texted him. I can't go to the Sutton party alone. These people make me feel like I'm in high school again. He would know what she meant. It was like keeping a secret, like passing, like choosing between getting along and being clear about who she was. She stared at the phone for a few minutes. Maybe he couldn't talk, but he could text. She took her prenatal. She finished her coffee.

She went back inside, turned her phone volume all the way up so she wouldn't miss him while she was in the shower. When the phone rang, it startled her. She hadn't really expected Nelson to call. She rushed out and saw that it was her mother, Lacey May. Noelle didn't answer.

It was a sick chain, she thought. *Nelson ignores me; I ignore my mother. I hunt after my husband; my mother hunts after me.*

Noelle left the house in her exercise clothes. She knew exactly whom she'd ask to go with her to the party, to help her get through. And Inéz would say yes. She was sure. They had forged their friendship in that golden stretch of years in college when they would do anything for each other, when nothing was more solid or mattered more than the love of your girlfriends. They'd pierced each other's ears, taken the bus to Babeland to buy dildos together. They had forgotten their families and clung to one another, as if their old lives might not ever resume.

In the car, she tried Nelson once more — "Headed to the city, hope you're getting the best pictures of your life" — then hung up and turned onto the freeway.

Golden Brook was less than an hour from the city, her old life, and yet she'd let her days shrink to the circumference of a few miles. She could spend a whole day driving between the house, the grocery store, one strip mall, then another. She and Nelson had loved living near downtown. It was a proper city, not like home. The skyline was blue and gray glass, the buildings shaped like spaceships. Her heart gave a thump as she coasted through the streets. She rolled down the window, breathed in the flowering trees and exhaust. She reached the studio just as the class was starting.

Inéz was at the front in a black leotard and tiny turquoise shorts rolled up to nearly nothing. She gave Noelle a quick arch of the eyebrows through the mirror, ignored the students as they filtered in. Her hair was pulled into a gumdrop-sized nub at the top of her head, her skin bare, her gold septum ring sparkling in her face. She was magnificent. Noelle stood at the back, reached her arms overhead as if she knew what she was doing.

Inéz counted them in, *Five-six-seven-eight.* It was hard for Noelle to keep up, and it was only the warm-up. Her limbs were stiff, heavy. She hardly left the ground when she tried to leap up. She had to steady herself with her hand when she sank her hips to the ground. Inéz had a parakeet's voice, high and sweet. *That's it!* she shouted with enough gusto that it was almost convincing.

At the end of class, Noelle hung at the back, watching the students hover around Inéz, as if they weren't sure whether to say good-bye or simply leave. She was aloof and beautiful, mesmeric. In this way, she was like Nelson. Perhaps that was all Noelle had been doing with her life: collecting stars that never wanted to be collected in the first place.

When the room was empty, Inéz found her. "Excuse me, ma'am, did you pay? I don't remember you signing up for a class pass." She crawled down to the floor where Noelle sat, bound her with her arms. "What are you doing here?"

Noelle took her friend's hand in hers. "I want to take you to lunch. When's your next class?"

"Is everything all right? Are you pregnant or something?"

"Far from it. I need your help, baby girl."

Noelle drove them to a place on the Westside with tinted windows and small bistro tables. They ordered eggs, a coffee for Inéz, a glass of wine for Noelle.

"God, it's been forever. I thought you'd gotten lost up there in the country. Golden Hollow, or whatever it's called?"

"It's the suburbs, not the sticks."

"Same thing. Nelson out of town? Where this time?"

"Paris."

"But of course."

Inéz smiled and shook her head. Fourteen years ago, she was the most beautiful person Noelle had ever seen, and she still was now. Even Lacey May had referred to her once, when Noelle was home from college for Thanksgiving, as "that pretty dark girl." She was no darker than her sister Diane, Noelle had said defensively, and then it troubled her that she had felt the need to point out that someone she loved wasn't all that dark.

Noelle took her wine down in gulps, and Inéz watched. It was eleven in the morning.

"Don't you miss it here, Nells? You must be bored out of your mind out there, without your work, your friends. Do you even see people during the day? Or just in the grocery store, as you roam the aisles searching for a chicken to roast?"

It pained Noelle how accurate her friend's parody of her was.

"If these months had gone the way I wanted, I wouldn't mind being somewhere quiet, with fresh air and green space."

"*Green space?* Do you hear yourself?"

"I wanted a change."

"Well, you got one, honey." Inéz poured a drop of maple syrup into her coffee, swirled the spoon around with grace. "Now, tell me

62

everything. I've got to be back in half an hour."

"We're a part of this homeowners' association."

"Naturally."

"And there's a party tonight. It would look awful if I'm not there, but I hate these things, especially when Nelson isn't around."

"Nelson isn't the best at parties though, is he? He just sits on the couch and pouts until someone asks him about his photographs, then you can't shut him up. Or if he's drunk, then he's fun for an hour or so until he sobers up and gets sulky again. No offense."

Noelle knew her friend's opinion of Nelson had turned sometime over the years. At first, Inéz, like all their classmates, had admired Nelson's cool. But eventually, she'd tired of how he seemed to live without moods, impenetrable. Everything was fine, nothing was a crisis, but nothing was a tremendous pleasure either. She didn't expect Inéz to love him, but she ought to leave him be. After a life like his, what did people want? For him to give a song and dance? He'd done enough.

"Please, Inéz. Every time I go somewhere without Nelson, I get asked a dozen times,

'Where's your husband? He travels a lot for work, hunh? Must be lonely, hunh?' It makes me feel like we're doing this whole thing wrong."

Inéz looked at her, as if to say, *Maybe.* "Who cares what they think?"

"It doesn't help that we already feel like anomalies out there."

"Because he's black and you're white?"

Noelle was taken aback that her friend would call her white — she knew about her family, her father, Robbie. She decided to let it slide. "Because we don't have children."

Inéz seemed unmoved.

"Please, I'd have much more fun if you came with me. We can get drunk and eat all their catered food, and then you can spend the night. I'll drive you back in the morning."

"The booze better be good, expensive."

"It will be," Noelle assured her.

"Fine, but only because I love you. I'll consider it a kind of social experiment."

"It's my life." Noelle leaned across the table to kiss her friend.

"I know," Inéz said as she swatted her away and drained the last of her coffee.

Noelle spent the day in the city, waiting for

Inéz to teach her last class. She parked in their old neighborhood. She and Nelson used to go for walks by the row houses, the rosebushes and hydrangeas in the front yards. Instead of going to church on Sundays like good Southerners, they went to the farmers' market, made elaborate breakfasts at home while listening to podcasts. They drank coffee, then had sex in the living room, took turns pleasing one another. Then Noelle left for the theater to work, and Nelson to the arboretum for one of his long runs. He couldn't go without ten or twelve miles on the weekend; it kept him calm, steady. So did the sex. She never made fun of his rituals, never let him go without the things he needed day to day.

Now Noelle had no place to go, no apartment, no office at the theater, so she stopped into shops. She bought herself tea, then a cheap necklace made of plated gold, then a clip for her hair. She didn't call Nelson because she was embarrassed at her small, dreary life. She filled the time with buying things, waiting out the day until there was someone to be with her again.

Being a wife, it seemed, was mostly waiting. Waiting for a phone call, waiting to be thanked, waiting for a delivery, the plumber, her husband to come home, to ask whether she was all right, to slip a hand in her underwear. Waiting with her legs up. Waiting because it seemed a way to love him. It hadn't bothered her as much when she was working, in the city. If he was remote, she knew it wasn't because he didn't love her. It was just his way. But now, without the theater, she felt that all she did was unnecessary; Nelson could fend for himself if he had to. If one shirt was wrinkled, he could wear another. If dinner never appeared, he'd make a sandwich. He could survive, handle his own needs; he was doing so in Paris. Perhaps that was why she had wanted the baby. To be needed, indispensable, at least for a time. Nelson gave the impression, always, of absolute independence. She was used to it, the off-and-on loneliness of feeling like an appendage to a man. She knew that becoming a mother was only a temporary respite. Any child would one day leave her; she could count on that. But wouldn't it be worth it for those delicious years? A soft skull nuzzled into her neck, the tug of gums at her breast, that precious infant smell of powder, crusted milk? She knew it wasn't modern. It was the kind of convention that her college degree and her years in the city were meant to cure, and they hadn't.

On the drive north, they got caught in traffic. Inéz rolled down the window to smoke, offered Noelle a cigarette.

Noelle shook her head. "I've quit. Remember?"

"Yeah, but you're not pregnant yet. Come on. I saw you down that wine at lunch. How long have you been trying now?"

"I've lost track." Noelle fixed her eyes on the road.

"There's no shame in that, Nells. Is that why you haven't been coming around as much? You don't want to talk about it?"

"It's the distance. I'm far away now."

They sat for a while through the discord of honks and running engines.

"I'm not going to let you off the hook that easily. It's not right — the way you disappeared." Inéz was staring straight at her now, her tongue pressed against her lower lip in annoyance, her head titled into her hand.

"Have you even been back to the Electric House? They just did *Orlando.* An all women and femmes cast, beautiful costumes — a few of the nights were even sold out."

67

"I outgrew that place, Inéz. You know that."

"And grew right into Golden River?"

Noelle pumped on the brakes a bit harder than she needed to. "I know you all find it backwards that I'm doing just what our mothers did when we could be doing anything."

"Speak for yourself," Inéz interjected. "My mother always worked."

Noelle saw no point in defending Lacey May. She had worked, too, but she had taken no pride in it. She had gone about her life as if it were put upon her. Noelle refused to do the same.

"I want a baby. What's so wrong with that? Isn't feminism all about getting to decide what you want?"

"Not exactly."

"You could have visited me, too. Or is the center of all life Atlanta?"

"Well, the idea of the suburbs is repulsive. And pregnancy —" Inéz shuddered. "Breastfeeding has always struck me as . . . bovine. What's the big deal with motherhood anyway? I feel like I've got everything I need."

"I want the experience of mothering. I can't explain it."

"*Mothering*. Is it a verb now?"

"It ought to be."

"And Nelson? Is he as nuts about *fathering*?"

"You leave him out of this."

"How can I?"

"If I have to choose between you and my husband, I know who I'd choose."

They sat in uneasy silence for a while. Noelle felt a fervent thrum at her temples. She tapped her fist on the wheel. Inéz caught her fidgeting hand and kissed the knuckles.

"I'm sorry," she said. "But I'm livid, too."

"Because I moved away?"

"Because you forgot about me, and yourself."

Noelle wasn't sure how to answer her. Inéz spoke as if selves should be fixed, as if they couldn't change. Noelle wasn't choosing to make herself less. To become a mother was to multiply.

The Suttons lived on a hill, their house flanked by a garage the size of the house Noelle grew up in. An immense magnolia was in bloom on their lawn, the porch strung with lights, the shutters thrown open. They had hired a small staff to pass around appetizers. Noelle breathed a sigh of relief when she saw they were white college

69

students in cheap vests. Inéz took her arm as they climbed the steep hill, and Noelle wondered whether she was fully forgiven.

A large mirror hung in the foyer, and Noelle took in their appearance quickly. Beside Inéz, she seemed somehow older, less vital. Her body was soft where Inéz's was hard. She was tall and pale, her hair ragged. She had thought her green floral dress was sweet, but she could see now it was dowdy. Inéz wore a wine-colored dress, cut close to her waist, all her usual jewelry glistening.

"You're beautiful," Inéz said, as if reading her mind.

"Look who's talking."

They turned into the living room, arms linked, where the crowd burst in welcome. They shook Noelle's hand and asked, predictably, after Nelson, but Inéz saved her. They were fascinated and stood agape at the glamour of her life — a dancer! the city! single! so beautiful! And, although they'd never say it — black! Her life was a puzzle to them, and Inéz didn't play it up or down. The two of them stole away as soon as they could, snatching bourbon and lemonade from a passing tray.

"They seem so old," Inéz whispered. "My grandmother is less astonished by my life."

70

"Welcome to the burbs, mami," Noelle said, and they laughed.

They found their way to the kitchen, the spread of bruschetta and olives, pungent wheels of cheese, dipping bowls of tapenade and oils, a few platters of quiche, a silver dish of spanakopita.

"That's the thing about white people in this country," Inéz said. "They always want to be from someplace else."

"Not in North Carolina," Noelle said. She imagined a spread with pimento cheese and hot-pepper jelly, crackers and deviled eggs.

They filled their plates and went to sit somewhere they'd be left alone to eat and finish their second round of drinks, but the Suttons found them, the Radlers in tow.

John Sutton was a willfully silent man. He listened more than he talked, his hair down to his chin, too long for a doctor. It was hard to know what there was to him, what he believed in. Nelson didn't like him, any white man who didn't spread his cards early on. His wife, Ava, was red haired and warm, impeccably mannered, but equally hard to pin down. They had two girls who played lacrosse. The Radlers were former North Carolinians, and Noelle felt that bond with them, although they'd lived outside Raleigh, on a farm with a house full of stained glass, chickens, and a band of sheepdogs. Brent was some kind of software salesman; Helene stayed home with their twins. Inherited wealth, Nelson had said, was the only way to explain it. Then he'd arched an eyebrow at Noelle and said, *How do you think white people got houses like that in North Carolina?* But the Radlers volunteered for the Boys & Girls Club. To Noelle, this seemed like an assurance.

"John and Ava. Brent and Helene."

Inéz repeated their names, pointing at each pair with her hands pressed together in a steeple.

"That's right," Ava said. "Around here, everyone comes in couples. If people get divorced, they move away." She laughed.

"Not as a rule, of course," Helene chimed in.

Inéz stretched her arms overhead, amused. "Of course," she parroted.

They politely asked Inéz about her latest production, and they nodded patiently, if confounded, as she explained it was an exploration of patriotism. The admission fees supported an organization working against voter suppression.

"There's an issue we can all get behind," John Sutton said, and he raised his glass unironically. Nobody toasted, but they all drank.

Ava looked toward the door as another couple swung in. "I do hope that new woman and her family show up tonight. Patricia — was that her name?"

"I wouldn't blame her if she didn't," Helene said. "Did you hear about that? The incident down at the pool?"

Noelle reached for another drink, her third, knowing it didn't matter. There was no life inside of her. "What happened?"

John Sutton started to explain. "A new family moved in earlier this week. A nice couple. They've got a son about the girls' age. Anyway, the newsletter hasn't gone out yet this week, so we haven't had a chance to announce their arrival. And this morning Patricia took her son down to the pool. She was reading a magazine, and he was diving in, splashing around."

"A very normal thing," Helene interjected.

"Yes, very normal —" Brent said.

Inéz slipped her hand into Noelle's, as if she knew what was to come.

"To make a long story short, another resident confronted her. Asked if she lived in the community, said he hadn't seen her around. He asked her for ID, and when she

73

refused to give him any, he called the police."

"Oh God," Ava said, although she'd certainly heard the story before.

"It all got cleared up. She showed the officer her ID, her key card to the pool, and he left. But her son, I think, was very upset. And the other resident —"

"Who was it?" Noelle asked.

"Do you know that salt-and-pepper-haired man who's always walking those dachshunds? Doesn't stop to pick up their waste unless someone is watching?"

"Such a nuisance," Helene said.

"Oh God," said Ava again.

"Well, what kind of repercussions will he face?"

The group turned their eyes on Inéz. She had put down her glass.

"I assume that what got left out of the story is what's obvious. That Patricia and her son are black. Am I right?"

"They're West Indian, I believe," said Helene.

"Jamaican," said Brent.

"Well, this man is obviously a racist. Why else would he assume they had no right to be at the pool?"

"Well, the newsletter's late this week —" John Sutton began.

"He owes them an apology," Inéz said.

John Sutton nodded. "He acted badly. An apology is not a bad idea."

"It's an absolute requirement. At the very least."

"What a terrible welcome to the neighborhood," Helene said, shaking her head, and Ava murmured something about the Lord and mercy, lifted another glass of sparkling wine off a passing tray.

"I wonder what it will be like for him to go to school with your girls," Inéz said pointedly to John and Ava. "I imagine the schools here are also predominately white? I hope for his sake that the neighborhood, at least, can be a place where he feels safe."

"Well, he was never really in any danger," Brent said. "The police out here aren't like the police in the city. They come to investigate, not to mow anybody down."

Inéz pushed her eyebrows together in puzzlement, disgust.

"But you never can be too careful," Brent went on, nervously now, and he turned to John Sutton. "Maybe you can put something in the newsletter," he said.

After the party, they sat on Noelle's back porch to sober up. They drank coconut water and swatted at their arms, the citronella tiki torches doing little to repel mosquitoes.

"I hope it works out for you," Inéz said. "This life out here."

"I think I'll invite that woman over — Patricia. And her family. Let them know they can count on us."

"You didn't say a single thing during that whole conversation about the pool. That's not like you, Nells."

"I know. But this is all I have right now. Those are my neighbors."

Inéz squeezed her hand. "Don't get lost out here, love."

"You know, I was pregnant before."

"And you lost the baby? Christ, Nells, why didn't you say anything?"

"At first, it was this beautiful secret, just between Nelson and me. And by the time I was ready to tell everyone, it was all over. Nelson took it in stride, said there was nothing to do but accept it and try again."

"That man is so strange. And it's not just thick skin either. It's not normal."

"He's not as unbreakable as he seems," Noelle said, guarding her husband, his secrets.

The first time Noelle had seen Nelson cry was toward the end of college. A girl Noelle knew from seminar had died. She and the girl had sat beside each other for months, shared notes, complained about the professor's illegible handwriting. She had been sick, but Noelle hadn't known. The professor made an announcement at the end of class. In her room, Noelle had sobbed, inconsolable, carrying on about the unpredictability of life, how they would all die, but they didn't know when. Nelson had tried to comfort her. He put his arm around her, cycled through every aphorism he seemed to know about cherishing every day. When he couldn't calm her, he grew more and more agitated, until finally he started to beat his own skull. He crumpled onto the floor and begged her to stop. There was no point in her suffering. It wouldn't make anything better; it wouldn't bring back her friend. She'd only derail herself. Noelle wound up rocking him, kissing him until he was still. They made love. They never talked about her friend again.

"Why would he break when he's got you looking after him?" Inéz said. "You're the one I worry about."

"I'm not as blameless as I seem. I've been a mess. I think that's why he took the job in Paris — to get some space."

"He'd be a fool to stop loving you."

Noelle shrugged. "We've been together a

long time."

"So?" Inéz asked, defiant. "So have we, and we've sustained our love." She smiled at Noelle, leaned her head back against the rocker.

Noelle didn't want to hurt her by saying it was different: the fuel needed to run a marriage, how exacting it was to be so close to someone, to see them with the same mixture of sympathy and scorn that you saw yourself. It didn't even take an unkindness to feel let down by the person with whom you had vested your whole life.

"He can't be everything to you," Inéz said.

"I know, I know, *never rely on a man.*" It had been their mantra in college, even as Noelle had dated Nelson year after year. She didn't believe it, but she knew it was what Inéz wanted to hear.

"No, no," Inéz said, the light from the torches coloring her face. "It's got nothing to do with that."

Inéz slept beside her, her breath filling the bedroom with the kind of presence Noelle had been missing. Still, she couldn't sleep. She ran a bath and brought her phone with her in case Nelson called. It was a new day in Paris.

She sank into the hot water, dropped in

the rose and calendula soak she had bought to help with fertility. The dried flowers bobbed in the bath. Noelle didn't believe they would ever work, but all the witchy remedies gave her, at least, something to do. She could drink primrose tea to soften her cervix, take fish oil and go for long walks, treat conception like a full-time job. It made her feel her odds were better. Nelson had said they could make another, but she wasn't so sure. She'd never get pregnant if he weren't around.

Nelson told her not to think of the miscarriage as a baby but rather a little maybe she'd been carrying around that had turned to a no. But her child had been the size of a mango when she lost him. He'd been anchored in her, by blood, a new organ her body had made. She knew that babies were conceived and died all the time when they were just the size of seeds or nuts, but that knowledge had made no difference. The little maybe had been hers, a life she was waiting on.

The phone rang and Noelle leapt for it. Finally. Nelson. She needed his voice, the sweet husk of it.

The voice that came through the phone was coarse and female. Her little sister Diane. She called every once in a while, usually on mornings she was alone on a long drive. They had kept up their small talk over the years, as if all they needed to know was that the other was fine. Noelle loved her sister, but she'd lost track of her somehow, while she was busy running from Lacey May.

"Chickadee, why are you up so late? Everything all right?"

"Mama collapsed this morning. She fell right off the front porch."

A sick shock ran through Noelle. She remembered her mother had called earlier, and she had ignored her. If her mother was hurt badly, she'd never live it down — the prodigal daughter, now even worse than Margarita. "Is she all right?"

"She's awake now. Bumped her head pretty hard though."

"Well, all right. So she's fine."

"The problem is she fainted cause she's sick, Noelle. They're saying she's got cancer."

The word hit Noelle like a physical blow, a straight shot to the chest. "Not everybody dies from cancer," she said.

"She's been asking for you. She's going on about how she knows you won't come, even if she's dying, cause you hate her that much."

"Mama sure knows what to say to convince people of her way of seeing things."

"Maybe you should come home. What are you so busy with anyway?"

"You call Margarita yet?"

"Yes. She was as indifferent as you are. Some sisters I have."

"Well, what am I supposed to do, Diane? I'm not an oncologist."

"Then come home for me, goddamn it. Did you ever think I shouldn't be the only one to go through all this?"

Noelle could sense her sister seething on the line, little Diane who didn't ask for things, who was good-natured and steadfast, the most peaceable Ventura.

"Fine, I'll come, but I'm not staying at Mama's."

"You can't stay with me — you know I've got a roommate. Things are tight around here."

"I don't mind. I'll sleep on the couch. You and Alma can keep your rooms."

"All right."

"I'll leave tomorrow."

"Good. You better hurry up."

"Come on, Diane, ease up. I don't like the way you're talking to me."

"I don't want to play peacekeeper between you and Mama once you're here. Or you

81

and Margarita, if she ever shows up. I've got my own life going on. My own problems. I don't know why I always wind up stuck in the middle."

"Little sis, it's only cause you're not like the rest of us. You're one of the good ones."

Noelle meant the words as a kindness, but Diane answered her with fury.

"Just get down here quick, and try not to cause trouble once you arrive. You might not care about any of us now that you've got a family of your own, but this is for real. Mama's got a tumor in her brain."

4

Jade put up a shrine to Ray in the kitchen. It was where he would have liked it to be. She hung his picture on the wall, potted violets underneath. She set out a fat black candle that smelled like tobacco when it burned, and nailed a wooden rosary to the wall. Jade didn't believe in God, exactly, but if there were one, she wanted him to look after Ray. And so, each morning, she lit the candle in the early dark, squatted in front of the shrine, and tried to pray. She would start off talking to God and wind up talking to Ray. His voice was the one she wanted to hear. So far, she had heard nothing, but she went on kneeling at the shrine, expectant. If he had a spirit, he would still be around, trying to reach her. All she had to do was wait.

At first, she asked for his forgiveness. It was her fault for getting him mixed up with her family — a crew of people she should have known to leave behind. She said sorry, and she cursed herself, cursed Wilson. Once, she was so loud, Gee woke up and crept into the kitchen without her noticing. She turned and found him leaning against the door, giving her a terrified look. She sent him to his room right away, told him everything was fine. She knew well that sadness was a contagion. So was rage. She couldn't allow him to see her swallowed up by grief.

Now, she mostly asked Ray for help. Help to rise early enough to do all the things that he used to do: fix breakfast and pour milk and wash dishes and iron clothes. Help to carry on. Help to find peace, whatever superpower had made Ray able to smile at life, keep cool, and be satisfied. That wasn't her. But she had to find a way now, for Gee.

And she was tired, so tired. It had been six weeks since Ray was gone, and she hadn't felt this drained since her first days with a newborn. All those hours she spent alone in her mother's house with a baby she didn't know how to soothe or hold or feed. The only thing she knew then was that she had to control herself. She couldn't lose her temper. He couldn't see her weep. They learned about the world by looking at your face, listening to the tone of your voice. A baby couldn't handle the raw force of her loneliness, her terror. And so, she had smiled at him, forced herself to stay calm when he spat up milk on her, to say sweet things she didn't mean when she crawled out of the bed to feed him in the middle of the night. All that effort in those days, and still her son had wound up a boy with a father who was dead. Now, she found herself playing that same role again. She was even. She smiled at Gee. She turned to him even when she'd rather stay in bed. She pretended she didn't miss Ray as badly as she did; she pretended it wouldn't be near impossible for them to go on. She stopped herself whenever she felt she would overflow; it was far too much for such a little boy.

On her first day off since the funeral, Jade sat at the shrine and waited on Ray. She was hollowed out, dazed from another string of bad dreams. Sometimes, they were benign: She was looking for Ray, wandering the halls of her high school, a corridor of empty hospital rooms that opened one onto another. She saw Ray ahead of her, and she chased him, but he'd vanish every time, just before she reached him. But other times, the dreams were terrifying. There was a fire, and Ray was walking into a smoke-filled house. There was a storm, and Ray was charging toward the center. There was an earthquake, and he was standing on the road, unshielded. Every time, she ran to him. Every time, he was going away from her.

Jade sat cross-legged on the carpet, and she hurt all over. Her knees hurt, her hip bones, her jaw. Grief, she knew, could take over the body. The social worker had left her pamphlets that said so. The pamphlets included bullet-pointed tips, as if mourning were like starting a new diet. Check the boxes, and you'd be on your way. *Talk out loud to your beloved* was the one she tried each morning at the shrine. So was *Lean on your higher power.* Another bullet point encouraged her to sit still and observe her thoughts, but she quit that one quick. Her thoughts were a dismal parade. *We never got married and I'm still a widow. Ray looked after me and it killed him. When I graduate from nursing school, nobody's going to be there. I don't want to love anybody else. Gee won't ever be able to unsee what he saw. Ray, where are you. Ray, can you hear me. Ray, Ray.*

Jade sat for a while, asking Ray for help, the only help he could provide — for an

86

idea. She had to do something about the bills. Electricity, gas, the phone, the rent. She was late on everything. Things had been tight since she went back to school, but without Ray, it was worse. She and Gee were already on cups of noodles, canned beans, bread and peanut butter. The night before, Jade had scavenged dessert from underneath the sink: canned peaches that she and Gee ate together on the couch with spoons, taking turns to drain the syrup from the can.

It had been easy when Ray was alive to ignore how much she depended on him. She loved him — that was clear — but he had guided her, too, in a way she would never have admitted. He was the one who administered their lives, who bought Gee the next size up in shoes, who turned down the thermostat at night, who bought detergent and set alarms, who drew a blanket over her when she fell asleep with her books, a drink.

After several minutes of nothing at the shrine, Jade gave up and told Ray good-bye. The day was calling her, and Gee would be getting up soon. She kissed her fingers, touched them to his face. The photograph was from a day they had gone to the park with Gee. It was nothing but a flat field and a few oak trees, and she remembered being bored, wishing she were somewhere else, by herself for once, or studying. But Ray had amused Gee, making up games and running around, pulling up grass and tossing handfuls at their boy. It had moved her, how much he seemed to delight in Gee, how content he seemed with their life. She had taken the picture of the two of them.

Without any intervention from Ray, wherever he was, she had to go on with the only plan she had: to move Gee in with her and rent out his little square of a room. Jade sat at the kitchen table and wrote out an ad. She wouldn't get much for it, but it was better than nothing. She wondered about the odds of finding a woman, someone safe enough to let in her house.

When she was done, she hauled herself to the stove, and made hot chocolate from two dusty packets she found in a cupboard. She browned bread in the oven, spread butter over the last two slices, and left the bigger one for Gee. She went to his bedroom and turned on the lights. "Up," she said. A few minutes later, he was in the kitchen in his pajamas, frowning at her.

"Mommy, it's too early."

"We've got a lot to do today." She pointed at his toast and chocolate. It was a command, and Gee sank into a chair, rubbed his eyes, and started nibbling at the crust.

Gee seemed fine, more fine than she had expected. Sometimes, he moved too slow, took too long to answer her, but he snapped out of it when she shook him. He went to school and did his homework, watched cartoons and colored at the kitchen table. He was still seeing the social worker for now, but as far as she knew, he wasn't doing much crying in there either. He seemed like himself, maybe a bit more turned off, but he had always been that way with her: somber, tentative. He was used to saving up all his play and sweetness for Ray. The biggest change was that he was asking her questions, and it made Jade suspect Gee didn't understand what had happened at all. He talked as if there were a small chance Ray would be coming back. *When the summer comes, who's going to take me wading in the creek?* he asked, as if she might say, *Your daddy.* Or *Who is going to teach me to play ball?* or *Who is going to make my roast beef sandwiches now?* Every question gave her a reason to break. Still, she answered him. What else was she to do?

Jade found suddenly that she'd lost her appetite. She slid her toast onto Gee's plate.

"What do you think about getting a room-mate?"

"Like another little kid?"

"No, like a nice lady. Somebody fun to eat breakfast with in the morning?"

"A stranger?"

"Some strangers are nice," she said. "Some strangers are nicer than your own family."

"But I don't want to live with a stranger."

Jade shushed him before he could say more. She knew whom he wanted to live with, and she couldn't bear to hear him say it. "Finish up your toast," she said, and he didn't protest. He ate, rose to put his plate in the sink. He was such a pliant child, she often wondered how it was that he came from her. Jade reached for him by the shoulders, looked him hard in the eyes.

"You know I love you, right, little man?"

As soon as she spoke, she realized it had come out all wrong. It shouldn't have been a question. Gee nodded at her and mm-hmmed, then shuffled back to his room to get dressed. She should have just told him — *Gee, I love you. I love you, I love you.*

When they finished hanging the flyers, it was ten thirty, and Jade drove them to Superfine, where they could get free breakfast, and she could talk to Linette.

They found it closed, the metal gate down, the windows shuttered. The mums planted in the window boxes were shrunken, brittle. Jade had a bottle of water in the car. She doused the soil, but it wasn't hardly enough.

"Should we get more water, Mommy?"

Jade shook her head. "It's too late."

"They're dead?"

She nodded.

"And they can't grow back?"

"No, they can't, baby."

She watched him puzzle over what it meant. She laid a hand on his shoulder, and the scent of the rotting flowers, the stale dirt, overtook her. She doubled over in front of the shop and vomited.

Gee thumped her on the back. "Mommy, Mommy," he said, and she snapped at him. "Jesus Christ, can you stop banging on my back?"

He stared at her, his face twisted with fear. She caught herself, wiped her mouth, and cupped his little chin in her hands. "Come on," she said. "We've got to find Ms. Linette."

She knew the way to Linette's house by memory. It was a brick and white town house wedged between identical homes on either side. There was a small courtyard full of crape myrtles. The purple flowers were all gone, the parking lot and walkway slick with rain and crushed petals. Gee walked ahead of her. Jade had to call to him twice before he turned around, took her hand. It was an act of obedience, as if he, too, found it unnatural for her to hold him.

At the door, Jade checked the two of them to make sure they were presentable. Linette had strange ideas about what people ought to wear. Jade was in a black turtleneck and skirt, her lace-up boots, and Gee in a secondhand wool sweater, sneakers, and jeans. He was bleary-eyed but neat. The old woman couldn't object.

"My little man!" Linette said when she opened the door. Gee stretched his arms up to her, and she hoisted him onto her hip. "You must be cold. Out here with no jacket? No coat? What was your mama thinking?"

Jade made a point not to roll her eyes and followed them into the house.

The living room was dark, velvet drapes hanging over the windows. Linette had grubby carpet that smelled of dust and recycled air. The plywood coffee table was scattered with porcelain figurines — a white lamb, two children drawing water from a well. Linette left Gee and Jade on the couch and went to fix a pot of tea.

Linette had answered the door wearing a rumpled blue housedress, her hair tied into a crooked bun at the side of her head. She was moonfaced, pale lipped without any makeup on. She came back with a tray, teetering with cups, a plate of shortbread cookies. Gee thanked Linette and dug in.

"You didn't have to do all this," Jade said.

"I didn't want to come over empty-handed."

"But here you are." Linette smiled, squinted her eyes at her over the porcelain cup. The cup had a gold rim, blue roses painted on the saucer. Jade wondered whether this tea set was one she'd used when her husband was alive, whether all the things Linette owned were relics of her old life. He'd died of a stroke one day while waiting in line at the bank.

"You admiring my china?" Linette asked. "These were passed down to me by my grandmother. She lived here, you know? Back when there was still a black business district, a whole city inside this city. Before they built the freeway right through it. Did you know about that? They didn't teach you that history in school, I bet."

Jade didn't like when older women talked to her as if she were their child, as if being old gave them a pass to mother anyone they wanted. It was hard for her not to fight back whenever someone talked down to her in that motherly way. They'd mean to say, *I'm looking after your own good,* but it always seemed closer to *You are no good.*

Jade felt a flutter in her chest, a surge of exhaustion that started behind her eyes and rolled down to her feet. She had the sensation that she might faint, and she knew she should have eaten more that morning, but the idea of tasting anything had made her sick.

"Mommy, what's the matter? Are you going to throw up again?"

Linette sputtered over her coffee.

"I'm fine," Jade said. "I've just been feeling funny since what happened."

"What's going on now?"

Jade tried to explain. "Sometimes, after a shift, I'll be walking to my car, and it's like I'm floating outside of my body. Like I'm not really there, like I could just fall right through the earth."

Linette was staring at her now, clenching and unclenching her hands.

"Gee, why don't you go out to the yard and play? Sometimes there's a big cat that likes to lay out there in the sun. Go on and see if you can find him."

Gee took one last gulp of his tea and went out the back door.

"You can't talk like that in front of him," Linette said. "You're all he's got now, and you've got to learn to be the solid one."

Jade felt bruised. She had been trying to confide in Linette, share something real. "You know I had Gee before I met Ray, right? I was raising him all by myself."

"You were raising him the way they raised you. Keeping him alive but not so much as looking at him."

"Give me a break, Linette."

"Ray told me about all the times Gee missed school because you were dead asleep, drunk. I hope you're ashamed of yourself."

"Shame's not really my thing," Jade said, and she decided there'd be no better time, no use in trying to butter her up anymore. "I came to ask for a loan."

Linette knit her fingers together, shook her head. "I closed Superfine. Since the story ran, I've been getting calls. Inquiries. People who want us to cater. But I don't have anyone to help me fill those orders. Not without Ray."

"I wouldn't need more than twenty dollars. Just something to hold us over until I get my check."

"You know, I haven't seen you since the funeral. You haven't dropped by to see me once."

"We've never had a habit of visiting each other."

"This hasn't been easy on me either," Linette went on. "First, I lose Billy. Then I lose Ray. It's no good dying, but sometimes I think it's worse being the one who's left behind."

Jade couldn't agree. She'd have done anything to have Ray back again — anything short of dying herself. She was certain that she wanted to live. It was all she wanted, too, for her boy.

Linette sighed and heaved herself off the couch. She looked wider than she had at the funeral. She came back with her tangerine leather purse, fished inside, and handed Jade a twenty.

"You must know how I feel about you," Linette said. "Or how I don't feel about you. I never kept it a secret."

"I'm not sure how you feel," Jade said, "but I bet it's mutual." She slipped the bill in her purse.

Linette leaned back on the settee, as if she were too tired to go on trading blows with Jade.

"Ray was the closest thing I had to a son.

I won't let you go hungry, especially not Gee."

"Thanks for being clear," Jade said. She headed for the back door to collect her son.

"Wait," Linette said. She stood with a huff and clamped her hand on Jade's arm. "I'm just trying to find someone to put all my anger on. I know it shouldn't be you." Linette looked at her pleadingly. She softened her voice. "I know you and Ray used to talk about having a baby together."

Jade wrenched her arm away from the old woman. She didn't want to talk about those times with Ray, times Linette could know nothing about. The way he used to whisper in her ear when they were making love: *Come on, baby, can't you just picture her — a girl?*

"You look different," Linette said. "I can't explain it. Something in your eyes, in the way you're moving around, your limbs. I saw it when you walked in the door. And then Gee said you threw up this morning."

"He's been dead six weeks, Linette. That's too long. I'd know by now."

"Well, did you get your period?"

"They say grief can affect all kinds of things. It's probably stress — I haven't given it any mind. It's not possible."

"Why don't you take a test?"

"He's gone, Linette."

Linette sighed, and Jade could see now that she was crying.

"It wouldn't be the worst thing in the world, Jade. Ray gave you a life once. Maybe he's giving you life again, one last time. Maybe there's a little piece of him that's still here."

At the supermarket, Gee darted ahead of her in the aisles, pulling down the things she'd said they would need. She wanted to get home and make him lunch so that she could sleep a few hours before dropping him off with her cousin Carmela. She didn't like leaving him with her, but there was no one else anymore. She wasn't talking to Wilson. When Jade arrived in the morning, she usually found Carmela snoring on the floor, the TV still on, and Gee huddled on the edge of the couch, as if he hadn't slept at all, chasing off bad thoughts by keeping his eyes open.

Gee had piled the cart with cereal, milk, bananas, and everything she needed for her specialty: chicken cutlets, roma tomatoes, a box of spaghetti, bread crumbs, a can of sauce.

"You know, before I met your daddy, I used to make dinner for myself, and there was only one thing I knew how to make. Chicken Parmesan. And it was the only thing I made because I never needed to learn to make anything else — it's that good."

She kissed her fingers for emphasis, and Gee giggled. She collected his laughter in her ears. It was the greatest accomplishment of her day.

"Go on and get me some cheese," she said, and he took off again. He was a good boy.

He returned, waving a green canister. She thanked him and did some quick math, counting up what was inside their cart. They could eat the leftovers for days, stretch the sauce over spaghetti, put the chicken inside sandwiches. She told him to return the tomatoes and meet her at the front.

In the pharmacy, Jade inspected the pregnancy tests. She felt foolish for even taking Linette's words to heart. She had always looked at Jade as if she had no right to be a mother — lots of women did that to her, especially when she was younger, carrying Gee around wherever she had to go. If she'd gotten an abortion, they'd have called her a murderer, but now they looked at her and Gee as if they were a waste of life. Why bring another child into this world?

She had been pulled over once for a broken tag light. She was five minutes from home, and four cops got out all at once. They shone flashlights in their faces, made Gee lie on the ground next to her, his cheek against the grit of the road. She had felt anger surge through her, an electric strength in her limbs. They sent her off with a warning. On the drive home, her leg thumped uncontrollably beneath her, the car lurching as she shook. Her anger gave way to terror, for her son, the world she'd never be able to shield him from. And all of this was before they'd lost Ray.

At the register, the cashier was a gaunt-faced man with chin-length hair. He wore a neon-yellow vest over a tattered plaid shirt. He asked her how she was doing, and she grumbled hello and turned back to the register to see if she'd been right about how it would all add up.

"That's a pretty little boy you got there."

Jade nodded at the cashier in thanks.

"He got all his good looks from his mama, didn't he? But it's not really right to call you good-looking. You're a lot more than that."

"Don't you talk that way to me in front of my son."

"I was just giving you a compliment."

"Any more compliments and I'll have to ask to talk to your manager."

The skinny man laughed and pointed to a tag on his shirt. It read TEAM LEADER.

"That's me, sweetheart. Would you like to file a complaint?"

"Just ring me up. I'm not your goddamn sweetheart." She handed him the twenty-dollar bill.

"You're short," the man said, and Jade saw it was by seventy-nine cents. She started rummaging in her wallet knowing she wouldn't find anything there. She picked up the box of cereal to leave behind.

"Easy there," the team leader said. He scooped a handful of change out of a plastic container beside the register. "I've got you." He spoke in a low voice, magnanimous, as if he didn't want to embarrass her. She wasn't embarrassed. He dropped the extra change into the register, withdrew her receipt, and handed it to her.

"What's your name anyway?"

"Onyx."

"Well, Onyx, next time you're in here, you come find me. This is my register. I'm here almost all the time. Come see me, and I'll take real good care of you."

He winked at her, and Jade felt her stomach turn. She knew what she wanted to say, *Fuck you, you nasty arrogant fuckface.* She wanted to drive her palm up into his nose.

Instead, she told Gee to step up on the cart. She pushed him toward the exit and made sure not to turn around. She was sure he'd be watching them.

"Mommy, you weren't very nice to that man. He gave us money."

"He didn't do what he did out of kindness."

"Why'd he do it?"

"There are bad people in this world, Gee."

"Like that man?"

She wanted to say, *Like him, like the man who killed your father, like my father, like Ray's father, like your father, like Wilson, like a lot of people.* She cleared her throat.

"Maybe. I don't know. But sometimes you're better off not sticking around to find out."

Their first date had been marred by Gee. Jade had never gone out somewhere with a man. She'd never had one show up at her house, drive her away, kiss her good night in the car. She and the college boy had only ever gone to the Cook Out drive-through after class. They'd listen to hard rock and split a joint, then drive somewhere to have sex in the backseat. There hadn't been dates.

She had told Ray she had no one to watch Gee, but he said to bring him.

He'd taken her to a café in the next county over. It wasn't far from the campus of the university, where she'd been accepted but couldn't attend because of Gee. The café was a little shack in the middle of the woods, tables scattered beneath trees, stone sculptures and dirt paths winding around the hilly grounds. Inside, they didn't ask for ID, so Ray ordered them beers, two slices of cake. They could sit wherever they wanted, so they found a stone bench underneath a string of lights. The night was breezy and the mosquitoes were biting, and Gee squirmed and cried. It was getting close to his bedtime. She stood to rock him, to get him to be quiet, so she could drink her beer, talk to Ray, but it was no help. He was ruining her dress with his drool.

Eventually, Ray asked if he could hold the boy. Gee was mesmerized by him, a new person. He put his hand on Ray's cheek, gazed at him. Jade rushed to finish her cake, to drain her beer, until she was fuzzy-drunk and calm. The cicadas were singing. She couldn't believe the café was less than thirty minutes from where she lived. He told her he wanted to own a café of his own one day, so he made a business of visiting them, memorizing menus, learning about flavors. The key was slowing down, he said. You had to slow down to taste.

When they were back in the car, Jade rode in the back with Gee in her lap, the seat belt over the both of them. *Next time bring the car seat,* Ray had said, and it surprised her that she didn't hear it as an order. He was sweet and matter-of-fact, and she wanted to see him again, too.

New Hope sliced through the forest. It was one of the newer roads, uncracked and brilliant black, snaking through the heart of the east side. The trees formed a tunnel around them. If she turned left for the freeway, she could ride back to that café she and Ray had visited that one time.

"Mommy?"

Gee snapped her back to the car, the present. "Hmm?"

"Did Daddy have other children?"

"Who told you that?"

"Carmela was saying Daddy wasn't really my daddy. So I wanted to know if he was really somebody else's?"

Jade looked through the rearview at her son. He already looked dejected, although she hadn't said anything. What could she say to dislodge the doubt her cousin had planted?

They were going forty-five on a two-lane road, the shoulder no more than dirt, but Jade pulled off quickly, slammed the car into park. She had to turn around and look at him, make sure he understood.

"Sometimes, people are your family because they're your blood. But that doesn't mean much on its own. The realest family are the people who stand by you. Your daddy would have stood by us every day for the rest of time, if he'd gotten the chance. He's not your blood, but he's your daddy. And the next time anybody tells you different, you tell them, 'Fuck off.' Even Carmela. That's right — 'Fuck off.' And if they say anything to you, don't you worry — you tell them your mommy said it's all right. Under this one condition, you have my permission. It's not nice, but sometimes you have to tell people so they can hear."

As soon as she got home, Jade called Linette. "I know you wish that I was pregnant," she said. "But Ray already has a child. He's already left someone behind for us."

Then she explained about Carmela, how she wasn't attentive to Gee, didn't cover him with a blanket when he fell asleep on the couch. Linette seemed unmoved.

"She's been telling him that Ray isn't really his daddy."

"I'll take him," Linette said.

Jade was so relieved she swooped down and kissed Gee on the mouth. He was startled but pleased, and he smiled back at her, stumbled off to unpack the groceries.

"But you've got to do something for me, Jade," Linette said, still on the line. "You've got to take a test. I just have a feeling."

"You're getting your hopes up for nothing."

"Please."

"Fine, but get ready for bad news."

Jade hung up the phone and got a beer from the fridge. It was old, flat. She took one long swallow and then another. If she were pregnant, one wouldn't do any harm, she figured, but she wasn't sure. She took another swig.

Gee had pulled a stool over to the sink. He was filling a big pot with water. He set it on the stove and then started fishing out the tools they'd need. He was quick around the kitchen after all the time he'd spent shadowing Ray. Even though Gee had Ray's imprint all over him, Jade couldn't help but be overcome with the sense that Gee was hers. It wasn't that he looked so much like her — he didn't — or that he had her mannerisms — he had Ray's. It was this feeling that she wanted him to live more than she had ever wanted anyone or anything to live. This feeling that her survival was mostly about him. It would be easy to chalk that up to nothing, but no one had ever loved Ray that way; no one had ever loved her. On the day Jade left home, her mother barely looked up from her can of beer. "Bye," she'd said, without stirring from the couch, without a wave. Her mother had slapped her, thrown her against a wall, cut off all her hair once with a pair of shears, but none of that had hurt as much as how indifferent she could be. Jade had left and hadn't looked back, and her mother had never gone searching for her.

If there was something she could do for her son, it would be to never be indifferent to the course of his life. She would advise him. She would watch over him. It would be either her or no one, and he deserved more than that.

They worked together in the kitchen, Gee salting the water, showing her where Ray had kept the red pepper. They ate spoonfuls of powdered cheese while they waited for the pasta to cook. The boy seemed content.

"This is good," she said, tasting the spirals

of the spaghetti. It was all she said out loud, but she hoped he'd get her other meaning — it could be good, just the two of them, together. She didn't believe it fully herself, but she didn't want him to feel alone. Would it be better, after all, if she were really pregnant like Linette had said?

With Gee, she'd had weeks of cramps she'd mistaken for a period taking its time to arrive. She'd felt nothing this time, but even if there was a churning within her, the buildup of new cells, would she have noticed? They weren't always careful. She didn't like it when there was anything between the two of them, and she felt fine about it because she was good at timing her cycles. After sex, Ray liked to get up and rinse off, and she would pin him down on the bed, try to get him to stay where she wanted him. It was one of the only times she let on how much she needed him. She assumed it was obvious from their life, all the ways they were one, but now she couldn't be sure she'd done enough to make him know. She shook the thought away — it was too bottomless. She heard his voice in her ears comforting her. *You didn't never know,* he said. *How short our time would be.*

Jade's mouth dropped open. It was the visitation she had been waiting for. His spirit. She strained to hear him again.

"Mommy?"

It was the first time she had cried in front of her son. She had done her best at the funeral, the ensuing days, to shield him, to be strong. She built the shrine for her private mourning.

"Mommy," he said again, reaching up to her. She brought his arms down to his side.

"Now, now," she said, "no more tears," although she was the one who was crying. "Remember what I told you? We've got to keep moving forward. Daddy would have wanted that."

Gee gaped at her. She patted him on the head, told him to bring down the plates. When Gee didn't move, she told him to pay her mind. She kept her voice soft, went on giving him directions. This was better: to calm him, turn his mind elsewhere. She went through the motions: serving food, eating, cleaning up, but she was waiting to hear Ray's voice again. She didn't. He'd already gone away from her.

That night at the hospital, Jade went to see the attending physician on her break. She brought him a cup of coffee and knocked on the door. She liked working with Dr. Henriquez, his full head of silver hair, his green eyes and thin face, his wide, pouting lips. He was always laughing at his own jokes, clapping staff on the shoulders to congratulate them on the smallest of tasks — a smooth handoff of a patient, a quick draw of blood. He didn't look past forty, despite his hair, and Jade wondered if he'd gone gray from all these terrible night shifts.

He offered her a wrapped pineapple candy from a crystal dish on his desk. Jade said no, still working up the nerve to say what she had to.

"You know we don't get insurance in this job, right?"

"You're part-time," Dr. Henriquez said. "And they keep it that way on purpose."

"My boyfriend died last month. I haven't brought it up cause there's always a different attending, and I didn't want to keep having to say it, over and over."

Dr. Henriquez snapped his jaw shut, relaxed his brow. It was the same composure she had seen him use with patients. She wondered if it was real, his ability to tolerate bad news, or if he'd learned how to switch something off inside himself.

"Jade, I'm sorry. You need some time off?"

"I can't afford that. I've got a little boy."

Dr. Henriquez didn't react to the mention of Gee, which Jade appreciated. She was sick of the doctors looking shocked and saying, *But you're so young!* It was worst with the female residents, who were older but didn't have any children of their own. They could hardly cover up their envy, disgust.

"That's a big burden, raising him all by yourself now."

"I used to think of him that way. Like a big old weight tied to my ankle. But it felt different with Ray. Like maybe my turn wasn't up yet. Like maybe I still had a shot at my own life. You know I'm in school, right? I'm not going to be a medical assistant forever."

"You'll make a great nurse one day. Your boyfriend was right to support you. Good man."

"He was. My son is, too. We call him Gee."

She took a candy from the dish. It stuck to her tongue, the tart, artificial yellow tang. "I think I might be pregnant."

"Then you ought to check."

"Could you give me a test?"

"All right," he said, rising. "Let's get this done."

Dr. Henriquez met her back in his office. He cleared off an area of his desk, handled the plastic canister that Jade had brought back from the bathroom. It was embarrassing to watch him hold the cupful of her pee. He dipped in one of the test strips, laid it flat on a paper towel.

"Now we wait," he said.

Jade nodded. She didn't want to look, to see if two lines materialized. She stared at the doctor. He must have been a pretty younger man once, before his gray hair, the little lines encircling his lips. She had known somehow that she could trust him, even if they had only shared small talk on these night shifts together. She believed, for whatever reason, that he'd keep her secret.

"Where are you from, Dr. Henriquez?"

"Miami," he said, then, "But you mean before. Peru. My parents were both doctors. They sent me here to study."

He didn't say that they were rich, but Jade could figure out that much. He nodded, as if he could read her thoughts.

"I've been luckier than I deserve in life. If there's one thing I've learned in medicine, it's that life isn't fair. Nature isn't fair, and we only make it worse."

"How much longer?"

"A few minutes."

"Are you married?"

"My wife left me during residency. She hated North Carolina, and I was never home. Once she was gone, I had no reason

112

not to stay. I like it here."

"It's fine."

"Honestly, it's not so bad being alone, under these circumstances. It's hard when you feel you're constantly letting someone down just by doing what you have to do." He drummed his fingers on the desk.

"I know what you mean," Jade said.

When Gee was born, Jade cried and cried. She could barely look at him; there had been so much blood. Before he was born, he had been mostly theoretical to her. First, he was a blastocyst, and she tracked the development of his cells. She had wanted to study molecular biology in college, and pregnancy had been like a science experiment that she couldn't halt, unfolding in her own body. Then he was a squealing purple thing they handed to her. He smelled medicinal, raw, and she had wanted someone to take him away.

She had never had a baby by a man she loved. Maybe it would be different.

"I'm sorry, Jade," Dr. Henriquez said. She leaned over his desk to examine the strip. A single pink line, the control line. She wasn't pregnant. Her legs buckled, and she sank to the ground. Dr. Henriquez went to her, held her by the shoulders. "I'm sorry," he said again. How could she explain that it was relief that brought her to her knees? It was better this way, a mercy. She had chosen Gee when she was a girl, and she didn't know any better. She wouldn't make the same choice now.

Her voice rose from within her, unbidden. "Ray," she said. She waited for him to speak, to return. To forgive her. "Ray," she said again. She heard nothing, so she conjured up his voice for herself. *How short our time would be.* It was no comfort, false. Why would he come to her now? She was selfish, and she knew it. It was a terrible thing to choose your own life, to be willing to live it.

5

Lacey May pretended she was still asleep, belly down, her arms covering her face. She flicked her eyes open to check the time. Thirty-four minutes until Robbie's bus got in. She felt her heart beat in her ears. He was closer and closer.

The front door clanged shut, and she heard Hank stomping toward her. She let out the long sigh of someone who was still out cold. Soon he was kneeling beside her, whispering a litany of pet names. This was the phase they were still in, even after more than a year: waking each other with kisses, fetching glasses of water in the night, murmuring *sweetheart* and *baby* at every chance. They were still trying to make it real, neither wanting to catch the other in a lie.

"Baby," he said. "Sweetheart. I got the car all loaded up. You ready?"

Lacey May mumbled unintelligibly, and

115

he shook her by the shoulders until she gave up the ruse.

"We can't leave yet. The girls have got to eat and get ready."

"We're going to the beach. They can go dirty. They can eat in the car."

Hank had on his swim trunks already; he had shaved, combed his hair back with water. It was no accident he had planned the trip for the precise day Robbie was set to be released. Lacey May glanced at the clock. Twenty-seven minutes.

She gave Hank a kiss to take the edge off, pressed his hand flush against her chest. It wasn't long before he was massaging her breast. "Baby," he said. "Sweetheart."

It wasn't bad, after all, this part of life with Hank. He was eager for instructions, zealous, and she could do so much for herself with a turn of her hips, the right picture in her head. What she had assumed was magic with Robbie had proven to be something cruder, more animal, a predictable spark that any two bodies could make together.

Lacey May kissed him, held his face in the crook of her neck. She kept her head up, one eye turned toward the clock.

She convinced hank to make pancakes, and the girls sat at the kitchen table in their bathing suits. Margarita was the only one eating, licking syrup from her fingers, reciting all the things she'd do at the beach — bury herself in the sand, find a popsicle stand, join in a game of volleyball. She was telling them the story of the day, as if it had already happened, and she could assure them it would all be fine. Diane was somber, slipping her bacon to Jenkins under the table. Noelle's eyes were fixed on the street, and she looked like a little lady, older than twelve, in her sundress. She had worn yellow, Robbie's favorite color.

Hank paced the living room, on his third cup of coffee. He swept the curtains aside.

"We got some clouds moving in," he said, as if the beach weren't one hundred miles away.

By now, the girls knew their father had been in jail. Lacey gave up on the story about the fishery job when they moved in with Hank and rented out the house. They had never visited him, but Lacey May kept on depositing money in his commissary. Hank couldn't begrudge her that. The money she earned at the store was hers to keep, and Robbie was still her husband, at least legally.

"I'm off for a smoke," Lacey May said, and Hank didn't stop her. He must have figured out they were all stalling, and there was nothing he could do.

It was as quiet as usual on the street. The bungalows down the lane were small and attractive, houses that had been built and sold after the war. Hank had inherited his from his father. It was simple, with brick columns, a shingle roof, a picture window that looked out on the hydrangeas on the lawn. Honeysuckle grew in the back, and there was an inflated pool covered in leaves, the yellow film of pollen. It was a fine place for her and her girls, although it wasn't the kind of place she'd have ever chosen for herself, except, of course, she had.

She had lived on this side of town before, west of Main Street, when she was in high school. Robbie had lived on the east side, where the South and Central Americans tended to land. The town had been largely split this way — white and black, then white and not white, for as long as Lacey could remember. It had been true even before they were born, when the millworkers dispersed at the end of each day. It had remained true, even as the west side had emptied out, and most people who could afford to leave the city did. Lacey's family had stayed. But she'd been grateful to move to the northern edge of the county when Robbie bought their house. Out there, they made more sense. Their neighbors were the river and fruit farms, a dairy plant, the old Civil War battleground.

Here, she'd caught some of the neighbors looking a little funny at her Diane. While nobody said anything, Lacey May couldn't help but notice. Noelle was the fairest, limber, big eyed, long haired. Margarita looked like her father: dark eyes and full lips, something alien about the way her face was put together. And Diane looked like neither of them with her high cheekbones and coiling hair, how brown she became in the summer. But Lacey May didn't see her daughters that way; as far as she was concerned, they were all the same to her, hers. Colombia was just a place their father was from, like Ireland, or France. Everybody was from somewhere else. Even the Native Americans. And what did it matter? The earth used to be all one continent; she had heard about it on a program.

Lacey was renting the house to two Brazilians. They were a pair of graduate students, hippies growing herbs in the yard, leaving their fat books out in piles on the porch. She often wondered what Robbie would think about some other couple living in their house, reading books and drinking wine or whatever it was they drank, talking about the future and where they'd live next. She and Robbie had never wanted to live anywhere else.

She heard him before she saw him. He was humming. She hadn't even lit her cigarette.

He was wearing the clothes he'd had on the day they took him in: jeans and a black button-up. He carried a plastic bag, and he wore all his usual jewelry: a stud in each ear, his gold watch. When he got close enough, she saw his wedding ring swimming on his finger. He was thinner, bronzed, as if he really had been working on the shore all this time.

He climbed the porch, still humming. It was one of his ballads. Lacey knew the tune. She could hear the horns, the congas, a piano in her head. She wondered whether she'd still look beautiful to him. She had painted her toenails pink. Her blouse was the color of sunflowers.

Robbie stood before her and smiled. He was missing a tooth on the right side, a molar. It tore her in two.

"Welcome back," she said finally, and a sorrow washed over Lacey that she didn't understand. She didn't want him to stay in jail, but she didn't want him here either. He reached for her, and she let him wind his arms around her shoulders. He held her too close, for too long.

The door swung open.

"Look who it is," Lacey said, waving at Robbie as if he were a guest, a surprise, not the man who had given her a life and then taken it away. Hank stood in the doorway, clenching his coffee mug and squinting at them. He looked jittery, feeble. Before he could speak, the girls came storming out the door, the dog barking after them.

Margarita came first, her long legs launching her off the ground. Robbie caught her in his arms as Diane grabbed him by the knees, crushed her face into his legs. Noelle was last, and she pushed past her sisters, thrusting them aside. She was the only one crying, her face contorted as if she were hurting physically. Lacey May knew the feeling. Robbie smiled and tousled her hair. "My girls, my big girls," he said, his voice as bright and easy as if he were telling a joke, as if his time away had all been a trick. Even now, he wanted to be the one who could make them laugh.

At the kitchen table, Robbie told a story about the man he sat next to on the bus ride home. He had more than a hundred multicolored tattoos, including a pouty pair of lips he could make blow kisses if he flexed his bicep. The girls laughed, ensnared by him. Even the dog sat at his feet, his ears flattened with pleasure whenever Robbie reached down to rake under his chin. Only Lacey May seemed to be ignoring him as she gathered up things for the beach — extra towels, baby powder to shake off the sand — but Hank could tell she was listening. Her eyes flitted to Robbie and then away, every time she came into the room.

When Lacey May brushed by with a gallon of lemonade, Hank grabbed her by the belt loop of her shorts. "Baby, are you going to take the whole house? Let's get moving."

"All right." Lacey May smiled, and it seemed real enough. How could he ever expect to know what went on inside Lacey May?

She ordered the girls to use the bathroom and run out to the car. They would see their father when they got back; he was spending the night. She turned out of the house, too, without saying good-bye. Soon only Hank and Robbie were left at the table.

The men stared at one another, and Robbie winked. He was as smug as ever, even if he looked ragged, beat. He'd walked nearly two miles in the heat from the bus station to the house.

"Shame we couldn't go pick you up this morning, but I thought we'd be gone by now," Hank said. "You know how long you'll be needing to stay?"

"I haven't thought that far. I'm just trying to soak it all in. My girls look good. Thank you for taking care of them."

Hank wasn't sure whether Robbie was sincere or trying to say he'd take over from here. He'd always had a way of making Hank seem like a fool, especially in front of Lacey. Hank offered him a cigarette, and Robbie waved it away.

"I remember, you know, the way you used to talk about her."

"I was young," Hank said. "And we talked about her together, didn't we?"

"That was before she was my wife."

"And before you were a junkie." Hank felt his face heat up at his own boldness.

"It's just a little problem I have."

Robbie stood from the table unceremoniously and started calling for the girls, their names different in his mouth. Hank followed him out. Lacey and the girls were all hanging out the car, the engine running. Had they been waiting on him or Robbie? The opportunity to invite Robbie along to the beach hung in the air.

"I was thinking I could make us some dinner," Robbie said. "We can all eat together when you get back."

"We'll probably eat on the road," Hank said. "Chicken sandwiches or something. Don't trouble yourself."

"Please," Robbie said, his tone forceful, as if he wasn't pleading at all, and Hank buckled inelegantly. "Fine, but you might be waiting a long time. Who knows when we'll be back." It was like an instinct, to give in and follow his friend, more handsome, more charming than he'd ever be.

Lacey May lent him the keys to her car, although they all knew good and well the car had been Robbie's, and it was still in his name.

On the coast, the land gave way to scorched yellow grass and salt marshes. The houses were slapdash and wooden, the air tinged with salt. Hank sped up to fifty-five, and the girls rolled the windows down and stuck out their heads. Lacey May was asleep, the skin on her thighs burned pink. A long-necked bird flew overhead, a heron maybe, its wings blue and gray.

Margarita unbuckled her seat belt to see, and, as if by instinct, Lacey's eyes flew open. "Margarita Ventura, have you lost your mind! You sit your bottom down and put that seat belt on now." She had to tell Margarita once more before she obliged. "You're just like your father! You think everything is going to be fine when, sometimes, everything isn't fine."

Diane had the dog crowded onto her lap. At the mention of Robbie, she asked, "Uncle Hank, why couldn't we bring Daddy to the beach?"

Hank tried not to cringe. The other girls called him by his first name, but it was as if Diane didn't quite understand the arrangement. No one had told her to start calling him uncle; she'd come up with it on her own.

"You were right there, chickadee. He didn't ask to come. He needs to rest. Besides, you'll see him tonight."

Noelle sucked her teeth. "Why are we even doing this dumb trip anyway? I hate the beach."

"Quiet," said Lacey May. "This is a nice thing. A day at the shore."

Hank turned up the radio, cycled through the stations. A dirty rap song, humdrum gospel. A report about a teenage boy who'd lost his arm in a shark attack at Atlantic Beach. The malaise in the car was suffocating, which was the last thing he wanted. He was burning up a tank of gas to bring them to the ocean, and they were all thinking about how they'd rather be back home with Robbie.

"I've got a headache," Lacey May said. "You got any aspirin?" She started unzipping the backpack Hank had set at her feet.

"Not in there," he snapped, and Lacey May dropped the bag. In the top pocket, he'd packed sunscreen and cigarettes, a black velvet box with a ring inside. It was a big beautiful aquamarine, flanked by two little white stones, on a thin gold band.

Lacey May looked stunned, and he smiled to make up for his tone, but then he remembered his teeth and clamped his mouth shut. He had teeth so twisted they faced one another. He was planning to get them fixed — it might help them both if Lacey could love his smile. Robbie had been gifted a perfect set of teeth. It wasn't fair, one of the many natural advantages he'd been given and squandered. He'd already lost one tooth, and, if he kept going the way he was going, he'd lose them all. Hank didn't want to wish ill on his old friend, but he didn't want to wish him well either.

Hank didn't know whether Lacey had ever explained to Robbie about how they'd started. To Hank, those were technicalities,

126

circumstances they had moved beyond to get where they were now. They were like roommates at first, except for when Hank reached for Lacey in the night, and she rolled toward him, willingly. He paid the bills; she cleaned up after him and the girls. Soon they were sharing rides to work, then sharing cigarettes, kissing on the mouth while he was inside her. Once, he overheard her tell another clerk at the store that her ex was in jail. Her ex. It gave Hank a wild hope that Robbie was out, and, maybe, he was in.

They reached the town and drove past dollar stores and hot dog stands, a string of new restaurants all with Spanish names. Hank wondered whether, at this rate, he'd even be able to read the signs around here in a few years. He parked on a side street in front of someone's green-and-white summerhouse. They unloaded the car and headed for the boardwalk, the girls sullen and complaining about the heat, until they saw the beach.

"It's paradise!" Margarita screamed in her ecstatic, showy way, and it made Diane laugh. They charged down the sand with Jenkins, his leash tangling at their ankles. Noelle lagged behind, headphones on.

"Why don't you help your mama with all the things she's carrying?" Hank said, and

Noelle raised an eyebrow at him.

"She's a big girl. She can live with her decisions."

She loped ahead of them, kicking up the sand.

Robbie didn't waste any time getting ready. He took a long, hot shower and anointed his body with all the little potions he found in the bathroom that belonged to Lacey May and the girls. Then he drove east toward the Súper Súper on Valentine Road. It was deliciously familiar, the *put-put* of the engine, the smell of the vinyl seats. There was dog fur, bundles of the girls' hair on the car floor, and the scent of Lacey — her smoke and perfume. It was as if he'd only just left, as if jail had been one interminable day.

This side of town had the carnicerías and pool halls, the barbershops and one-room churches, the paper ads in Spanish stapled to trees. The highway became a five-lane road, dividing rows of low brick ranches and pine trees, purple coneflowers sprouting from the median. He'd left New York because an uncle had promised life was better, cheaper in the South. His mother brought him to the east side when he was a teenager, and a few years later, she left. She had done what she set out to do — see her only child through high school — and then returned to Bogotá.

Robbie entered the Súper Súper and prayed he wouldn't run into anyone he knew. He wasn't ashamed to say where he'd been, but he couldn't bear to admit he had nowhere to call his own anymore, and his wife was living with another man.

The store was bright and big, and Robbie wheeled around his cart, feeling the strangeness of being out. He picked things up and put them down. Nobody watched him. It was awkward and familiar, like resuming an old part he had once known by heart.

At the back of the Súper Súper, there was a butcher, a Western Union, a cell phone vendor, a shaved ice stand, and a small carousel you could operate for a quarter. The Súper Súper was like an open-air market enclosed in concrete, a one-stop shop for the Mexicans and Salvadoreños who came in. There were Caribbean customers, too, but Robbie hadn't found other Colombians. There were Colombians, he knew, in Raleigh and Charlotte, but they weren't like him. They arrived already speaking English, enrolled in programs at NC State and Duke. He had learned to see other Latinos as his countrymen. He sang rancheras in bars, bought pupusas for his daughters from the carts in front of the Catholic church downtown. It was better this way, helped him feel less alone.

The cashier was a pretty girl with a big bump in front of her, a sparkly stud pushed into her chin. She made small talk in Spanish while she rang him up. *How has it gone for you?* He felt a rush of blood to his groin. It had been so long since he'd been with a woman. She was pregnant, but Robbie was only looking. And what was wrong with that? Did he even have a wife anymore? A wife was a woman you kept your promises to, who kept her promises to you. Robbie had kept the most important ones. Even high, he'd been a saint — he'd never fucked another woman, not once that he could remember.

Robbie asked the cashier for her phone number. She told him no, and he left quickly, carrying his bags across the shopping center to the bar.

He sat alone in a booth, ordered tamales, a shot of tequila, beer. The paintings on the wall were new. A red chili pepper in a sombrero rode on horseback, gunning down a gang of green chili peppers, and rescuing the yellow pepper in a white dress they'd been holding captive. Robbie stared at the mural and drank. Maybe everyone was high, more people than ever let on.

Amado must have spotted him first because when Robbie looked up, he was already crossing the bar, headed toward him. Robbie cursed. He'd been out only a few hours, and here was Amado, sliding into his booth.

"Roberto," he said. "You got lost. We heard what happened to you."

Robbie shrugged. "I needed wheels. I wasn't thinking straight. You know how it is."

Amado wore his shirt unbuttoned, his gold chain on display. A diamond ring glinted on his pinkie. He was older than Robbie, muscular, and slim waisted. Beside him, Robbie looked scrappy, too skinny.

"They put you to work?"

"All the way east. They had us building roads. I learned a lot. If the garage doesn't need me anymore, I think I could get a job in construction."

"I'm happy for you, hermano. You got off light."

"I'm a lucky man," Robbie said. He gulped his beer.

"It's not easy out here, you know — at least in jail you know what to expect. But out here, things are always changing. Police are always getting smarter. They know everybody's face."

"I'm not coming to work for you, Amado."

"But I'm thinking about you, man. Before you had the garage. It might not be so easy going back now. You're a felon. You should thank God you have your citizenship, otherwise, they'd be deporting you."

"I've been here my whole life."

"What do they care?"

"I'll make my own way."

"So valiant." Amado laughed. "Optimistic. I've never looked at the world and thought, *It will all work out.*"

Robbie said nothing. He wasn't afraid. What could Amado do to him that he hadn't already learned to survive?

"Well, hermano, I won't count it against you if you wind up eating your words. You come see me if you need a job. Or if you need anything else." Amado pointed at the empty shot glass, asked if he wanted another.

Robbie stood. "I better be heading home. My wife is waiting for me."

"That's fine." Amado smiled at him. "I'll be seeing you, hermano."

By afternoon, the girls were restless, sunscorched. They had sand in their bottoms, they were hungry and cranky, but they couldn't go home. Not when they'd come so far, and the sky was bright and unending. A day at the beach was a prize, no matter how miserable they all became.

Lacey May and Hank bought Margarita a kite to appease her. She twirled beneath it, whenever it caught on the wind, putting on a little show, whether anyone was watching or not. Noelle was in the water, leaping over the waves, talking to a gang of slightly older boys, who seemed about fourteen. Only Diane had stayed close. She was piling sand into a bucket, digging out a moat. Hank needed to send her away. Lacey May was chugging beers, and if he didn't muster his nerve, she'd be drunk before long.

"Aren't you hot, chickadee? You're just sitting there, roasting. Why don't you go and play with Jenkins under the pier? Get some shade?"

Diane, obedient by nature, sprang up and ran off with the dog. Hank turned to Lacey and grabbed her hand. "I've been meaning to ask you something. I want to know if you could make a little more room in your heart for me."

Lacey drained her beer and reached for another. "You're already in my heart, Hank." She kept her eyes on the sea. The crash of waves along the shore. A faraway bark.

"What I mean is," Hank said, rummaging in the backpack beneath his chair. "Goddamn it."

He heard Diane scream, and when he turned to the pier, he saw her and Jenkins, a large, rust-colored dog circling them both. Diane was stuck between them, Jenkins tangling her legs in his leash as he tried to dart away. The rust-colored dog growled, lurched. Soon Hank was running down the beach, Lacey May close behind.

Hank shoved the dog, thumping its chest with one hand. He used the other to push Diane, and she tripped backward onto the sand. He managed to unclip Jenkins, who ran off, away from the snapping maw of the red dog. He kicked the dog once in the face, and again, then Lacey May was there, scooping Diane into her arms. Both of them stared wide-eyed at Hank.

A man in aviators ambled over, not nearly fast enough. He grabbed the red dog by the collar, knocked him on the nose. Hank started in on him.

"You son of a bitch. What's wrong with you bringing a dog like that to a family place like this? He could have killed my daughter."

Lacey May turned at the word.

The man started to mutter excuses, and Hank shook his fist in the man's face. "Control your goddamn dog, man, or I'm calling the police."

Diane whispered in Lacey May's ear. "Uncle Hank saved me, Mama."

Lacey May kissed her and carried her away, squeezed her belly to check for wounds, but she was thinking of Hank, how he'd thrown himself between her daughter and the dog. The way a real father would. She had never seen him so angry, so strong. He had noticed the trouble before she had. She had been busy watching Noelle and those boys. She had been daydreaming about the way she and Robbie had been young together, while a dog tried to eat her baby.

The other girls were with them now, and Jenkins weaseled his head between Lacey May's ankles. Noelle shivered and shouted, "Dee, are you okay?" and Margarita, stunned and speechless, held her crumpled kite to her chest.

When Hank joined them, he slung an arm around Lacey May, another around Diane, who was red-faced, trying hard not to cry.

"Let's go have some sodas and calm down," Lacey May said, and the girls went ahead with Jenkins, their slim bodies pressed together. They were rarely harmonious, the girls, but in moments like these, they had a way of falling together, like a single organism.

As they climbed up the dunes, Hank leaned into Lacey May, pressed a lip to her ear. "I hope that wasn't a sign. A bad omen or something. I was fixing to ask you to marry me. I'd reconsider, but I love you too goddamn much."

A shiver ran down Lacey's neck. Perhaps the residue of fear, and something else. She turned to face him. Hank's eyes were a cloudy blue, his skin lined and leathery. He sealed his lips together to hide his teeth, his expression pleading and pitiable. He was harmless in the end. The way he looked at her, he could have been one of her children.

Hank kissed her, and she could feel his hands quivering around her shoulders.

"If you say no, Lacey, we can keep going on the way we've been," he said. "I won't cast you out. But I hope to God you'll say yes, and let me make you my wife."

It was dark when they pulled up, the headlights sweeping over the living room, where Robbie had set the table with everything he'd made: rice and beans, plantains, and carne mechada. At the last minute, he'd

136

dashed out for an ice cream cake — Diane's favorite — strawberry with a cookie crust. It had started to melt, but he couldn't bear to put it away. He wanted them to see it when they walked in, to clap and to climb on top of him. He knew he'd win the girls back eventually. He was their father; it was in their DNA to choose him. Lacey would be harder, but he was ready to fight. Sometimes you had to work against the universe, the fucked-up order of things, your body, your own brain, to keep the things that were yours.

Take his friend, that baker. A man with talent, a good heart. He had been judicious, stayed out of trouble, and still, the universe had blown his dreams away. Life was a gust of wind, a puff of air, and nothing more — Robbie had to remember that. He couldn't afford to waste any time.

The girls came crashing in, sandy and red-skinned. They surrounded him, kissed his cheeks solemnly, and immediately Robbie knew something was wrong. Lacey May and Hank hung back, holding hands. Hank grinned too wide.

"We might as well come right out with it," he said.

Robbie's eyes drew instinctively to Lacey May's hand.

"But Lacey and I are still married," he said. "I haven't signed any papers. She hasn't asked me to sign any papers."

"I'll go on and put this cake in the freezer," Hank said, and he called the girls into the other room. Lacey May yanked Robbie by the hand out to the porch, but he couldn't feel her holding him. The night was humid. Lightning bugs flickered across the lawn.

"I should have let you visit," Robbie said. "We lied to the girls, and they found out anyway. Maybe if they'd seen me, we wouldn't be here. Maybe you wouldn't have forgotten you love me."

"Robbie, none of this is about love." Her voice was a pin sliding under Robbie's skin.

"You don't need him anymore, Lacey. I'm here. I'm going to get back on my feet."

"It's not about money neither."

"Oh God, please don't tell me it's physical."

"He's a good man. I can count on him."

"He used to take high school girls behind the store to feel them up. He used to pretend to squeeze your ass when we worked at the restaurant. Why would you trust him? Noelle will be a teenager in a couple years."

138

"Those were just rumors. Besides, he was lonely then. It's different now."

"How could you wear that ring in front of me? I just got out."

"I don't believe in fairy tales anymore, Robbie. I don't believe love solves anything. We're still family, you understand? I'll never keep you from the girls. But I can't be your wife."

Robbie had a flash of running into the house and swinging at Hank, bringing his fist down on his skinny head until it was all pulp, ripe. He shook the vision away; he had to act fast. A ring was nothing; a promise wasn't the same thing as a life lived. He had more to offer her: a future, yes, but also their past. You couldn't change your roots, and he was hers. Lacey had grown from him, like Eve from one of Adam's ribs. There wasn't one of them without the other. He had to help her see.

"You remember, Lacey, that time we went to the quarry together? You were teaching me how to swim?"

"Robbie, we've had a lot of good times. It was all so long ago."

"You remember?" he asked again.

They had left the Hot Wing early. Lacey drove them to a deserted parking lot with a knocked-over trailhead. She led them to the old rock quarry lake. There were other teenagers there, drinking and diving off the rocks. The lake was sunken in a ring of trees, the water green and warm, sixty feet deep at the center. They started close to the edge, where it was shallow. Robbie went too far out, and when he couldn't reach the bottom with his toes, he panicked, slipped under. He remembered it as if he'd been able to see Lacey May gliding across the surface, her pale arms cutting through the water. She wrapped an arm around his chest, hauled him back to land.

They had laughed, as if Robbie hadn't nearly drowned. His mouth was already open when Lacey May tilted him back onto the grass. The earth stuck to their wet skin; there were ants. They went on kissing for a long time. Robbie had a gummy, hot sensation in his shorts, a lightness in his head. It was the best he'd ever felt, and the best he would ever feel, until he had cocaine.

"When I was in there, I used to put pictures in my head. To motivate myself. To make me do the right thing. And even when I knew you were with him, the picture I held on to was you, dragging me up. I'd see myself with my head underwater, and then I'd see you bringing me back."

"You ever think anyone else could use

some rescuing besides you?"

"It's a sickness," Robbie said. "I'm sick."

"If you're sick, then so am I."

"Then let's be sick together."

"Two sick people can't run a house. Robbie, I've made up my mind."

She embraced him, but it wasn't the way he'd wanted her to. She fluttered her fingers against his shoulders, angled her hips away. It was worse, far worse, than if she hadn't touched him at all.

They settled on a routine of weekend visits. Robbie drove up in an old blue Chevrolet, honked, and the girls would go running to meet him. He had become a celebrity to his own children, whisking them away to the mall or bowling or for milkshakes. When he dropped them off, the girls would be sullen and smart with Lacey May, as if she were the one who had gotten high, stolen a cop car, and ruined it all.

She was wearing Hank's ring, though he had promised to give her time to square away her affairs. He meant the divorce, the house. He hadn't told her to sell it, but it was obvious what he wanted. He sulked whenever she left to tend to the house, as if she were off to meet a lover. She'd come back from clearing the gutter or mowing

141

the lawn, and Hank would ignore her until they were alone in bed, then he'd be rougher with her, grab her by the hair, flip her around, and hold her where he wanted her. It wasn't quite mean, but it wasn't sweet either.

He was at the store, and the girls were hiking the state park with Robbie, when she finally arranged a meeting about the house. She was waiting for the Realtor when her old neighbor, that fat nurse, climbed onto the porch, uninvited, in a pair of pink scrubs and rubber shoes.

"Hey there!" she said, and Lacey May couldn't help but scowl at her. All this time, and Ruth Green was still here, living in these woods, driving her cream-colored car with the hospital parking pass stuck on the windshield.

"Can I help you?"

"I hear you're getting the house appraised. Your tenants told me."

"Unh-hunh."

"I wondered if I could talk to you."

"Aren't we talking now?"

"I was hoping you'd come over. I made us some lunch."

Lacey said yes before she could catch herself, her own eagerness surprising her. Was she so desperate that she'd accept an offer from Ruth Green? She had watched Lacey lose her life, return to tend to the house, and never once had she said good morning. She had denied her the little loan that might have spared her everything. Still, Lacey followed her across the yard.

Ruth's house was plain and pretty: pale wood floors and seafoam-green walls, her son's toys and her knitting in straw baskets strewn through the rooms. They drank sweet tea and sat looking out at the garden, where Ruth's boy was watering his tomatoes. Lacey complimented her on her home, asked whether she was thinking of selling, too.

"God, no. We love it here, me and Bailey. I want to die in this house."

Lacey remembered when she'd thought the same.

"There's some developers who've got a plan to buy up all this land. They want to build a community with town houses, a playground, a pool. I'm worried if they get your land, they'll just build around me. They'll clear out the woods, and my view will be of some big old gate."

"You expect me not to sell my house because you'll miss the trees?"

Ruth pointed at Lacey's finger. "You re-married?"

"Not yet."

"You going to try for more kids?"

Lacey laughed. "I got my tubes tied right after I left my husband."

"Your fiancé know that?"

Lacey shrugged. "He hasn't asked. Sometimes it's better to just let a man dream."

"As long as you don't get caught up in the fantasy."

"Please. I couldn't forget my circumstances if I tried."

"No, you can't. Not when you're a mother. Your circumstances stare you in the face every morning, ask you what's for breakfast."

Lacey May laughed, and Ruth went on. "My ex always had his head in the clouds. He was all, *Let's travel here, let's move there, let's have ten kids.* I had to be the boring one who said things like, *But what about the car payment?* and *Bailey needs new shoes.* He called me a killjoy." Ruth shook her head, sipped her tea. "He gives surf lessons now, lives with his girlfriend on the coast. Well, it's always a new girl, and he's always living with her on the coast. He doesn't get out to see Bailey much."

"I'm sorry about that," Lacey said.

Ruth grew somber. "I wanted to ask you not to sell the house. But it's not about me

144

or my view. I've been carrying around this guilt since that winter you left. I didn't help you, and I've never stopped wondering what it cost you. That's why I never say hello — I've been too ashamed. You see, I was raised to be hard, and you seemed so . . . Would you believe me if I said I thought I was helping you back then?"

"What I needed was a loan."

"I was relieved you didn't wind up having to sell the house. And I'm telling you not to do it now. That house is your wealth. It's your future."

"That house is a monthly payment, and my ex is no help."

"What about your girls? It's their inheritance."

"My fiancé doesn't want me to keep it."

"Well, his name isn't on the deed, is it? You can't let these two men yank you around so you forget what really matters."

The woman had some nerve. Lacey May rose to leave, and Ruth stood and stammered.

"I'm not very good at holding my tongue. Please forgive me. I hope you'll come back. Next time, I won't have a lecture prepared. We can just have tea. You can bring the girls."

Lacey made no promises, moved for the

door. It shocked her when Ruth pulled her into a hug. Lacey didn't resist her strong arms. She let the woman hold her. It was as if Ruth were a deep-rooted tree, as if she knew that what Lacey May needed was a steady thing.

The Realtor didn't mention a developer, and the number he gave Lacey wasn't much more than she and Robbie had paid for the house. Lacey didn't like to think she was being cheated, but it bothered her even more that he genuinely couldn't see how much the house was worth. She and Robbie had loved that house and loved in that house. That kind of love did something to a place, it lived in its walls. You could feel it when you walked in. A house was more than windows, wood, and frame.

The girls were waiting for her on the porch when she got back. They were covered in mud, electric, babbling about their morning with Robbie.

"Papi caught a snake!" Diane said. "He picked it up with a stick and his bare hands!"

"He was so brave!" Margarita swooned.

"Oh my," Lacey said because she didn't want to stamp out their joy. "What kind of snake?"

"A copperhead," Noelle supplied, and they rolled into the house, the girls going on about how he'd taken them to a food truck after. Among them, they had devoured eighteen tacos: potato and chorizo, beans, eggs, cactus.

"Cactus?" Lacey May asked, playing along.

"Cactus!" they shouted, shedding their outer layers in a heap for her to wash. They were in a better mood than usual, as if they'd forgotten they were angry with her for reasons they never named. They argued about who would get the shower first before the hot water ran out, and Lacey carried the clothes down to the basement.

The downstairs belonged to the girls. They'd brightened it up with pink armchairs and a rainbow rug to make up for the meager light that came through the window. There were bunk beds for Diane and Margarita, a pullout for Noelle, a TV, the washing machine. Lacey May started a load and went upstairs, where Noelle, unsurprisingly, had claimed the shower. Diane and Margarita were down to their underwear, watching cartoons beneath a blanket on the couch. Even after all those tacos, they were sharing a bowl of cereal.

"What are you two doing? Don't let Hank

147

catch you out here half-naked."

Lacey May was ordering the girls to go and put on some pants when she saw the bundle of wildflowers, tied up with twine, on the coffee table.

"They're from Papi," Margarita said. "He sent them for you. Sorry we forgot."

"He took us to pick them —" Diane began, but Lacey didn't have to hear where he'd taken them. White and purple aster grew all along the trail that led to the quarry, the lake where she had taken him when they were kids, where Robbie had nearly drowned. They could have been the same flowers that were growing all those years ago, their skinny, gorgeous buds.

Lacey muttered that she needed to run to the store and pick up something for dinner, and she left before the girls could ask her any questions. She drove in the direction of Valentine Road, trying to remember the name of the motel where Robbie had said he was staying.

Robbie answered the door in his undershirt and jeans, a bottle of beer in his hand. His shirt was thin, and she could see his skin right through it. Lacey May looked at him in a way so that he would understand. He locked the door, drew the blinds. She sat on the edge of the bed, unable to say a thing, and Robbie kneeled in front of her, waiting. She kissed him first. They kissed for a long time, as if they were trying to relearn the taste of one another: his brand of beer, her cigarettes. They lay back on the bed, and Robbie unbuttoned his jeans, made plain what he wanted. It surprised her this would be the thing he craved after so long, but she was fine to give it to him. It was all about Robbie for a while, his pleasure and her seeing to it, which somehow felt right, after everything. He'd suffered. He'd gone away. He gave little sighs, knotted his fingers in her hair.

When it was her turn, she hollered and writhed, as if she didn't want him to make her come, as if she didn't deserve it. She let herself rise and crest on the wave of feelings Robbie drew out of her, and soon she was crying. Robbie rushed to hold her, but she didn't want to be held, she wanted to be fucked, and she said so, and he did, and there was no more crying.

After, he wrapped his arms around her. She was still in her blouse, the long skirt she had worn to meet the Realtor. Her hair was heavy with sweat. She smelled. Robbie sank his finger into her belly button, an old habit.

"I'm sorry," she said, and Robbie spared her the pain of saying for what. He kissed her.

"I thought that was how you'd welcome me home."

"We don't have a home anymore."

"Sure we do," Robbie said, picking up the bottle he'd set down on the soiled carpet.

"You got another?" Lacey went to the miniature refrigerator and fished out a bottle. She wanted to ask Robbie how many other women there had been besides her in the time since he'd been out, but she knew it wasn't fair. She wanted to hear zero. She wanted to hear no one. She slammed the cap off the beer with her palm, took a long drink.

"I saw somebody about selling the house today."

"Now why'd you do that?" Robbie said. His voice was light and lilting, as if they were playing a game. It was that effort he put into making everything seem all right, funny even.

"Look at where you're living, Robbie. It's only our house on paper. And it'll get more complicated once we get divorced."

"What do you mean *divorced*?" Robbie sat up in bed. The thing about his humor, his ease, was that once Robbie lost it, he went wild. "You came in here, and you asked me to fuck you, and you're still thinking about becoming Hank's wife?"

"I'm confused."

"Let me clear things up for you." Robbie patted the spot on the bed beside him. He was all gooseflesh and dark hair, his long limbs. He was beautiful naked, his shoulders broad, a new scar running the length of his ribs. "Come here."

"We can't fix all our problems in bed."

"What else is there to say? Didn't we just say it all with our bodies? The way we touched each other?"

Lacey didn't want to talk about what they had done, now that it was over. If there was one thing she had never imagined herself being, it was an adulterer. Who was her husband? To whom did she owe her loyalty, her life? Nothing made sense anymore.

Lacey sucked her beer down to the last drop. "I ought to be going."

Robbie crossed the room, put his hands around her face. "Lacey May, we've still got time."

"I've got to make dinner before Hank gets home."

"I don't mean right now. I mean, you're alive, and I'm alive. Anything is possible."

Lacey hated when Robbie brought up dying like this, like they had to be grateful no matter what life brought their way because one day they'd be dead. She wasn't like him — she didn't need a rush from drugs to feel thankful for her life; she didn't need a friend to die to know each day was precious. She never would have tired of their old life, even if they could have gone on living forever, the two of them in their little blue house, the girls never growing any older, the leaves never falling from the trees, and Jenkins running circles eternally in the yard.

"Goddamn you, Robbie," Lacey said. "Why'd you go and ruin everything?"

Robbie shushed her. "We can figure it out. We'll keep the house —"

Lacey wished she could believe him. He'd make a fool of her, if she let him. She kissed him hard and left before he could say anything else to get inside her head. He had always been the one who led her. Without him, she had no idea what was right.

Lacey May had left him burning. He had tried to be good, to calm himself down, but he didn't last very long alone. He hit one bar, and then another. First, it was dusk, then night, and he couldn't piece together all he'd done in the hours since Lacey. And the burning — he couldn't get rid of that.

The first girl he drew into the bathroom was beautiful, but Robbie couldn't bear to look at her. He shut his eyes. Her tongue was sweet, made him grow huge, muscular, warm. He asked her how much she liked him, and she said very much. He asked her if she loved him, and she said, yes, very much. Robbie pinned her to the wall, and they slammed into each other a few times. The girl moaned in his ear. His bones were vibrating, his cock enormous. Music streamed underneath the door, accordion and plucky guitar. She took his hand and led him back out to her friends. Of course she wanted to be seen with him; she was proud of what they had done. He bought her a beer, and her friends beers. The girls had dark hair and unbuttoned blouses, and he was making them laugh. He was funnier in Spanish.

How old are you? he asked them, and his favorite girl said, *How old do you want me to be,* like in a movie. He decided it was fine — these girls were old enough, at least, to be in the bar.

On the dance floor, he saw the devil in the corner — Amado and his big pinkie ring. The girl he had taken into the bathroom led Robbie over to the booth. She was one of Amado's girls; he called her by her name — something beautiful, a kind of flower. Rosa or Lila or Flora. She slipped a baggie into Robbie's pocket. A gift. He kissed her, like a man, in front of Amado. He wished it were Lacey May who could see. He whispered to Lila all the things he wanted to do to her, and she laughed. They danced; he held Flora by the hips. Amado bought another round. What more did he need? If Lacey sold the house, if she never came to see him again, he'd be fine, in his new life, with Rosa, and they'd see. They'd all see that he was the one who had given them everything they counted as theirs.

The next weekend Lacey May pulled into the motel parking lot and honked the horn, ordered the girls to get out. She was late for an appointment to get a second opinion on the house. Robbie had never shown up that morning, and she had called and called until he finally picked up. She had wondered if he was punishing her, taking out what happened between them on the girls. She honked the horn again.

"Jesus, Ma, cut it out," Noelle said.

"Who's it going to bother? The neighborhood association? Now go on and get out."

The girls climbed onto the hot asphalt and stood together, unmoving.

"Is there a problem?" Lacey May said.

"We don't know which room it is," Noelle answered.

"Right." Lacey May had forgotten the girls hadn't been here before, and, as far as they knew, neither had she. "It's that one." She pointed. "Number forty-three."

Lacey May honked once more for good measure, then tore away.

The girls had been knocking for a while when Margarita flopped onto the curb and folded her arms. "Can't you dummies see he's not in there?"

Diane tried to peer through the blinds. "Where else would he be?"

"He's probably just passed out," Noelle said.

"Like asleep?" asked Diane.

"Yes, chickadee. Just like that." Noelle banged on the door harder.

Margarita rolled her eyes. "Let's just come back later. I'm hungry. I want to eat that cactus taco again."

"It's called a *nopal,*" Noelle said, "And we can't go over there by ourselves. Are you crazy?" They knew what she meant — the east side wasn't safe to wander.

"It's the middle of the day, Noelle."

"We can try and catch another snake, too," Diane said. "Maybe there's one in

155

those woods." She pointed across the five-lane road to a chain of businesses: a used tire dealer, a fabric store, a row of squat fast-food huts. Behind the strip mall loomed a hedge of pines.

Margarita took her little sister by the hand, started marching down the stairs.

"Where the hell do you think you two are going?"

"You can stay here and bang all you want. We're going across the road."

"You don't have any money!"

"Guess you better come along then."

Noelle screamed and stomped her foot. She followed after her sisters, Margarita in her too-short shorts, Diane in an old motorcycle T-shirt that had belonged to Hank. There wasn't a stoplight, so they had to wait for a lull in the traffic to run for the slender median. They perched on the little island of concrete while the cars rushed by. They waited and ran again.

When they made it across, Margarita was panting, exhilarated. She pushed her sunglasses onto her forehead. "You liked that, manzanita?" she asked, and Diane clapped her hands. Noelle wanted to smack them both.

"Let's go in the woods first, work up an appetite, then we can find those tacos," said

Margarita. *"Nopal, nopal, nopales,"* she sang, and Diane laughed. They sprinted toward the stand of skinny pines ringing the lot.

The trees gave way to a clearing, all grass and two silver pipes running aboveground. They followed the pipes to a creek rushing mud brown. Diane announced she was going to look for snakes and edged down the bank. At the water, she started to cross, leaping between the stones jutting out of the stream. Margarita sat on a tree stump to watch.

"It's pathetic," Noelle said. "You don't even like the woods. You're breaking the rules just to break them."

Margarita stuck out her tongue at Noelle, turned smugly back to the water.

"I can't wait to go to college," Noelle said, louder now, hoping to hurt her. "I can't wait to leave this stupid town, this stupid family, all of you."

"I can't wait for you to leave either. It's a good thing Mama loves you so much, cause she's the only one. You're a bitch, and we all know it."

Noelle shoved Margarita off the stump. She fell hard on her bottom. She lunged at her sister, tried to wrestle her to the ground, but Noelle was bigger. Margarita clawed at Noelle's arms, slapped her face, punched spitefully at her growing breasts. Noelle tackled her, and soon they were rolling down the bank, snapping twigs, swinging and kicking. They had never fought before, not like this; it felt good, feral. Noelle took her sister by the shoulders, slammed her head against the ground. Margarita bit her sister's hand, let out a triumphant scream. They were rolling in the mud when they heard a splash behind them, the sound of Diane slipping into the water, and then a terrible thump, the sound of her skull as it made contact with the rocks.

Robbie woke to the sound of Lacey May. She was knocking, calling. He found his way to the door, opened it. The world was too bright. What day was it? How long had it been? He'd spent one night, two nights, three nights at the bar with Amado, his girls. Robbie wondered if Lacey May could tell. He waited for her to come into focus; he knew the hazy shape of her, her moving mouth, her long hair. Something about the girls. He hadn't seen them. Why would they be here?

Lacey May pushed past him into the room. She called their names. She swept into the bathroom and out again, while Robbie stood at the door. He was willing himself back to awareness, staring hard at her, trying to tune in. She was naked, she loved him, they were making love.

Lacey May shook him by the shoulders, said a string of things he didn't understand. And then, too clearly: "You're useless."

She slammed the door, and Robbie stumbled after her. The sun had burned the whole sky white, and Robbie could feel the heat annihilating him. He was soaking it up, all the light. He wanted to hide inside, shrink under the covers, but he followed her somehow, fell into the passenger seat of the car. The skin of his head threatened to burst.

"Right now I hate you, Robbie Ventura," Lacey said. He heard that. He could grasp her more distinctly now. She was all bug eyes, hunched over the wheel, scanning the motel parking lot. She drove out to the road. They had to find a payphone, she said. Lacey was going to call 911.

They had an hour before the officer would call the phone in Robbie's room, so Lacey said they'd use the time to search the strip mall across the road. They entered every store, checked the aisles, and Lacey begged the managers to make announcements over the loudspeakers. She described each girl, down to the moles on their shoulders, the precise shade of their brown hair: Noelle, ash; Margarita, honey; Diane, Coca-Cola. They had no luck, made it through two more shopping centers, Lacey May a flash ahead of Robbie. She turned around once in a while to egg him on, to curse at him. He tried to keep up, blinking through the fluorescence, her insult revolving in his head. *Useless.*

When they got back to the motel, Lacey had hardly parked when she sprinted out of the car. Robbie pulled the emergency brake and followed her. He wanted her to notice, to thank him for his soundness of mind. He got out of the car and felt his head balloon. It was the size of a beach ball. He thought he might vomit. He put his head between his knees and breathed until it passed. When he got up, he saw them: the girls and their mother at the top of the stairs. Lacey May had his room key. She swept them indoors, examined them at the foot of his bed.

The girls were covered in mud, shivering, Noelle and Diane holding on to each other. Lacey May was yelling. Robbie asked what had happened.

"They nearly drowned," Lacey said, and she bared her teeth at him. She was pulling apart Diane's hair, pressing her palm into the girl's scalp. Her fingers came away with blood.

Robbie felt again that he might vomit.

"I've got to take them to the hospital," Lacey said. "Girls, you all go on and wait in the car."

Robbie couldn't watch them go. He looked at his feet. He was wearing a pair of flip-flops, his feet pale and hairy, his toenails ragged, long. In his sweatpants and under-shirt, he was sure he looked like a bum. And his head. If you put a finger in his ear, with all the pressure in there, he'd explode. He needed water. He could fall down dead in front of Lacey and she wouldn't care. The girls vanished without saying good-bye to him. Another failure. He slumped against the bed. He figured he should speak before she did. He knew he couldn't bear whatever she had to say.

"How could you come in here and make love to me, Lacey? You tore me up inside."

Lacey May laughed.

"Why couldn't you just tell me you wouldn't sell the house, that you love me, that you could never replace me — I was locked up."

"Don't you blame this on me! You go on a bender and it's my fault? Please. And I haven't replaced you. I'd never replace you

161

because I don't want someone like you in my life! To bring me trouble! To bring me grief! You ruined my life, Robbie, you ruined all our lives, and you had no reason to. You should have loved me more. And if I knew exactly the drugs you needed to do yourself in, I'd give them to you so you could stop wasting our time. We all know where this leads!"

Lacey May was quivering and flushed, her fists balled at her sides. He felt the urge to raise his arms, to cover himself, as if she might hit him. She was glaring at him, her lips pressed together, her head rocking from side to side in a rhythm she couldn't seem to control. There was a word for the way she was looking at him — *asco,* like when you see a dead animal on the side of the road, *asco,* at someone with filthy hands reaching toward you, *asco,* the sight of a man's guts, a rotting tree crawling with maggots. Maybe this was how she had looked at him every time she found him high, and he had lodged it away somewhere in his brain, because he recognized it now. It was her deepest feeling for him — he could see that. He wanted to say, *It was just this once.* He wanted to say he'd clean up his act. He wanted to say, *I'll get help.* But it wouldn't change the way she was looking at him. He could do nothing. Robbie sank to the floor, crossed his legs beneath him, and cried. Lacey May didn't stoop to comfort him. She left, again.

He looked up when he heard the bathroom door swing open. Margarita emerged from the rear of the motel room with a fat lip, blooming purple, a cut under her eye. He hadn't known she wasn't with the others. He wondered what she'd heard.

"Pepita," he said and crawled onto his knees. "I am sorry, mi hija. I am so sorry. I need you to understand —"

Margarita shook her head, quieting him. "It's okay, Papi. It's not your fault. It was my idea. It was me."

6

AUGUST 2002
THE PIEDMONT, NORTH CAROLINA

Jade's lips were burning for a cigarette, her legs jumping underneath the seat as she pulled into the lot of Central High School. She parked and turned to look at Gee. He was slumped against the window, his face pressed against the glass. She shook him by the shoulder and called his name.

"This is a good thing," she said. "I wish this had happened to me when I was your age."

Still, he wouldn't look at her.

"I'm not saying it's going to be easy."

Gee tuned out his mother and surveyed the lot. It was nearly full, although the town hall wasn't set to start for another half hour. He'd been dreading the start of the school year all summer. He hadn't had a good night's sleep since he got the letter approving his transfer to Central. He was gnashing his teeth again.

"You don't know," Jade went on, "what a

difference this is going to make. This is a good school. I've been lucky. I don't want you to have to count on luck."

Gee's mother was good at pep talks, reminding him to double-check his homework, put lotion on his hands. She liked to monitor, advise, steer him the right way. Sometimes he thought he ought to be more grateful. But she didn't seem to notice that his insides were quaking. Gee felt his jaw clamp shut. He pried it open to speak.

"What's the point of this meeting anyway? What is there to discuss? It's all final, isn't it?"

"It's supposed to be a welcome."

"Will it be?"

"Sure. One way or another." Jade gave him a tight smile, then patted his leg and said, "You've got to trust me." They climbed out of the car, and Jade flung her arm around him. It felt strange, but he let her hold him anyway.

The school was four stories, a brick building with white windowpanes and eaves. Dogwood trees guarded the small lawn between the lot and the entrance.

There was a clatter of car doors opening and closing. Gee recognized a few of his classmates and their mothers trudging toward the school. Adira was approaching

165

the school in a fuchsia windbreaker and faded jeans. She had come in regular clothes, and Gee felt conspicuous in his collared pinstriped shirt, his good pants. Adira was calm and easy all the time, even now, sandwiched between her tall parents, the Howards. She was one of the few kids at school Gee could call a friend, but it wasn't saying much because Adira was friends with everyone. She was the kind of girl who kissed her friends on the cheeks, complimented strangers on their sneakers or hair and meant it. She could reach for you, hug you, wink at you, laugh, and it didn't seem like flirting. She bounded toward him, snatched up his hand. It felt natural, good. It didn't set his skin on fire.

The Howards relieved him of Jade, and the adults went ahead, snapping together into a knot, lowering their heads and their voices. Gee couldn't tell if they were worried. The papers said the initiative to merge the city and county school systems was popular. They were piloting new programs to make all the schools attractive so county kids would want to transfer, too. Most students would get to stay where they were. But it was hard for Gee to believe people were coming to this meeting in droves all because they wanted to shake hands. There had been talk of a band of white parents who planned to protest. He had no particular fear of white people; Gee sorted them into good and bad, safe and not safe, the way he did with everyone else. But he knew even good people could turn, let alone good white people.

Adira had linked her arm with his, and she didn't seem to be thinking about the meeting at all. She was fawning over Jade. She admired her knee-high boots, her black dress cinched with a silver chain at the waist. "She's so glamorous," Adira said. "She doesn't even look like a mom."

Jade had recently cut her hair into a mohawk, long on top and buzzed around her ears. Since becoming a nurse, she had stopped wearing her nose ring, but her ears were studded with gold, her nails painted a red so deep it seemed black. She liked to stand out, even now, a day when Gee needed to blend in. Gee shrugged at Adira, and she looked confused, as if he should be flattered, as if he should want people to assume that Jade was his sister and he was a parentless freak.

"What's the matter? Aren't you excited? I've never even been inside here before. Look at these windows! It's so bright."

"My head hurts," said Gee. It was his

go-to line when he had to explain why he wasn't coming along for a soda after school, or why he hadn't raised his hand in class, or why he didn't want to go and meet some girls. Even when it didn't work, and people saw that it was a lie, he got what he wanted anyway: to be left alone.

They followed the signs down the hallway. The crowd was mostly kids Gee didn't recognize, shepherded by their fair-headed parents.

They reached the auditorium and saw that nearly every seat was filled, the murmurs of the crowd a low roar. Linette stood sentinel over three seats in the front row, among a contingent of students from Gee's school and their families. He recited their names to himself like a psalm — *Rosie, Ezekiel, Magdalena. Humphrey, Austin, Elizabeth, Yvonne.* He'd known most of them since elementary school, and although they were all clumped together now, soon they'd be dispersed, just a handful among the two hundred new students at Central this fall. Would it matter they were all there together? Would they be able to find each other then? Without willing it, his teeth began to grind against each other, back and forth. A sound like tearing paper filled his ears.

Linette could always seem to sense his

nerves. She kissed him on the cheek, which did nothing to still his trembling, but he was thankful for her all the same. They settled into the battered, cushioned seats, unlike the hard-backed chairs at Gee's school. Gee sat between the two women, and they turned their eyes toward the stage.

The blue velvet curtains were swept back, and a dozen school officials sat in a row before a long wooden table. Gee recognized one of them as the principal. She wore a gray suit and pointy heels, her hair pinned into a severe blond bun. Gee had met her at that first meeting in June for the new students who'd be joining in the fall. She had shaken his hand but seemed harried, reluctant. It was a relief that she hadn't said much, and that he'd had to say nothing, although her silence and her tepid smile had left him wondering whether she was repelled by him.

A black man sat at the edge of the officials' table, and Gee wondered who he was. He was broad shouldered, clean-shaven, handsome in a blazer and tie. Maybe Gee should have worn a tie, too? He strained to read the little paper sign in front of him that bore the man's name and title, but he couldn't see, and soon the principal was calling everyone to order.

She welcomed parents and students, old and new. There was scattered, cheerless applause. Gee made sure not to look at his mother. He could feel the energy of her body. She was burning, desperate to say something out loud. It made him want to disappear.

The principal announced all the good things they had to look forward to: a nearly unchanged student-teacher ratio, class sizes kept under thirty, funding for a whole new line of programming: a choir, a kiln in the art room, a drama club that would put on productions in this very theater. It was what they'd been promised in exchange for the new students. Other high schools had gotten microscopes or specialists to redo the math curriculum; Central had gotten money for the arts. They were gaining more than they were losing, and that was before even accounting for the new students, whose differences would make the community even stronger.

"Now we can say we're an even better reflection of the city, the county, and the changing face of North Carolina. And above all, the law has spoken. Our representatives have spoken. It's our duty, as citizens, to open up our doors and move into the future."

A chorus of boos rolled over the room. The principal held up her hands. "We're not here for debate. This is a time to look ahead. We'll open the floor now for questions, words of welcome — that's why we're here."

Before she was through, a line had started to form at each of the microphone stands in the auditorium, one in the rear, the other in the aisle next to Gee, Jade, and Linette. Gee sank lower in his seat. His teeth scraped together, and he felt a familiar shock run from his jaw to his ear. He winced from the pain and listened as the speeches started.

A woman with gray hair and Coke-bottle glasses was first. "I hear everybody here talking about welcome. New beginnings! But what about good-byes? What about mourning?" She was met with applause, an echo of *Yes!* "To make room for these two hundred new kids, we've had to let go of two hundred kids who have been at Central since they were freshmen. All because the school board and the city have got an agenda? My daughter is losing every single one of her best friends to this new program, and she's going to be a junior! It's a critical year, and she's going to have to start all over! How is that fair?"

By the end, she was shouting, and the

cheers went on for so long, the principal had to stand and ask the crowd to quiet down. The deluge kept coming.

"Okay, we're keeping our teachers; okay, class size is staying the same. That doesn't mean this school is the same. Everybody knows it's the students that make the school. And now we're going to have these kids — these kids who are coming from failing schools — making up twenty-five percent of every grade. Twenty-five percent! They're going to hold our kids back! These kids aren't where our kids are in their education or their home training. And it may not be their fault, but it's not my kid's fault either!"

A meek-mannered woman with a short black bob and glasses edged to the microphone as if it caused her great pain to do so. She began in a low voice. "Everybody deserves a fair shot in life — I believe that. I always have. That's what America is about. My son is applying for college this year, and I've heard it on good authority that this wasn't random. That these kids were hand-picked because they're star students. And now, my kid's ranking is going to fall. What has my son been working for if these new students are going to come in underneath his nose and steal everything he's been working for, and everything we've all been working for? Everything we do is for him."

"I know this isn't about *integration*. It isn't about *what's right*. They put nice words in the pamphlets, but I'm not fooled. This is about money, money, money, and the city being greedy. They're playing around with my kids' future. Central might not hit that county quota of no more than forty percent of students on free or reduced lunch. Because we may leave. A lot of us may leave. I'm looking into private school for my girls because I can't trust the administration here, and I can no longer trust the city I've lived in, and that my family has lived in, for generations, for over one hundred years!"

Gee felt Linette stir beside him. Her leg thumped underneath her, and she knotted her hands in her lap. She was nervous, and it was catching. He leaned away from her in his seat. Jade reached over to take Linette's hand and steady her. The women locked fingers. Jade was swinging her head from side to side, disagreeing with the latest speaker at the podium. Gee knew it was only a matter of time before she burst.

Next there was a man in a plaid shirt, a long beard and sideburns. He pointed at the floor for emphasis with every sentence. He was so steady, so even, it was terrifying.

"Am I the only one who will say it? These kids could be *bad kids.* What about background checks? How are you going to keep our kids safe? Are we going to put in metal detectors? What about in the hallway, when my daughter is walking between her classes? And what about the parking lot? We ought to put cameras out there."

Gee felt his vision tunnel, the room around him turn to black at the edges. He mopped his forehead with his sleeve. He was turning inward, closing up. He nearly missed Adira sliding to the microphone, her hands clasped primly in front of her, her head high.

"My name is Adira Howard, and I'll be a junior here at Central next fall. I came tonight because I was excited. Because I want a future too —"

Gee wondered at Adira. She was stupid and brave and beautiful all at once.

"My family has been here for generations, too. And I deserve my future as much as anybody else. It hurts to know I'm not welcome here, at a school that's only fifteen minutes away from my house, all because of the color of my skin."

There was an encouraging whistle from the front row, and the Howards stood up, clapping for their girl. A few white grown-ups stood, too, to applaud Adira, and Gee wondered why they hadn't spoken yet. Where were all the people who had published op-eds in the paper about the benefits of the program? Where was that majority who supported this change?

When the boos started up again, while Adira was still at the microphone, Jade sprang up to stand in line. A balding man in a crimson polo shirt was set to speak first. He shook his head for a long while before he began.

"This is not about race," he said. "This is about fairness. We don't have to give up our rights to the whims of whoever is in office right now. I know it must have taken guts for that little girl to stand up here and speak, but, young lady, you're dead wrong. This has nothing to do with the color of your skin. I taught at North Carolina A&T, a historically black college, for twenty years before moving here — I am not a racist, and it's criminal for you, or anyone, to suggest I am."

There was hooting and screaming for the man at the microphone. The principal hammered at her podium with a gavel she hadn't used before. The school officials fidgeted onstage, except for the black man who sat calmly on the edge of his seat, his hands folded into a steeple. His eyes were invisible behind the sheen of his glasses. Gee wondered how he managed to sit up there, with all those people watching, whether it was better to be onstage or in the crowd in moments like this. Next, it was Jade.

"My husband wanted the best for our son. We've spent our lives trying to figure out how to give it to him. We haven't had our lives handed to us, like some of the people in this room. For a lot of you, your kids coming to this school is just them inheriting what's rightfully theirs — the future they've been headed toward since they were born. But for my son, it's a change in his fate. And his fate has been changed more than once, and not for the better, and none of that was his fault."

Gee felt himself shrink.

"And now that he's got this chance, we're not going to let anyone take it from him. He's not going to be left behind. And I'm going to be here, every morning, and every afternoon, to make sure he's welcomed the way he ought to be, the way the law says he deserves. Put in your metal detectors. Put your cameras in the parking lot. Let me tell you — you'll be seeing my face."

There was whooping and hollering as Jade returned to her seat. Gee felt his anger focus on his mother. She slid into the seat beside him, and he crossed his arms away from her.

"What did I do now?" she asked, and he wondered whether there was a point in being honest.

"I just want to fit in, and you're talking like you're ready to go to war."

"Do you hear these other parents?"

"I don't care about them. What about me? I don't want any trouble."

Jade shook her head. "These people are just talking cause there's nothing else they can do. You'll see. You just got to let them know they can't take you for a punk, that you'll fight back —"

A shrill voice startled them. Someone at the back of the room was speaking right to Jade.

"To the young woman who just finished up here —"

A fair, slender woman stood at the microphone, her hair large and feathered around her.

"How dare you say anything in my life has been handed to me! If your husband wanted the best for your son, he should have done what I did and moved him into this district fair and square. I made sacrifices to get here. It cost me. It cost my children. And I'm not just going to give it up so you can get *handed* what you think you deserve — that's not right, and that's not American."

The applause that erupted into the auditorium was the most riotous yet. People stomped and rose in their seats. The principal banged her gavel uselessly. The large-haired woman went on, and Gee couldn't bring himself to look away from her narrow face, the bright aperture of her eyes.

"There's a bunch of us," she said. "We're putting together a march! And we're not going to stop there. The school year hasn't started yet. We've got time. I'll be standing right back here with flyers for anyone else who wants to get involved. Come find me. My name is Lacey May Gibbs."

After the town hall, Gee rode back with Linette. He could see Jade's headlights shining through the rear of the car as she followed them down the road. He wondered whether she was headed home with them, too, or if she'd turn off somewhere, and go wherever it was she went when she wasn't working or at home. She never announced when she'd be leaving; she just left. There were hours where neither he nor Linette could account for Jade. He couldn't say either of them missed her much. When she was home, she just listened to music on her headphones in her bedroom, or drank whiskey-and-coke and read her medical books. So far, she was still trailing them, and Gee wished she'd signal, disappear around a bend.

"Are you punishing your mama by riding home with me?" Linette peered at Gee from the corner of her eye. "You don't like it when she speaks up. Even if she's doing it for you."

"She just loves being right. You know that."

"She was speaking from the heart."

"She said they were married. She was talking about him like he's still alive."

"Maybe that's how she sees it," Linette said. "Maybe that's all true to her."

Gee rolled his eyes.

"Your mother's come a long way. You know, you could have turned out lots of different ways after what happened. But look at you. She stepped up. She spared you."

Gee didn't like when Linette talked this way, as if he were some project of his mother's, and all the credit for who he was could be given to her. As if, without her, he was a tragedy, a boy destined for a lifetime of nothing.

He rubbed his jaw where he was sore. His teeth seemed to be vibrating; he could still feel the pressure of them sliding together even when he stopped.

"I could hear you, you know, in the auditorium. Grinding those teeth. If you're not careful, you'll crack another."

"I can't control it, Linette."

"Have you tried? You can't let people bother you so much, Gee. I don't need to tell you what it might be like for you at this school. You were there. You heard them."

Linette and Jade were always telling him how hard his life would be, like he could ever forget.

"Those were just the parents," he said.

"You think teenagers are going to be much better?"

"Can we talk about something else?"

"Fine. Adira was looking cute today."

"Oh God, Linette. Please. I don't want to talk about girls."

"Why not? There's nothing wrong with a little crush."

"She's my friend."

Linette wiggled her eyebrows at Gee. It was so goofy he couldn't help but laugh. Linette had dressed up for the meeting in a crisp blue blouse, her nails polished. He couldn't remember the last time he had seen her that way. Usually, she looked rundown, her hair undone, gunk at the corners of her eyes. She spent most of her time watching the television, cooking their meals, and keeping the house together while Jade was at work. She didn't seem very happy, but she wasn't miserable either. She was tender with him, and she got along with Jade fine. The two of them orbited each other, ate their meals together, as if this life wasn't really theirs; it was temporary, filler, and they were biding time, counting down the days until something changed. What? Until he went off to school? Until they were all far enough from what had happened to Ray?

They rolled farther east, down the wide, quiet roads.

"It can be good, you know, to let somebody close," Linette said.

"Like you and Ma?"

"You mind the way you talk to me, young man."

"Sorry." Gee didn't mean to be rude with Linette, but he had nowhere to put all his bad feelings. He made a point of sighing, fluttering his lips, to ease the tension in his jaw. It made no difference.

Through the rearview, he saw Jade's turn signal blink. They were still a mile from home. He watched her make a left, and then she was gone. He turned to make a face at

Linette, as if to say, *See how much she cares?* But she kept her eyes on the road.

At home, Linette parked herself in front of the TV. Whatever attention she'd had for him had dried up now, and she went straight for her needlepoint and the evening news. He left her, retreated to his room upstairs. It had been a walk-in closet, but now it was his: a narrow bed, a desk with his computer, big speakers to play music, a hanging light bulb, and a picture of him and Ray.

It was the photograph that had hung in the shrine before Jade took it down. She said Ray was in their hearts; they didn't need to keep him on the wall. It was the same year his nightmares started, although he couldn't remember how old he'd been, whether it had started in the old apartment or here at Linette's. First, he was sleeping too much, then he wasn't sleeping at all. Then he had headaches, real ones that gave credibility to the fake ones he used as excuses now.

The dreams were all the same at the beginning. He was in a car, riding somewhere. Then he was alone: on a dark street, or in the woods, or the old fairgrounds. They all ended with him being snatched from behind, someone dragging him away, although he didn't know where. He woke one morning because he felt himself choking; he spit a pearly shard into his hand and saw he'd split his front tooth in two. He didn't know how much it had cost to repair, but he knew Jade had put it all on a credit card and it took her a long time to pay it off. The dentist said he had other internal fractures in his teeth, and it was only a matter of time before they cracked, too, if he kept grinding. He had said it as if Gee had a choice in the matter, as if he could stop, if only he put his mind to it.

He had retrieved the photograph of him and Ray at the park from a box in Jade's closet, put it up on his own with thumbtacks. It wasn't that he liked the picture much; he didn't. It was the portrait of a stranger, a dead person. And he didn't recognize himself, either, in the dimpled, sun-lit little boy. It didn't capture how it had felt to be Ray's son, to sit with him in the kitchen in the morning to test out recipes, to fall asleep against his shoulder in the windowsill at Superfine. All his memories of Ray were hazy, so it wasn't that he missed him, exactly, but he thought of him every day. When he saw a boy his age with his father. Or a happy pair of parents with their child. When he ate a good slice of cake, when he saw rusting old sedans, green, like

183

the one Ray had driven. He didn't remember watching him die, although Linette and Jade had asked him what he saw, and they had asked him, too, in court. He remembered only saying he didn't know and feeling he had disappointed them, all those watching grown-ups with faces that betrayed there was something more they had hoped to hear.

Alone in his room, Gee flopped into bed, started tapping his tongue against the veneer. It seemed fine for now, still intact, unlike the mouth guard he used overnight, which was covered in dents. He didn't know why he did it; he didn't go to sleep worrying about anything, and the nightmares were rare. But there was evidence of his habit every morning. His jaw ached, and it took a few moments to unseal his teeth, open his mouth, and feel again that he could speak.

It didn't seem to be a problem in his mind — no matter the kind of day he had, no matter his thoughts, the grinding wasn't any better or worse. The trouble was in his body. It wasn't only his receding gums, the blood in the sink when he brushed his teeth. Sometimes, he found himself standing with his shoulders up by his ears, or his fists clenched, or he'd be lying in bed listening to music and he'd notice suddenly that his legs were as rigid as planks of wood. He tried to help himself by discharging the ugly feelings. He did it in the bathroom at school, under a blanket in front of the TV, here in his room. The trouble always came back, but it still helped to snuff it out for a while.

Gee reached up to turn off the light, slid his hands into his jeans. He started working on himself. His skin was dry, but it felt good, and he ignored his routine unease about what he was doing. There was no question that he wouldn't stop. He rubbed harder, and it became smoother, more fluid. His hand glided along, and he helped himself with his thoughts. These were not his fingers; this breath was not his breath. There were women in his brain, women in his room. Women who were older, women who loved him. Women with no faces, with body parts he'd never seen close up. Women who didn't exist, except for now. They told him he was perfect. They told him he should come. They told him and told him and told him. Soon he took off, the pleasure where he was holding, and elsewhere, too: his toes, his buzzing skin, his warming face. He was nowhere, free. He felt himself lighten; he felt himself float. Everything inside him flowed into the air, became big energy, rippling around. He was empty. He was wet and spent and fine. His jaw unclenched.

There were some who said the initiative started in the county. The city was changing. People were moving closer to downtown; the business council had a five-year plan for revitalizing Main Street; the old millhouses were being converted into single-family homes. Money was coming back to the city, and they had to get ahead of the changes. If they brought together the city and county school systems, they could redistribute the kids — and the taxes — the right way.

There were others who said the mayor dreamed it up. He was a black man who would be retiring at the end of the term, and this would be his lasting legacy: undoing the white flight that had damned the city schools so long ago, especially on the east side, where he was raised. He was hoping for a plaque in his honor, downtown, catty-corner from the Confederate soldiers' monument.

And still others said it was a long time coming, overdue, what federal law had required for decades. The school board was finally putting their money where their mouths were. They were busing the kids, piloting programs in vocational training, computer science, the arts. It was the chance to transfer your child to a school with new programs that got most parents on board.

The first pamphlets used the words *integration* and *equity*. There was a slew of op-eds in the local paper threatening legal action, arguing the problem of considering race in public schools. A band of white parents called it discrimination; they cited the inconveniences of busing. They held living room meetings, papered the storefronts downtown with their hot-pink flyers.

When the pamphlets were reissued, they used the words *opportunity* and *choice,* laid out quotas for the number of students on free and reduced lunch in two short paragraphs. The rest of the pamphlets highlighted the new programs, the way to apply for a transfer. It was wildly popular, a trick. But they hadn't fooled Lacey May.

She hadn't planned on getting involved, but all the talk of inequality, giving every family a fair shot, rubbed her the wrong way. There were problems in this life, sure, but they were mostly the result of people's own doing. You could blame the world, Lacey May thought; you could make up arguments, you could blame the past. But it was like blaming a shadow, searching for a reason, when the reason, at the end of the day, was you.

She was making signs at the kitchen table when Noelle finally came up from the basement. She had shut herself down there after they got home from the town hall and skipped dinner. It was dark now and she slipped in, filled a glass of water at the tap. She halved a lemon and squeezed it in, seeds and all. She inspected the signs her mother had made. *Our Taxes, Our Schools! Protect Our Kids! Not Our Problem!*

"Feeling sick?" Lacey May asked.

"Well, I do want to vomit every time I look at those signs." Noelle drained the glass and filled another. "You know we live *in* the city, right? And your friends are trying to keep city kids out of the county schools?"

"The west side is different," Lacey May said. "Our schools are the good ones. Why do you want it getting ruined? The least you could do is help."

"No chance in hell."

Noelle crossed into the living room, where her sisters were watching a vampire show on the TV. Margarita was swooning over the pale-faced lead, Diane watching with Jenkins belly up in her lap. Hank drank a beer in his armchair, winced at all the punching and grunting onscreen. Noelle crouched on the floor to tie up her boots.

"You going out?" Hank asked. "It's late."

"I'll be back before morning."

"Very funny," he said and turned back to the vampire show. He had learned to give Noelle a wide berth, and she had learned to expect it. There was a honk outside, and Lacey May charged into the living room.

"Just where do you think you're going?"

Noelle went on crisscrossing her laces.

"You think I'm some bigot, but I'm a realist. Do you know what that is, Noelle? It's somebody who prepares for the future by paying attention to today."

"Thanks for the lesson." Noelle clomped out of the room, and Lacey May followed her.

"You think you're so special, that no matter what happens, you'll be just fine. Well, let me tell you, this is no land of plenty. When you're grown, you've got to fight for everything you call yours, and no one is going to make it easy for you. Nobody is going to help. I wish I had a mother looking out for me! You go around like your future is guaranteed."

Noelle spun around to face her mother.

189

"Don't you worry about my future, Mama. I won't get stuck marrying Hank." Another honk. "That's my ride," she said, and stepped into the night.

Duke was waiting for her in his car, and Noelle crossed the lawn quickly. She was quaking with rage and embarrassment. Her mother had never cared about school, never so much as baked a brownie for a bake sale. But for weeks she'd been hosting other mothers in the kitchen for coffee and folding mailers. She had even signed her name to an op-ed in the paper. Noelle had been grateful her mother had changed her name and that there was nothing there, in print, that tethered her to Lacey May.

Once she was inside, Duke handed her a beer. She kept the open can between her legs as they coasted through the west side toward the highway. When they reached the cover of speed and darkness on 85, she took a sip. It was warm and flat. Duke slid his hand up her leg, brushed his fingers against her groin. She didn't move against him. She drank until the can was done, then she crushed it, stuffed it into the glove compartment.

"Are you going to that march?" she asked.

"Maybe. There's a bunch of us walking over after church."

"Then you can go with my mother."

"What's the big deal?"

"It's like a movie. People are making signs, trying to keep the new kids from coming in. You'd think it was the sixties."

"Don't be so dramatic," Duke said. "It's got nothing to do with them being black."

"Don't be such an idiot. Of course it does."

Duke turned to her in shock, his face flushed from the beer.

"I'm sorry." Noelle leaned over to kiss him behind the ear. "I'm not feeling good tonight. I've got a lot that's bothering me."

Duke looked at her disapprovingly, but he didn't say anything. He picked his battles, and he didn't like to disappoint, not his mother, not Noelle. It was one of the reasons he made such a decent boyfriend. He had sculpted his red-blond hair into spikes for the show, put on the Black Sabbath T-shirt Noelle had bought for him at a record store on one of their dates.

"Let me make it up to you," she said and slipped her hand between his legs.

Duke looked at her, measuring. He had eyes the clear green of pines. She unzipped his fly, untied his belt, and he lifted his hips, which was how she knew she'd been forgiven. She rooted around in his pants, and he was sighing even before she stroked him. He set the cruise control in the car.

"Put your seat belt on," he told her, then, "Faster." He kept his eyes on the road.

The club was fifty miles west, and Duke paid their way in. They were checking IDs at the bar, so he got them sodas with lime. Noelle chewed the limes, hers then his, separating the pulp from the rind with her teeth. "My stomach hurts," she explained, swallowing down an acid taste in her throat.

The stage was in a dingy, windowless room, papered with banners from old shows and black-and-white stickers that said things like *Meat Is Murder* and *Support the Police — Beat Yourself Up.* The band was in town from New Jersey, and both Duke and Noelle considered themselves devotees. Their music was loud and simple, the guitar parts easy enough for Duke to imitate on his guitar, the singing mostly shouting. There was fury and energy to their sound, a thumping bass to move your hips, a drum solo to bash your head, breakdowns where you felt your body soar, the music lifting you. The chain store in the mall didn't carry their CD, so Noelle had downloaded their whole EP over her dial-up connection, waiting an hour for each track.

The first set started, the crowd surging toward the stage to welcome them. In the crush of bodies, Noelle felt herself a part of something, a movement of misfits who weren't sure what unified them besides that they didn't fit in anywhere else. It was this feeling of being out that had led her to start wearing black rubber bracelets, stacked a dozen high, and to start painting her lips blood red. It was part of why she'd chosen Duke. His parents may have been deacons in the church, but he wasn't quite a square.

In a way, it made sense to her to feel adrift, out of place, in North Carolina. The band was from close to New York, where she imagined it was easy to find other vegans and anarchists and feminists, other white boys who wore their hair too long. She screamed and thrashed alongside the teenage boys in eyeliner, the girls with titanium rings pushed through the cartilage in their ears. They batted around blown-up condoms, inflated like balloons. They smashed their bodies together and slid across pools of sweat.

The first set was nearly through when Noelle spotted a crew of brown kids, all boys, except for one girl, whose face Noelle couldn't see — she'd tied a red bandanna just below her eyes. She wore a cropped white shirt that exposed her long, hard belly, a large indigo bird rising out of the hem of her sweatpants, flying across her rib cage — a tattoo. Noelle sometimes fantasized about getting a black butterfly on her hip bone, a seashell in the cleft between her breasts. All she needed was the cash, a ride to Charlotte, an artist who wouldn't care she wasn't yet eighteen. But here was a girl, not much older, who wasn't stuck dreaming, who had done it. Noelle watched her windmill her arms, grab white boys by the collar, and swing them around. The girl and her friends made a little protected knot at the center of the mosh pit, and Noelle, at the edge of the circle, held her hands out in front of her to shove away anybody who came too close. The beautiful girl with the bird on her body never did. Noelle would have liked to touch her. Duke kept his arms tied fast around her waist.

The set was nearly over when the nausea came on hard. Noelle felt as if liquid were collecting in her throat, and she went off running, pushing her way through the crowd. When she reached the stall, she threw up.

She sat down on the seat to recover. She felt dizzy and warm. She was at the sink, rinsing her mouth, when the girl strode in, her bandanna pushed down around her neck. She had a wide, beautiful face, her makeup smeared around her dark eyes. She nodded at Noelle.

Before she knew it, Noelle had sputtered her name, her whole name, out at the girl, who smiled at her indulgently. She said she was Alexandra, a student at UNC, and she and her friends came to all these shows. They had started a band of their own, in the style of the Chicano hardcore bands from Chicago and L.A., although they were all North Carolinians, only two of them Mexican. Alexandra was from El Salvador.

"You half?" Alexandra asked, offering Noelle a stick of gum.

"My father is Colombian."

"Nice," she said. "Well, look us up. We're called Mega Fuerza. Come and see us play." The girl finished retouching her makeup and left. It was only when she was gone that Noelle admitted to herself that she was in trouble. The vomit had confirmed what she already knew, and so had looking at Alexandra, her sweat and radiance, her lean torso. Noelle wasn't the same. Something had shifted inside her.

Duke was waiting for her outside the bathroom, clutching another soda and lime. He looked nervous. "Take me home," she said, and they headed out into the night, their ears still throbbing.

Duke led the way through the dark, unfamiliar downtown. Noelle wondered whether she'd come to school here, or whether she'd be able to go away, much farther. Duke wasn't the kind of boy who would follow her. He'd stay in his church and meet a girl, work some job, buy a house on the west side. He'd take off his studded bracelets, cut his hair, and live out the life he was always going to have lived.

Noelle wanted more. She wanted to be far away from Robbie, who was here and then wasn't. She wanted away from her mother, who held up hateful signs and pretended not to hate, who had married Hank but still gave money to Robbie, held on to their old house. She was weak, small. Noelle wanted to be different. She wanted to live in a big city. She wanted to have friends who spoke Spanish. She wanted to order coffee from a coffee bar. She wanted to make things, to be around people who made things. She wanted out of the basement, a room of her own, where she could bring home boys, maybe even a girl, like the one from Mega Fuerza. She didn't know what she'd do, or where she'd live, but she could go anywhere, be anything. If she could leave now, she would. She didn't want to see how things would go at Central.

"Noelle." Duke was calling to her. She snapped back to the warm night, his cool, soft hand. "Are you okay? You only had one beer."

He was a sweet boy, and what they had for now was good and easy. Before they got home, they'd pull off somewhere, make out in the car. They'd put their tongues in each other's ears. They'd go at it until he came, one way or another. He was her first boyfriend, but she'd found ways to do this, with her hands, her mouth, climbing on top of him. It made her feel competent, powerful. She could make him moan. She could make him say her name.

"Noelle," he said again, still worried.

She smiled at him and kissed his knuckles. "I'm fine," she said. "It's just a little thing."

7

The café was modern, an oddity on this street in the eleventh arrondissement. It was brightly lit and industrial with concrete walls and floors. A glass wall separated the front of the shop from the back, where the bakers were molding dough, folding and beating, brushing butter onto croissants. Nelson sat by the window and watched them slide trays from the oven. The café had a euphoric name, something like La Bonne Espérance, and it was tucked into the corner of a frantic boulevard not far from the Bastille. Noelle would have liked the shop, its polish and grit. He thought of her as he looked out on the street.

The neighborhood wasn't as picturesque as the ones closer to the Seine, the rue de Rivoli. Out here it was all bus stops, two-euro crêpe stands, eyeglass shops, and pharmacies, a green square where children kicked around a soccer ball. Nelson could see the column of the Bastille, a quarter mile away, towering green and gold. The bronze nude atop was a man, winged, a torch in one hand, a broken chain in the other. A star over his head. *Le Génie de la Liberté, The Spirit of Freedom.* Nelson remembered enough of his college French to know that *génie* meant "spirit" and not "genius" in this case, which he appreciated since he didn't believe in genius. There was only luck and social capital, as well as capital capital. It was true even for him, his career, but what did it matter? He was here.

Rumor was that the café was black owned. He ordered a beignet and a coffee, turning down the espresso for drip, *un café américain.* Even across an ocean, he couldn't deny his roots.

The beignet was airy and fat, sugar dusted. He bit into the soft dough, the tart smear of raspberry jam, sifted clean of seeds. It was simple, perfect. There were many arts that weren't considered arts but should have been. He ate with his eyes shut. He didn't notice Jemima had breezed in, until he heard the scrape of a stool across the floor.

"What's the matter? Are you crying?"

"Just communing with the dead," Nelson said, and when she tilted her head at him, questioning, he went on. "Never mind. I

199

was having a meditative experience."

"Sure," she said, flipping over the menu. "Whatever. Do they have real food here or just pastries? It's almost lunchtime, you know."

Jemima was dressed like a Parisian teenager in a silk floral dress and white sneakers, her bangs cut straight across her forehead. She had coffee-colored hair and olive eyes, a cell phone she kept glued to her palm. She had worn purple eyeliner every day he'd known her, today included. She was twenty-four, and Nelson was fairly certain this was her first job.

She asked him how he'd spent the morning, and Nelson said he'd gone for a walk in the gardens, then a run. After his shower, he caught a taxi here to the eleventh for a coffee, dessert.

"Hard at work, hunh?" Jemima waved over a server.

"It's my first day off."

"Do you think you could incorporate calling your wife into your day off?"

"Noelle called again?"

"Last time, she tried eleven times in a row. I was this close to blocking her number. But thank God, I haven't heard from her in a few days."

"Me neither."

"And that doesn't worry you?"

"She left some messages about a party in the neighborhood. Nothing important."

"Not to you, no," Jemima said and shook her head at him, too familiar. He liked this side of her, how frank she was, how she didn't measure her words, worry about how she might be received. It was obnoxious, the product of her whiteness, her youth, her too-good fortune in life. It put him off when he noticed that unflustered air in men, but it was different somehow with Jemima.

He watched her shuck off her leather jacket, so small it seemed to be a piece of clothing for a doll. A constellation of sweat spread over her upper lip, the mounds of her breasts.

Jemima was a junior publicist at the French office of the house that had agreed to put out his book of photographs. She had served as his handler the last few weeks while he worked. She coordinated his meetings with the editor, people, and businesses of interest. The book was tentatively called *Paris in Black and Brown,* and while he was sure he would never earn out the advance, the deal included this trip, and it had come at the perfect time, just when he needed out of Golden Brook. There was a clause in his contract about the option of another trip, if he needed more shots. He didn't think he'd have to use it, although it all depended on Noelle.

A server wandered over to collect his plate. Nelson pressed his finger to the dish, licked the sugar off his fingers, the memory of butter. Jemima ordered them salads, a carafe of white wine.

"So is this a real meeting? I thought we were all done. I leave in two days."

"I know, I'm the one who booked your flights, remember? I'm here to ask you to stay."

Nelson stared at her, disbelieving.

"Please." She rolled her eyes. "It's a request from the house. They've got an offer for you."

A playwright had heard of the project and wanted to work with Nelson. He had written a play about a French woman, a widow, whose son was killed by a terrorist. She was having an affair with a Muslim man, and the death of her son threatens to tear them, and their community, apart.

"*Community?*" Nelson repeated. "Is this a joke?"

"He wants to incorporate your photographs in the set. Blow them up, get them printed on silkscreens. It would be a beautiful way to show the work. You've heard of this guy before, right? He does very edgy stuff. Likely to get a lot of buzz. French nationalism, Islamophobia, suicide bombing, cross-cultural love — it's all there."

Their salads arrived, and Jemima went on, trying to sell him on the project, while she divided their food. She picked out the eggs and baby potatoes from her salad, depositing them on his plate, so that soon she was left with nothing but vegetables and hunks of pale pink fish. It wasn't one of her more charming qualities, the way she ate, as if she didn't want to, as if food were a nuisance to be tolerated with the fewest number of calories allowed. She stayed away from the bread basket, too, although they were here, in Paris. This was perhaps the only way in which she wasn't entitled, the only way in which she denied herself. Nelson helped himself to the bread. He doused the salad in oil. He asked how many days the project would add to the trip.

"You'd have to go through the script together and do some mockups of the set. It could take a while." Jemima was noncommittal as she guzzled her wine.

"I'll have to talk to my wife."

"One more thing, it isn't paid."

Nelson laughed. "Then I'm out. What do they think? This is my summer internship?"

"You'll still get your per diem, and we'll keep you at the hotel. Just think of how good this will look on your CV. Think of it as free publicity."

It was absurd to take career advice from Jemima, he knew. She was shortsighted and young, and she wasn't an artist. She dealt in emails and lunches, buzz.

"I can't work for free. I've got a family."

"Correction — you have a wife. And you don't seem too worried about her most of the time."

Nelson didn't like the way she was talking, as if she knew anything about him and Noelle.

"Don't make that face," Jemima said. She was talking and chewing at the same time, a sliver of fish lolling around in her mouth like a second tongue. "I didn't mean to upset you. But there's no way you can turn this down, and I don't mean because of the book. You're not ready to go home. I can tell."

Afterward, in his room, Jemima put on a robe and went to the balcony to smoke. They were visible from the street below, Jemima bare legged, Nelson back in his pants and undershirt. The wind whipped her hair around her face, she offered him her cigarette, and Nelson couldn't help but think they were merely acting out their parts — the artist and the lady, two Americans in Paris, a white woman on the verge of the rest of her life, and her black lover.

Sometimes, he had this feeling that his life was being watched, that other people could see not only what he was doing, but into his mind. He tried to revise his thoughts, as if they were a soliloquy someone might overhear. There was nothing romantic about this moment, the traffic below, Jemima tapping away at her phone.

Nelson took in the view of the blue rooftops, the maze of sand-colored buildings. It was spectacular, more impressive than the faraway spire of the Eiffel Tower, the green corridor of the Champs-Élysées, all the sites that were reproduced on postcards for tourists. The city had changed so little since he'd studied abroad. He'd been a boy then, scrappy, in love with Noelle. He was in love with her still. He was just fucking someone else.

"Read this." Jemima handed over her phone. "It's the first scene of the play. It won't take you long."

Her cheeks were still flushed, and Nelson had a vision of how she'd looked, flat against the mattress, facedown. He had moved in and out of her slowly, the way she liked, although it had been hard to pace himself. It was worth the effort to watch her pant and squirm. He could please her consistently, deeply. And she was a shouter, which he loved. He had memorized her gasps and moans, replayed them for himself later. He had done a terrible job of containing what they had.

Nelson leaned against the iron railing and scrolled through. "Oh God," he said.

"I know, it's hardly Shakespeare."

Nelson read aloud. *The thing about endless war is that there is never a victor but always carnage."*

"That's sort of true."

"It's melodramatic and didactic."

"You've got to see the theater where the show's going up. Maybe that will convince you."

"This is supposed to be my day off. I've hardly had a chance to be a tourist."

"You'll have plenty of time once you agree to stay on."

"You know, my wife used to be a theater director."

"I thought she was a housewife."

"You thought wrong."

Jemima put up her hands. "Easy there. I've got the utmost respect for housewives.

My mom stayed home with me for years." She tapped her ash over the edge. "You know, you never talk about your parents. You bring up your wife sometimes, as if you don't want me to forget, but she calls so much, how could I? But you being married — that's not very interesting. Your bio doesn't even mention where you grew up. All your portraits of the South but no mention of how you know it. Whether you lived there, or visited grandparents over the summer. If your ancestors were slaves."

"Of course they were slaves."

"It's like you want people to believe you came out of the ether. You think it's mysterious, but that's not what people want. They need a good origin story."

"The better questions are the ones about my art and not about me."

"It's not just the art that's for sale, you know."

Jemima got up on her tiptoes and kissed him on the cheek. Her lips were warm from the cigarette. "So you want to see this theater or not?"

Nelson had started taking photographs on his road trips with Noelle. Neither of them wanted to go home for breaks, so they'd rent a car and drive. They went to Savannah, Charleston, the Smoky Mountains, once as far as Florida. Nelson took pictures of men at roadside fruit stands, orange groves and swamps, the high grass that presaged their arrival at some gray-water beach.

He used an old point-and-shoot to take self-portraits in motel bathrooms and close-ups of Noelle, nineteen, pimply, and beautiful, underneath bristly, stained sheets. He liked the way a photograph could preserve the secret life of a person, a place. It was as if the world were offering itself continually if you would only look.

He scraped together enough money from his campus jobs to pay the studio fee for a photography class. He won grants, got funding from the dean. He studied abroad in Paris one summer, Brazil the next. With his photographs, he was spared backhanded compliments from his classmates and teachers — there was no denying he was good. It was a consolation to be a natural.

His first show after college drew a decent crowd, mostly Noelle's theater friends. He hadn't set out to create a series from his travels; he had just photographed older black men whose faces he found beautiful. He got a nice review and sold very little. Their lives went on unchanged. He worked production on film shoots, took dinky family photos on the weekends. He and Noelle filled the gaps in their paychecks with stints as bartenders, baristas, which made them feel noble, as if they were paying their dues. That phase lasted only a few years. Eventually, Noelle became director at a reputable company; Nelson got magazine work, started showing at galleries more.

Soon they had plenty for dinner and cocktails and plays, long weekends to the Caribbean, where they snorkeled and drank on the beach, ate fried fish with their hands. They were solidly middle-class but felt rich, and it was more than just the luxuries. Their little life was peaceable. They worked; they came home; they saw friends. They cooked vegetables, drank oat milk, took vitamins. They went for night walks in the neighborhood and felt safe. They weren't sick or broke, dead or dying. They had no addictions they could name. Their framed degrees hung in the foyer. They were better off than Nelson had ever known two people could be.

Sometimes, when he was running, Nelson would be struck with the terrible presentiment that something bad had happened to Noelle. He didn't experience it as a fear but as fact, a catastrophe he could sense, preternaturally, in his bones. She'd been hit by a bus, attacked by a stray dog, caught in a shootout and bled out when a well-meaning bystander couldn't stop the wound. He'd run hard and fast in the direction of home, find her on the couch, glasses on, reading a play. He'd kneel before her, put his head in her lap, say nothing of what he'd seen.

He would calm himself, and they'd go on, their little domestic life unspoiled. He might have been ambitious, but it was clear to him that all he really needed was her. Noelle was his key to a good life.

There were other women only when he was away. A caterer he took back to his hotel room at a convention in Rio. A curator at a Manhattan gallery who lived in a loft with plum-colored walls. A graduate student at a lecture he gave in Chicago. A painter at an artists' colony in Maine.

They didn't mean anything, except that, without Noelle, there was no way to steady himself. No one had ever usurped her place in his heart. He had called her, returned to her, always. But there was something new in what he was doing with Jemima. He was gallivanting with her around the city as if he belonged to her. And he was ignoring his wife. It was repulsive, even to him.

Maybe he was trying to beat the universe

to the punch. He'd ruin his own life before it got snatched away from him. But even to see his motivations that way was too generous. Maybe he merely wanted to punish her. Noelle had broken their first, most vital promise: to live well, to never look back. To go beyond what should have been possible for either of them. She had let herself sink, and he couldn't follow her down. If he fucked Jemima, if he sent Noelle to voicemail, maybe she would hear: *You won't take me with you.*

The performance space was in a converted church not far from the Sorbonne. It had high ceilings and gilded walls, dusty velvet chairs. There were five hundred seats, which, Jemima was careful to point out, meant more people would see his work during opening week than likely had over the entirety of his career.

When they left, Jemima looked triumphant. She slid on her sunglasses, waved good-bye, and sauntered off nonchalantly, as if she knew she'd see him again; he wasn't going anywhere.

He sat on the church steps to collect himself. The day was warm and windy, and he itched in his clothes. He clicked through his phone history, saw the string of unanswered calls from Noelle, and then nothing from her over the last few days. She had too much dignity to keep chasing after him when his silence had made plain that he wanted to be left alone. He knew it was petty to avoid her, but it would have undone the purpose of the trip to answer. Her sadness would hook him, drag him back. He hadn't invited her along precisely to avoid her obsession with the miscarriage. Her presence didn't soothe him anymore; she unwound all his efforts to maintain equilibrium. He would return from a run, and she would assail him with her theories: Her baths had been too hot; her cortisol levels were too high. She should have taken more fish oil; she should have avoided caffeine. He would emerge from a dark room, his evening meditation, his mind clear, and find her staring blankly at the TV, still wearing her clothes from the day before. He'd turn to her in bed, reach for her waist, to find her quivering, weeping noiselessly.

For all his daily terror at the thought of losing Noelle, it had never occurred to him the baby might be lost. It was a sign of how all his luck, the good life he didn't deserve, had twisted his mind — he had expected everything to be fine. It was one of the things that had first attracted him to Noelle:

her understanding that life was unfair, brutal, and all you could do was treasure the good when it came along, while it lasted. And yet, he had taken their lot for granted, pictured it all unfolding easily. She would grow larger, give birth; they'd welcome and watch over their child. He had no fantasies about being a father; he was certain he wouldn't know how. But to grow with Noelle, to change with her and undertake an adventure, felt natural, as if it were a life they were entitled to. He might have been more like Jemima than he wanted to admit.

Nelson tucked away his phone. He wasn't ready yet to call her, and he hadn't made up his mind about the play. He didn't know whether Noelle was ready for him, or if he would go home and find only more of the same. He did pity her that she was still in Golden Brook. It was impossible to be home and not to grieve, remember. But here, there was so much beauty to turn to, so much more to consume his attentions. Bridges and rivers and narrow cobbled streets, wine and beignets, gardens and moonlight, and sex, *Le Génie de la Liberté.*

He headed for the metro to Belleville. He wanted to find a park he had been to once as a student. It had been full of black and brown Parisians, and he'd felt himself blend in, disappear. It was one of the remarkable things about traveling while black. There were places in the world where he could be anyone. He could be Brazilian, Jamaican, Dominican, a black Londoner, an African émigré to France. And there were places where it was impossible: Austria, the South of France, but also Boston, parts of North Carolina, near where Noelle's family lived. Places he had felt even more acutely that he was on display, being watched for a misstep. But not here, not today.

He surfaced and asked around for the Parc des Buttes Chaumont. He stopped in a grocer's along the way to pick up peaches, a bottle of wine, seeded bread, and Camembert. Before long, he found the park, its sloping greens and muddy lake, the jagged outcrops of white rock overgrown with vines. At the top of a hill, he could look down on dozens of couples spread out on blankets, their limbs tangled up as they kissed or read or slept in the sun. The view was what he had needed.

Nelson uncorked the wine. He poured a few drops into a plastic cup and let it sit without tasting it. He bowed his head. Then he poured the wine out on the grass, refilled his cup.

That first summer he'd spent here, his

scholarship had paid for the art history class, the airfare and dorm, everything except what he'd need day to day. He had eaten just like this — baguettes and rationed cheese. He bummed wine and weed off his classmates. He walked a dozen miles a day to avoid the metro fares. He scrounged together entrance fees to as many museums as he could, resolved to walk around and take pictures when he couldn't afford a ticket. His classmates went out for escargot and duck, the forty-euro dinners they'd deemed indispensable to the experience. Nelson ate falafel with hot sauce, butter and sugar crêpes, sheets of ham he washed down with white wine. He ate by the Seine; he ate on park benches; he ate squatting on a curb in the Marais. He wrote Noelle postcards in his stilted French. He masturbated and thought of her breasts and tried to intimate this whenever he borrowed his roommate's cell phone to call her — she was back in North Carolina, miserable under her mother's roof again, and sometimes she snuck away to the bathroom, and they'd touch themselves in tandem. After she came, he'd raise his voice and talk about all the things he'd seen that day, mostly bookstores and gardens, anywhere that was free, then he'd wipe his hands and return the phone without looking at his roommate, and go back out into the night alone, taking long-exposure photographs of birds and graffiti, children climbing into fountains, the stained glass of the cathedrals, the river lapping at the stones.

He had felt that summer like a man with no past. He was anonymous, and he found his life glamorous. He had slipped out of his skin; he was a new self; he was in Europe. He felt far from where he had started. The only piece of home he had wanted to keep was Noelle. He had wished she could be there with him; he'd imagined taking her to the Jeu de Paume to look at the photographs. He'd fantasized about buying her ice cream and wandering the Tuileries, where Noelle would marvel at the red flowers and insist they take a picture together. She'd have slicked his eyebrows back into place with her spit and her thumb. He would have led her through the Père Lachaise, and they would not speak of their dead, or anything they'd lost; they would press their palms together, stand close. To the passersby, they'd seem blithe, carefree. He had adored her even then; his love for her predated everything he knew about himself.

The first time he cheated on her, they

were seniors. Noelle was at a wake for a girl she had known who had died suddenly, disappeared from class. She hadn't told him where she was going, but he had known. Without her, he went down to the commons, the lounge in the basement of the dorm. He wasn't friendly with the people on his floor, but he didn't know what else to do with himself. They were watching football, splitting a milk crate full of beer, passing around enormous bags of chips. There was a girl with big eyes, bangs that covered half her face. She sat hunched over, her skinny legs in fishnets, crossed at the knees. She kept looking at him sideways, passing him beers. When he drank, she drank, as if she were his mirror. He had been good for so long, and he tried not to think of her that way. She must have known he was with Noelle. She didn't care. When he rose to leave, she followed him. They climbed the stairs, and she brushed his hand with hers, clutched his fingers. He pressed his palm into hers, and it was over. Soon they were in his room, and he was inside her, and she was biting down hard on his pointer finger, a thing Noelle had never done, a thing that thrilled him beyond measure. He came too soon, which was for the best, because he wanted her to leave.

He did a load of laundry, wishing he could boil his sheets. He streamed in more and more bleach. When Noelle came to his room that night, she was red-eyed but said nothing about the service. He held her while she slept, and felt sick at what he'd done. But the days passed, and no one found out; the big-eyed girl never came knocking. It was a secret he could keep, another life to stow away, to pull out only when he needed. He could protect her from it, or so he told himself. He had never before let it get out of hand.

He decided to call. He'd hear her voice, and, in it, there would be an answer. She would be his Noelle again, and he would come to his senses, go home. Or he'd hear that she was still sinking, and he'd bring her here. Show her the bakery, the Seine. The phone rang and rang. She didn't answer, which he deserved. He poured himself more wine. Then his phone was buzzing, her name on the screen, *Noelle,* his wife, her picture. It was a cell phone snapshot of her with wet hair, cross-legged on the floor of the old apartment while she held up the newspaper, open to a review of her last production. The critic had called it *resplendent.* She was resplendent. Nelson answered her.

"Babe," he said. "We've been missing each other." It wasn't a complete lie to suggest he'd been calling, too. "How you been?"

"Will you look at who was lost and now is found."

It was his mother-in-law, her voice brittle and too high.

"My prodigal son-in-law. Is he coming home now? Does he expect a fatted calf? Should we throw him a party?"

Nelson heard muffled coughing. A steady beeping filled the quiet. He tried not to let on that he was surprised Noelle had gone to see her. It had been years.

"Where's my wife?"

"She's running an errand for me with Diane. I wanted Coke and licorice. I'm in the hospital. But I bet Noelle already told you that?"

"She left her phone with you?"

"The hospital line isn't working, and I'm expecting a call from Margarita. Or Robbie. They're both missing."

"Missing?"

"Well, they won't answer their phones, and we don't know where they are. I'd say that's missing. How about you? Are you missing?"

"I'm working."

"Your mama called me. That was kind of

her. Noelle must have mentioned I was sick. I told her I'll never live to see my grandchildren, and that's sad. She understands it. I'd have liked to meet them. And I'd have loved them like crazy, if you can believe that. Even after everything. Even if I never wanted Noelle's life to go this way."

Nelson winced. Her reasons for disliking him were as plain as they had always been. His racist mother-in-law. He wouldn't miss her if she died, but he'd rather she lived, for Noelle. Losing a parent was like losing a part of yourself, even if it was a part you'd rather forget.

"Enough about me," said Lacey May. "Can I take a message?"

"Tell Noelle my trip's been extended. I'll explain later when she calls."

"And call she will. You know my girl — she's the kind that keeps her promises."

"I hope you don't die before I see you again." It was the crudest he'd ever been with his mother-in-law, but he couldn't help himself. The way she talked to him — it was as if she knew what he was up to.

"Hmmm," said Lacey May. "Well, we'll see how it all goes, won't we? One thing I've learned is we don't always get what we wish for. And some of us get more than we deserve."

"Just tell her to call me."

"Sure thing," said Lacey May. "But don't you rush. Take your time. There's none of us that want you here, and if I go before I see your face again, that would be just fine with me."

8

Margarita left before dawn. On days she had a job, she liked to watch the sunrise as she drove down the 405, away from Cerritos. She liked to use the extra time to clear her head, to visualize getting all the things that she needed. She cranked down the windows, checked her hair in the rearview, and chanted to herself: *This face is going to work for you. You're going to work this face.*

The commercial was for a banking app that let all your money live online. It was a solid job, and the client had chosen her. Before she came to L.A., she had told herself she was pretty. She had won pageants, appeared in a print ad for squeezable yogurt tubes. Now that she had been here for years, she knew that it wasn't quite true. She was versatile, interesting, but she never got *gorgeous* or *stunning,* like her business partner Celeste. In a way, she was lucky — to be ordinary was worse. Out here everyone was gorgeous, and not just the models.

The trouble was her chin. It was broad, and it made her face resemble a square. She had inherited the shape from Robbie, and she'd have given anything for her face to come to a fine point like a heart (Diane), or a neat horizontal ridge like a diamond (her mother; Noelle). But her face got her work, and she couldn't complain. It was going to be a good day.

As the car glided down the freeway, she visualized herself nailing the job. The line producer would hand her a check. She'd show up at Celeste's house in Venice Beach with a box of chocolate cupcakes, a bottle of rosé, and a twisty-tied baggie of coke. They'd post a selfie of themselves licking frosting off their fingers, a looping video of their clinking glasses. After, they'd go to that brick-oven place on Abbot-Kinney, share plates of beets and eggplant and artichoke hearts, and resist all the free bread. Margarita would pick up the bill, flirt with the waiter, fuck him in Celeste's bedroom. In the morning she'd drive back to Cerritos and pay the building manager what she owed him. She'd drink her coffee on the balcony facing the Home Depot and plan her content for the day. What couldn't she do with all that cash?

When she was close to downtown, she listened to her voicemail to see if her agent had left any last-minute advice about the job. All three of her messages were from Diane.

I'm here with Mama at the hospital, she said, as if Margarita didn't already know. *Noelle's here, too.* Naturally. *Look, I know you've got a lot going on, but you've got to at least let us know whether you're coming. Noelle says we should just assume you aren't, but maybe I haven't made it clear. Things are looking real bad. Mama's been asking about you. If there was ever a time for us to all be together —*

Margarita deleted them all. Diane was too sentimental, brainwashed by Lacey May. It was why the poor girl didn't have a life of her own. And Noelle was a big phony; she didn't care about any of them, she just wanted to save face, avoid being the sister in last place. They were kidding themselves if they thought she'd leave L.A. Her life was here. And they had her number. When the brain scans came in, they could text.

The city came into view, the dry-earth hills, the glimmering fleet of buildings downtown. It made a beautiful backdrop. Margarita angled her phone overhead, smiled up at the little image of herself on the screen. Her hair rippled behind her. She kept an eye on the traffic as she typed a caption, Home Sweet Home, then set a geolocation for L.A. and applied a filter to brighten her skin. She sent it out to her followers.

She pulled into a lot and didn't even flinch when the attendant said parking was forty dollars. Nobody was going to bring her down today — no one.

On her walk to the warehouse, she spotted a pretty peach wall, and stopped to take another video. So excited to be working with a new brand today! She pressed a finger to her lips. BIG SECRET! Can't say who it is yet, but I'll be posting clues & pics all day.

She checked the engagement on her last post — over two hundred views already — and it buoyed her. She visualized herself back at Bikram, Celeste taking a picture of her in dancer's pose, the perfect thumbnail (her long legs, her solid breasts, her head not so square in profile).

When her phone rang, she went to ignore Diane instinctively, but she saw that it was her building manager, Gavin.

"Babe," she said in her softest voice. "Good morning. What can I do you for?"

"Margarita, where are you? I am outside your door knocking. The owner wanted me to tell you in person that we're changing the locks tomorrow. He sent you a final notice."

"But I'm getting paid today. Can't he wait one more day?"

"He doesn't believe you anymore, Margarita."

She had given Gavin more than one blow job. Not in exchange for rent, not in exchange for anything, really, besides his goodwill, some reason to believe he'd be on her side when she needed.

"Can't you do anything? Help me?"

"I don't make the rules, babe. He's my boss. And he's being nice. You're so far behind he could have kicked you out a long time ago."

Margarita took her oceanic breaths as she rode up the freight elevator. All would be well. How many people were lining up for a place in Cerritos anyway? It was too far inland, too regular. It could have been anywhere.

A man in a ratty T-shirt was waiting for her in the reception area. He carried a clipboard and his shoes were suede, expensive. She turned on a smile.

"Margot?" he said, sizing her up. His eyes seemed to snag on her chin. "You're on time."

"Of course!" Margarita laughed. "Why wouldn't I be?" She laughed again and wondered if it was too much cheerfulness.

"You never know with talent," he said. She shimmered at the word.

He was the producer, Ollie, and when they entered the loft, he introduced her to the team. The director was dark haired, beautiful, not quite white, Colombian maybe or Lebanese. Oblong face. Margarita wiggled her fingers at him, and he glanced back at his phone. The DP was a plain-faced woman in a black T-shirt, her mangy hair tucked under a Lakers cap. She slurped her coffee with one hand. Margarita was certain they'd have nothing in common. The prop stylist was much more L.A., in clogs and a linen dress, her red-and-gold hair piled on her head. Margarita decided she'd get her handle by the end of the day.

The set was tiny: an oak bed with pale sheets, a straw rug, a brass nightstand arrayed with delicate objects: a crystal paperweight, a navy-blue alarm clock. Margarita wanted it all. Her bedroom was nothing more than a mattress on a frame with wheels. It slid around when she was having sex.

When they started filming, she'd sprawl out on the bed and pretend it was the end of her day. She'd repay a girlfriend for brunch, order flowers for her grandmother in a nursing home, and, last, zap money to a handsome white man on a crowded street in Bangkok. He'd get her wire, check into a lavish hotel, plug in his laptop, and call her. She'd laugh at the screen, blow a kiss. Et fin.

They were starting at nine sharp, so she had to hurry to hair and makeup. Ollie showed her the breakfast spread: boxed coffee and greasy sandwiches. She had expected better from a brand like this: cold brew, avocado toast, yogurt, and melon.

"Oh my gosh, this is so yummy!" she said, biting into a croissant stuffed with ham and orange cheese.

The makeup artist had violet hair and false lashes. She was old and trying not to look it, but then again so was Margarita (twenty-nine).

"Aren't you striking," she said. "Look at your skin. I won't have to touch you at all."

Margarita knew this wasn't true. The makeup artist would make her face disappear, then bring it back again. It was a process she loved to watch, like being born, or something. She propped her phone against the mirror to record a time-lapse. She watched her face grow creamy, uniform, more square than ever, and then there was bronzer, blush, and she had dimensions again; she was different, rosier, *Margot.*

The makeup artist traced gold dust along her brow. "You've got an exotic look to you," she said. "But it's not too much, you know? It's really subtle. You're not niche. You could go all kinds of ways. You know, one of my clients, she's as white as they come, from Vermont, but you'd never know looking at her. She's got freckles, and this big, crazy hair. She's working for this brand that I bet would love you. They're starting a hair-care line for women of color, and you've got that look."

Margarita's phone buzzed. It was her mother. She dismissed the call.

"I'll call her later," she said, in case the makeup artist had noticed. "I see her all the time. We're very close."

She checked to make sure her video hadn't been lost, then uploaded it with the text Every Girl Is Beautiful. She listened to the message from Lacey May.

Margarita. Why won't you call us back? It's been days now that I've been trying. I don't know what it is that you're trying to prove. They're saying they can't start me on any treatments yet because there's too much swelling in my brain. I'm on these drugs to

229

bring it down. They're talking about surgery. I want to get the whole family together before then. Just in case something goes wrong. Have you heard anything from your father? I can't reach him either.

Margarita felt herself sink. It was bad enough her mother had never asked her to come home before. She'd waited until she was dying. And now, she was really after Robbie — he was the one she couldn't do without.

Ollie came over, tapping his foot. It was nine thirty. They'd lost track of time. "She looks fine," he said, and rushed her off to change. At ten, she padded onto set in a pair of skimpy pajamas. They handed her a tablet loaded to the home screen of the banking app. She had a fake name, Emmy, and a fake account balance — $38,292.06.

They started shooting, and from the first take, it was all wrong. She tapped when she should have scrolled, flopped onto her belly when she should have rolled to her side. And she wasn't exuding a sense of pleasure at all — online banking was supposed to feel good. The director kept leaning over to whisper to Ollie. What was he saying that he couldn't say out loud? *This isn't working* or *Look at her head*?

Margarita tried to channel ease, exhilaration. She visualized the Pacific, gray on a cloudy day. She and Celeste paddling out. The warm water, a quiet rush. Instead she saw her mother gasping for air in a hospital bed. Her sisters on either side of her, all their hands clasped together in a knot on Lacey's chest. Margarita heard Ollie calling her name. She'd forgotten where she was, what she was supposed to be doing. The director called for everyone to take five.

She ran into the DP and the prop stylist in the bathroom. They were washing their hands at the sink, talking about the president. On the news, he had compared the people who crossed the border to livestock.

"My parents came over on a plane cause we're Korean, right?" said the DP. "They didn't cross the border, but he's still talking about us when he says something like that."

"I don't know," the prop stylist said. "He's probably talking about, like, drug addicts and people in the cartels." She looked at Margarita, waiting for her to weigh in.

"Right," Margarita said, "like people who don't belong here in the first place."

"Exactly." The prop stylist smiled at her. "Where do you live, Margot?"

"Oh, I live in Venice. It's just this little pink house, super small, but I love it."

"I thought you looked familiar," the DP

said. "We're neighbors. I just bought a place off Rose. Where are you exactly?"

The prop stylist saved her. "You ever been to Black Bear? They've got this thyme syrup they mix into Sazerac. I know what you're thinking — what the fuck am I doing drinking Sazerac . . ."

The women wandered back to set together, the DP complaining about closing costs. Margarita commiserated and asked whether either of them knew when they would be cutting checks. No one had mentioned anything to her yet about when she would get paid.

The director cut in, looking Margarita in the eyes for the first time all day. "Does anybody even read their contract anymore? Why do we even bother making contracts if they don't read?"

Margarita saw then the only way to win was to show him she was more than he thought of her. She asked to start from the top again. Ollie coached her through. *You remember the bottomless mimosas. Your grandmother loves the tulips. You miss your boyfriend in Thailand.* Margarita nailed it all. The last thing she had to do was fling herself back on the pillows, shut her eyes, and sigh. She imagined an orgasm, a gorgeous line of coke, and they were done.

There was a brief smattering of applause.

Margarita went around to shake hands as the crew started setting up for another shoot. Even the makeup artist had a different woman in her chair. Margarita showed herself out. She was waiting for the elevator when she heard Ollie running down the hall.

"I asked about the check for you," he said. "You were paid half on signing. It should have been deposited into your account a while ago. You get the rest after they greenlight the clip."

Margarita did her best to cover her shock. She had blown through the money already, hadn't even noticed when it came in. It might be weeks until she got the rest, if she ever did. She thanked Ollie and left.

She had an hour before her business meeting with Celeste, but she wanted to squeeze in another post first. It was lunchtime. She wandered until she found a café with outdoor seating, an empty bistro table where someone had left a paid bill and an unfinished plate of risotto. Margarita sat down swiftly, discarded the squeezed lemon, ground pepper over the plate. She took pictures of the table, herself, the view of the street. She uploaded them and promised more food content later in the day.

She and Celeste were making another

recipe video this afternoon, although Margarita's agent thought they were a waste of time. But Celeste said that if people liked you, then brands liked you, and that was all that mattered, more than your reel. Margarita had seen it work for other people. Why couldn't it work for her?

She closed her eyes. They would make a good video today. They would get fourteen thousand likes. She'd get tapped for a sponsored post for nontoxic moisturizer or smoothie home delivery, then move to West Hollywood or Silver Lake. Fuck it — to Venice. She'd go to Black Bear, and run into the director at the bar, order Sazerac. She would know what he wanted, pull him into the bathroom, an expensive candle burning on a shelf. He'd slip his hands in her underwear, stand her up on the toilet. She'd brace herself against the ceiling while his tongue split her apart.

She could see it all; she could see her problems flitting away. A server tapped her on the shoulder and told her to move along.

They filmed themselves in Celeste's kitchen, in short, halting clips, as they drank sake and assembled the cold ramen. They wore cutoffs and swimsuits to show off Celeste's rib tattoos and the large bells of Margarita's breasts. They spiralized squash and soft boiled eggs, Celeste chopped tomatoes and swung her hips, and Margarita placed a bonito flake on her tongue, squeezed her eyes at the sharp taste. At the end, they bowed.

They went back and forth about whose account should host the video. In the end, Celeste won because she'd bought the ingredients, and they were in her house. Margarita could repost it on @Margot-_doez_LA, but it wasn't the same as being the originator of the content.

"What are you complaining about?" Celeste said. "You're already going to look prettier than me." She was referring to the professional makeup, but even she didn't seem to believe it. Celeste was blond and brown eyed with golden skin for a white girl. She had bleached teeth, a flesh-colored mole on her cheek that added interest, long jawbones, and a tiny, rounded chin (diamond).

They had locked Celeste's grubby Maltese, Annelise, in the bathroom while they were filming. They let her out and went to the yard with the vape and a bottle of whiskey. It was sunset, a magic hour in Venice. They sat under the lime tree, and Margarita stroked the dog between the ears.

"I used to have a dog. He went missing."

"No shit," Celeste said and dragged on the vape. "I wish she'd go missing. I'm kidding. I just don't have the headspace for a dog these days. You should take her, honestly. Venice is a circus. A guy on a unicycle nearly ran her over the other day."

Celeste's parents rented the house for her. It was pink with bougainvillea growing up the walls, a single bedroom, but there was an attic with a little moon of a window.

"So, how'd the face work for you today? You a rich bitch yet?"

"The shoot was fine, but I've got to wait on the money. Actually, I think I'm in trouble. I owe a lot of rent."

Celeste shook her head, handed her the vape. "Do you ever think, like, what's the point?"

"Of modeling?"

"Of cities. You pay all this rent. But you don't want to spend time at home, so you hemorrhage all this money so you can go out. Lunch, happy hour, Pilates. It all adds up. Now, you turn thirty, and you can't even buy a house unless it's, like, in Long Beach. My parents, they had it easy. They had a mortgage, no traffic, everything was five minutes away. But our generation? We could be in L.A. forever. And, it's like, how'd we get duped? Into this expensive, shitty life? I hate it here."

"You're good at it," Margarita said. Even now, in the vinyl lounge chair, Celeste was an ever-ready image for her followers. At @Celestial_LA, she had nearly twice the number Margarita had.

"I'm lonely," Celeste said. "I'm twenty-seven, and I'm totally alone. No offense."

"Why don't we become roommates? I'm here all the time anyway."

Celeste sucked on the vape, the colored lights blinking. "You idealize this place too much. I'm telling you, Venice is not that great. You can never find parking at the beach."

"It's not about Venice. They're going to kick me out."

"Didn't you fuck that guy? Gavin?"

"I've got until tomorrow."

"That's what I'm saying about cities. They pump you for your money, and you have nothing to show for it." Celeste fidgeted with her phone.

"Nobody is bankrolling my life out here," Margarita said. "I don't have anyone to rely on."

"What about your parents?"

"My mom is sick."

"Holy shit. Since when?"

"She's got cancer. She's in the hospital."

"What about your sisters? Maybe they can help you out."

"We're not those kinds of sisters. Can't I just stay here? I'll sleep in the attic."

"Margs, you know my deal with my parents. If I move anyone in, they stop paying the rent. This is my sanctuary. It's supposed to help me focus."

"You wouldn't have to tell them."

"My mom's got a sixth sense. She'd know."

They sat in an uneasy quiet. In all the years she'd known Celeste, Margarita had never needed her for anything but to go out — to sushi, to bars, the nail salon, a bonfire on the beach with some guys she'd met surfing. Celeste always said yes. Margarita had never asked her for anything else.

Celeste smiled and proposed they drive to Malibu to cheer themselves up. They could get drinks cliffside, watch the waves.

"I just told you I'm broke," Margarita snapped, and retreated into her phone.

The videos they had posted already had hundreds of views, and she had a dozen direct messages. She clicked through them, ignoring Celeste, and stopped dead when she saw a message from Noelle. Her sister didn't even follow her on any of her accounts, but there was her profile picture, a tiny orb on her screen. The message was a single line.

Nice to see you're not answering your phone because you're busy doing big, important things.

Margarita stood and snatched the whiskey from Celeste. "Fine, let's go," she said and drank straight from the bottle, swallowing as much as she could in a single swig. "But we're getting something stronger on the way."

Of all the drugs she had tasted, shrooms were her favorite. The way she felt the edges of herself melt away, how close she became to everything, as if she were swimming through existence. It was a pure, ecstatic feeling. But afterward, she could spend days in bed, crying for no reason she could name, which wasn't like her — she wasn't the sort of person prone to feeling sad. Weed was fun, but she only liked the head highs, traipsing around L.A., giggly, loose, allowing herself ice cream and cold soda. MDMA and alcohol were standbys, precursors for nights out. Fun, electric. Hazy. Cocaine was all right if everyone else was doing it, a ritual that roped a group of strangers together for

239

the night, but she watched herself with that one.

They got edibles: a dark chocolate square for each of them. Celeste drove fast along U.S. 1 so they would get to the beach before it hit them. The sky was velvety blue, the waves cresting one after the other.

They were bowled over by the high once they reached the beach. Celeste was giggly and yammering about nothing. Margarita splayed out on the sand and watched the clouds morph, felt herself sink into the earth.

Since she was a girl, she had been haunted by the sense that she was no one. It wasn't a voice in her head; it wasn't even a conscious thought, really. It was a feeling, like a blanket draped over her body to disappear her. It wasn't because her father went to jail or used; it wasn't because her mother had no self beyond her marriages. It wasn't being mixed and knowing she was always half-in with white people, half-out with people of color. It wasn't any of that — or, it wasn't only that. It was the way she slid out of the watchfulness of everyone she wanted to see her. It wasn't classic middle-child bullshit, either, because she knew other middle children.

Margarita closed her eyes, wished for the

ocean to sweep up to shore and carry her away.

She felt Celeste kick at her side. "Get up. I'm hungry. I want In-N-Out."

Margarita sat up and glared at her. "Why won't you let me stay with you? What will it cost you? You already have everything. Your house, your parents, your diamond face —"

"Don't start with that square-face bullshit, like you're some victim."

"I have nowhere to go."

Celeste squatted beside her, put her hands in her hair. "You'll figure it out. You're resilient! And so pretty."

Margarita shoved her away. "You selfish cunt."

"You don't know what you're saying," Celeste said. She hoisted Margarita up with both hands, dragged her in the direction of the road.

Once, Margarita found Robbie in the yard. It was fall, and there were leaves on the ground. They crinkled under her feet, soft and cold, as she walked toward him. He lay flat on his back in the dark. Margarita often woke before her sisters and watched TV by herself in the living room. She had heard a noise, followed it onto the back porch, and saw her father, his breath streaming above

241

him in warm clouds. It might have been a year before Robbie left, before Lacey May said he'd gone without saying good-bye to take a last-minute fishing job on the coast.

He was in his work clothes, his name embroidered on the pocket in shiny thread. His eyes were closed, but she could see his eyeballs zooming underneath the lids. His lips twitched, as if he were trying to say something. She called him, and he said nothing. She gripped his shoulders, and his eyes fluttered open. They closed. He started to hum. Margarita screamed, and Lacey May found her. She scolded her for being dramatic, sent her inside.

Margarita watched from the window as Lacey May hooked her hands in his armpits, tried to haul him toward the house. He stood, and then he fell. Lacey May tipped him over onto his side and he vomited.

A while later, they entered the house, and Robbie collapsed onto the couch. Lacey May called Margarita into the kitchen, away from her father, and she obeyed. Her mother fixed her a cup of hot chocolate, a piece of toast. She told her that Robbie had been sleepwalking. Margarita had asked who kept them safe at night if their father was outside wandering around.

"That's why he does it," Lacey May had said. "To watch over us."

Margarita woke to vomit. Celeste had placed a paper Whole Foods bag on her side of the bed. Margarita missed. She was thirsty; her head throbbed. Somehow, they had gotten back to Venice. Somehow, they had eaten burgers. Wrappers littered the bed. Celeste snored beside her. The lights were on, and it was one a.m. She fumbled for her phone.

She checked her texts, her voicemail, her email, the messages on each of her social media apps, but she hadn't heard again from her mother or her sisters. They had given up. Of course. But the videos she and Celeste had posted had over ten thousand likes altogether. It lifted her. She clicked to Celeste's profile and saw her followers had ballooned by at least one hundred. Margarita navigated back to her own account and counted her new followers: sixteen.

She looked over at Celeste, her slender body curled around the dog. She had vomited, too, yellow crust on her pretty chin, chunks of noodle and tomato on the bedspread around her. Her blond hair was pasted to her face, her bare breasts hanging out of her tank top. She was no better than

243

Margarita, and yet Margarita had affixed herself to her. Why did she always forget she was enough on her own?

Margarita stood and aimed her phone at Celeste. She took in her face, the dog, the circle of vomit, her sickly pink nipple. She placed a cartoon golden crown atop Celeste's head, used every hashtag she could think of for models in L.A., actresses in L.A., working in L.A., and California style. She tagged @Celestial_LA, set the location to Venice Beach, shared the video, and left.

The street was quiet, the houses dark behind hedges of palms, the sky black and clear. Margarita sat on the curb and told herself she'd only be gone for a little while. Her commercial money would clear and she'd come back, rent a better place, out of Cerritos. Find a better agent, a better friend. It was a delicious vision. She gathered it close and dialed her father.

It was loud wherever he was. Rancheras played in the background. A bar.

"Hi, Papi."

"Hija?" He didn't know which one she was.

"It's me, Margarita. I'm in L.A.?"

"Qué hubo, pepita? Are you all right?"

"I'm fine, Pa. It's Mama —"

Her father groaned. "Oh, don't talk to me

about that, hija. It's the worst news of my life."

"They've been calling you, too?"

He didn't answer, as if he didn't hear. There was roaring and clapping in the background, someone calling his name, *Robbie, Robbie,* in Spanish.

"Papi, I want to go home, but I don't have any money."

"It's not going well for you over there, pepita?"

"It's good, Pa. My career is really good. I just did a commercial for a tech company. Like Apple? One day, they could be as big as Apple. I'm just waiting for the check, but I know the family needs me now. I don't want to be away anymore."

Margarita knew he wouldn't deny her. Robbie was good at covering up his guilt by giving her whatever she asked. Margarita knew she should have been relieved but she felt small and faraway, her body a shell left behind by an ocean wave receding.

"Give me a few days, pepita. I'll get you the money."

"Thank you, Pa. I'll see you at the hospital."

"Oh no," Robbie said. "I'm not going. I can't see her that way. But you should go. She needs her daughters. She's always loved you all more than me."

It was a strange thing for him to say, as if he would have preferred if Lacey May had loved them less. She didn't want to deal with Robbie's self-pity tonight. She had to sober up and drive to Cerritos, put her things in storage. She had to figure out how many nights she could charge at a hotel before she'd have to sleep in her car.

"Just hurry up and get me the money, Pa. I'll go and be with Mama for you."

"And your sisters."

"As long as they need me, I'll be there."

The music in the bar switched from rancheras to cumbia, and Margarita heard strangers chanting her father's name again, calling him back to the dance floor. Robbie shouted at them to leave him alone, and he seemed to maneuver himself to a quieter corner of the club.

"I am so happy," he said, although it sounded as if he was crying. "I may have lost you all, but you didn't lose each other. No matter what happened, the family survived. It's a blessing. Amen."

9

SEPTEMBER 2018
THE PIEDMONT, NORTH CAROLINA

The day camp became an even greater refuge for Diane after her sister arrived. She would leave before dawn while Noelle was still asleep, a pot of coffee brewed for her, a plate of biscuits left steaming on the counter. She'd drive west to the camp, where she and Alma unlocked the gate, knocked cobwebs and dew off the banner strung up by wire. It read PAWS & FRIENDS, pictured colored balloons and cartoon dogs galloping across a field. The camp was nearly two acres, divided into a play area for the big, boisterous dogs, and another for small dogs or timid ones who would rather sniff grass and lick their paws than romp around. Each side had a kiddie pool for splashing, a plastic slide, tubes for crawling, and ropes for tug-of-war.

It was calm in the early morning while Alma and Diane cleaned up the office, a wooden shed they had converted with shelves and a phone line. One of the dogs, a docile basset hound with drooping ears and amber eyes, had been sick overnight, and Alma went to the kennels to check on him. Diane stayed behind to talk to Cora, one of her favorite workers, who gave her the report on how the hound had fared.

Cora was ten years younger than Diane, fresh out of high school, a girl with creamy lean legs she seemed to bare no matter the weather. She wore athletic shorts in summer, wool skirts in winter. She scarcely wore a bra, which Diane liked to take as some sign that teenage girls today were more liberated than she had ever been.

Cora started loading the van to get ready for pickups, and her varsity volleyball T-shirt rode up, exposing the curve of her waist, the green rivers of her veins. Diane didn't mean to ogle her — it was just that Cora had blossomed into a woman somehow, and she was no longer the plucky intern who wasn't afraid to fish a rogue stone out of a Labrador's mouth, to pinch together the legs of a Havanese resisting being lowered into a bath. She'd stopped needing to dash out early to study for tests, to miss weekends for away games. And her bralessness had become more noticeable, the shape of her nipples visible through the thin cotton of her T-shirts. It made Diane feel old and full of a lust she knew would never drive her to do anything but lurch for Alma in the night, or circle her own nipples with her thumbs in the shower, Cora's face flashing in her mind before she pushed it away and replaced it with someone more suitable — an actress, older, a woman Diane would never meet, whom she'd never have the nerve to talk to, even if she did. She liked that actress who did the boxing movie once, a Latina with big arms, brown eyes. She liked, too, that actress from the vampire show, although she was too skinny, too blond. But Diane had read somewhere that she was queer, and that had changed everything. They were all beginning to be younger than she was. She was at that tipping age, when the girls singing on the radio and acting in her favorite sitcoms were all younger than she was. She was twenty-seven.

When Cora hauled out, Diane turned to Alma and told her what she'd been thinking. They were drinking their coffees in the last minutes of calm before they opened. At seven thirty, they would let the boarded dogs into the yard, lift the shades, and any customers already waiting in the parking lot would come pouring in.

"It's normal to think the way you're thinking," Alma said. "Death makes everybody horny."

"It's probably my mother. I think I'm fine, but then my mind keeps turning to fucking."

"Too bad I can't help you with that."

"We talked about this," Diane said. "My sister."

Alma's face betrayed nothing, and she went on drinking her coffee. In the fluorescent light of the office, Diane could count her freckles. A well-meaning customer had once told Alma she was a lovely girl, but that she looked strange, like a beautiful alien. It was her features with her auburn hair, how she was light skinned but clearly not white. Down here, people didn't know to read her as Puerto Rican; she simply seemed mixed in a way they weren't used to. But she had been familiar to Diane from the first day she'd seen her at the orientation for the veterinary school they'd both dropped out of to open Paws & Friends. Diane wasn't sure whether she believed in other lives, beyond this one, but if they were real, she wouldn't be surprised if she and Alma had known each other in them all.

She smoothed Alma's hair off her forehead and kissed her forcefully, to make her know how much she was loved.

"If you're going to kiss me like that, you

ought to check the blinds first," Alma said, her voice cool and unforgiving. She left her coffee behind the desk, unlocked the door, and headed out to the yard. Diane didn't have a chance to call her back before Mrs. Wilkins burst in, carrying her corgi-collie mix, Camille. She was too large a dog to be carried, nearly forty pounds, but Mrs. Wilkins cradled the dog all the same.

"She's having a terrible morning," the woman said. "I had to wrestle that leash onto her. And that was after I told her, *Miss Camille, we're going to play. We're going to your favorite place.*"

Alma appeared in the office to clip a leash onto the dog. She led her out without looking at Diane. Diane was rattled as she typed the drop-off time for Camille into the computer.

"You know I've been thinking of swinging by to see your mother," Mrs. Wilkins said.

"That's kind of you."

"I've been praying for her. And for you, too. I know it's got to be affecting everybody in the family. That's how these things go."

"These things?"

"Cancer."

"Right." Another customer swung in with a wide-eyed Pomeranian, and Diane waited for Mrs. Wilkins to slide off to the side.

"I know your mother never has been one for church. I'd have never gotten to know her except for that campaign at the high school all those years ago. Do you remember that? A bunch of us ladies from that time are in the same home group from church now."

Another customer clanked in, this one a ruddy-faced man with a leaping terrier.

"And how are your sisters? Have they been coming around?"

"Noelle's here, and Margarita arrives tomorrow." Diane avoided looking at Mrs. Wilkins and hoped she'd get the message. The customers were starting to line up, and she didn't want to talk about her sisters at work when they were already swallowing up her life everywhere else.

"You know I follow Margarita online!" Mrs. Wilkins said. "I love her posts. So glamorous. But Noelle I haven't heard a thing about in years. She's married, isn't she? Living off in Atlanta? I'll tell you, there's nothing worse than having family all spread out. Your mama is blessed to have you close. I bet she tells you so all the time."

"My mother isn't the kind to thank her children for things she thinks they ought to be doing anyway."

A man in reflective sunglasses and a fishing vest strode in with a tremendous mastiff. A new customer would take much longer to check in.

"You'll excuse me, Mrs. Wilkins," Diane said. "I've got to help these other customers."

"Look at me," she went on. "Holding up the line. Well, if you ever want to come to the home group, you let me know. If there's any one of you all I can see coming, your mother included, it's you. You've always been such a sweet girl, even when you were little, I could tell —"

Alma marched back into the office and tugged Diane by the arm. "Go on outside," she whispered. "I'll handle it." Diane obeyed and stumbled toward the yard.

A half-dozen dogs were already circling in each pen. It was a hazy, wet morning, the white sunlight just beginning to bear through the clouds. The day was cool and smelled of packed dirt, the still water in the blow-up pools. Diane spread her legs apart in the sod, let the wind sift through her. A few of the dogs ran up to her, and she patted their trunks, sent them off to play. They'd be worn out by noon, crawling into the kennels to rest while the staff refilled the water bowls and handed out their lunch. Dogs were simple, even when they weren't.

The things they wanted were predictable, good: food, fresh air, attention, touch. It was easy to be with them.

Diane had gotten used to no longer being seen as one of the Ventura girls, a small figure in the tableau of her sisters. She had a life in town outside of them, even outside of Lacey May, Robbie and all his trouble. Part of it was Alma, the little existence they'd made together. They had the camp and the dogs, their brick house. At night, Diane worked in the garden while Alma made dinner. Sometimes, they went for drives, to get milkshakes or pick up Q-tips at the supermarket. They used any excuse to zoom around at dusk, under a pink sky with flecks of gold, endless, marred by nothing but the spires of the pines. On their off days, they hiked and drank beers and had sex, and she never tired of Alma's body, she never tired of Alma, her convictions and her crankiness before her morning coffee, the accent from her Bronx girlhood that surfaced whenever she said *water* or *quarter,* the way she'd taught Diane the word *jíbara* to explain her insistence on composting and herbal deodorant, the way she loved the trees. She talked to Diane in Spanish, even if she only half understood. They had their fights, but nothing ever left a mark, not even

Diane's requirement that she go to her weekly dinners with Lacey May and Hank alone. Alma would stay behind, and when Diane came home again, she could forget about her family, their small disruption in the usual course of her life. But it was different now, with her sisters. Noelle was staying in her house, and Margarita would be soon.

Dusty, one of Diane's favorite dogs, trotted over to her, her tail wagging. She was a blue nose pit bull, her pelt velvety gray. A meek girl. She had recently been moved to the large pen and was still disquieted by the big dogs' mouthing and wrestling. Diane squatted down to nuzzle her.

"Hey, good girl," she said. "You're fine." She kissed her nose to give her courage, then sent her off to play.

Dusty wasn't three yards away when a galloping Lab knocked her to the ground. Dusty snapped in fear, and the red Lab pinned her, its jaws at her neck. Dusty yelped and went still. A camp staffer reached them first, lifted the Lab's hind legs to pull her off, then leashed her and drew her away. Diane crouched over Dusty. She whimpered, but there was no blood. If the Lab had wanted to hurt Dusty, she could have, but she hadn't wanted to bite her, only to prove her dominance.

They took Noelle to the new barbecue place not far from the camp for dinner. It was on an otherwise desolate road, all trees and unlit houses. Hidden entrances to the state park were strewn between the trees, a creek snaking through them. This was the part of town where it was most common to find Confederate flags posted in the yards, but the barbecue joint was modern, all glass and neon lights. Nearly half the space was taken up by a wraparound bar in the center, the glittering bottles lined up in rows. It was a gastropub, or so the sign said: FINE BARBECUE AND FINER SPIRITS.

It embarrassed Diane how much she wanted her sister to like the place, to join in her life and approve of it. Noelle played along, oohing and aahing at the bourbon list. She ordered a fourteen-dollar shot and kale salad, while Diane and Alma got their usual: creamy draft beers and a towering plate of pulled-pork nachos. Noelle praised the food, too, but it didn't make Diane feel any better. It was as if Noelle was indulging them, making do, although nothing was really up to her standards.

"I don't know why it's taken so long for a

place like this to spring up," Noelle said. "The university has always been close by. There have always been people here with money to spend. You used to have to drive to another city for a dinner like this."

"Well, it's whiter now," Alma said. "Even in the time I've been here, it's changed. The New Yorkers I used to meet were black women who moved down here in the nineties. Now the New Yorkers I meet are white women who just left Brooklyn."

"Where are you meeting all these New Yorkers?"

"Book club. Yoga. Around." Alma shrugged and drank her beer.

"Yoga? Your life is so cute," Noelle said, and Alma answered her instantly: "I love it here."

"I bet you do," Noelle said, and sipped her bourbon. "I couldn't picture you living in the suburbs. You'd stand out like a sore thumb."

Alma went red and rose from the table, flustered. Diane watched her go. She hadn't learned yet that Noelle didn't mean to antagonize. When she was upset, she grew smug and started telling everyone who they were and who they weren't.

"You know, for all your disdain for Mama, you can sure be a lot like her. You take out what's bothering you on everyone else. You offended Alma."

"I didn't mean to," Noelle said and gazed out the window, toward the black road. She looked almost penitent, although she had been icy since she arrived, as if she were bored by the whole ordeal: their mother's cancer and North Carolina, the fact that they were back together. When they went to the hospital, Lacey May pursued her. She complimented Noelle's hair, offered her fruit from her lunch tray, handed her the remote to the flat-screen. Noelle ignored her, reading or taking naps in the corner of the room with her sunglasses on. Occasionally, she chimed in on their conversations about neutral subjects — the weather, the kindness of the nurses — never politics or the president. Eventually, she would announce she was going for a coffee and leave. Ten minutes would pass, then an hour, and Diane would go and find Noelle in the parking lot smoking a cigarette. This was how Noelle transmitted to Diane she was ready to go — she left, and Diane followed.

If she didn't want to be with them, why had she come at all?

"I noticed Nelson isn't calling."

"I'm not calling him either. It's mutual."

"I thought things were good," Diane said

and realized she didn't know if it was true.

When they spoke on the phone, Noelle didn't share much about her life, as if she couldn't trust Diane simply because they were blood. They had been close once, or at least, that was what Diane remembered. Sometimes she wondered whether she had made it up: the ease of being together when they were girls.

"You think you two will sort it out?"

"Nelson isn't really one to talk about things. Usually, I can draw him out when I need him. But he doesn't seem to want that right now, and I'm not going to beg. I know how to take care of myself."

"Sounds healthy," Diane said, and she scanned the restaurant for Alma. She wanted to go home. A nice dinner with Noelle was impossible; she was a fool to have tried.

"It hasn't been that long," Noelle said. "I just knew I couldn't handle trying to reach him on top of everything else. I stopped calling when I got here."

"That was a week ago."

Noelle shrugged. "A marriage is never harmonious."

"I suppose it depends on who you marry."

Noelle shook her head. "You think you know a person, and the problem is you do.

You know exactly who they are, and you marry them anyway." She sipped her bourbon. "At least with a friend, you never expect the other person to take away your loneliness." Noelle nodded at the empty seat across from her. "Take Alma. You two are so bonded. I can tell. And you make it all work — your friendship, being roommates, the business. You could never do all that with a man."

"Probably not," Diane said.

"Please don't tell Mama." Noelle wiped her eyes. "This is all temporary. We're going to get back on track."

"I won't say anything."

"And don't tell Margarita. Do you really think she's going to show tomorrow?"

"Sure. Papi gave her the money for her flight."

"Jesus, she had to bum money from Papi? Is our Hollywood empress not empressing?" Noelle was back to form, ready to focus all her judgment on their sister. "How'd she reach him anyway? He knows I'm here, and he's not returning my calls."

"He's the same with me. I'll see him every once in a while, and then one day, I'll call and he'll say he can't come and visit because he's in Delaware. Like it's nothing. Like he shouldn't bother telling his daughter that he moved out of the state."

"Some family we've got," Noelle said and drained her bourbon.

Diane considered pointing out that Noelle had left, too, but decided against it.

That night, after Noelle was asleep, Diane crept off the couch. Her sister was in the guest room they had told her was Diane's; Alma was waiting in their bedroom. She had been aloof after dinner, but now she opened her arms for Diane. Her curls were tied up with a crimson head wrap, and she already smelled of sleep, musty and warm. Diane kissed her, and Alma reciprocated, but it was all too mild, as if Alma simply didn't want to turn her away. Diane tried slipping her tongue into her mouth, sliding her hand between her thighs, but they never caught a spark. She gave up and put an arm around her. What she wanted most was to be close to her. She told her about the blue nose pit, how defenseless she had been in her terror.

"Maybe she just couldn't get unpinned. Maybe she's not as strong as she looks."

"She is strong," Diane said. "A strong, sweet girl."

Alma rolled her eyes. "They're all sweet to you."

Alma cared for the dogs, but to her the

day camp was mostly a business. She didn't rely on the dogs, like Diane. She had a much wider life. Her Spanish book club and her knitting group. She was open with them about their relationship, and Diane didn't mind. Her only hard line was her family, which was a relatively small exception in the scope of their whole lives.

"This is getting ridiculous," Alma said.

"You saw how Noelle can be. She has something mean to say about everyone."

"So what do you care if she says something to us? It's just the way she is."

"She's my big sister."

"And you're a big girl. Besides, she probably knows already. You really think she believes I'm your six-year roommate?"

"They wouldn't expect it from me."

"Wouldn't expect you to love me?"

"They have no idea who I am. And they like it better that way. It's convenient for me to be Diane, the baby, the sweetheart. It keeps me out of the way while they wage their wars."

"You like it that way, too," Alma said quietly. "You're the one who's hiding now."

Diane reached for her hand, but Alma pushed her away.

"It's getting to me. Soon Margarita will be here, and I'll be putting on a show for her, too."

"You don't get it — this isn't New York."

"Please don't start with your *this is the South* bullshit. You and I both know plenty of dykes in this town."

"My mother still hates Nelson. And he's a man."

"She may be a bigot, but I still want her to know who I am."

"She grew up a different way —"

"Jesus Christ, is this some Ventura family tradition? All this lying and pretending? No wonder they call you the good one. You cover for them all."

"What do you want from me? It's not like you get to choose your family."

Alma squinted hard at Diane in the dark, thrust a pointed finger straight into her chest.

"Yes, you do, Diane. Yes, you fucking do."

They picked up Margarita from the airport next day, and it struck Diane how natural it was to see her, to put her arms around her and inhale the blast of her perfume. She and Noelle embraced, too, and Noelle asked about the flight, offered to help with her bags. Margarita had brought them matching gifts: bath salts and fancy soap made with ossified flower petals. They piled into

263

the car, Noelle riding shotgun, Margarita in the backseat filming out the window. "I forgot how green it is here," she said.

It gave Diane a sliver of hope. Maybe being sisters was simply this: seeing each other after a long time and finding it was wholly ordinary to be together again.

A pop song came on the radio, a duet between two nineties stars. They all surged with recognition and sang along softly, instinctively. Noelle swayed her shoulders, and Diane tapped her hands on the wheel. Margarita hit a high note wrong to make them laugh.

"You know, you should think about comedy," Noelle said, raising her voice over the music. "At the theater, I used to meet people struggling to make it as serious actors, but they were so funny. So funny, and they couldn't see it —"

Margarita stopped singing, and Diane knew that Noelle had done it.

At the theater, Margarita said, affecting a rarefied accent. "I don't need pointers from you, Noelle. Atlanta independent theater isn't exactly the big leagues."

"I'm just trying to be supportive."

"How could I forget?" Margarita was shouting now. "My big sister, my greatest champion. What were your last words of encouragement?" She scrolled through her phone. *"Nice to see you're not answering your phone because you're busy doing big, important —"*

"We didn't know if you were coming. I was pissed."

"How about 'I'm sorry'? You think you could try that? I'd wait for you to come around, but I'm not Diane."

"Leave me out of this," Diane said and turned off the music. "Can you all behave yourselves for just one day? This isn't about us. It's about Mama."

Margarita laughed. "Of course it is, manzanita. Even after all these years."

The girls arrived after lunch, and Lacey May couldn't remember ever having seen them like that, all grown up together. It would have been the perfect time to take a picture if not for how worn she looked in her threadbare robe, her body bloated from all the machines whirring and pouring fluid into her.

Margarita looked like a star, her hair streaked an artificial caramel color, her breasts larger than Lacey May remembered. Yet somehow, she was all Robbie. Diane seemed homely beside her, stocky and dark, her hair curling around her ears. The only pretty thing on her was the emerald charm around her neck, the one her father had given her when she was a girl. And Noelle was a great beauty wasted; she seemed so much older than thirty-two. Her body was soft and dimpled in strange places — her arms, her knees — and thin and brittle in others — her hands, her neck. She looked like a woman who had been changed by the swells and vacancies of pregnancies, one after another, and never enough time in between to put herself back together. But Noelle had no reason. She should have remained intact. Lacey May said none of this out loud.

"My girls!" she said. "Come here, my girls!"

There was a round of hellos and kisses as they descended on Lacey May. Hank stood at the foot of the bed, nodding at the girls, waiting to be embraced. Her poor man. He still acted like an extra in their lives, a man so happy to have been cast, he tried mostly not to be a bother. The girls hugged him limply, and Lacey May squeezed his hand. Any lives they had, they'd had because of Hank, whether the girls saw it that way or not. She would be eternally grateful.

Within a few minutes, the commotion subsided, and the girls assumed their places:

Noelle slumped into her usual chair in the corner; Margarita climbed onto the windowsill and tapped at her phone. Diane stayed beside Lacey May and fussed with the hospital bed, cranking it so she could sit upright.

Lacey May wondered how to snap them into awareness of one another. They were all unmarried except for Noelle, who seemed unhusbanded. One day Lacey May would be gone, and they'd only have each other. How could she make them see?

The doctors didn't know yet whether she'd need radiation or chemo or surgery. They were holding off on promising treatments until they brought down the swelling in her brain. They had warned her she might feel confused, and there might be pain. The worst of it, so far, was the nausea, which reminded her of labor. She had thrown up with all her girls. She imagined dying would be something like childbirth. A splitting open. A transfiguration she couldn't fully believe in, until she was in it, crossing over from one state of being into another, with no say in the matter at all.

Lacey May cleared her throat. "The doctor came by this morning. He said the swelling isn't coming down the way they want it to, but the good news is I haven't had another seizure."

Noelle snapped to attention. "What do you mean *seizure*? I thought you fell off the porch and hit your head."

"Well, they think it was a seizure, and I can't say any different cause I don't remember."

"Maybe the way you described it led them to the wrong conclusion. You've always had a tendency to blow things out of proportion."

Margarita burst out laughing from the windowsill. "I ought to just record Noelle. Point my phone right at her. Her grudges are pure entertainment. Better than reality TV."

"If it'll help your failing career, go right ahead."

"At least I work. What do you do? After all your big talk about getting out, it must kill you to be where you are."

"Where I am? What about you? You had to ask Papi for money. Who do you think is using more these days, you or him?"

"My God!" Lacey May roared. "The way you girls talk! I didn't raise you to talk like that."

"Sure you did," said Noelle. "Has anybody even heard a prognosis? We're all gathered here like they've given Mama a death sentence, and we don't even know the facts."

"Mama's sick," said Diane.

"I know she's sick, but we can't take her word about how serious it is."

"This girl thinks I made up my cancer!"

"I'm not saying that —"

"Don't you all see this may be it?" Lacey May slammed her wired hands down on the bed. "This may be the last time we're all together, and we're wasting it. We've got to get a hold of your father. If we wait for him to turn up, it might be too late."

It had taken all her strength to shout at them, and the girls were stunned into silence.

"Oh, Mama," said Margarita. "Now you're in the running for best performance in a drama."

"I'm serious. I need you girls to help me find your father."

"Margarita was the last one to hear from him, but that was days ago," Diane said. "There's nothing we can do. He'll show up when he wants to, Mama."

Hank finally spoke up. "That's your father. Never around when he's needed. Only shows up when it's convenient for him."

"If I were you, Hank, I wouldn't be talking about *convenience*," said Noelle.

After that, Lacey May was on her, screaming and calling her ungrateful. Margarita egged her on, and Noelle snatched up her purse and left. Diane felt woozy and sank onto the bed. Maybe Alma was right, and she was only lying to herself, pretending she could keep the peace among them. She took her mother's hand.

"You can't take it to heart, Mama. She's just afraid."

"Something's going on with her. I bet it's Nelson."

"Mama, every time there's something wrong with Noelle, you blame it on Nelson."

"And ninety-nine percent of the time I'm right."

Margarita sighed heavily and stood from the window. "If I had known we were all coming here for a conference about the state of Noelle, I'd have stayed in L.A."

"She's your sister," Lacey May said.

"And the center of the universe. Go on and make your plans to save her from herself. You let me know what I can do for my beloved sister when I get back."

Margarita bowed her head beatifically, her hand on her heart, then turned and left, too.

Lacey May could have wept at the ease with which her daughters left her. They had seen her, in her gown, the wires needled

270

into her hands, and she had won no sympathy. She wanted to wail, *What did I do?* and Hank would put his arm around her. Diane would reassure her: *Nothing, Mama, nothing.* And she could say, *You can't control your kids — you can only love them,* or, *They turn out how they turn out.* But these were lies. There was plenty she could have done differently. She could have stayed with Robbie; she could have never gotten involved in that campaign at the school; she could have loved and welcomed Nelson; she could have let her daughters be. But she couldn't bring herself to wish she'd taken another course. She was their mother, and she'd tried to use her influence for good. If she had the chance to do it all over again, she would do it all exactly the same.

When Diane returned to the camp, Alma was out front fiddling with the banner. It was sagging, and she cut and rewound the wire to string it back up.

"Your dog is here," she said. "The blue nose pit. I moved her in with the small dogs and she's happier. So far, everybody's behaving."

"I wish I could say that for the Venturas and the Gibbses."

"Was it that bad?"

"I've got to find my father. The doctor finally gave us the rundown."

"Is she going to die?"

"I don't know. It was all numbers. Just because forty percent of patients live doesn't mean you've got a forty percent shot. It's either you die one hundred percent, or you live."

Alma dropped the pliers in her hand and reached for Diane. Diane buried her face in Alma's neck, inhaled the tinny odor of her sweat, her floral hair gel, and her underarm funk. They pulled apart, and Diane could see Alma was near tears.

"I know it's not a good time to push all this. But it would break my heart if your mother never knew who I was, not really."

"I can't talk about this now. It's too much."

"Fine. Tonight then."

"I can't sneak off and see you anymore. Margarita's sleeping on the couch with me now, and she'll notice if I disappear."

Alma released her and frowned. "Is there anyone you're related to who isn't on the list of people who can't know about us?"

"It isn't a very long list."

Alma looked down at her high-tops, smeared with mud. When she looked back up at Diane, her face had changed. It was softer, but more closed, and Diane wondered whether this was the moment when she would begin to lose Alma, if in a little while, she'd give up and move on.

Alma spoke gently, her face half in shadow, the rusted wire spooled around her wrist.

"It's only our life if we say so. Otherwise it belongs to them."

10

The enrollment at Central was higher than anyone had expected. There had been talk that students wouldn't rise to the challenge when they saw what it required of them: inconvenient bus routes, early mornings, the awkwardness of being new. But Central was at capacity with transfers — two hundred across the four grades — and Gee sensed them, the others, when he wandered the halls, when he sat at lunch with kids he recognized from elementary school, and in PE, where the black boys scheduled for sixth period had drawn together into a little band. They changed together in the locker room, ran laps in sync, and separated only when the coach divided them into teams.

There weren't many new students in Mr. Riley's English class, although Gee couldn't be sure. He knew there were white kids, too, benefiting from the program, but they didn't stick out nearly as much. Besides himself, he counted a Cambodian girl who sat in the last row, scribbling poems in her notebook, and a Salvadorian girl who arranged the long puff of her hair to cover her face whenever Mr. Riley asked for volunteers. Gee, too, hunched over in his chair, drew his hood around his face. All three of them were hiding.

For homework Mr. Riley had assigned the first scene of the first act of a Shakespeare play. Gee had read and reread the lines but understood nothing. He knew he wasn't alone because they'd spent nearly the whole class period rereading the packet aloud and then translating. Mr. Riley asked questions and answered them himself.

Gee knew Mr. Riley would call on him before he did. The teacher had some kind of thing with him. He called him to the board to take notes more than anyone else; he asked him to read aloud, although Gee made a point of keeping his voice so low Mr. Riley wouldn't ask again. When he had seen him onstage at the town hall, Gee had been curious about him, this black teacher who seemed so cool while all the other adults shouted at one another. He could see now that it wasn't poise; Mr. Riley was fake. He smiled at the students even when they weren't doing anything remarkable; he wore a tie, which few of the other teachers did; in between classes, he lint rolled his blazer and brushed out his waves. He was the kind of man who seemed to always be thinking about who was watching, while Gee liked to think mostly about how he could disappear.

"Will you read for us?" he asked in front of everybody, as if Gee had a choice.

He brought the pages close to his face so that no one could see and raced through the lines.

Heaven doth with us as we with torches
   do,
Not light them for themselves; for if our
   virtues
Did not go forth of us, 'twere all alike
As if we had them not.

His tongue twisted and tangled, but the teacher let him suffer through it.

"Now, what's Shakespeare saying here?" A customary silence rolled over the room. "Gee?"

Gee felt his bottom teeth slide in front of the top ones. Mr. Riley stared at him, as if he were trying to transmit an answer to Gee's head. If he knew it, why didn't he just say it?

"I don't know," Gee said finally. Mr. Riley

didn't skip a beat.

"He's saying you shouldn't be afraid to shine. Well, not you — all of us."

Gee felt he should say something, anything, to make Mr. Riley move on. "Unhhunh."

"Like a torch. A torch doesn't exist for itself. It exists for others."

Mr. Riley waited for someone to pick up the conversation, to offer a thought, but, thankfully, the bell rang, and the class scrambled to leave. Mr. Riley shouted instructions for the next day's homework, and Gee, his book bag on his shoulders, was turning toward the door when the teacher called him to the front of the room. He handed Gee a folded sheet of loose-leaf paper.

"It's my address," he said. "Your mother and I made plans for dinner."

"We're going to your house? Is that allowed?"

"It's totally appropriate. My wife will be there and my daughter."

Gee wondered now whether he was being set up. "Your daughter? Does she go to Central?"

Mr. Riley laughed. "She's seven months."

Gee slipped the address into his pocket and turned to leave. Mr. Riley caught him by the arm.

"You've been doing very well these last few weeks."

"All right."

"Even if I can tell you're hoping I'll skip you. I see you slouching down in your chair."

Gee said nothing.

"People notice you, Gee. Whether you want them to or not."

Gee sometimes had the strange sensation he was being recorded, as if this footage would be played back for him later so he could see how he'd acted and decide whether it was right. Mr. Riley talked to him, too, as if Gee's whole life were a test, or an after-school special, and the objective was to choose wisely, otherwise everything would be lost. Jade was the same way. No wonder the two of them had bonded.

"I've got math," Gee said.

Mr. Riley patted him on the shoulder. "See you Friday night."

In the hall, students were dawdling and shuffling, trying hard to avoid going to class. Gee headed for his locker and saw Adira there waiting for him. She leaned against his locker, her arms held tight to her chest. He got closer and saw that she was crying.

Gee ran to her, and she threw her arms around his neck, her mouth at his ear. A girl had never come at him like that, and Gee was stunned. He tried hard not to think of how she felt in his arms. Something was wrong.

"These girls," Adira sobbed. "These white girls. They pulled my hair."

Her hair was tied into two buns, uneven now, drooping on either side of her head. She must have looked so cute before — she always did — in her pink turtleneck and faded jeans, her cream-colored sneakers. She was always putting together outfits like it was the eighties or something.

"They started asking me if my hair was real. They just came up behind me. And I ignored them, but they kept going, so I turned around and said yes, and then they said I was lying, and it was fake, and they started pulling my hair. I caught one of them by the hand, and I pushed her away, and then her friend got in my face and said, 'Don't touch her, you black bitch,' and then they walked away, like it was nothing."

Adira started weeping again.

"You want to tell somebody?"

"They were just trying to make me mad. If I go to the principal, then they win."

Down the hall, a few other kids were

watching them, but no one came over to ask what had happened, to see what they could do.

"We should get them in trouble," Gee said. He was channeling Jade, he knew. It was the kind of thing she would have done. She had never worried about being a snitch.

Adira groaned and pressed her fists into her eyes. "You think they'll get in trouble? I love you, Gee, but sometimes I swear you don't know nothing."

She shook her head at him and grimaced — he disgusted her — then gathered her backpack and stomped away. Gee called after her, but she didn't turn around. Across the hall, two white girls leaned against their lockers, watching. The blond girl gaped at him; the other, a redhead, seemed to be smiling at him meekly, as if to commiserate, but Gee couldn't be sure; she wouldn't look him in the eye.

He didn't open his locker to drop off the address or pick up his textbook. He drifted down the hall, dazed. He kept hearing Adira crying, telling him he knew nothing. He saw her tears spilling freely, her wet cheeks, and destroyed hair. Without wanting to, he found himself defending the Central students in his mind. *It's not most of them,* he thought. *There's always one.* And then, involuntarily, before he could stop himself: *One is all it takes.*

Gee had few memories of the trial for the man who killed Ray. When he tried to piece it together, he could conjure up a vision of himself taking the stand, a little boy in a too-big blazer, although, of course, the memory wasn't real, and he hadn't watched himself testify from the benches in the courtroom. He knew a woman with a squeaky voice had asked him questions he hadn't known the answers to. He had said he couldn't remember, or he didn't know, and each time, he had the sinking feeling that it wasn't what anyone wanted him to say — not the judge or that questioning woman, or Wilson, or Jade. But they had told him to only tell the truth, and nobody had explained whether there was something that he was secretly meant to prove.

In Gee's memories, the man who did it wasn't there, although he must have been. If Gee tried to recall him, he managed to, but he knew this, too, was all invention. He dreamed up a man who was a composite of images he'd seen on TV: a broad male body in orange clothes, a tattoo circling a muscular neck, handcuffs linking wrists.

Gee didn't know his name, and he didn't

know what he and Wilson had been fighting about. No one had ever explained it to him, not then or in the years after. He didn't know whether Wilson had been caught up in a debt, a deal, or something else. His mother had given him the version of events appropriate for a six-year-old, and never bothered to fill in the rest.

Wilson had disappeared afterward. He had been their family, and then he was gone, cut off, probably by Jade. His sister Carmela had disappeared, too, although she had watched Gee for a while. Weeks? Months? He couldn't tell. Everyone they'd known before was gone, except Linette. Even Ray had been wiped away the moment Jade took his picture off the wall.

After school, Noelle caught the bus from the station downtown, half a mile from Central. She rode north, and the bus left her on the side of an access road with no sidewalk. She kept far onto the shoulder as she walked, the mud mucking up her glossy black boots. It was a while before she reached the old gravel road, its long slope down through a cavern of trees. Then the three houses: the first painted salmon pink, the second, the one that had belonged to them, still midnight blue. The last belonged to Ruth, her mother's only friend.

Bailey was reading a comic book on the porch swing. They waved at each other. He was an eighth grader, like Margarita, but he seemed younger than his years. He loved his comics and gardening, and whenever Noelle and her sisters came over with Lacey May to visit, he went on doing whatever he had been doing before. He wasn't bad or boring, just quiet.

Noelle asked for Ruth, and Bailey led her inside their pretty green house. Ruth was in her bathrobe, eating yogurt from a giant tub and watching the news. There had been a fire in Raleigh, a whole family burned alive in the middle of the night.

"Noelle, honey, what are you doing here? Is everything all right? Where's your mama?"

"It's just me."

Ruth seemed to read her situation instantly. She sent Bailey out front, led Noelle to the yard.

They sat on the brick patio overlooking the vegetable garden. Bailey was growing beets and cabbage, radishes, and raspberries, the fruits edging out of their buds into the sun.

"He sure loves these plants."

Ruth mm-hmmed at her. "They keep him company. It can get lonely out here, you know. Your mama called this morning to invite me to some emergency meeting for concerned parents. That's where she is right now, isn't it?"

"Why didn't you go?"

"People get all worked up over nothing. What do I care if these kids have a better shot now than they used to? Who am I to stand in the way? We all get good breaks and bad ones. That's life."

Noelle didn't see the point in arguing with Ruth, in saying that maybe she ought to care about what happened to other kids in the county, maybe she ought to care about the trouble Lacey May and the other parents were causing. She didn't want to upset her, not when she needed her help, not when she was already so much better than her own mother.

Noelle didn't realize she was welling up until Ruth started digging in her robe for tissues. She thrust a crumpled twist of paper under her nose.

"Honey, what's the matter? This will all blow over, one way or another. Your mom is just agitated right now."

"It's not about her. Or school."

"Go on."

"I need to set up an appointment at the hospital. Women's Health? Maybe I could

284

ride with you one day you're going to work, and you can show me where to go?"

"You need pills or something, honey?"

"I'm past all that."

Ruth stared at her. It didn't feel bad to have the woman look at her, and Noelle wasn't ashamed. All the women she knew were having sex or had had it. And Lacey May hadn't been much older than Noelle when she'd married Robbie. What she felt instead was trapped, like she'd been cornered into confessing to what everyone did in the dark, as if she were the only one.

"You can't go to the hospital," Ruth said. "They won't be able to help. But there's a clinic forty minutes away. I'll take you there. How far along are you anyway? It might be too late."

Noelle told her how long it had been since her last period, and Ruth squeezed her shoulder.

"That's good news," she said. "Don't you worry. It's probably no bigger than a prune."

Noelle let Ruth hold her, and it felt good to be drawn close. She wished Ruth hadn't said anything about the size. It was easier not to wonder what she thought about it all, the big questions they posed during the debates at school — *When does life begin? Where do one person's rights end and another one's start?* They were questions without answers, as far as she was concerned, but what was clear to her was that she couldn't have a baby. It would bind her to Lacey May, to Hank, and that house forever. She'd amount to nothing, no one, her life swallowed up before she'd ever had a chance.

She knew Ruth would understand, not only because she was a nurse, but because she'd chosen to be a free woman: to live alone, to raise her boy, to have a career. Even if they weren't kin, Noelle was struck with pride every time Ruth rose from one of their visits to say, *I've got to get to my shift.* She'd disappear into the bathroom and emerge smelling like roses and hot soap, her face gleaming and red, her eyebrows plucked too thin. She'd pour out fresh coffee into a shiny thermos, kiss Bailey good-bye, and leave him with money for a pizza or instructions on how to warm up his dinner. Lacey May would leave, too, drive them all back to Hank's house, where she'd sit on the couch with him, watching television and drinking the beers he liked, until she followed him into their bedroom, and Noelle could hear them from the basement, her mother's disgraceful moaning, all their creaking and bumping, the shuddering floor. It was payment for a life Lacey May never could have afforded on her own. What would be the point of anything Noelle had ever dreamed, if she wound up just like Lacey May?

Ruth took her by the hand and helped her stand, as if she were in a delicate condition. "Come on," she said, steering her back toward the house. "We'll sort this all out."

Mr. Riley and his wife lived just east of downtown, in a part of the city that was rough but being revitalized. It was mostly old millhouses, empty lots, and a few larger houses, bought up and awaiting renovation. The Rileys lived in a complex with a hair salon, tattoo parlor, and bicycle shop. Their unit was at the end of a bare courtyard, across the road from a row of sagging blue houses.

Gee and Jade had to be buzzed in, and they climbed up a pristine white staircase that reminded Gee of school. They reached the third floor and found Mr. Riley and his wife waiting for them in the hall. Mr. Riley was wearing a bow tie and slacks, a crimson apron around his waist. His wife wore a blue-and-white head wrap, blue stone earrings, a matching denim dress. On her hip she held their baby girl, in a onesie printed with the words i am magic.

They greeted Jade and Gee with hugs and kisses on the cheek. Mr. Riley introduced his wife, Andrea, his daughter, Katina; they both bore his last name.

The apartment was a single room with floor-to-ceiling windows, a couch and sitting area, an eat-in kitchen. Two bicycles were mounted on the plaster wall. A long staircase led up to the loft where they must have slept.

It was smaller than Gee would have imagined but also more beautiful. He found himself thinking Mr. Riley had too much and too little all at once.

"I know what you must be thinking about the stairs," Andrea said. "But we're very careful with Katina. And we're going to move as soon as we've saved up for a house. Where do you all live?"

"The east side," Mr. Riley answered for them. He was pouring Jade a glass of wine she hadn't said she wanted.

"That makes us neighbors," Jade said.

Mr. Riley shrugged. "I suppose. This is practically downtown."

"It's the east side, baby," Andrea said, and she changed the subject by asking Gee if he wanted root beer, carrot juice, or coconut water.

Gee went to serve himself, but Andrea

waved him off. She moved quickly, even with the baby tucked into her side. She had heavy breasts and tired eyes, a wide, open face. It was a surprise to Gee how pretty she was, and he wondered how Mr. Riley had found a woman like her.

They poured drinks and set the table, and when they sat down to dinner, they found they didn't have much to say to one another. Gee had asked in the car what the point of all this was, and Jade had said, *Connections are a good thing, Gee,* but even she didn't look so sure anymore.

Andrea had made a big salad full of squash and red onion and raisins, and a creamy pasta filled with vegetables Gee couldn't recognize under the thick yellow sauce.

"I hope nobody's got any allergies." Andrea had the baby in a sling now. "This has got soy and nuts and all the things that will make you sick if you've got an allergy."

"But no seafood," Mr. Riley said with a smile. "Andrea is vegan. Kept it up all during her pregnancy, too."

Gee felt his stomach turn. He gazed down at the pasta, which had smelled appealing, like hot cheese, a moment ago. They didn't say grace or anything, so they all ate up, and it was quiet, until Jade asked what had brought them to the area.

The Rileys mentioned Jersey smog and too much rent. They said this was a good, growing city, where you could still find free parking downtown. You never had to wait for a table at a restaurant. You could drive west to the mountains, east to the coast. And there were black people, which mattered to them both. Andrea explained her job at the university to Gee: she took donors out to play golf and to watch football games, and, in exchange, they wrote the checks that built new dining halls and science labs.

Gee wasn't surprised anyone would write Andrea a big check. He imagined her playing golf in a striped shirt and pants, a little white beret. He felt himself go hard, and he was washed over with guilt. She had been so nice to him, waiting on him, asking how he liked the food. She was too good for Mr. Riley, too beautiful. Gee liked her big, soft body, her thick eyebrows, how her daughter clung to her. It was almost too much when she slipped a breast out of her dress to feed Katina. When he looked up again, he was relieved that he couldn't have seen anything even if he tried.

Was this what his mother had wanted him to see? Mr. Riley's big-breasted wife, his apartment with fogged-up windows and a bedroom hidden upstairs? Was it supposed to make him grateful for Central, for the chance to go further than she'd been able to, as far as someone like Mr. Riley? It didn't seem like that exceptional a life, but it was still more than he had ever imagined for himself and more than he knew how to get.

Jade was the one stoking the conversation now, explaining how relieved she'd been to meet Mr. Riley at the town hall.

"I knew it would make a difference," she said, "for my son to have someone to look up to at Central. Somebody who looks like him."

Gee glared at his mother. She sounded so corny. He hadn't heard her flatter anyone ever in his life. What was so special about Mr. Riley anyway?

He thanked her, beaming, holding up his wineglass, as if he were going to propose a toast to himself. "You know that's why I went into education," he said. "For our boys. When I was in school, I was always looking for a vision of a successful black man. I didn't know my father either."

"I knew my father," Gee said. "He died. But I knew him."

"I'm sorry to hear that," Andrea said. "How long has he been gone?"

"About ten years," Jade said, skimming over how he'd died. She never told people that Ray had been killed, and Gee had gleaned it was the kind of thing he shouldn't mention either. He felt heat pooling in his chest, his hands. He needed to find a way to empty himself, to discharge his embarrassment and rage, but he stayed put, his teeth clamped together.

"He was a baker," Jade went on, "like my mother-in-law, who made that pie." Linette had sent along a plum pie that was cooling on the counter. "Like I was saying, it means a lot to me that Gee's got someone at Central looking after him. Those concerned parents have been quiet since school started, but the rumor is they're working on something. I don't think they'll get the program reversed, at least not until after Gee graduates. It's the environment I worry about, the messages he might get."

For all her boldness, Jade was good at citing risks, naming all the things that could sabotage a life. In the weeks after a homicide in the neighborhood, elementary school kids did worse on tests. Teenagers without fathers were more likely to wind up parents before graduation. Black boys got sent to the principal's office more. He'd been listening to her spout these facts for years, as if they were land mines he could avoid, if only he knew where to look.

"Gee is lucky to have you," Mr. Riley said. "My mother didn't know how to guide me. She wanted to, but she didn't know how. I had to figure things out for myself, especially in college and ed school. Over time, I came up with this mantra that got me through —"

"Oh, Lord." Andrea rolled her eyes. "Here he goes."

"I don't mean to preach, but maybe it'll help the young brother." He pointed his glass at Gee and cleared his throat. "You ready?" They were all quiet, even the baby, waiting for his grand pronouncement. *"If they're going to look at you, then you've got to give them something to look at."*

"Come again?" Jade said, but Mr. Riley went on, speaking to Gee.

"They're always going to be looking at you. To see if you measure up. To see if you'll make a mistake. They'll try and see if you're really as smart as they're afraid you are. And you've got to answer their question. You've got to show them what's what. *Don't hide your light under a bushel* — that's in the Bible, but it's the same as what we were talking about in class. *A torch.* You've got to be a torch."

Jade's voice cut soberly through the room. "My son doesn't have to be anything. He's got a right to be at that school, and if those white kids don't have to prove they belong, then neither does he."

"Well, there I disagree with you. You see, the torch is a metaphor —"

"I don't care about your metaphor."

"It's Shakespeare's."

"When it comes to my son, my opinion is the only one that matters."

"And Gee's," Andrea said, her voice sweet and clear, but Gee didn't miss the challenge in it.

The women smiled at each other.

"That's right," Jade said. "What matters is what Gee wants."

There was an opening then for someone to ask him what it was he wanted, his opinion, but no one did. It was Andrea who broke the quiet, asking who wanted pie. Mr. Riley rose to help her, and they busied themselves brewing coffee and making plates. Jade remained at the table with Gee. She smiled at him and arched her eyebrows at the Rileys, their backs turned, but Gee didn't smile back. He wished he were home, in his room, a picture of Andrea in his head. His shoulders ached from the way he'd been sitting at the table this whole time: too stiff and alert.

He thought about Adira, those white girls who had pulled her hair. He hadn't told his mother, and he didn't think he ever would. If there was someone he knew who was a torch, it was Adira, and it hadn't spared her. Her parents couldn't spare her, and neither could Mr. Riley, or Jade. Whatever was going to happen would happen — to Adira, to him, to everyone. There was nothing the grown-ups could do to watch over them, really, although they liked to talk as if they had control. They could go on talking, as far as Gee was concerned. It was mostly for themselves anyway. It was what they needed to get by.

Gee was especially quiet on the drive home, and Jade played the rock station hoping they'd air the tracks she knew, the songs that had helped her say, *Fuck you,* to anyone who didn't like her precisely the way she was. The music gave her courage, the clarity of rage. It was the perfect antidote to Mr. Riley's influence, but Gee didn't seem interested.

A Nirvana song came on, and she turned the radio up. "Listen," she said.

Gee kept his eyes away from her, the lights reeling past on the freeway.

"Listen," she said again, and he indulged her.

The song had its own kind of groove, the beat a hypnosis that sent her head swinging from side to side. Gee stayed still.

"What's this song even about?"

"I don't know," Jade said, realizing it for the first time. She knew the lyrics, but they didn't matter much to her. It was more about the way the music made her feel. It was Kurt Cobain, his gruff voice, reciting the same line over and over. It was a prayer, an incantation. The guitar riff cracked her wide open.

She wanted Gee to know this music was for him, that irreverence and rage weren't just for white boys. He could get a little drunk if he wanted to; he could play in a band; he could say shocking things, wear a dress, pierce his ears, any part of his body that he wanted; he could scream and break things, as long as they belonged to him and it wasn't in her house. She didn't want him to act out, but she didn't want him to worry too much about how the world would see him either. He'd wind up only punishing himself. She wanted him to be free.

"So, what do you think?"

"I have no idea what he's saying," Gee said. "But it's all right."

He started to bop his head along, and Jade felt her heart might explode. To be a mother was like this: to fight desperately to hold on to yourself most days, to struggle against the snare of your child, to focus on his future instead of your own. And then, suddenly, to feel bowled over by your love for him, to feel his breath is your breath, your music his music, and you are the same. It was a sensation she hadn't had in a long time. She let the feeling fill her.

When she dropped him off at home, she didn't offer any vague excuses about where she was going. She told him good night and then she left.

León Henriquez lived in a cul-de-sac on the southern edge of town, off the road that ran between the two university hospitals. The houses in his neighborhood were tall and white; they looked like wedding cakes lit up in the dark. The cars were parked on large paved circles at the bottom of the pitched lawns. Jade pulled into a spot and climbed to León's door, let herself in.

He was in the parlor, sitting cross-legged in an armchair, a book open in his lap. He held up a finger for her to wait a moment, then he snapped the book closed and went to her. He kissed her, softly, wetly, then brandished the book before her.

"Epigenetics," he said, tapping the cover. "It's not all bad news. There's good evidence that we can rewrite ourselves, our genetic code, for the better. We can, in a way, rewrite our history."

"Is that right?" Jade shrugged off her jacket, led him back to the armchair, and settled into his lap. León was always reading about the world's problems, one tome after another. It seemed to calm the unease he felt about his big house, the gap between his life and his patients'. The reading, at least, gave him an outlet, but Jade didn't care to hear his case studies about inequality, trauma. She took his book and set it on the side table.

"So how were they?" León asked.

"They were the uppitiest black people I've met in my life."

"Ever?" León laughed, disbelieving. His hair and beard were all silver, a fan of lines around his lips and temples. He had clear green eyes, little amber orbs around his pupils. She loved to look at him.

"You're too far in now, no? Gee will want to be seeing them again."

"How do you know what Gee wants?"

"Weren't you saying he needed a mentor?"

"All that teacher wants is to try and get

298

him to prove he's just as good as those white kids in his school."

"That doesn't sound so different from what you've been trying to teach him."

"It's one hundred percent different," Jade said. "I'm teaching him how to live up to his own standards — not anybody else's."

"Ah," León said. "My mistake. Still, he's at an age where he'd benefit from a man in his life."

"Don't start," Jade said, and she tried to pull away. León held her tightly. "What would you have me say? *This is Dr. Henriquez, I sleep at his house sometimes?*"

"How about, *This is León. I've known him for many years, and we care about each other very much?*"

"Gee doesn't need any more challenges."

"Don't you think it would bring the two of you closer if he knew the truth?"

"I'm his mother. We don't need to know every little thing about each other."

Jade crossed her arms to show that she was displeased and done with the conversation. She could be petulant with León, and it wasn't just that he was thirteen years her senior. He wasn't afraid of her moods, even the ones that were infantile. She could be petty or fussy or ecstatic, and he would look at her, every time, as if there were no piece of her that he couldn't enjoy.

"I suppose I'm jealous." León tilted her head upward, kissed her chin. "They got to have dinner with you and your son, and I still haven't had the pleasure." His voice turned low and serious. "One day he'll go away, and you'll have to start living your own life again."

"I can't see the point of looking that far ahead."

"Fine," he said. "Then let me preoccupy you with the here and now." He kissed her throat, used his tongue to trace a curve along her neck. Jade capitulated eagerly. Why argue when there was this?

León carried her into the library, set her atop a cabinet filled with books. When they were together, he played the role of devourer, and it felt good to surrender to him, to rest. Jade shut her eyes and leaned back, turned all her attention to the feeling of León, what he was doing to her body. Her head scraped against the wall, and he sank into her, the books rattling inside the cabinet. She came first, León after, and when she opened her eyes, he was staring at her, stern and resolute. She left for the shower, and he followed.

They stood under the water, soaping one another. His body was lean and golden, patterned with hair along his thighs and chest. His severe expression was gone, and he was grinning, exultant, ready to approach the same topic, as if this time she'd change her mind.

"Maybe you could come live here after Gee leaves."

"I don't think so."

"Are you worried about Linette? She's welcome, too." He winked, but Jade couldn't play along. She had to speak so he would hear.

She knew she wasn't very old. By the time Gee left, she'd still have years before she turned forty. She could conceive a child. She could marry. She knew women doctors her age who were just beginning to get engaged, to plot their lives. But it was the openness of her life after motherhood that she liked to envision. She knew she couldn't pick up where she'd left off as a teenager with her fishnet stockings and heavy metal albums, but she wouldn't remain standing still either. Gee would enter his future, and she hers.

"The life you want, I've already had it, even if it didn't last long." She kissed him. "Maybe if I'd met you first," she said, even though it was blasphemous.

"I'm not talking about you becoming

some kind of housewife. I want you to have your own life. I am so proud of you, and all you've done."

"I think when Gee is gone what I'll mostly want is to be alone."

"We could be alone together." He smiled at her, unflappable, even as she was turning him down.

She cupped his face in her hands. "Hear me, León. I can't see it. I won't live the same life twice."

The clinic was two floors, brick, and a gray-tiled roof. If not for the reflective windows, it could have passed for a squat and sprawling house.

The building didn't unnerve Noelle until she entered the lobby and saw the reception-ist encased in bulletproof glass. She slipped her ID through a shallow trough, waited to be buzzed in. It was only when they were in the waiting area that Noelle realized the security wasn't to protect the staff from patients; it was in case someone came in with a gun, shouting about the sanctity of unborn life.

Ruth seemed unfazed, fishing through a stack of magazines for something to read. She was dressed in her scrubs so that she could go straight to work after she dropped

Noelle off at Central. The appointment wouldn't take long. She'd be back before sixth period.

"I'm missing an English test," she said.

"That's all right. Think of all the things you'd miss if you weren't here."

Noelle had wondered whether Ruth would try and talk her out of it, but she hadn't tried, not even once. She reached for Ruth's hand, and Ruth gave it, without looking up from her magazine.

When it was her turn, Ruth waved her off with a smile. The room was large and smelled of castile soap and hot water, as if someone had just been in to clean. A quick and forceful nurse weighed her, took her vitals, sat in a chair across from the examining table to explain the procedure. It took a while for Noelle to recognize her; she looked so different in her mint-green scrubs, without her dark lipstick. She was the woman who had spoken at the town hall, the one who had pissed off Lacey May so bad that she decided to stand up and speak about the campaign.

The nurse asked whether she had any questions. "We'll go through the consent forms in a moment," she said, "but only once you're ready and you understand."

"Your son goes to Central."

Jade startled and looked up from her clipboard. She searched the girl's face and couldn't place her. "Do you?"

Noelle nodded. "My parents — they won't be informed, will they?"

"The only people who know will be the people you tell," said Jade. "You can tell everyone you know, or no one at all, for the rest of your life. It's up to you."

The girl screwed up her face in concentration, folded her hands primly on her knees. Jade watched her and resisted the urge to say more. Plenty of providers gave pep talks, especially to the younger patients, to say they were fine, it was fine, everything was fine. Jade had learned it was better to say less, to be swift, unceremonious. At sixteen, she'd been full of lust and opinions, capable of real feeling and sound judgment. She hadn't needed lectures or coddling; most girls didn't. They needed choices.

Jade gave her time.

"I'm ready," she said finally, and signed the forms.

Jade explained they'd give her an exam, then if everything looked good, they'd move on to the procedure. She placed her hand on top of Noelle's knotted fingers to give her a pat, and the girl started to weep.

It wasn't that she was unsure or worried it

would hurt. She wasn't afraid. It was this woman's hand — soft and brown and perfumed. It encircled hers so easily, and it embarrassed Noelle how good it felt to have a woman touch her, an elder who was beautiful and warm, and who had nothing to say. How did women get to be like this, so tender and wide open?

Jade handed the girl tissues. When she had calmed down, Jade asked her how she had known about her son and the school.

"I don't know him, but I remember you," she said. "My mother was at that big town hall. She's one of those concerned parents. She's a racist."

Jade looked at her, measuring. "Well, we don't get to choose our mothers."

If Noelle had to pick, she'd have chosen someone like this nurse, like Ruth.

"Your son," she said. "What's his name?"

Gee started sitting with Adira at lunch to make up for that day at the lockers. She forgave him quietly, and he saw that she didn't need his company or protection at all. She had already formed a little crew at Central, a mix of kids she'd known before from church and her neighborhood, as well as new friends who'd already been at Central, including a few white girls. Gee wouldn't have been surprised if, by year's end, Adira was elected homecoming queen. If someone could do it, it was her. She was beautiful and funny and real. It comforted him to imagine her in a crown. It would be a victory for all of them, a symbol that the drama among the parents couldn't touch the school. They'd cast their own votes, choose their own queen.

At lunch, Gee busied himself with his food, let everyone else do the talking. He made sure to laugh from time to time to register his presence, to show he was there and he wasn't a weirdo. It worked fine. He was doing just that when a girl approached the table, asking for him by name. She was long haired and slim faced, too sweet-looking for her dark clothes.

"You're Gee, right? I'm Noelle. I want you to audition for the school play. *Measure for Measure.*"

"Did Mr. Riley send you?"

"It was my idea. I wanted to find you."

Someone at the table oohed, and Gee knew enough to suck his teeth, murmur at them to shut up.

"Gee?" Adira interrupted. "In a play? What kind of play?"

"It's Shakespeare," Noelle said. "Can I speak to you alone?"

Gee followed Noelle as she weaved through the lunchroom. She brought him to a quiet corner by the vending machines. She dropped in her quarters, asked what he wanted. She bought him a bag of sour candy and a cherry soda. He didn't know why she was being so kind.

"I made a deal with Mr. Riley. I missed a test, and he said he wouldn't fail me if I agreed to stage direct his play. It's kind of perfect. I needed a distraction anyway."

"But he's not the one who sent you?"

"I already told you, it was my idea. This play is going to be a lot of time, a big commitment, and I want to make sure it's cool people doing it, not a bunch of jocks or whatever."

"You don't even know me."

"I've heard good things."

"From who?"

"Around. You interested?"

"You sure this isn't Mr. Riley? Cause he's weird. He's got a thing with me."

"Look, the truth is, I've got an agenda."

Gee laughed without meaning to. Noelle was strange, in her trench coat and big boots. She talked as if she were much older, so direct, so plain.

"I've been thinking this could be a good way to bring us all together. You know, old students and new. We could work together on something, really piss off those shitty concerned parents or whatever. Plus, it could be fun."

"That's cool," Gee said, without knowing whether he meant it or not. He was so used to saying things he didn't mean just to get through a moment, to get someone to look away.

"But I don't know," he went on. "I don't think I'd be good at acting. I'm not really a big talker."

"Then you'd be perfect," Noelle said. "All the words are already written for you."

11

Noelle's phone rang in the dark. Nelson. She fumbled to answer, desperate to hear his voice. She pressed the phone to her ear and heard nothing. "Hold on," she said, "let me step outside." She rushed to pull a coat on over her pajamas, a pair of slippers. She was groggy but quick.

She stepped onto the porch, and it was still quiet on the line. "Hello? Hello? I'm here," she said. She wasn't afraid to seem eager anymore. He had broken the silence between them by calling, and it was a sign they could find their way back. It had been their custom for one of them to seek out the other after an argument, or a long spell apart. They would come together briefly and kiss, as if to touch the cornerstone of their marriage, to be sure it was still there. Nelson would find her reading on the couch, lay his head on her lap, and thread their fingers together. She would find him in the kitchen, scrubbing counters, and she'd grab him by the waist, lean her body against his, to let him know that he was loved.

The sky was the deep blue black of night; it was probably lunchtime in Paris. She sank onto the steps and peered across the yard at the woods. A coyote stood by the dumpster at the end of the lawn. It turned its shining eyes on her and then slipped back into the trees.

Noelle heard a voice on the line, but it was muffled. She strained to listen. "Nelson?"

The voice was high, thin. It belonged to a woman. She went on listening. Eventually, she heard Nelson's voice, too, but not well enough to know what they were saying. There was no background noise of cars or clinking glasses or other conversations. They were somewhere private, just the two of them, their voices volleying back and forth, although Noelle still couldn't make out their words. Noelle kept the phone pressed to her ear. She felt her blood beating behind her eyes, in her throat. It must have been no longer than a few seconds when she heard the first moan. It rose suddenly — hers — and then it was met by a gasp, a groan she recognized. Nelson's. The moaning went on for a few moments, and then a slap, a louder grunt. Noelle hung up before she knew she'd done it, without deciding whether she wanted to hear more. It was instinct, unthinking. She threw her phone down on the porch, and then she was lurching to stand, bowing over the stairs to vomit. She retched into a patch of monkey grass, high and blue in the dark. When she was empty, she wiped her mouth, fell back onto the porch steps.

She decided to call back. She rang once, and he didn't answer. She rang again. A third time, a fourth. Every time he didn't answer, she hung up and dialed anew. She didn't know what she would say to him if he answered. She thought, briefly, there was no way he could see his phone, not while he was with another woman; and, if he could see it, he wouldn't be fool enough to pick up. It would take just a few clicks for him to realize what had happened, and the horror would overtake him. She supposed some part of her expected he would try to make things right — he was, after all, her Nelson. She was crying when the phone rang the ninth time, the tenth. She wondered briefly if she'd misheard it all, but then she shook the thought away. It made perfect sense, although she hadn't entertained the thought before, not really. It was an ill thought that crept around the edges of her mind from time to time but that she never indulged. A delayed flight, a turned-off phone, the vestiges of perfume on his coat. Why would she have given in to wondering? Her life was held together by trust and vows and benefit of the doubt. To be aloof was not to be out of love; to not answer your phone was not to be fucking someone else. She had no reason to think herself an idiot until it happened to her.

He answered on the twelfth time. This time there was noise: street sounds, the wind. He was somewhere outside.

"Sweetheart," he said. "Everything okay? I saw all your missed calls." He was playing it calm, waiting to see if she knew anything.

Noelle was sure he would hear all the crying she'd done in her voice, but she played along. "I'm just returning your call. You called me."

"Did I? It must have been an accident."

"Of course it was an accident. You haven't called me in weeks."

"You haven't called me either."

"We're even then."

"Noelle, I tried. I wrote to you about the play, and you never answered."

"What was I supposed to say? I couldn't reach you for days. I even tried your assistant, and then I get an email that you're extending your trip."

"I was afraid."

"Afraid of what? Afraid I'd break up with you? You're my husband."

"Maybe that's not the right word — I am ashamed."

Noelle caught her breath, waited for him to confess.

"I've gotten so caught up here — I suppose I wanted to forget. I'm not proud of it. I was so embarrassed that I didn't know you'd gone away until I spoke to your mother. Did she tell you I called?"

"She didn't mention it."

"It's so good to hear your voice. Maybe I dialed subconsciously. Maybe it was meant to happen."

Noelle could feel her every intake of breath. "Where are you?"

"I'm at this café, in the middle of a work lunch."

"Oh yeah? What are you having for lunch?"

"I wish I could talk more, babe, but, actually, I —"

"You fucking coward."

"Noelle."

"I'm used to you lying to yourself, but you will not lie to me."

"Noelle, let me explain. What did you hear?"

"You're a fake and a fraud, and I hate you. I hope I never see your face again."

"Noelle, you have to listen to me. Calm down."

"Is this the part where you tell me the problem is my reaction? All my feelings —"

"There can be more than one problem at a time, and, yes, part of it is the way you lose control —"

"Oh, shut the fuck up." She said it before she could stop herself, and soon Nelson was yelling back at her, "No, fuck you!"

She could hear him breathless on the phone, and she sat stunned. She had expected Nelson to grovel, to say sorry, beg her not to leave. She spoke to him in a hush.

"Can you imagine if he were here? If he could see us? If he were unlucky enough to have us as parents? Maybe it's better that we lost him."

"You don't mean that."

"I mean every word. Don't you bother coming back."

She hung up and felt her resolve collapse. She was sobbing when the screen door rattled open and Diane came onto the porch, dragging a sweatshirt on over her head. She rushed to Noelle, sat beside her, circled her with her arms. "What's the matter?" she said, and Noelle let herself unclench. She told her sister everything she'd been holding on to — the lost child, and Golden Brook, her pathetic, domestic life, Nelson's remoteness, the rustling and fucking she'd heard on the line.

"I'd say it wasn't his fault," she said. "I did become kind of a loser afterward. But, of course, it's his fault. I hate him."

It felt forceful and good to curse Nelson, to shed her instinct to shield him from her disappointment, to spare him.

"I can't believe he's cheating." Diane yanked her close. "I have half a mind to call his mother. I bet she'd set him straight."

"I always liked her, you know, but Nelson doesn't really talk to her anymore, so neither do I. Not officially. He just sort of drifted away."

Diane considered this. "Maybe this is a pattern of his, Nells. Maybe this is what he does. He reaches a new stage of life, and he leaves some woman behind."

"But he married me. We made promises." She tried to still herself, but her eyes filled with tears. "Please don't tell Mama."

"I won't tell a soul."

Diane held her sister, and Noelle laid her head on her shoulder. Her baby sister's body was firm, solid, and it felt good to let Diane hold her up.

"Maybe you two will work this out."

Noelle pulled away from her sister, looked her squarely in the eyes.

"I'm not saying you should, but some people stay together after a thing like this." Diane didn't say it aloud, that she was thinking of Alma. If Alma ever cheated on her, Diane was certain she'd take her back. Any life without Alma seemed worse than a life with her in it.

Noelle shook her head, disbelieving. "I'll never be able to forgive him. I'm not going to wind up like Mama, hung up on a man she can't trust."

"Give yourself some time," Diane said. "It's all too fresh. You don't have to decide now."

The sisters let a hush fall between them. They held hands and sat together on the porch, looking out at the yard.

Despite the dark, the birds were already singing in the trees. When it was light out, they'd zip across the yard, ribbons of color, flying from one bird feeder to the other, bluebirds and cardinals and chipping sparrows. Sometimes a mourning dove. Noelle liked to take her coffee on the porch and watch the birds fly back and forth between the wooden posts. There were often deer on the lawn, chewing at twigs; they scattered as soon as a car approached. The land reminded her of where they had all grown up, before moving in with Hank, although Diane's place was smaller, a ranch style. But it was all familiar: the lush scent of the mulch and grass, her garden, the pines, the critters in the yard, the scant light that pierced the trees, all the humble space and quiet, the spiderwebs in the windowsills on the porch. Crickets sometimes got into the house, and sang and leapt around the living room. Noelle had seen Alma catch them in her hands and release them outside.

"You know, if this wasn't where I was from, I'd love it here."

Diane chuckled. "It's divine. You shouldn't have stayed away so long."

"It's easy to take good things for granted. Don't assume you'll be able to have kids when it's your time, Diane. It's not as easy as you think it is. Start as early as you can. Start yesterday. Do you want kids?"

"Sure," Diane said noncommittally.

"You'd make a beautiful mother."

"You too."

"Maybe," Noelle murmured. "It's easy to be a good mother when it's all imaginary. I'm not sure I'd offer the right kind of example. You know, sometimes I think back to high school and that play I was in my junior year. Do you remember that? I think about how brave I was then, how determined. I felt like anything was possible — all I had to do was get out, leave North Carolina."

"You achieved all that."

"In some ways, that was the best time of my life. I was in love. I loved Gee."

"Don't let the nostalgia get to you now," Diane said. "This isn't the time for idealizing first love."

Noelle nudged her sister. "What do you know about *first love*? You've never brought anybody home."

"Neither has Margarita."

"No, but you could always smell the men on her. We saw her hickeys. I didn't have to wonder about her."

"You wonder about me?"

"All the time, baby sister. And one day, I know, you're going to surprise us all with all the secrets you've been keeping."

Alma made them breakfast: buttermilk biscuits and eggs, a salad of kale, cabbage, and fennel, all from the garden. Diane made coffee and juiced carrots. They played romantic salsa while they whirled around each other in the kitchen. Margarita scrolled through her phone, and Noelle rifled through a day-old copy of the paper, while they waited to be served at the table.

"This is cute," Margarita said. "Your morning routine. Do y'all do this every day?"

"Not usually," Alma answered. "But today is special — you're all here."

She joined them at the table, her plate heaped with vegetables and eggs, a biscuit glittering with orange jam. She'd painted her nails in the night, a blood red. She wore a blazer over a Sleater-Kinney T-shirt, cutoff jeans, and knee-high leather boots.

"You dress like that to spend time with the dogs?" Margarita said. Alma had a look, and she liked it.

"I just wear what I want to wear. Otherwise, I'd be in jeans and a T-shirt every day."

Diane laughed and slid next to Alma at the table. "You're going to get mud all over that outfit." She stopped herself from reaching for Alma's hand, palm up on the table. It was too easy to touch her.

"I almost had a roommate in L.A.," Margarita said. "But she was a total bitch. It's probably for the best we never moved in together — I might have killed her. And her little dog, too."

Noelle arched an eyebrow at Margarita, turned back to the paper. She had been unusually quiet this morning, her face pallid, her eyes pink around the edges. Margarita had caught Diane throwing glances at her, and even Alma kept offering her more salad, more coffee. They were doting on her, and Margarita could tell something was up. If she asked outright, they'd never tell her. She smashed up her biscuit with her fork so it would look like she'd eaten some of it, and tried to figure out how to get them to spill whatever was going on. They were talking about a story in the paper — a blighted strip mall was closing; a bowling alley and brewery would replace the crafts store and laundromat.

"All that effort Mama put into that campaign, all her worrying, and will you look at this town? Even the east side is getting nice now." She turned to Alma. "Diane hasn't told you? About our mother, the activist? You won't like the story. And you probably won't like Lacey May after you hear it — if you even like her now. The truth is both our parents are totally crazy. They just have different brands of crazy. The only sane member of our family, ever, has been Jenkins. Did Diane tell you about our dog?"

"You all are going out to look for your

father today, right?" Alma swiftly defused the minefield Margarita had laid out. She hadn't followed her lead, but she hadn't cut her out of the conversation either. Margarita was impressed.

With her dark nails and big curls, the pink Planned Parenthood mug she held with both hands, Alma was a perfect shot in black and white. Margarita took her picture with her phone.

"What are you doing?" Alma said.

"Just capturing the moment. I love your whole aesthetic."

Alma left the table under the pretense of clearing her plate. She leaned against the sink and went on eating, angling her body away from Margarita, her phone.

Margarita quickly uploaded the shots from that morning: the view from the porch (Tree Therapy), their spread for breakfast (Farm to Table), Alma (The New South), and her sisters (Catching Up and Old Friends). She didn't mention she was home.

"We should be leaving," Diane said, and she started to explain the plan for the morning. She and Noelle would take Alma's truck. They'd drop her off at the camp and then work their way through the motels Robbie had frequented over the years, the auto shops where he'd picked up work.

Margarita could take Diane's sedan around to the east side, check out the businesses there, the bakeries, the carnicería, the Súper Súper.

"So, I'm going to the east side? Alone? While you two ride together?"

Diane looked flustered. "That's what I was thinking, but we could always change the plan."

"You can ride with Diane," Noelle offered in a rare motion of magnanimity.

"Or you two can ride together," Diane said.

"Forget it," Margarita said, picking up her plate and shoving it into the sink. "I should have known that's how it would be. Let's get a move on then."

At first, Margarita had been bothered mostly that her sisters had left her alone. But then she figured something was wrong with Noelle, and it was in Diane's DNA to go to the person in need. She was like a dog. Dogs sat at the feet of the most reprehensible people. They found sick people, lonely people, mean people, and chose them, because dogs knew who needed to be comforted. She decided she couldn't blame Diane, and then she felt better, more even. She released her anger into the universe.

She didn't have to sit in the parked car anymore, alternating between banging on the wheel and trying to observe her breath.

She started making the rounds, stopping into the different shops, asking after Robbie Ventura and flashing his picture, describing his stature. Sometimes, she had to speak in Spanish, and she stumbled over her words. She knew *mi papá,* but she couldn't figure out how to say he was missing, he'd disappeared, so she'd say, *Él no está aquí,* which didn't help things. They would agree with her and repeat, *Él no está aquí.* She spoke to cashiers and stock boys, the waiter at a taqueria, and eventually they'd piece together a definitive no. Nobody knew where he was, and most of the time, they didn't know who he was. At best, he looked familiar, but they didn't know his name, and they couldn't say where they'd seen him last.

It was an hour before lunchtime, when Margarita was set to see her sisters again and debrief about their progress. They were meeting downtown for sushi. So far, Diane had been paying for everything, and that was fine with Margarita. She'd amused herself as she drove between places, by imagining what rolls she'd order, how she'd arrange everything in front of her, the little ceramic dish of soy sauce for the pictures she'd post in the afternoon. But after her seventh stop with no luck, she was tired, and she needed something to enliven her. She didn't like the feeling of incompetence, the way people furrowed their brows in confusion at her, the way her tongue malformed the words. And she didn't like how they'd cast her out — her sisters. If she had to name her feelings, it would be *piqued.* So she stopped early for lunch, for herself, a liquid lunch.

There was a terra-cotta-colored restaurant folded into the corner of a shopping center just off the main artery of Valentine Road. In the window blinked a sign: TAMALES, CERVEZA Y MÁS.

Inside the restaurant, there was a bar, vinyl booths, a bad mural of a chili pepper cartoon hero on a quest. The lights were dim, although the scene inside was relatively wholesome. The seats were crowded with pairs and families, eating beans and rice, drinking soda from frosted glasses filled with ice. A waiter approached her and said, "Señorita, how can I help you?" Margarita liked that. She asked to sit at the bar.

She ordered a beer and a shot of tequila, and the bartender blinked at her but didn't fuss. They arrived along with a basket of tortilla chips. She plowed through the chips, the burning salsa much hotter than she'd expected. She shot back her tequila then asked for another to keep company with her beer. When the bartender returned with her fresh pour, she showed him a picture of her father.

The photograph was old, from around the time Margarita had been in high school. Her father looked as if he were in his late thirties. He was tan, the holes in his ears empty, the diamond studs gone, likely lost or pawned. He was too lean, the sinew of his muscles visible, as if he were a man who had done manual labor that wore his body down, although his work in the auto shops was hardly that — he rolled under and out from cars, fixed up the paint jobs, and anything heavy was lifted by machines. He was bronze skinned, smiling despite his missing teeth: one in the front, a lower canine, a few molars in the back. His eyes were slitted, as if he were boring a hole with his gaze at the photographer. Margarita didn't know who had taken it, or where it was from. Lacey May had given it to her.

"Well?" she asked.

"No lo conozco," the bartender answered, and she knew enough Spanish to understand that. He asked her if she wanted to order any food, and she asked for another tequila instead. Margarita felt the liquor searing her stomach. The sharp edges of the chips bothered her gums. Everything was wrong, and it was taking over her body, too. Her mother was dying, possibly, maybe. They all were dying, but Lacey May was dying sooner, much sooner than they'd expected. And, for all she knew, her father was dead. When Robbie first started disappearing, they worried he'd been hurt, but he always turned up afterward. It became the pattern, a normal thing, but Margarita never lost sight of the fact that one time the disappearance would be for good. She didn't think of it much — what was the point? When he died, he died, just like any of them, but she wondered about it now. Whether the plot twist none of them expected would be that Robbie was already gone. She'd get her fare back to California no matter what, but she didn't like to think about her father no longer being alive. It was easier for her if her parents stayed stuck in the same rhythms — Lacey May and Hank working at the store, living out their little makeshift marriage, and Robbie, fixing cars, getting high, vanishing, and reappearing, calling the girls drunk to tell them how much he loved them. She knew what to expect that way; she could focus on her own life, her career. For years, her parents had been a familiar act, playing on the television set on mute. She didn't have to watch, but they were always there.

She called herself back to reality. Robbie was probably fine, up to the usual. It had only been a couple of weeks.

When the bartender returned with another shot, he paused in front of her, measuring. He must have been around her age, brown eyed, gaunt. He had a chipped tooth, but otherwise, he was handsome. Margarita waited for him to come on to her, or to ask her if she was sure she could handle another drink. The answer was, yes, of course, either way.

"Señorita," he said. "Here's that drink you ordered. But do you desire something a little bit stronger?"

"Stronger how? Like a double shot?"

"Not a drink. Something else."

He bit his lip and looked over his shoulder, as if there were someone else lurking behind the bar. He was nervous, and suddenly Margarita got it.

"What? Like pills?"

"Pills, powder, rock. We have everything."

"In the restaurant?"

He shook his head. "Just me. I'm connected."

He looked so innocuous in his blue polo shirt, his clean shave. Was this how things worked in North Carolina? Margarita doubted he had shrooms, but maybe he did. Weed wasn't worth the high if she got busted here — it wasn't L.A. She'd heard of friends from high school getting in trouble just for the paraphernalia — bongs, pipes — even when they didn't have anything on them. Besides, she had to meet her sisters.

"Just give me the tequila," she said, and he nodded, slid a fresh glass across the counter.

"But if you change your mind," he said, polishing the countertop, stalling. "You know where to find me."

"Yeah, yeah," she said and waved him away. She knew it was rude, but she had to stay clean if she was going to survive these days with her sisters. They'd know immediately if she were on something. Then Diane would be circling her, like she was the one in need of healing, and Noelle would be scoffing at her, the way she already did, but with reason. She'd stick to what was easy to handle, what wouldn't interfere. One more beer, and then she'd go.

The hood of the sedan was smoking when Margarita pulled into the spot in front of the sushi restaurant. The bumper sagged, and the left rearview mirror was smashed, the wires exposed and dangling, the headlights cracked.

In the restaurant, she found her sisters huddled at a table by the window. They had already started eating without her, a platter of soybeans between them. They were sharing. Of course they were. She clattered into her seat and saw both of them staring agape at her.

She said nothing and picked up the menu.

"We tried to wait," Noelle said. "But we got hungry. You're an hour late."

There was something conciliatory in her tone, but this didn't make Margarita feel any better. Any gestures from Noelle would be temporary — she always went back to thinking of herself, assured she was right and that only she could see the truth: about their family, this town, the world.

"Oh, fuck off," Margarita said. "I'm not surprised." She felt her eyes burn as she said it, so she reached into her purse and put on her sunglasses. She stared at the menu again, although the items on the list swirled before her.

"Are you drunk?" Diane put a hand on her shoulder, and Margarita shrugged her off.

"I might as well tell you now while you're feeling concerned," Margarita said. "I rear-ended a guy. Just a little bump. But I convinced him not to call the cops. We exchanged numbers. I'll handle it."

Diane stood from her seat and craned to look out the window toward the street. She saw the plume of smoke rising from the hood of the car.

"Oh my God."

"It's fine," Margarita said. "I'll take it into the shop when we're done here."

"While you're drunk?" Noelle said. "You're going to keep on driving that thing?"

The server arrived wearing a trim lavender blouse with a ruffled collar. Margarita followed the line of her pencil skirt down to a pair of black heels. She noticed, for the first time, the white tablecloths, and that the menu was a slip of paper in a leather folder. This was a *fancy* sushi place.

"Hi, there," Margarita said. "Would you mind taking a picture of us?"

The woman obliged. The phone was humongous in her hands. Margarita jerked her chair closer to her sisters. Noelle and Diane sat in silence, while Margarita flung an arm around their shoulders, straightened her back, lifted her chin, twisted her face to the side.

"Say *sushi*," she said. She examined the picture, deemed it beautiful, and then asked the server for seaweed salad, a spicy tuna roll, and the sake list.

She felt she had collected herself enough to push the glasses up on her forehead to look her sisters in the eyes. Diane had her arms folded in front of her chest and was looking down at her lap like a cranky little girl. Noelle was shaking her head side to side in a rhythm that seemed involuntary. She was wearing pearls in her ears, her hair pulled back into a ponytail that exhibited the clear six points of her diamond face. She was so fucking pretty.

Margarita tilted her head at Noelle, waiting for her to explode.

"You must be trolling us," Noelle finally said. "You think this is all a game. Papi's missing, and Mama's in the hospital. I'm not happy to be here, either, but we're all here for a reason."

"And what reason is that?" Margarita said. "Besides that none of us has anything better to do? Mama isn't dying. We're not the ones filling up her IV, giving her shots. Tell me, why are we all here?"

"To be together," Diane said. "Isn't that obvious? That's what families do in times of crisis. They come together."

"That's beautiful," Margarita said. "You should put it on a card. Did you ever think of that as a side hustle besides your little dog camp? You were born to write Hallmark cards, Diane."

Diane looked stunned. Usually, Margarita didn't come after her with such force. Margarita seemed to balk at herself, too. She looked away from her sisters, out the window. It was a bright day, the leaves green and gold. Pedestrians ambled along the street. The converted tobacco factories were pristine, all glass and brick office buildings and condominiums now. She observed the serene lunch hour outside. When she looked back at the table, Noelle was fuming, Diane wiping her eyes quietly with her fist.

"You're right," Noelle said. "I have nothing better to do. I left you all because I wanted to build my own life. The life I built is falling apart. I quit my job. I had a miscarriage. Nelson is cheating on me."

Margarita awakened to the news from her sister. Noelle went on.

"But that doesn't mean I was wrong to leave. And neither were you. I've been thinking. Our parents are always going to have their problems, but that doesn't mean we have to stay away from each other. We can be family on our own terms."

Noelle put her hand on the table, palm up. She was waiting for Margarita to take it.

"What are you talking about?" Margarita said. "What's going on?"

"I don't know why I'm always so hard on you. I was thinking about it today, while I was out with Diane. And I think it's just because I'm angry. I hate being here. But that's not your fault. You didn't make it that way."

"You all were talking about me?"

"It wasn't like that," Diane said. She was sniffling.

Margarita thrust a napkin at her. "Oh, go on, cry it out. The baby needs to feel her feelings."

"That's enough," Noelle said. "Why are you turning on her?"

"I don't need you to stick up for me," Diane said. "I'm twenty-seven years old, and I'm tired of being stuck between you two."

Diane was whispering at them, but her voice was hard. It rose above the happy chatter of the restaurant.

"You all see me like someone who will always be around. Like some pathetic kid who hasn't grown up, who just wants everyone to get along. And I do. But I don't need it to happen. If it doesn't happen, I'll be fine. I don't need any of you anymore. I've got a family of my own. Alma."

"No offense, sweetie, but all that stuff about *friends forever* is a sham," Margarita said. "Friends break up just like lovers do. Friends let you down, too."

"I'm not talking about friendship. Alma isn't my friend. She's my partner."

Her sisters stared at her. Diane felt herself shake under the table, but she wasn't frightened. She was enraged. She felt the charge surge through her limbs.

Noelle was the first to speak. "That's wonderful," she said softly and reached for her sister. Diane swatted her away.

"I'm leaving," she said. "I've had enough of both of you and your problems for one day. It's not just Mama and Papi and Hank. The two of you are a burden. I'm taking the truck, and I'm leaving. The two of you find Papi. I'm out. And, Margarita, you better fix my fucking car."

Diane shot up and sent the water glasses on the table toppling. She slapped down her napkin and headed for the door. Her sisters didn't try to stop her. They watched her through the glass. She climbed into Alma's truck, revved up the engine, and peeled away.

The server returned with Margarita's food, her little cup of sake. Noelle and Margarita sat in silence, both of them peering out the window, watching the vacant spot their sister had left. Eventually another car pulled into it; another family piled out of the van and onto the street.

"Go ahead and eat up," Noelle finally said. "We've got to find Papi." She took the cup of sake from in front of Margarita. She took a sip. "I'll drive."

They left Diane's car at the garage and walked a mile together to the rental place. Noelle took out a car in her name, and together they cruised around Valentine, wondering where else they should check.

"So, it was going to be a boy?"

"I never actually checked. Nelson wanted it to be a surprise. And once it was gone, it didn't make sense to know."

"How far along were you? Like, was it a baby or just a clump of cells?"

"I was at the beginning of my second trimester. I'd felt him move."

"Did it feel like butterflies? That's what

335

they say."

Noelle smiled at her sister. "It felt like gas."

They laughed. Noelle kept driving.

"You stopped following me online," Margarita said.

"I did."

"How come?"

"You seemed so happy, but I knew you weren't. It depressed me."

"Who's really happy nowadays anyway? There are more important things than happiness."

"Like what?"

"Inner peace," Margarita said, but Noelle could tell she wasn't joking.

Margarita fished in her purse for her pack of cigarettes. "Do you mind?"

"I'm not pregnant anymore," Noelle said. She rolled down the window.

They were passing the stretch of Valentine that was just a row of fast food. Hot dogs, fried chicken, glazed doughnuts.

"I want a doughnut," Margarita said, pointing with her cigarette. A sign announced they were hot and fresh.

Noelle smirked at her. "Are you high?"

"Hungover. I can feel my headache already."

They sat on the curb in the parking lot,

eating the fat, frosted doughnuts in front of the green SUV Noelle had rented. Noelle drank a burnt black coffee while Margarita guzzled a lemonade, licked her fingers.

"How do you stay so skinny when you eat like that?"

"It's all math," Margarita said. "You just have to keep track. Indulgence and then restriction."

"As long as it's not drugs," Noelle said. "You remember how skinny Papi got? I hope you're staying away from the hard stuff. Only party drugs."

"They're all party drugs," Margarita laughed, then it hit her, and she lurched off the curb, sent her lemonade cup flying. Ice and liquid spilled across the asphalt.

"I've got it," she said. "I know how to find Papi."

They parked in front of the TAMALES, CERVEZA Y MÁS sign. Margarita led the way directly to the bar. The bartender she'd seen before wasn't there, so she called over the new barkeep.

"Oye!" she said, using what little Spanish she had before she ran out. Noelle slid up beside her, resisting the urge to tell Margarita to lower her voice. She started describing the bartender she'd seen earlier in the day, explaining that she needed to speak with him. The woman behind the bar understood, and she left to go find him — he was still on his shift.

Margarita was holding the old photograph of Robbie, curled up in her fist. Noelle took it from her and flattened it on the bar.

"This is from after," Noelle said. "After Papi mucked it all up for good."

Margarita laughed. "Which time?"

"You know which time."

"Oh, right. And he tried to make it all better by buying us gifts. As if that would make any difference."

"He gave Diane that necklace she wears. The emerald charm?" Noelle shook her head. "And he gave me a leather jacket. Could you believe it? It was too big for me. A men's size."

Margarita looked at the picture of her father. Usually, she felt neutrally toward him: neither good feeling nor bad. It had taken years.

"What did he give you?" Noelle asked. "To make up for it all?"

"I can't remember," Margarita said. She looked away from his face, the photograph bleached of color, as if it had been a hundred years.

"You look like him," Noelle said, her

finger landing on the expanse of their father's cheekbones.

Margarita pointed at the expression in their father's eyes, the impression he gave of scowling even as his mouth split into a smile. "So do you," she said.

The bartender arrived, taking in the two sisters, and he grinned. Before he got the wrong idea, Margarita told him what it was that she wanted. Her specificity startled Noelle — she hadn't known there were so many varieties, so many preferences you could tease out when you ordered. The bartender seemed as if he hadn't known either. Noelle resisted the urge to tell Margarita, *This isn't L.A.* The bartender said he could handle it and started writing his phone number on a napkin. Margarita caught his pen out of his hand, set it down. She shook her head.

"If I'm paying for it," she said, "I want to meet your connect. I'll pay you both — I don't care. I just want to make sure I'm getting something good."

12

OCTOBER 2002
THE PIEDMONT, NORTH CAROLINA

When Lacey May realized Noelle was missing, she ran out to the yard to tell Hank. He was hosing down the dog, its hide covered in bubbles.

"She's gone," Lacey May said. "I can't find her."

Hank seemed unalarmed as he turned off the water. "It's the middle of the day. Maybe she stepped out."

"You wouldn't understand," Lacey May said. "I've got a feeling. A mother can tell when something is wrong."

"Let's go and find her then."

She had already checked the living room, the kitchen, the front and rear of the house. Margarita and Diane were giggling in the bathroom, putting mayonnaise in their hair. But she hadn't seen Noelle all morning, and she would have assumed she was sleeping in, but when Lacey May poked her head downstairs, the girl was nowhere.

They returned to the house, and Jenkins padded after them, trailing soapy water. Lacey May paced in the living room, wondering where to check first. She knew it was possible Noelle had simply gone somewhere without telling them, and she'd come back with a new black T-shirt and a frozen Coke, evidence she'd been at the mall, although she'd still refuse to answer any of Lacey May's questions. But Lacey May couldn't shake the sick feeling she had. It was like that time she went to collect the girls from Robbie's motel, and they weren't there. Diane had needed stitches. Lacey May felt as if she'd swallowed a stone, its weight in her stomach.

Noelle was dead. Noelle was pregnant. No, it was neither of those things. If she was honest, she knew what it was that worried her. Noelle had been sleeping late and skulking around. Noelle was high. There had been warnings in those pamphlets, the ones they'd given her so long ago, that first time Robbie was hospitalized, before the cop car and jail. He'd been babbling, senseless, and she'd driven him to the emergency room, only for them to tell her he was coming down, and she had yelled, *From what?* She'd felt ashamed that the doctors and nurses, who didn't live with Robbie, didn't love him, had known something about him that she hadn't. They'd warned her — *Addiction runs in families.* She had folded up the fact and stowed it away for some other year. The girls had been small then. If there was one of them who was susceptible now, it was Noelle — she was the oldest when Robbie left, the most likely to be ruined.

Margarita strode out of the bathroom, laughing and wringing her hands with a towel. She went to the refrigerator and retrieved a lemon, sliced it in half on the counter. As she crossed through the living room, she was struck motionless at the sight of her mother pacing.

"Mama?" Margarita inched toward her, the split lemon in her hands. "What's the matter?"

Hank answered. "She can't find Noelle."

"Did you check downstairs?"

Lacey May shot her a look.

"She's probably downstairs," Margarita said in defense of herself.

Lacey May pointed a finger at her face. "You know you live with your head in the clouds, Margarita. The rest of us are living down here."

Margarita stood quietly, holding her lemons.

"Just go on and carry out your beauty

342

experiment. We'll figure this out."

Lacey May turned away from her, and Margarita knew she had been dismissed. She found Diane back in the bathroom, sitting on top of the toilet, her clothes soaking wet. She reeked of eggs.

"Margarita," she sang, still giggly from the cold water, the fun they'd been having. "¿Qué pasó, Margarita?"

"Shut up and put your head back," Margarita said. She squeezed the stinging lemons over her sister's scalp.

In the living room, Lacey May had collected herself and decided they should make a round of calls before they left to search. They tried Duke and got no answer, so they called Ruth. She answered right away.

"I haven't seen her in a couple days," she said. "Lacey May, why didn't you tell me? Why didn't you tell me you'd decided to sell the house?"

"What's that about the house?"

"You lied to me. I saw the old tenants move out, and you told me you had new ones lined up."

"I do. They needed until November, and I told them that was fine."

"Well, this morning a man came by for an inspection. I went out to meet him as soon as I saw him pull up in his truck, and he told me the new owner was coming by in a few hours."

"Oh God. What else did he say?"

"He said the house was sold."

"Robbie," Lacey May said. "Goddamn it. It was Robbie."

"Calm down, maybe I misunderstood. He can't just sell the house on his own. Isn't it in your name, too?"

"Maybe that didn't stop him. I've got to go, Ruth."

Lacey May hung up the phone, her heart thumping. She sensed one of the girls enter the room. Noelle had her hair tied into a knot on top of her head, the skin under her eyes plump and pink, like bruises.

"Where the hell were you?"

"I was downstairs listening to music in the closet."

"In the closet?"

Noelle nodded, and Lacey May was too numb to lecture her daughter, her mind too foggy. She stood, and Hank stood with her.

"I've got to talk to him," she said. "But I ought to go alone."

She could see now that feeling inside her hadn't been about Noelle. It had been a premonition of this catastrophe, whatever Robbie had done with the house.

"I didn't think he was capable of a thing

344

like this," she said, staring at the kitchen table, the grain of the artificial wood. "You think you know a person," she began, but she didn't say anything else.

The rehearsals for *Measure for Measure* were in full swing at Central, and Noelle was grateful for the long hours. As stage manager, she was the first to arrive and the last to leave, which was exactly what she needed. She helped Mr. Riley with blocking and cataloged the props. She directed the group to the appropriate pages of the script. But there were long breaks, too, when she wasn't needed, and she sat with Gee in the auditorium.

She was the one who had started going and sitting with him. And while he didn't seek her out on his own, he didn't object. When they talked, he sat stick straight, facing the stage, peering at her sideways, as if he didn't want to look at her head-on. She didn't mind that or the way he never spoke more than a sentence or two at a time. He listened to her go on and on about her theories about the play, the classic rock albums she was listening to in order to edify herself. She talked about everything besides what was going on with Lacey May and Robbie, the phone calls she'd overheard between her mother and a lawyer. She didn't know why, but she had a feeling that if she ever decided to tell him the truth, he wouldn't look at her the way Duke did: as if she were no good, destined to be bad because of her family. Lately, she'd been wondering if that was the only reason Duke wanted her: he saw her as broken, easy.

Gee seemed like a boy with his own secrets. He was smart and staid; he had the air of a man, except for when he drew the hood of his sweatshirt tight around his face, started chewing on the strings. All his quiet didn't make her think there was nothing there, but the opposite. Inside, Gee was stirring.

Besides, he was cute. He had long dimples, sparse, unruly eyebrows, skin that was mostly clear for a teenage boy. He wore the beginnings of a mustache, neat and trim. He had long lashes, deep-set eyes. And while most of the boys at school reeked of too much cologne and deodorant, or musty towels that had never finished drying properly, Gee smelled like green soap: grass and limes.

He had been perfectly cast as Claudio, who was at the center of the drama, but silent for most of it. Without him, there'd be no plot to act out, no problem for the other characters to solve. When he was set free, the play found its resolution. He had one big speech and a few occasional lines that he had to deliver with heart. The rest of the time, he had to crouch behind bars, fall to his knees, and beg for his life. He hadn't done any good acting yet, but neither had anyone. He had mumbled his lines at the read-throughs, and Mr. Riley had told him over and over to *e-nun-ci-ate.* But the key to Claudio was quietly transmitting endurance and fear, and Gee could do it.

They were sitting together, sharing a peanut butter sandwich. Noelle handed half to Gee, and he accepted it without saying anything, which seemed to her a sign that they were almost friends. Mr. Riley had called five, and the rest of the cast was on-stage, miming actions with props from an old chest. Adira wore a plastic gilded crown and made nonsense pronouncements using *hither* and *thither* and *prithee* and *thou.* A knot of boys surrounded her, laughing, charmed. They were Shawn, who played Angelo; Beckett, who played the duke; Alex, who played Lucio, a friend to Claudio; and a few cast as townspeople. They watched her admiringly, and jousted at the air with rubber swords, striking each other underneath the arms.

Gee and Noelle saw their classmates horse around onstage, and they knew they were different, too old for childish games. They were better off watching, shoulder to shoulder, from the empty seats.

"It's such a weird play," Noelle said, licking peanut butter from her fingers. "I hope Mr. Riley doesn't get in trouble for putting it on."

"Nah," said Gee. "I don't think anybody's going to understand it."

They laughed.

The play was about a duke who pretended to leave Vienna so that he could observe how the citizens acted in his absence. Angelo, the deputy appointed to watch after things, was a pervert, corrupt and cruel. He put Claudio in jail for impregnating his own fiancée, Juliet, who was played by a sophomore named Rosa. Claudio and Juliet were the only ones worth rooting for, although they spent nearly every act apart. They were victims, they loved one another, and nearly everyone else was detestable, too stuck in their own ideologies to ever do what was right.

The star of the play was Isabella, Claudio's sister, who eventually won his freedom by outsmarting Angelo. Mr. Riley had been wise to cast Adira as the lead. Noelle knew she'd be stunning even in her habit and veil, but it wasn't only that she was pretty. She was easily one of the more popular new girls at Central. She got invited to senior parties on the weekends, flitted around between groups of friends, old and new, studious and cool, black and white. She would draw a big crowd, and so would Beckett as the duke. He was popular with the kids who went to Duke's parents' church. Together, they'd bring plenty of students, as well as parents, concerned and not, to the play. They'd all be in the same audience, subject to the same drama. They would witness Adira's virtue, and Beckett's self-righteousness, Gee's despair, the consequences of legalism and wrongful judgments. The play might be important; it might *say* something. Noelle said as much to Gee, and praised Mr. Riley's vision. Gee said nothing.

"The only thing I can't stand is how much Shakespeare hates women," Noelle said. "At least, he hates women who have sex. Everybody's a whore, except Isabella, and she's a nun."

Gee didn't know how to respond at the mention of sex. He didn't want to say the wrong thing and offend Noelle, or reveal too much. When he'd first read the play, he'd wondered why Mr. Riley had cast him as the man who couldn't control his impulses, who had impregnated a woman he'd promised to make his wife before it was time. It was as if Mr. Riley knew there was something wrong with him. Gee knew he couldn't be alone in the things he did: futilely searching for free porn on the internet, masturbating to sleep, masturbating to wake, fantasizing about nearly every girl or woman who so much as looked at him, who brushed past him in line at the supermarket. But it was hard to know whether it was normal. Sometimes, he felt crazed and manic, like he might die if he didn't find a release, a way to feel good. Other times, it had little to do with his body, and he wanted to watch those pixelated videos so he could be someone else: a man, wanted, powerful.

"Stop that," Noelle said, and he wondered whether she could read his thoughts.

She reached for his face, cradled his chin in her cupped hands. "You're clenching," she said, and traced her thumb along his jaw up to his earlobe. He felt himself shiver and hoped Noelle couldn't see.

"You know you've got the opposite problem I do — I say everything I'm thinking, and you look like you're always thinking things you don't say."

"You think it's a problem?"

"It's different. Like a mystery. But it's cool — not everyone gets to know you."

Gee shrugged. "I don't know. Nobody says everything they think."

Noelle smiled. He had caught her in her own lie.

"You want to go out after rehearsal?" she said, and proposed Cedar's, the sandwich shop at the bottom of the hill.

Gee wondered what Noelle wanted, why she had picked him.

"Don't you have a boyfriend? That goth kid?"

"So?" she said.

"My grandma is picking me up."

"That's fine. She can come, too."

Linette drove them to Cedar's in her grimy golden sedan. The day was bright and breezy, and they sat at a picnic table outside. He and Linette shucked off their jackets and gulped their sodas while Noelle waited in line for their food. Linette didn't comment, but her eyes on Gee made him squirm, as if he were doing something naughty, and she was happy to be his accomplice.

"Come on, Linette," he said finally.

"What's that? What did I do?"

"She's just my friend."

"Mm-hmm."

"How could it be a date if you're here?"

"That's a good point." She winked at him. "How could it be?"

Linette paid for their food, and Noelle thanked her profusely. She did it like it was nothing, although Gee knew she hadn't earned an income in years. But Linette seemed more awake than he'd seen her in a long time, enlivened and pleased to be out, even if the food Noelle had ordered wasn't the kind she favored: chili dogs and Tater Tots, wings, and soggy fried okra.

"You know I used to own a bakery not far from here. Long before Cedar's, or any of these other businesses opened up. Superfine — you ever heard of it?"

Noelle shook her head.

"Gee's father was my baker. He was very talented, you know. Right after he died, there was a story in the paper about us. There was no picture of him to run with the article, but they had photos of all the things he made his last day in the shop — morning buns and biscuits and devil's food. Was it cake or doughnuts? I can't remember."

"Doughnuts," Gee said.

If there was something he remembered clearly about Ray, it was the food he would make for him — roast beef with melty

352

cheese and onions, oatmeal cookies and steaming cocoa, red pepper soup, and hot cereal with mashed banana, a heap of brown sugar in the center.

"Your father died?" Noelle said.

"He looks just like him, too. When you're looking at Gee, you're looking at Ray."

Gee's eyebrows went up, disbelieving.

"I'm serious," Linette said. "Do you know that when you love somebody it changes your brain? The shape of it. Why couldn't it change your face, too?"

"It changes your brain?" Noelle shuddered.

"That's why you've got to be careful who you love."

Gee felt his face go hot; he started chewing on the gummy inside of his cheek. First, Ray, and then all this love talk. He shot a look at Linette.

She seemed to get the message, mumbled something about condiments, and got up to give them some room. As soon as she was gone, Noelle leapt at him with her thoughts.

"I can't believe your father died. You seem so normal."

"Thanks."

"What I mean is, something tragic happened to you, and you're all right. So solid. No one in my family is like that. My father's a big loser, and my mother's worse cause she keeps forgiving him. Even if she's married to someone else. I swear it's like a tragedy. Everybody's so pathetic and weak."

"You don't seem weak."

"It's the all black," Noelle said, flipping up the collar of her trench coat, and they both laughed. "I don't even have a reason as good as yours, and I'm all messed up."

Gee liked the way she talked about herself, so naked, so open. He had the same feeling — he had no reason to be the way he was, not after everything Jade had done, the person she had managed to become, the years that had passed, and how little he remembered.

"Maybe I'm the same way, and I'm just good at hiding it."

"Then you're really good," Noelle said, her eyes the color of honey in the afternoon light. He felt an unexpected pang. She didn't seem to notice.

"You know my favorite part of the play?"

"You really like this Shakespeare stuff."

"Don't you? Otherwise, why are you doing it?"

Because you asked me, he wanted to say. She had been so determined, so direct, but he hadn't felt she was trying to push him around. It was natural to be near her, even then, standing by the vending machine while she punched in the numbers, handed him his candy.

"Okay, what's your favorite part?"

Noelle described a part of the play Mr. Riley had cut, and Gee was amazed she'd read the whole thing. There was a scene where the drunken prisoner Barnardine refuses to be executed. The duke wants his head to play a trick on Angelo. But Barnardine simply refuses. *I swear I will not die to-day for any man's persuasion.* And miraculously, everyone listens. He is left alone in his cell, and the play goes on.

"All he does is say, *No, I won't be the one. I won't be caught up,* and it saves him. It *saves* him."

"That's nice," Gee said. "But it doesn't sound like real life."

"It's real for Barnardine."

"It's all made up anyway."

"You're too serious."

"Then make me laugh," Gee said, flirting before he knew it. It wasn't a line, and he wasn't imitating anyone. It had slipped out of him. It was what he had wanted to say.

Noelle smiled at him. "Too much pressure. Besides, I think it's your turn."

Linette returned, and Gee was relieved to see her. Looking at her dissolved the heat

355

he was feeling all over, the heat he worried Noelle could sense radiating off his body. He was loose and buzzing, happy. He wanted her to stay, but Noelle announced she ought to head back. Linette offered to drive her, and she said she'd make her own way. She hugged Linette as if they were old friends, and waved good-bye to Gee. She started walking slowly uphill, along the old baseball field, dusty and fenced in, back toward the school.

Lacey May was waiting for her in the parking lot. She yelled at her for a good long while, and Noelle looked at her serenely, refusing to say where she'd been.

"You knew I had a meeting. You knew, and you held me up on purpose."

"A meeting?" Noelle said innocently. "What kind of meeting?"

"You know what kind."

"The campaign is dead. It's October. It's too late. What are you going to do now?"

"We're talking strategy."

"You going to make your signs and stand in front of the school yelling at all the black kids? Is that your plan?"

"You get in this car right now," Lacey May ordered, and although Noelle obeyed, Lacey May knew that she had lost.

They sat, waiting for the engine to warm up, and Noelle extracted a big stack of papers from her backpack, and started sifting through them. She was pretending to go over the pages.

"You have no idea what's going on," Lacey May said. "You're focused on this dumb play, and your life is hanging in the air right now."

"Is that cause of the transfer kids or cause of Papi?"

"You shut up," Lacey May said and yanked out of the lot. She tried to focus on the road, the wheel, the pattern of clouds overhead. If she didn't fill her mind with something, she'd lose control and slap Noelle, and the girl was too old for that. She wouldn't stand for it.

"You shut your mouth," she said again.

She hadn't spoken to the girls about everything that had happened, but she knew they'd overheard her talking on the phone to Robbie and Ruth and the lawyer. It was her mistake not to keep it a secret. She'd been too caught up in her anger and confusion. She should have explained it to the girls after everything was settled. She should have been calm; she should have comforted them. But Lacey May hadn't been thinking of the girls, even if she'd held on to the house for them, their inheritance. She'd mostly felt pity for herself, pity that Robbie had wronged her, again, and that she'd become a woman so scarcely loved.

When she had confronted Robbie, he played dumb. He said he didn't know what she was talking about, he hadn't been the one to sell the house. It had been the same way when she figured out he was using. He'd denied and denied, tried to make her feel the fool. She left his apartment, crying, in a rage. He called her a few days later, high, and she went during her lunch hour to see him. She found Robbie curled up on the floor of his kitchen, weeping. He told her the truth. He said he was sorry. He owed rent, he owed other money, he was in trouble. He'd needed it. She had held him, and he'd wet her work vest with his tears. No one else knew what it was to see a man you loved so reduced, to be in the presence of the one you'd chosen and still to feel him as an absence, a missing thing, although you had him close. The last thing he needed was to be punished, no matter what Hank or Ruth said. Every time she punished him, she punished herself, the girls. Hadn't the years taught her that?

She had kissed him once, softly, and then again. She stopped before he could get the wrong idea, before she could get carried away. It wouldn't take much. His smell, his warm skin, his yawning need — it tore through her. Maybe that's what it was like with his drugs. If she gave in, she knew she would never be able to say no again.

At home, Margarita and Diane were watching a teen drama with their arms wrapped around each other. The show was about teenagers climbing into each other's bedroom windows, and Lacey May didn't have the heart to object. Hank was in the bedroom avoiding her, Noelle already downstairs. Lacey May poured herself a coffee, lit a cigarette. She called Ruth just to have someone to speak to, but no one answered.

Margarita pretended not to watch her mother from the couch. She had never known her mother to smoke inside the house; she didn't rise to crack the window. The teenage couple was kissing on the screen, and Margarita tried to focus on memorizing their movements, one lip sliding under another, a mouth opening wide, a flicker of a tongue.

Jenkins wobbled into the room, and Diane patted the couch, called for him to jump up. The old dog couldn't manage it, so she scooped him up between them. The girls watched one of the rebuffed lovers — he'd caught his girlfriend and his best friend kissing — row across a creek.

"We should go get Noelle," Diane said. "She's missing it."

Margarita rolled her eyes. "Noelle doesn't know what's good. I don't know why she's in that play. She doesn't even like TV."

"She's the stage manager."

"That's cause Noelle always has to be the boss."

"So do you."

"Shush."

Margarita snuck another glance at her mother at the kitchen table. Lacey May had her eyes shut, the cigarette pressed between her lips, her head tilted back.

Margarita leaned to whisper in her sister's ear. "Mama would have been a good actress."

"How come? Cause she's pretending she isn't mad?"

"Because she's beautiful," Margarita said. "Even when she's sad."

Hank made dinner: steak smothered in onions, with buttered peas and carrots. Noelle didn't come up when they called, so the four of them sat at the table, shoving food around their plates. Even Hank didn't try to close the silence, and it worried Diane. Maybe he was going to leave them, too. They were at the table when they heard the high pitch of Robbie's whistle from the front porch.

"You invited him?" Hank said.

"Of course I didn't."

"Well, something you did must have made him feel welcome."

"Girls, go downstairs," Lacey May said.

"But Papi —" said Diane.

"Right fucking now."

The girls left in a flurry. Margarita climbed onto her bunk bed, and Diane nestled next to Noelle, who was on the pullout, flipping through a stack of papers. Margarita could tell Noelle wasn't really reading. She was doing what they were all doing: straining to listen to what was going on upstairs.

"You skipped dinner," Margarita said.

"I already ate."

"With Duke?"

"Nope."

"You don't like him anymore?" said Diane. "But he's so tall."

"Did you know love changes your brain, chickadee? I don't want to have a brain like Duke's. Besides, I like someone else more."

Margarita cackled from her top bunk. "Your life is like that show."

361

"No, *their* life is like that show." Noelle pointed up at the ceiling. "It's a soap opera."

"That's not funny," Margarita said. "Papi has nothing. He's all alone. And now Mama is going to send him to jail."

"Papi's going back to jail?" said Diane.

"Oh, shut up. You watch too many shows," Noelle said.

"And you're a big old slut."

Noelle sprang up as if she might slap her, and Margarita jumped down from the top bunk to show she wasn't afraid.

"Girls!" Lacey May called from upstairs. "Your father wants to speak to you."

They found Robbie by the front door, as if he hadn't moved any farther into the house since he arrived. He was wearing a red shirt, unbuttoned too low. A gold chain swung from his neck. He smiled at them, and he was missing a tooth: his left canine. Margarita and Noelle hung back while Diane fell into him, wrapped her arms around his waist. Lacey May and Hank left the room.

"Mis hijas!" Robbie said. "It's been so long. Have you missed me?"

The girls murmured their assent.

"I brought you presents. Come sit down."

They saw then the large paper bags on the couch, Jenkins prostrate between them.

362

"That old dog doesn't recognize me," Robbie said, sitting beside him, ruffling his ears.

"We haven't seen you in weeks," Noelle said, but Robbie seemed not to hear her. He picked up one of the bags.

"First, Diane — I got you something, preciosa."

Robbie placed her palms, faceup, on his knees, and handed her a long, shimmery box. He told her to open it.

A gold medallion hung from a chain so thin Diane worried she'd break it. The medallion looked misshapen, like an oblong coin. A pale green stone glittered at the center.

"It's an *esmeralda,*" Robbie said. "They're from Colombia. I used to have one — a ring, but it was stolen. But that won't happen to you. Not with the life you'll have, mi niña."

He took up the necklace, and Diane bowed her head solemnly so he could fasten it. She held the medallion between her fingers, turning the emerald in the light. He called Noelle next, and she stepped forward, her arms crossed in front of her.

Robbie shook a jacket from one of the bags. It had boxy shoulders, a few tortoiseshell buttons, the leather pebbled and black.

He held it against Noelle's body, and it was so long it reached her knees. Noelle started shaking her head. Robbie went on smiling at her.

"For your concerts," he said. "So you can look like those roqueros you like to go and see."

"How could you steal from us?"

Robbie held up his hands plaintively. Noelle stomped her foot, repeated herself.

"The house is mine, mi hijita. I paid for it. You all lived there, but I paid for it."

"That's not true. Mama's been finding renters."

"You don't know how grown-up things work yet, Noelle. That's why you're so angry, because you don't understand."

"I understand perfectly. I know what you need the money for."

"Your mother and me, we worked it out."

Noelle picked up the leather jacket, stuffed her face into it, and screamed. Then she flung it to the floor and ripped out of the room. They heard the basement door slam. Robbie picked up the leather jacket, folded it neatly, and set it on the couch.

Margarita was the only one left, and she felt her whole body pulsating. She was furious, but she wasn't sure with whom — Noelle for being a brat, her mother for leaving them alone with Robbie, or herself for being the last to get a gift.

"And for you, pepita," Robbie said, "I got half a present."

Margarita felt herself sink. Of course she would get only half. Of course she was the one who would be forgotten.

"Now, now," Robbie started. "You know I love all my girls. I love you all the same. But you, Margarita — you're the one who when I look at, I see myself. I look at you and say, *There's the one who came out like me.*"

Robbie opened the box in his hands, lifted out one gold ring, and then another. The first was small, and he pushed it onto Margarita's ring finger where it spun, so he moved it to her middle finger. It was a signet engraved with an *R.* He slipped the other ring onto his pinkie; it was engraved with a cursive *M.*

Margarita held her ring aloft, watched it gleam in the pale light. How had her father known? The way she saw the two of them? The way she saw herself? Noelle and Diane were both so clearly made of their mother, not just in terms of their looks, but in their temperaments. But every time her father left, she fought the feeling that she should have been going with him, that they belonged together. She was his blood, and he was hers. All along, without saying so, he had known.

She went to thank him but couldn't speak. She felt that she would burst.

"You keep that one," he said. "And I'll keep mine. That way no matter where I am, I'll be with you. That way we'll always be together."

After Robbie left, the girls went back to their TV, and Lacey May climbed under the sheets. She didn't want to talk to Hank, and he huffed around the bedroom, putting on his pajamas, straightening things, until he couldn't hold his tongue any longer.

"We could use that money, you know. Your daughters could use it one day."

"Robbie promised to give me some for the girls."

"And you believe him?"

"Stay out of it, Hank."

"I'm your husband."

"And so was Robbie. I've got my business with him, and I've got my business with you."

"You're going to lose them."

"Is that right? But if I take Robbie to court and ruin his life, I'll get to keep them?"

"You're focusing on all the wrong things. That campaign. Helping Robbie. Your girls need you."

"That campaign is for the girls! One day, Margarita and Diane will go to that school. I'm doing this for all of them. To protect them."

"Maybe they don't need protecting anymore. You got them out. Maybe their futures are already fine."

"A woman's future is never fine," Lacey May said, and left the room.

Margarita and Diane were sitting on the couch, the dog at their feet, as if Robbie had never shown up, and there had been no disturbance at all. They were wearing their new jewelry. Noelle was nowhere to be found, but this time, Lacey May knew not to go looking.

She sat beside her daughters, reached her arm around their shoulders. To her astonishment, they nuzzled close.

On the screen, a flimsy blond girl was throwing men with bloody jowls against brick walls in an alley. The girls leaned toward the glowing set. The blond girl on-screen yanked out a pointy stake from the sleeve of her leather jacket, turned toward her assailants, blew them to dust, one by one. The girls gasped; they clapped. Here, it was plain to see: her girls wanted a hero. How could Hank ever expect her to step away and leave them be?

During commercials, a preview aired of the late-night news. There had been a drive-by shooting on the east side. A house party, a teenage girl struck dead through a window, someone who had nothing to do with the dispute. They showed her picture, the big purple scrunchie in her hair, her face too young. Lacey May sucked her teeth, and shook her head, but before she could say anything out loud about girls at parties, crime in the city, she had an idea. It was fire bright, the kind she'd been needing all along.

At the next rehearsal, Noelle didn't sit with Gee in the audience. Instead she left the auditorium during the breaks and wandered back in right before Mr. Riley called them to scene. She seemed distracted, missed giving a few cues. Gee wondered what was wrong with her, but she didn't meet his eyes when he looked in her direction.

Mr. Riley seemed to sense her malaise, the way it penetrated the room, because he cut their rehearsing short and suggested they play an energizer to end. It was a half-hearted round of Zip Zap Zop, and Adira stood next to Gee, whispering in his ear.

"You like her. And if she doesn't know

already, she'll know soon. You keep staring at her."

"I don't date white girls," Gee said, as if it were policy, although he'd never dated anybody.

"She's not a white girl. Her last name is *Ventura*."

Gee shrugged, zinged one of his castmates.

"Don't be so backwards. I've never seen you talk so much to anybody."

"She's the one who does most of the talking."

"Unh-hunh."

"And she's not talking to me today."

They were still playing when the auditorium doors burst open and Noelle's boyfriend swooped in. He was a tall boy who wore rubber bracelets, his red hair sculpted into spikes. He had on a pair of reflective shades, even if they were indoors. His knee-length jacket fanned behind him; a wallet chain swung from the belt loop of his pants. He sat in the front row, as if his presence wouldn't perturb them, disrupt their flow. He was skinny and menacing and pale.

It was Noelle who eventually said, "Mr. Riley, it's ten past," and Mr. Riley looked deflated, told everyone they were free to go.

Noelle met Duke, and he shoved his face

at hers to kiss her, slipped a hand into the back pocket of her jeans. It was territorial and nasty. Gee looked away. Adira caught him and raised her eyebrows at him. Her face seemed to say, *Yeah right, you don't like her.*

Adira linked arms with Shawn, and they walked out of the auditorium together, laughing. Somehow, they had coupled up. Gee had missed the signs. Maybe it was the real reason so many of them had joined the play. When it came to love, few people could resist. Everyone wanted it badly, whether they said so or not. Even his mother was different when it came to Ray: his memory, his name. But even that love hadn't lasted; she had put him away like a secret. People loved each other for a while, then they forgot; they buried one another.

It was funny that Gee had been cast as the only man in the play who was really loved. Angelo and the duke both wound up with women, too, but those couplings were strange. It was one of the reasons Mr. Riley said *Measure for Measure* was a problem play; it ended with marriages instead of deaths, so it wasn't a tragedy, but it was too dark, too unsettling, to be a comedy either.

Gee was the last to leave, and he slipped out the back door so he wouldn't run into his castmates on the front steps, hanging out and making plans for Cedar's or the mall. He'd sneak out to the parking lot and find Linette, ride home, race up to his room, where he'd lie down first thing and rub himself fast and rough, a picture of some nameless woman in his head, one with big nipples, an open mouth, one who was saying his name.

He was starting his daydream, the illusion keeping him company, when he ran into Noelle, crouched against the side of the school building. She was poking a twig at the underside of her big boots, scraping off grass and congealed dirt. Her mouth was twisted into a frown, and she was red-faced, as if she'd been screaming.

"What are you doing?"

"Waiting for you," she said, and Gee didn't believe her.

"What about your boyfriend? You left with him."

"He stopped by cause he was helping our mothers do something for the campaign. You know that bulletin board outside the main office where parents can post notices? Apparently, they took it over, papered it three inches thick. The secretary is the only one who stays in the main office this late, and she's a sympathizer. She goes to Duke's

371

parents' church."

"What did they put up?"

"Flyers. Stupidity. I don't know. I almost dumped him on the spot."

"Why didn't you?"

Noelle shrugged, and Gee understood. If he had somebody, he couldn't imagine dumping them either.

"He talks about *the transfers* like they're not kids we know. Like he's not talking about you and Adira and my friends."

"Maybe he does know who he's talking about."

Noelle paused for a moment, considering it.

"Will you go with me to see what they posted? It feels less scary if I go with you."

"All right," Gee said, not because he wanted to see, but because he wanted to be with Noelle.

At the front entrance, a few kids loitered on the steps, laughing and punching each other on the shoulders, running around the railing. The parents who had papered the bulletin board were gone now, and so was Duke.

The halls were empty. Besides the drama club, the only students who stayed at school this late were the jocks, and they were still off practicing at the fields. The school officer nodded at them as they reentered, genial and disinterested in whatever they were up to. Gee wondered if he'd done the same as the parents traipsed in with their stacks of paper and rolls of tape.

When they turned in to the hall toward the main office, they saw the walls of the corridor were covered in huge white sheets of paper, some as long as Gee's torso. They spread from the baseboards of the floor up to the ceiling. They were taped up in crooked rows, haphazard and overlapping, so the pages seemed to have erupted from the walls.

Gee and Noelle crept deeper into the hallway, and Gee saw that they weren't flyers; they were newspaper clippings the parents had printed and blown up. It took him a few moments to realize the pattern, but the headlines gave it away.

First Shooting Death of the Year read one. *Former High School Teacher Charged with Assault. Eleven-Year-Old in Critical Condition. Late-Night Flat Tire Scam: What You Need to Know.*

The articles spanned years. Burglaries, kidnappings, drug busts, all on the east side. Gee could see they had printed and posted many of the articles more than once; the duplicates were of the most gruesome stories.

Noelle gasped and covered her mouth with one hand, reached for Gee with the other, but he was already drifting ahead of her. He felt his blood rushing in his ears, his feet lifting off the ground, his vision razor sharp. He scanned the walls.

There was no order to the posters, neither chronology nor class of crime. They had included things as minor as car pileups on a busy boulevard, as dire as a child caught in the crossfire in a drive-by. The sheets were large and washed-out, the print fuzzy, the photographs distorted.

Gee must have found the article, but it seemed as if it had found him. The large print of the headline was a terrible beacon calling him forward. *Local Man Murdered on Ewing Street.* Gee hadn't known the street name. He'd never seen an article about that day.

Raymond Gilbert, it said. *Twenty-four,* it said. There was no mention of Superfine, or the other article that was soon to run in the same paper, as if they were different men, the baker and the murder victim, Ray and Ray.

Wilson wasn't named; neither was *the assailant.* There was no mention of the blood, or all the big pieces of furniture on the lawn. An image sailed into Gee's mind: a boxy pink armchair, an oak dresser. He had run among them, as if in a maze. The article mentioned a disagreement, a debt. The assailant had done time before for assault and battery, illegal possession of a deadly weapon. He owed alimony. In the altercation, no one else had been harmed.

A photograph of Ray hovered between the two slender columns of the story. The picture was inky, too granular to really give an impression of his face, but he looked younger than Gee ever remembered him being. Had he been that young when he died, when he was his father? He looked as if someone had taken the picture before he was ready, his mouth only beginning to smile. It was stiff, posed, like a high school portrait.

Gee had seen many articles like this, so many photographs of people he had no trouble believing were gone because to him they had never existed. But to see Ray's face was different; it was as if a faraway fact, a thing he had known without knowing, had resurfaced, monstrous and real.

Raymond Gilbert had left behind a girl-friend and his girlfriend's son. It didn't say he'd been his father, and it didn't mention his name, except for Gilbert, his surname, but that alone wouldn't be enough for anyone to know.

That was what he wondered: whether anyone would know. Gee felt himself tremble. He slumped to the ground. He wished Ray had never died, and even more he wished he'd never had a father who had died. He was disloyal; he was selfish. He lowered his head to the ground, felt the cool tile of the floor. His teeth fastened together, his jaw sealed tight. He felt his ribs heave and contract as he tried to breathe.

He heard Noelle calling him, her voice far, getting farther, even though he knew she must be getting closer. She was watching him. She was reaching for him. Her hands on his shoulders. If he wasn't careful, she would see. Gee found a way to steady himself. He pushed off his hands. He stood up.

13

The hospital chapel was one austere room. A golden crucifix was mounted on a pine-wood altar, folding chairs arrayed before it in narrow rows. Robbie sat in the rear beneath a painting of a stained-glass window. The sanctuary was airless, musty.

He had decided to pray. In the derelict room, he said to God all of the things he'd lose the nerve to say to Lacey May when he saw her.

In the years since the divorce, he had never stopped believing they would find their way to one another. In his vision of death, when it came, they were together. One of them would go first, the other soon after. They would be old. It wasn't such a crazy dream.

He didn't doubt that she had learned to love Hank, in the way one loved a distant relative, or a dog, or an old lady from church — it was love that was mostly fondness, gratitude, the vague desire to see someone again. It was mild, and it was pleasant, but there was a limit. It wasn't what he and Lacey May had, the feeling he was sure she still harbored for him, the feeling she would give herself over to if he were ever ready for her, suitable, but he never was.

Noelle had left, then Margarita, and Diane, and he had missed every window to win her back. It was his own fault. He would wish that he had never started, but it would be pointless. Prayers couldn't undo time, undo who you were.

If he were ever good enough one day, what would it matter that he'd left her alone for so long? What would it matter that he'd stolen from her? She wouldn't hold it against him if he were her man again, if she could trust him, if he weren't so useless. She had been good to him, never kept the girls away, only herself, which he understood. If he could have kept away from himself, he would have, too.

There were times he had gotten close. He worked, saved money, blew it, started over again. He got fired, moved on, got fired again. In between, there were women; there were apartments; there were days that seemed like the bottom but weren't. The highs weren't what kept him alive; it was Lacey May. She was the reason he went on cycling through motel rooms and cities and years. The girls didn't need him, not anymore, maybe not ever. But Lacey, the promise of Lacey, of getting clean and loving her again, was enough to go on painting cars, checking his brakes and changing his tires, brushing his teeth, stamping out his cigarettes at night so he wouldn't set fire to the bed.

He had meant to pray about the cancer, but he had wound up talking about himself. What was there to say to God? *Please don't take her?* Death would come for them all. *Help me let her go?* That was impossible, even for the Heavenly Father. Finally, he prayed, *Not yet,* and, *Por favor, Señor, give her a little time for me.* It was selfish, but there was no use in lying to God. The Lord already knew it all, knew Robbie didn't deserve anything. But He also knew that Lacey May had been his wife all along; in his heart, he hadn't betrayed her. That wasn't nothing.

The chapel doors creaked open, and Robbie turned to see Margarita, his tall girl in knee-high boots. She wore a skirt that hardly covered her thighs, a flimsy shirt with big sleeves. He put on a big smile for her, although he ached everywhere: his knuckles, behind his eyes, his gums. It hurt to be this sober.

Margarita sat beside him, her skirt disappearing underneath her. He didn't ask how she'd known where he'd be. The girl had a sixth sense. The rest of them, they were always underestimating her.

"Where's your sisters?"

"Noelle isn't coming. Diane and Alma are already in the room."

"La novia?"

Margarita nodded.

Robbie sighed. He hadn't been surprised by the news about Diane; his American daughters had their American lives. They were adults. And even he had to admit Alma, and that hair — she was really something.

"Noelle's going to miss me if she doesn't come."

"You're not leaving again, are you? Diane's paid up the motel through the end of the week."

"Why wouldn't my own daughter want to see me?"

"She said it's too much for her. She's just being dramatic."

Robbie smiled mischievously. "I wonder where she gets it from."

"The both of you." Margarita was sharp and didn't return his smile, but Robbie didn't mind. They had all found their ways to survive; Margarita had hers.

He had never asked her how she got in touch with Amado's men, whether they had given her any trouble. He had never confessed that when she and Noelle arrived at his room, two hours southwest of town, he was expecting them to be a delivery, and he was nearly jumping out of his skin, eager, waiting.

Margarita crossed her arms, and Robbie saw that on her pinkie she was wearing the ring he had given her — the *R* etched into gold.

"My God," he said, pointing. "You still have it."

"I just got it from Mama's house. She saved it for me."

Robbie felt a little pained she'd left it behind, never took it with her to California.

"And yours?"

"Lost," Robbie said, although he couldn't explain how. He might have left it in a soap dish in a motel. Someone might have wrenched it from his finger, robbed him one night he was high. He might have pawned it. It might have been ten years since it went missing, or five, one. He wasn't sure.

If Margarita was disappointed, she didn't show it on her face. "Come on," she said. "Mama is waiting."

"Maybe I should leave." He made up a lie about how Lacey May probably didn't want to see him. He knew she'd been asking for him, but he was terrified to see her sick, to see her irritated with him, to see how far they were from his dreams of growing old together.

"Oh, shut up," Margarita said, and Robbie was startled, chastened by her. "Stop pretending you don't matter."

"All right."

Robbie stood and crossed himself. They left the chapel together.

Lacey May was out of the bed, sitting in a chair in the corner of the room. She wore a thin robe the color of wine, and she had crossed her bare legs. They were freshly shaven, lotioned, and Robbie couldn't remember the last time he had seen so much of her body. Her legs were wider, the threads of her veins thick behind her knees, at her ankles. She was eating grapes from a carton and looked more or less like herself, perhaps a bit paler. Hank and Diane were sitting on the windowsill, and Alma was beside Lacey May, perched on the arm of the chair. Together, they pinched the red grapes from their stems.

It was uncannily placid, the television playing the weather report on mute. Clear skies. High winds.

"Robbie." Lacey May smiled at him. She rose to meet him, and Alma offered her arm to help, but Lacey May was fine.

Robbie shuffled forward to meet her. They embraced, and she smelled of antiseptic, the grainy hospital sheets. When she returned to the chair, he kneeled beside her, and she offered him a fistful of grapes. They were sweet and hard; they burst against his teeth.

Robbie saw they had a spread laid out on the bench at the foot of the vacated bed. A platter of waxy orange cheese, a box of crackers, a fragmented chocolate bar, broccoli, a bottle of ranch dressing.

"It's like a party," Robbie said because he wasn't sure what else to say. He flashed smiles at them all — Alma, Margarita, Diane, Lacey, even at Hank, who hadn't turned to look at him, hadn't even nodded his acknowledgment when Robbie entered the room. He was tapping on his phone.

Now that he was here, Robbie wanted to make them laugh, wanted to help them see how good it was to all be together. There was too much you couldn't control in life, too many terrible things. They should be happy, even if only for a little while, even just for right now.

The doctors had said Lacey May could lose her vision, her ability to speak, if the tumor went on growing. But for now, the swelling was down, and she'd be going home soon. She'd come back in for radiation; they would zap the tumor, and she'd get better, go into remission. Or, she would need surgery, and they would cut open her skull and lift out the mass. Or chemo. Or nothing would work, and she'd die. Robbie didn't like her odds. But Lacey May seemed animated, calm. Unguarded. She grinned at him, and he wondered what kind of drugs they were giving her.

"Have you seen Diane's house yet?" Lacey May asked. "It's beautiful. It's got land, just like our old one."

Robbie felt the girls stiffen at the mention of the house. Even Hank looked up from his phone, which he had been toying with as if it were totally engrossing.

"It's brick," Lacey May said. "Not blue like ours was. But I think they should paint it. Gray. All the new houses are gray. The ones that are selling downtown? They're all the same shade of gray, and they have pretty silver house numbers, lanterns on the lawn."

Lacey May twisted her mouth to the side, as if she were about to whisper a secret. "I warned Alma already. I told her, be careful with my daughter. She's a Ventura. Even if your name is on that deed, you better know a good lawyer."

Lacey May threw her head back and laughed, and the girls looked on in horror. Hank turned back to his phone, and Robbie decided he might as well laugh along with Lacey May.

"She's delirious," Margarita said. "She doesn't know who she's talking to."

"I can hear you, you know. And I know exactly what's going on," Lacey May said. "I'm just happy because I'm with my family. Everyone is here — or, almost, once Noelle arrives."

Hank mumbled from the window that he was off in search of a coffee, and he left before anyone could stop him. Lacey May watched him go.

"You know how they say when you're going to die, everything is suddenly clear?" Lacey May leaned into Robbie, as if he were the only one in the room.

"Nothing is clear," she said. "None of it. Nothing makes sense. But when I woke up this morning, I was happy that I was going to see you. It's been years, Robbie, hasn't it? But it's the most natural thing in the world to see you. After everything that's happened, I want you close now. You're my family. I'm so glad the girls could find you."

Alma and Diane were the ones now exchanging looks. Diane invented an excuse about checking on the car. They left, and Margarita got the idea. She hesitated, unsure whether her parents ought to be left alone. They were acting more like dopey teenagers than fifty-year-old exes who had been separated half their lives. Plus, her mother was probably high. Still, she gathered up her purse and left, said she was off for a walk and green tea. Lacey May and Robbie hardly looked after her as she went. Lacey May clasped both of Robbie's hands in hers. They were cold, and he wanted to breathe onto them.

"Where have you been?"

"Oh, here and there."

She stared at him, their hands locked.

"I would have come eventually," he said. "I wouldn't have made you wait too long."

Lacey May nodded, although they both knew it wasn't true. Robbie could easily have waited too long, waited until she had died, if that's how things would go. She didn't say this. She kissed his hands, firmly, across the knuckles, once, and Robbie found himself confused, heart hammering. He imagined Lacey May slipping off her robe, tucking herself naked into his arms, the hospital room door still open. She did none of these things, but she kept his hands cocooned in hers.

He decided he might as well tell her. "Lacey, I still think about you and me together."

"Me too. I think about those good years we spent in the house. Sometimes, I wake up, and I've been dreaming we're all back there."

"I mean right now," Robbie said. "Or in the future."

"The future is for the girls, Robbie. I stopped worrying about myself, dreaming, a long time ago. The day I knew I couldn't wait until you got out was the day I knew it was over for us. That's why it's good, in a way, that the girls haven't settled down yet — well, Margarita and Diane. They'll never go through what I did. When I lost you, I lost everything except what you'd left for me."

"The girls?"

"The girls and the house."

Robbie didn't see the use in apologizing for the house now. Lacey May was looking at him too calmly, her smile too easy. Robbie felt that he wanted to kiss her, but she wasn't signaling clear enough that that was what she wanted, too, and he didn't want her to turn him away. Was this all she wanted — to hold his hands? Or was she ready to admit now what he had long known — that it had always been, would always be, the two of them?

Robbie decided he ought to offer her something to look forward to, a promise. Maybe it would help her, carry her through the treatments. Maybe it would even be true.

"I can get clean," he said. "I know you need me now. Lacey, if you need me —"

She shook her head and shushed him. "I have what I need from you, my love."

Robbie felt his heart in his ears. He was breathing hard. "What are you saying, Lacey May? Is there something you're trying to tell me?"

Lacey May took his hands, pressed them to her heart.

"You're not listening, Robbie. I'm not trying to say anything. There's nothing I'm trying to change."

The taxi ride from the airport was more beautiful than Nelson remembered. The trees were green and amber, lustrous. They sheltered the road from the construction on either side, the tractors churning through sunken sand pits. He stared at the leaves, the unbroken sky. It filled him with momentary ease to behold something so beautiful. Soon, he was passing downtown, its meager small-town skyline, the light-up billboard beckoning drivers to take the exit toward Main Street. The car pushed on west, toward the edge of the county. It turned off the freeway and rattled down a gravel driveway. Nelson willed his calm to return. He would need it to convince her, to convince himself that everything would be fine. He repeated his intention, over and over to himself, like a mantra, *I am here to get my wife. We're going home.*

He paid in cash, the multicolored fan of euros still clipped inside his wallet. The taxi was climbing back uphill when the door to the brick ranch house clattered open, and there stood Noelle. She was mostly undressed, in a silver camisole and shorts, and a fat flannel robe that didn't belong to her, or hadn't the last time he had seen her. It had been nearly eight weeks, the longest they'd gone without each other. It was unnerving to look at her, to see how familiar every inch of her was, even from across the yard: the hair piling on her shoulders, the silhouette of her thighs, even the way she was twisting her lips into a frown, holding her arms close to her chest.

He strode toward her, and he couldn't stop himself from smiling. He had missed her. He loved her, and she still loved him. That would be enough to see them through.

She didn't move from the porch, didn't uncross her arms, not even when he reached her, wrapped himself around her. He kissed her cheeks. She was stiff and still, didn't say anything as she opened the screen door and led him into the house.

It was warm and bright inside, the windows facing the woods and the lawn, the crop of crimson and orange leaves on the grass. The remains of breakfast were on the table, different items of women's clothing flung around the house on hooks, the backs of chairs. It was ordinary and disorderly, more inviting than anywhere he'd been in weeks.

"What are you doing here?" she asked finally. She flung herself down at the table, where she lifted a piece of toast to her mouth, bit the edge, took a long time to swallow it down.

Nelson explained that he'd spoken to Hank; he had told him she wasn't at the hospital this morning and given him the address. Noelle looked at him, bewildered. She'd never known him to be one to contact her family, let alone Hank.

"I thought it better not to involve your sisters. If I told them, they might have warned you, and you'd have left."

"Don't I have that right? This is bad timing. My mother is dying, maybe."

"How are you feeling?"

Noelle laughed. "A feelings question? From the man who never lets himself feel a thing?"

Nelson refused to take the bait and said nothing, although she was wrong about him. He could feel, and feel, and feel, even when it did no good, even when there was no bottom.

Noelle went on. "It was a lot easier enduring my family when I knew you and I had our own. I could tell myself we'd made something different. It was like having a back door." She poured herself orange juice from the carton. He reached for her trembling hand.

"Nells," he said.

"I'm surprised you're here. I know how you feel about North Carolina."

"I came for us."

Soon, she was crying, and Nelson wiped

her eyes with his fingers. It was a little thing, but the gesture made her cry harder. He caught her fingers and kissed them, and she crawled into his lap. He held her as she wept, and then she was kissing him, and Nelson was kissing her back. She was frantic, quick, and Nelson helped her to slow down. His tongue touched hers, and she tasted of the morning, her sleepiness, the sour juice. Her shampoo, her lotion were different, but they weren't enough to have changed her smell, the one he knew: the composite of her scalp and her skin, the particular funk of her sweat. She wrapped her legs around his waist, wet his face with her tears. He picked her up, with effort, and carried her down the hall. She shed her robe, her top, and directed him into the bedroom where he could lay her down.

They didn't discuss it; they didn't use anything. He was still her husband, she his wife. They moved together for a short time. It was all liquid and soft muscle, a warm mess. He kept his eyes open, and Noelle's face was somber, focused. He wanted to make her feel better, to offer what pleasure he could. He came with a groan, and Noelle started crying again. He wanted to keep going, and he said so, but she rolled away from him and covered her face with her hands.

He tried to lift her fingers away to kiss her. "I'm sorry," he said. She stared at the ceiling and shook, and, eventually, he resigned himself to shut up, lie beside her, and let her sob. It wasn't easy. He could sense her feelings creeping into him. They were indistinct, amorphous, and they seeped like a poison. He closed his eyes and breathed. Eventually, her crying subsided to hiccups, and she turned to him.

"I've been trying to find an answer. I won't let this be one of the things in life that you just never understand. Is it because you never got the chance to be with other women? Were we too young? Did you get tired of our life? What was it?"

Nelson tried to shush her, and Noelle snapped.

"I don't need to be calmed down. I need you to answer me."

"It just happened. I let it happen."

"That's not good enough. I deserve the truth."

An old line returned to her, but she couldn't place it — *Truth is truth, to the end of reckoning.*

"It felt good to be wanted. There's nothing more to it."

"Bullshit. I've always wanted you."

She was right, in a way, but Nelson

couldn't see the good in explaining any-more. Jemima had wanted him in a way he found irresistible. She wanted him because of whom she suspected he might become. She wanted his name, a story for her life about the weeks she'd spent in Paris with the artist, the photographer. She was a mir-ror to reflect the image he had fashioned for himself. With Noelle, he couldn't be anyone else. He was always himself, in focus, too clear. It was sweet, but it wasn't titillating. Is that what she wanted to hear?

"I wanted to get away from my life," he said. It was the mildest version of the truth he could conjure. "I wanted to be someone else. After the miscarriage —"

Noelle sprang up in the bed, naked and fierce. "Is that where it started? You've been confused for a long time, sweetheart. And it isn't my fault." She rose and dressed quickly, violently. She left the room.

Nelson found her on the beat-up turquoise couch, covered in pillows and blankets, dog hair. The sun stuttered through a spotted window. He sat beside her. She spoke without looking at him.

"I can't forgive you for this, Nelson. I can't forget."

"You can forget anything, Noelle. You haven't given yourself a chance."

"I've had time to think. I've been with my sisters."

"You mean, your mother."

"She has nothing to do with this. I haven't told her what you did, and I doubt I ever will."

Nelson's jaw went tight. "I don't want to live without you."

"Neither do I, but I'm not the kind of woman to just go on after a thing like this."

"So, you're going to leave me based on principle? You're too hard, Noelle."

"I thought it was the opposite, and I was too soft?"

"You're both," Nelson said, and he didn't intend it as meanness. Neither of them was perfect. She was too brutal and too tender all at once.

"You don't get to tell me how to be anymore."

"Why not? We've always tried to push each other, to make each other better, haven't we?"

"I never promised to make you better. I was your wife. I promised to love you, and I kept my promise."

Her voice was calm and stern, her face swollen and serene. Nelson sat beside her, chastened. He had seen this Noelle — the cool composure that signaled she had shut a door inside herself. He had seen her do it when the doctor delivered the news to them, and she'd gone perfectly still, thanked her for the explanation. He had seen her take note of anyone who had been discourteous to him at a party, or a dinner, and she'd grow taller somehow, superior, turn a chill on them that let them know they'd never be in her good graces again. It was the way she had kept herself apart from Lacey May, without cruelty, but with a vicious, elegant coldness. She had done it even with her father, whom she tolerated but had learned to no longer need. In some ways, it was a comfort to him, to see the old Noelle return; there was that spirit, that steadfastness he'd loved. But it was then that he knew it was all over. For years, she'd had one conviction about him; now she had another. She wouldn't be weeping Noelle, or rapturous Noelle, or sweet, or naked, or curious Noelle with him ever again. She had closed a door that he couldn't force open if he tried. In this way, they were alike; Noelle knew how to put any part of herself away.

He reached for her hand, and she let him take it. There was more that he wanted to say to her. He said it all in his head. They sat locked together, as if she were listening, until Noelle took her hand away.

"I ought to go and see my mother."

"I thought you'd decided not to see her."

"I was avoiding my father, actually. I didn't want to feel any worse than I already did, but there's no point in that now. Besides, what more is there for us to say?"

It was terrifying to hear her speak so matter-of-factly about the end of their life together. He wanted to say so, to beg her not to leave, but it would be pathetic, make no difference. He couldn't fathom that they'd ever be done talking to one another. He put the thought out of his mind. There was only this moment and the next. There was nothing else that he could do.

"I'll head to the airport then."

"You're going to turn around and go right back to Europe?"

"What else is there for me here?"

Noelle was sunlit and sedate. "I wish you wouldn't think that way," she said. "So this is good-bye."

She walked him to the door; in a daze, he followed; he went to hug her, and she shook her head; she opened the door and shut it, uneventfully; he found himself alone on the porch.

He leaned against the frame of the house to steady himself. He strained to hear Noelle inside the house, just on the other side of the door. He heard only insects and birdsong, the rush of air through the trees. He watched the woods, the lean of the pines. He felt himself sway inwardly.

When he had left for Paris, she cried and cried. Usually, they said their good-byes swiftly, unsentimentally, but she had been crying so hard as she searched for her keys to drive him, he said it was better if she stayed; he'd call a car. The truth was he wanted to leave her quickly, didn't want to watch her sob. It made him feel desperate, and if he wasn't careful, he would say something he'd regret: *It's been months* or *I can't take away your pain* or *You're only hurting yourself.* But he had held his tongue except to say he wanted to ride alone.

In an instant, she had calmed herself, tranquil on the bed, her legs folded beneath her. Perhaps that had been the first moment that she started to let him go. *I hope you find what you're looking for over there,* she had said, and he had felt that she could see right through him.

He had left, longing for Europe as an interlude. The book, the play, and the other woman were all meant to be temporary. He had planned to come home. Noelle was his life.

He had kept the truth hidden for so long;

it had been his fortune to keep it from her. But now it was out in the open, and he couldn't hide. He was no good, and she knew it.

Hank was sitting on the curb when Noelle arrived at the hospital. He drank from an enormous coffee cup and squinted across the lot. He didn't turn to Noelle, and she wasn't sure whether he genuinely couldn't see her or whether he wanted to be left alone.

"Hey," she called. "What are you doing out here?"

"I thought you weren't coming."

"Nelson found me."

"Must have gone well if you're feeling better and decided to come here."

"Is that why you're here? Cause you feel so good?"

Hank chuckled, and Noelle sat beside him. They stretched their legs into the street, watching the cars that rounded the curb to make sure no one ran them over. Noelle peered into the cup and saw Hank was nearly done. She'd never known him to drink more than half a cup of coffee in the morning and finish the rest once he got home.

"Are you avoiding my father?"

"It's that obvious?"

"I was avoiding him, too," Noelle said. "And my husband, until you interfered." She reached for Hank's cup, took a long swallow of the cold, stale coffee. "My marriage is over. I don't know if I'll ever see him again."

Hank made a disbelieving face. "You think you're through with a person, but you're never through, not when you've loved someone like that."

"You know, I used to hate you and Mama for shacking up as fast as you did. I thought, *How could you leave someone you'd vowed to never leave?* But I see it now. I don't care what I promised. Nelson didn't care if he was ruining our life, and that tells me everything I need to know."

"I won't ask you what he did. I suppose you wouldn't tell me anyway."

"I should be heading back to Georgia. Get my affairs in order."

Hank frowned. "I'm not looking forward to you girls leaving. I've got a feeling about your mother — that she'll only last as long as you all are here. You all keep her strong."

"We keep her mad. That's her life source," Noelle said. "Rage." She laughed. Hank didn't seem amused, and she tried to comfort him. "Don't go and assume the worst.

She's just getting started with her treatments."

Hank shook his head. "I'm not so worried about her dying. You all think about that because you're leaving — you're trying to tell yourself she'll be here when you come back. But I'm thinking about what's ahead right now, for days and days. Probably longer. Mood swings and appointments and treatments. I'll be the one who's with her. I'm the one who's been with her all along."

Noelle hadn't given much thought to all the years Hank and her mother had spent together after she and her sisters left. She hadn't thought about the conversations they had likely had in the dark, or all their mornings and afternoons together, the quiet hours they'd spent in the unceasing, secret waltz of marriage.

She had seen Hank mostly as an interloper; she had never cared to look at him as a husband, a man in love. She reached for his hand.

"Come on," she said. "Let's go and see them."

"I don't know," Hank said, but Noelle was firm.

"You belong there," she said. "That's enough."

If there had been a provisional harmony at Central before, as much as could be expected of any high school teeming with kids from across the county, it started to fracture after the posters. There were two assemblies: the first about the concerned parents, whose actions the principal called shameful. She didn't say the word *white;* she didn't say *black.* She said instead that schools were a place for students' ideas, and not their parents'. After, a league of black girls founded a club called Concerned Students for Justice, but they couldn't get a room assignment for their meetings because they weren't recognized by the school as an official group. Adira started a petition, and the signatures surged toward one hundred before the administration granted them club status, claiming all they'd needed to do in the first place was fill out a form. There was no uproar from the students whose parents had papered the hall. It seemed they mostly wanted to go undetected; they didn't want to upset their parents or be found out by their peers. Still, there was talk, and everyone knew.

The high school carried on with its usual life of cliques and crews, flirting in the lunchroom and kissing in the stairs. There was a pie sale to raise money for the senior trip. The new students came and left by bus; the teachers oversaw their arrivals and departures. In the classrooms, they conducted courteous debates about history and war, clashes that seemed faraway. Mr. Riley counted down the weeks until opening night.

The first instance of graffiti was the N-word in permanent marker inside a stall of the boys' bathroom. The principal called the second assembly to announce an investigation, how seriously they were taking the vandalism, and how it was their duty not to jump to conclusions. It could have been a custodian, a visitor, a student scrawling out rap lyrics, unaware. Then a swastika appeared on a white wall facing the athletic fields, and there were articles in the city paper, a disquieted hush.

The play was an alternate universe where they put on costumes and spoke funny words, and the drama was about whether Claudio would live or die, whether he'd marry Juliet, whether the duke would win Isabella, and Angelo would finally get what he deserved. It was peaceful, mostly, except for the rehearsal when Shawn confronted Beckett, whose father owned the print shop where the concerned parents had made their posters. Beckett had lurched at Shawn, waved a finger in his face and shouted, *Free speech! I've got free speech, don't I?* Shawn had warned him to calm down, his own fists clenched at his sides, until Mr. Riley stepped between them, called everyone to sit in a circle.

He said the play was meant to be a refuge, for everybody; the rehearsals were *a safe space.* And if they all did their jobs, they might be able to *spark a conversation* and provide a service to their community through *the arts.* It was corny and went on for too long, but no one nodded their heads along more vehemently than Noelle and Adira, who sat together, their hands clasped. Noelle had joined Concerned Students for Justice and invited Gee to come. When he had asked what they were planning, Noelle said nobody knew yet; it was mostly a place to talk. He steered clear, but Noelle kept asking. Whenever he said no, she said, *Why won't you come? What's wrong?* and he knew she was fishing for an answer about what had happened that day in the hall. Just thinking of it, the terrible headline *Ewing Street,* made him feel as if the room were being swallowed up, a dark film slowly washing over his eyes.

Noelle found him in the hall one day, between classes, and told him to meet her in the auditorium a half hour before rehearsal. "I'm not asking as your friend," she said. "I'm asking as your stage manager." Then she clomped away in her boots, her ponytail swinging behind her.

When he arrived, she was onstage, kneeling over a long scroll of paper. She was painting prison bars in gray, the gaps between them. She had painted many of the sets mostly by herself, coming early and staying late. She worked as if she believed all the things Mr. Riley said were true and her efforts could make a difference to the school, the parents. She might have been naive, but he couldn't help but admire her. He didn't want to stay away.

"You've been messing up your lines," she said. "I want you to run them with me. There aren't that many, and I know you know them by now."

"Maybe I don't."

Noelle sighed. "You either do or you don't, Gee. Which one is it?"

Gee shrugged, and Noelle shook her head. It was the first time she had shown she was annoyed with him.

"You want to know something?" she said. "I like you, Gee, but I'm not sure you like me."

Gee felt his heart thumping in his ears.

"You don't tell me anything, and I ask you questions, and you shrug, and you mumble, and that isn't how you're supposed to act with your friends."

He deflated at the mention of friendship, although he supposed it was true — they were friends.

She asked what had happened that day in the hall, why he had been so upset, why he hardly spoke a word while they walked back out to the lot to wait for Linette.

"I thought you wanted to run lines," he said.

"Fine." Noelle snatched off the hot-pink scarf she had tied around her neck and re-tied it like a bandanna around her crown. "How about I tell you something first then. Sit down."

He sat beside her, and she told him about her father and his drugs, how he was there sometimes and sometimes he wasn't, about the stupid leather jacket he had given her, the house he'd bought and stolen and sold.

"I hate to say it, but I'm pretty sure he's a bad person. So is my mother. I come from bad people."

"You say it like you're proud."

"I'm not ashamed. I didn't do any of that stuff."

"But once they know, people see you different."

"I don't care how people see me."

"Come on," Gee said.

"I don't. I really fucking don't."

"Well, I'm not you."

"I wouldn't want you to be."

She took his hand and pressed it to her chest, a flat spot at the center, below her throat. It surprised him, filled him with a warm gush of feeling.

"Everybody's got secrets," she said. "Everybody. That's what I love about music, plays. It's everybody's worst business all laid out."

"But you didn't tell me your business — you told me your parents'."

Noelle told him about the abortion.

"Why are you looking at me that way? What, do you think I'm bad now, too?"

Gee shook his head. "My mother got pregnant in high school. If she'd had an abortion, I wouldn't be here."

"Well, she didn't."

"Was it Duke's?"

"It was mine."

"So you're trying to trade or something? A secret for a secret?"

Noelle said nothing, waiting on him. It made him want to tell her everything, as if to tell her here, in the auditorium, might keep the truth safe. He felt that they were somewhere else, far away from the town, as if the auditorium weren't a part of the school at all. It wasn't the place where he'd attended that first town hall. He was different here. He said things aloud he never would have said elsewhere, like, *Death is a fearful thing* and *I am so out of love with life that I will sue to be rid of it.* He could say these things here; they were bone-deep, real, even if someone else had written the lines.

He told her about Ray. He didn't say, *It was an accident.* He didn't say, *He passed on,* because nothing about the way he'd gone was natural. He told her he had been killed.

"He loved me," Gee said. "Even if I don't remember him much. That was his picture on the wall. Did you see it?"

Noelle listened quietly, her arms wrapped

408

around her legs, her chin on her knees.

"You were five?"

"Six."

Noelle reached for Gee and pressed him to her chest. She said nothing as she held him, and Gee felt himself wilt pleasantly, his body losing form against hers.

When she pulled away from him, her face was serious.

"I'm going to help you," she said. "Now let's run those lines."

It was Beckett who saw them together. He'd snuck into the auditorium through the rear to look for a pair of headphones he'd left at the last rehearsal. He knew Noelle and Gee were spending time together, but not alone, not like this. He saw them onstage, too close. He slipped into the wings to hear.

The next day Gee was walking to class when an anonymous white boy shoved him against the lockers. There were two others with him, neither of whom Gee recognized, and they took turns slamming him against the wall. He spoke without thinking, the words spewing out of him. *What the hell are you doing?* and *Get off me.* It was a reflex, too, when he pushed one of the white boys back.

He couldn't see the span of the hallway,

the figures of the other students. There were only these three before him: their cursing faces, their collared shirts. They called him a thug and said he didn't belong at their school, his father was a gangbanger and that's why he was dead. They said he ought to stay away from other people's girls. One of them pushed him so hard Gee's head snapped back, made contact with the steel locker. There was a ringing in his ears.

He swung at one of the boys, landed a punch on his cheek. Gee had scuffled with other kids when he was young, but they had been play fights, and you could quit, complain if someone hit you too hard. You were never in a corner. This was different — clumsy, rough. No way out. They pinned him to the wall. They shook him by the collar, grabbed him by the straps of his backpack, swung him to the ground. Gee collapsed on himself defensively, felt himself being kicked, stomped. They pummeled any part of him they could reach. He heard a girl scream, someone call for a teacher, but Gee couldn't imagine that help would arrive, that anyone would intervene. There was only this moment, the feeling of pressure in his stomach, blows to the side of his face, his shoulder, his groin. The sensation of air being pushed out of him. One eye closing and then another. The boys above him blotting out the light. He tried to get up, but they held him down. He was drowning, and they were water. He struggled, until all went dark.

At the hospital, Jade asked every nurse who came to check on Gee when she could expect an officer to arrive to take down a report. It shouldn't be taking so long; it was protocol. There had been a crime, and they'd better be ready to treat it like one.

They had Gee in the ER, a room sectioned off with hanging sheets. He sat up in the bed, his cheeks swollen, one finger set in a splint, his speech slurred at first from the painkillers. There was a cut over his eye, another on his hand that had been stitched up. Jade had seen a hundred patients, more, receive sutures in places more tender than their hands, but she had still gagged as she watched the doctor seal his flesh with wire.

You're a lucky young man, the doctor had said because all of Gee's X-rays had come back fine. Jade had started yelling and requested a different doctor. They were waiting now for someone new.

Through the haze of the medication, Gee watched her. She was agitated, pacing the small stall. She hardly looked up when

411

another doctor swept aside the privacy curtain and came in. He had gray hair and light eyes, round spectacles. He introduced himself as Dr. Henriquez.

"I used to work with your mother." He offered his hand. "I've always wanted to meet you. I'm sorry it's like this. How are you feeling?"

"I'm all right," Gee said. "When can we go home?"

Jade asked to speak to the doctor privately in the hall, and they stepped beyond the curtain. Gee couldn't make out their back-and-forth, and when they came back in, Jade was wiping her eyes. Dr. Henriquez said he'd find out as soon as he could when Gee could be released. He promised Jell-O and a fresh round of painkillers in the meantime. He winked good-bye and let the curtain fall.

Jade sat in the lone chair next to Gee's bed. "I'm going to kill whoever did this to you," she said.

Gee wanted to warn her she shouldn't be saying that kind of thing — maybe someone was listening, maybe, after everything, she would be the one who wound up in trouble — but he let her rant and rant. He was numb, his head foggy. He knew lots of people who had been beaten up before, but

412

he'd never been one of them. He had survived it; it was over; he was on the other side of it now. What had stuck with him was the feeling of being overpowered. He had been feeble, trapped. There was nothing he could do but give in. He remembered that.

He wasn't expecting to see Noelle when she appeared in the makeshift room, parting the curtains suddenly and thrusting herself among them. She was crying and started crying harder when she saw his face. Gee wondered how beat-up he looked; he hadn't wanted a mirror.

Noelle latched her arms around his neck, and Gee let himself be held. When she pulled away, she turned to Jade and said, "I know who did it. I know who did this to Gee."

She looked familiar, but Jade couldn't place the girl. She wore a pair of battered, mammoth-sized boots, a black vest pierced by a half-dozen safety pins.

The girl explained it had been three boys from the church where Duke Redfield's parents were deacons. They were friends with Duke, knuckleheads acting on his behalf. They'd taken it upon themselves to send a message, although what the message was she couldn't be sure.

"I have an idea," Jade said, but the children didn't seem to be listening. Noelle was holding Gee's hand in hers, and Jade quickly grasped what was going on between them. She staggered out to find León.

Jade lurched through the halls wearily. She felt dizzy, light boned. When they had called her from the school and mentioned the assault, she had braced herself and thought, *My baby is dead.* She flew out of the clinic and did eighty-five, ninety, as she maneuvered down the highway. *Ray,* she prayed as she drove. *Come and help your son.* After all these years, it was still the most natural thing to do, to call on Ray to help her, help them. There was no one else she needed close, to hold her up, so that she could face Gee, survive what those boys had done to him.

Jade found León at the nurse's station surrounded by a cadre of women in scrubs. They were idly chatting, the women smiling, and Jade wanted to shake him for being so at ease, so calm, while her son was beaten, bloodied. Jade waited for him to finish with the nurses. When he turned to her, he spoke officially, medically about Gee. They'd be released within the hour.

"An officer hasn't been by to collect his testimony. We can't leave until that's done."

León spoke delicately, in a tone Jade

recognized as the one he used for volatile patients. "I spoke to the attending. Gee told the officer he didn't have anything to report. It was before you arrived. They can't make him talk."

"I bet I can."

"Jade, I'm sure he has his reasons for keeping quiet. Maybe you should listen to him."

"And let those boys get away with what they did? If it had been the other way around — if Gee had jumped one of them — he'd already be behind bars. Maybe he'd be dead."

"Let's just thank God he's fine. And let him make his own decisions. That's a part of his recovery, too."

"This has nothing to do with you," Jade scoffed. "You have zero say in this."

León reached for her shoulders, although they had an agreement against touching in public. "Technically, I'm his doctor."

"Technically, you're no one to him."

León dropped his hands, and she could see that she'd wounded him.

"Why do you have to push? Why are you trying to get in the middle of this? You're not his father. He had a father. His name was Ray."

"I'm not trying to replace anyone. I'm just

trying to help."

"So send an officer."

León shook his head. "You can't always protect him, Jade."

"Are you kidding? That's the *main thing* I'm supposed to do. And I'm failing."

León reached for her again, drew her toward him.

"What are you doing? They can see us."

"I don't care."

She pushed him away. "You're not listening. If you won't send an officer, then we're done here. There's nothing else that I need you for."

Back in the room, Jade found Gee with a worried expression, his mouth twisted to the side, as if he were waiting for a pain to subside. She asked him if he was all right, but before he answered, she heard his friend on the other side of the curtain. She was talking to an older woman, the two of them standing just beyond the curtain. It rippled with their movements. Jade listened and realized quickly why her son was so upset.

"I thought you knew better than to get tied up with boys like that."

"It was Duke and his friends. They're the ones I should avoid."

"This is exactly why I didn't want things

at the school to change, but you didn't listen. All you wanted to do was criticize me when I've been trying to help you."

"Gee didn't do anything wrong."

"Gee! What kind of name is that? Noelle, I thought you were smarter than this, smarter than me."

Jade pushed past the curtain and found Noelle beside a woman she could only assume was her mother. She had her hair tied up with a large clip, the ends splayed like the spokes of a wheel. She was lean with a mean, pretty face. She wore a yellow vest Jade recognized from the grocery store. She wore a pin that read TEAM LEADER.

"Would you mind moving your conversation somewhere that my son can't hear? And, to be honest, I don't want to hear it either."

Noelle apologized quickly, and the woman sneered defiantly at Jade. "Who are you?"

"I'm Gee's mother — you know, the young man with the funny name. Who the hell are you?"

"I remember you. From the town hall." The woman narrowed her eyes at Jade. "Tell your son to keep away from my daughter."

"Mama, I came to see him," pleaded Noelle. "He's my friend."

"You don't need friends who will only

bring you trouble. You don't need friends who will derail your life."

Jade was stunned at how frankly this white woman was talking in front of her, how unafraid she seemed to offend. It was as if she thought her words were unimpeachable truth, and it was a service to say them. She was an ignorant woman, dangerous. Another woman's child was laid up in the hospital, and all she could see was the imagined threat to her own.

"Noelle, I think you better leave. Take your mother with you."

"This is a free country, and I'll go wherever I like."

"Don't you have any decency?" Jade said. "My son was just assaulted, and you're out here calling him names. Some example you're setting for your daughter."

Lacey May looked stunned. She hitched a hand onto one hip and went to snap back, but Noelle seized her hand and yelled, "Leave it, Mama." She started dragging her down the hall, and Lacey May followed reluctantly. She turned around more than once to glare at Jade, but she said nothing. Noelle was sobbing again.

Fury surged through Jade. She wondered whether she should have done more to put that woman in her place, to defend her son.

She heard Gee calling her, and she came back to her senses. He was the one who needed her. Chances were, they'd never see that awful woman and her daughter again.

Noelle announced she was moving out that night. She wasted no time packing up a bag with her clothes, a cardboard box with her shoes and schoolbooks. Then she called Ruth and asked her to come and get her.

"Now, you know I can't do that," Ruth said.

"Either you come and get me and I'm staying with you, or I'm leaving this house and looking for somewhere else to stay, starting with the bus station."

"All right. Bailey and I are coming."

Lacey May didn't stop screaming the whole time Noelle was putting her things together. Hank shut himself in the bedroom so he wouldn't have to watch. Margarita sat impassively at the TV, mostly watching her show but occasionally interjecting to point out how both Lacey May and Noelle were wrong, that they were two peas in a pod and they deserved each other. Diane followed her eldest sister around, tugging at her knees and weeping.

Jenkins, perhaps, was the most distraught. The dog, who mostly lay on the floor by the couch these days, was alert and whining sharply now. He followed Noelle around, barking at her, as if he knew what was going on. He bit at the hem of her shirt to get her to stay, but she swatted him away. After that, he kept close, shadowing her, until there was a honk from the street, and Noelle left, carrying her suitcase and cardboard box down the lawn. Lacey May had given up by then, slammed the door behind her. Jenkins stayed at the door, sniffing and whimpering, until Lacey May told him to shut up and kicked him good in the ribs. Diane picked the dog up into her arms and carried him down to the basement; he couldn't handle the stairs on his own anymore.

It wasn't until Lacey May was alone in the bedroom with Hank that she finally let herself wonder aloud. "Am I wrong? Am I crazy?"

Hank was in his pajamas, cross-legged on the bed, reading a motorcycle magazine. He looked tired, his graying hair long around his ears.

"He isn't Robbie," he said.

"He's black."

"Jesus Christ, Lacey May. What's that got to do with anything?"

"Nothing on its own. But you've got to look at things in the big picture, think about how he's been raised, where he's from. And his mother —"

"You don't even know the boy."

"Please tell me I can still speak my own mind in my own home. Goddamn it, Hank."

She had come to him for consolation, and he had let her down. She pulled on her nightgown with a vengeance, as if she wanted it to rip, and Hank sighed, called her to him.

"You speak your mind all you want. Meanwhile, your daughter's run off to another house."

"Are you saying I'm wrong?"

"What's it matter if you are? You've got to decide whether you'd rather be right, or you'd rather have your daughter."

It felt like no kind of choice to Lacey May.

The first few days at Ruth's were peaceable. Noelle stayed in a spare room with a day-bed, an exercise bicycle, boxes full of Bailey's old clothes and toys. She had plenty of company. They ate breakfast and dinner together, the three of them, every day. And Ruth drove Noelle in the mornings to the mouth of the freeway, where she waited on a little patch of grass for the bus to arrive in the early dark. She did her homework in the room, and sometimes Ruth came up and rode the bicycle while Noelle worked. Still, she was lonely, lonelier than she had ever been. It surprised her, since she was sure she didn't miss Lacey May.

Gee hadn't been to school for days, and the boys who had gone after him had been suspended. Noelle waited until lunchtime to tell Duke it was over, so she could make sure it was in front of all his friends, the kids of his parents' friends from church. Even in public, he had tried to plead with her, and it had felt good to yell at him, to say, *I am through with your bullshit,* as if they were getting divorced, as if it had been years, as if they were on reality TV.

Mr. Riley asked Alex, who normally played Lucio, to read Gee's lines at rehearsal. He said he had a hunch that Gee wasn't coming back. "I tried to help him," Mr. Riley said. "But you can't help anyone until they're ready." Noelle had wanted to say to him, *You have no idea.*

When the quiet got to her — it was so unlike living with her sisters, the dog — she would go find Bailey in the garden. He never sought her out, but he never objected to her presence either. She had helped him harvest his carrots and cabbage. Now they were laying down sawdust and leaves before the next frost. Bailey gave orders without being bossy. He had ruddy skin, a spate of brown freckles across his nose, hair that he kept buzzed around his ears. He was nearly fourteen, and he had the slender body of a boy, but his voice was changing, breaking sometimes when he laughed.

They didn't talk much — he wasn't the kind who felt the need to fill up silence. Noelle realized that she was. She was a Ventura, whether she wanted to be or not.

When they were done in the garden, they went inside and rinsed off all the vegetables they had picked. Sometimes they sat on the porch with the vegetables still in the colander, a tea towel underneath to sop up the draining water.

They took out a batch of green beans and sat on the swing, the colander between them. Bailey read his comics and snapped the beans between his teeth; Noelle read the play, going over the lines she liked. They stirred something in her, even when she wasn't totally sure what they meant: *Go to your bosom; Knock there, and ask your heart what it doth know.*

She had been staying with them for six days when she finally asked Bailey about his father.

"Don't you ever think about him?"

"All the time. Probably more than he

thinks about us."

"Sometimes, I think my parents are all I think about. It's pathetic."

"What about that boy from the play? You must think about him."

"I think it's a lost cause. He's probably going to quit."

"Maybe he won't. Maybe he'll do it because of you."

Noelle couldn't help but smile. Bailey talked plainly, as if life were easy. He still had all the clarity and candor of a child. She nudged him. "What about you? You got a girlfriend?"

Bailey began to blush. "No. But your sister Margarita sure is pretty."

Noelle grimaced. "Her face is weird."

Bailey looked taken aback, and Noelle saw how her meanness looked to him. He wasn't like her. He was a sweet boy, his mouth full of metal, dirt caked under his nails. He couldn't understand all the things she had inherited, the way she was. After all, he had Ruth for a mother, not Lacey May.

"Sorry," she said. "Sometimes I can be a shit person. It's my DNA."

"You shouldn't talk that way about yourself. Maybe you are the way you are for a purpose."

"A purpose? You been going to church or

something, Bailey?"

"Maybe your quirks are what make you who you are. Maybe you're not supposed to be any different. Not just you, but everybody."

"I don't think I like that," she said. "Maybe we are supposed to be different."

Bailey shrugged.

"But that's kind of deep. Where'd you get all that stuff anyway?"

"There's this manga that I like," he said, and Noelle laughed.

When Hank pulled up in his truck, he took them by surprise, and Noelle leapt down from the swing. She crossed her arms, ready to protest that she wasn't going back. Bailey called for his mother.

They had hardly come to a stop before Diane burst out of the truck and darted up the driveway. Her face was puffed up and red.

"Jenkins ran away!" she wailed. "It's been two days, and we can't find him. Is he here?"

Margarita came loping behind her. She was frowning, her arms crossed, as if to copy Noelle's stance. "I already told her he probably ran off to die."

Diane's eyes filled with tears. "If he's dying, why would he want to be alone? If he's dying, I want to hold him." She turned to

Noelle. "I think he left looking for you."

Noelle opened her arms to her sister, but Diane didn't move. She dropped her head into her hands and sobbed. Bailey called again for his mother.

Hank joined them on the porch, his hands in his pockets. "She's been like this since you left," he said.

Diane ran for Ruth as soon as she opened the door. Ruth gathered her into her arms and shushed her, then carried her inside. Hank followed without a word. Noelle found herself reeling. She thought of how she'd shoved the dog away, how he'd whimpered and followed her.

"You think Jenkins is really gone?"

Margarita fidgeted with the ring Robbie had given her. "We all knew it was coming. I just didn't think he was going to run off. I thought we'd find him in the yard or something."

"Diane probably thinks it's my fault. She wouldn't even let me hold her."

"She just misses you. That's the real reason we came."

"What about you?"

Margarita shrugged. "Mama's at the store, and they wouldn't let me stay home alone."

"Unh-hunh," Noelle said, and she felt closer to her sister than she could remember feeling. They were alike in this way; they both refused to let on how much they needed. Noelle regretted saying what she had about her sister's face.

"The thing about dogs is you get used to them," Margarita said. "Just being there, around."

"I know what you mean."

Noelle slid back onto the porch swing, patted the place between her and Bailey. Bailey's face was burning red now, and he left without a word, the screen door clapping behind him. Margarita hesitated, staring at her sister, measuring. Finally, she climbed up on the swing beside her.

"Can you believe we used to live there?" Noelle pointed to the empty blue house next door, the SOLD sign pitched into the cold earth.

"No," Margarita said. "I can't."

They swung their legs together, shared the sweet, hard beans.

At home, Linette fussed over Gee more than was necessary. She made him chili smothered in cheese, cup after cup of warmed milk. His tailbone ached, so he couldn't sit at the table, or at his desk to play at the computer. He ate in the kitchen, standing up, and then he went up to his room and lay on his bed under the swinging bulb, listening to music on his CD player. He took naps, and when he couldn't doze off, he stroked himself to sleep. There wasn't always pleasure in it, but always release. His humming fingertips. His blank mind. His loose jaw.

Jade had allowed him to stay home from school; he had a doctor's note; the days passed in boredom and peace, except for his nightmares. He ran through alleyways and fields of grass; it was dark; he was alone; he couldn't see who chased him. What Gee knew in every dream was that he couldn't outrun them. If he stayed sleeping, he'd be gone. Once, he woke up crying, which was embarrassing. Usually, he lurched awake with a feeling that he'd swallowed a mouthful of cold water; his teeth ached, vibrated. He went down to the kitchen to drink mugs of steaming water. One night, he boiled water and drank, then opened the back door, and sat on the steps.

The town houses at the complex were narrow brick. They were close together, separated by little seas of grass that the neighbors used as yards. They kept grills or bicycles or tools under large tarps. A wooden fence divided the complex from the road, the squat houses on the other side.

The ground was covered in fallen pine needles, sharp cones. It was dark, a night without a moon.

The cool air felt good on his skin. His face was still swollen, and he wondered how he'd look by the time he had to return to school. There would be rumors. People would know what had happened; they would know about Ray. What was worse was that Gee was certain most of his classmates didn't even know who he was. *Which one is he?* they'd probably asked. *Who's Gee?*

Adira had called a few times to check on him; so had Mr. Riley. He hadn't come to the phone for either of them, although Linette tried to encourage him. There had been no word from Noelle, and he wondered whether what had been brewing between them was over now, if she had been scared off by their mothers. He hadn't had the chance to see whether knowing the truth about Ray had changed how she saw him; he hadn't had the chance to hear what she meant when she said she liked him. Maybe he was just another project to her, the way he was to his mother, to Mr. Riley. Maybe she just wanted to be the kind of girl who could be friends with a boy like him. Maybe she was just trying to show she knew wrong from right. Whatever the reason, he didn't want her to change his mind.

"What are you doing out here?"

Jade stood in the doorway, her face bare and serious, her earrings off. She wore an oversized T-shirt for some band he'd never heard of and a pair of men's boxers, knee-high socks.

"You need your rest," she said. "Come on, it's cold."

"Sit next to me," Gee said, and to his surprise, she did.

"What's wrong?"

"Nothing. Can't we just talk?"

"All right."

The silence leached between them.

"You ever been in a play?"

"I used to dream sometimes about being in a band," Jade said. "Playing the drums."

"I thought you wanted to be a scientist."

"I used to dream about a lot of things."

"But you never dreamed about Daddy. You just found him."

"We found him. You were there, too."

Jade talked about that day at the DMV the way some mothers talked about their children's births: it was where Gee began. He knew nothing about the day he was born; he supposed it was a day she didn't want to remember. He didn't bring up those circumstances, how young she'd been. He didn't ask about his biological father. He knew his name and that he'd left; he didn't need to know anything else.

"So what's going on?" Jade asked. "Are you in love or something?"

Gee shrugged. "She's my friend."

"I don't like that girl for you. She's got too many problems."

"You don't even know her."

"I can tell by looking at her family. You can't escape the people you come from, at least not when you're that young. Girls like that get good men in trouble."

Jade rubbed her thighs against the cold. She looked up at the dark stamp of the pines against the sky.

"Whatever happened to Carmela? And to Wilson?"

"I don't concern myself with them anymore," Jade said. "And neither should you. I'm talking to you now about that girl —"

"Noelle."

"Is she the reason you're doing that play?"

"Mr. Riley gave me a big role."

"I was reading about that play. He cast you as a man in jail. That Mr. Riley is not your friend."

"I like being Claudio."

"Please, we both know you're no actor. This is about her."

Gee felt his voice rising. He was sick of his mother telling him who he was and who he wasn't. "You're the one who wanted me to go to Central in the first place."

"And I still do. I don't think those boys are going to cause you any more problems. They're just some little punks who did what they did cause they thought they'd get away with it. Cause there were three of them."

Gee felt himself shrink under the idea that he was an easy target.

"But they won't do it again. I've already called their parents to let them know I'll make it my personal business to send those boys to jail if they ever so much as look at you again."

"Ma, I told you I just want to leave those boys alone. I want to forget about this."

"So they get to put their hands on you and walk away free? Gee, I swear, I'll never understand you. It's like you've got no pride in yourself at all."

"What's there to be proud of? You just want to fix my life because you couldn't fix yours."

"That's not how I see you at all."

"How do you see me then?"

Gee felt himself clamoring for his mother. What would she say? He waited to hear.

"It doesn't matter how I see you. It matters how you see yourself. When are you going to learn that, Gee? I don't know how else to show you." Jade stood up and sighed. "You're going to quit that play. Leave all this drama behind."

"I am not quitting," Gee said quietly.

There wasn't a trace of rage in her voice when she answered him. "We'll see about that."

15

APRIL 2019
A TOWN NEAR THE CRYSTAL COAST,
NORTH CAROLINA

On weekday afternoons, the theater was a holy place, emptied of its congregants. It was cool and unlit, the curtains drawn back from the stage, the austere rows of stiff metal chairs. Noelle felt like a small seed at the center of the dark, cavernous room.

The next production was *Frankenstein,* and Noelle was painting the North Pole: blue-black water, the iridescent fragments of glaciers. She tipped her paintbrush in teal and silver to make the edges shimmer, where the ice touched the water. She worked over a scroll unfurled on the floor of the stage, listening to music from her portable speaker. She sang along in her tongue-tied Spanish.

Sombras nada más, entre tu vida y mi vida . . .

The day outside was bright and warm, breezy. It was spring on the coast. She had a few hours before she met Ruth, and she hadn't been able to resist a morning in the theater. It was soothing, peaceful to work under the sweet light streaming in from the street, her hands stained blue. When she was done, she sprayed the paper with fixative, clipped it to a rack to dry.

She rode her bicycle the few miles from the theater to downtown. She rolled past the graveyard, the rows of Queen Anne houses, many of them boasting bronze plaques engraved with their build dates. The sound glimmered around her as she rode over the bridge, but it was the vegetation, not the water, that reminded her most she was somewhere different: her new home. The myrtle shrubs and goldenrod, the fans of palmetto on the front lawns, the red cedars and wild olive trees. Noelle liked to think these would be beautiful names for a child — Cedar, Olive, Myrtle. Even Palmetto. Why not? If Hollywood actors could name their children after fruit and bugs, then she could name hers after a tree, a bush.

Ruth was waiting for her on the boardwalk in a little park, shaded by craggy, windblown trees. She sat on the edge of the fountain, her hair peroxide blond, twisted into a fat braid. She wore navy exercise pants, a sun visor, and a bright green T-shirt that read

Clementine Farms. Her body was heavy and firm. She threw open her arms for Noelle.

"Aren't you a vision," Ruth said, and Noelle looked down at herself. There was nothing special about the cork sandals she wore, her black pants and gingham blouse.

"It's all here," Ruth said, and caressed her face. "You look happy. Are you happy here?"

"Yes, ma'am. I am. Where's Bailey?"

"Oh, he went off to give us some time, just the two of us. You'll see him before I go."

"I haven't seen him in — how long? — sixteen years. He's still a little boy in my mind."

"He's a man now. I couldn't be prouder of the two of you. Come on. Let's eat."

Noelle led Ruth to her favorite pub. They had tables on a wooden deck overlooking the water, the boats anchored in the marina, the birds pecking around the boardwalk. They could see, too, the wild horses roaming the sliver of island in the bay, digging for groundwater with their hooves. They ordered quickly so they could spend their time together talking. Noelle ordered the fried shrimp and a green salad, Ruth the blue crab cakes and cheddar grits. They had beers: Ruth's tasted of peach, Noelle's of cucumber and ginger.

"Well, it suits you," Ruth said. "This little town with its craft beer and fancy menus."

"This is all for the tourists," Noelle said. "But I do like the breweries. They remind me of living in a big city."

"You're a city girl at heart."

"I'm not sure anymore. I love it here."

"How could you not?" Ruth waved her hand over the view, the glittering water.

"It's good for right now. But it's very white."

"You're very white, honey. I'm sure you've figured that out by now."

"Maybe," Noelle said. "But my child won't be."

"You still saving up for that adoption? You should set up a website. Crowdfunding. That's how Bailey got his farm."

Ruth had been visiting Bailey at his farm, about ninety miles northwest. When Ruth told Noelle she'd be so close, Noelle had invited her down to lunch. The coast was in the opposite direction of home, and she'd have a longer journey back, but Ruth said she didn't mind. Now they had these hours together. Noelle was grateful.

When the food arrived, Ruth inquired about the theater, and Noelle filled her in eagerly. She was the manager of the company, which meant more here than it had in her last job because the operation was smaller, the budget infinitesimal. All the staff was part-time except for her. She designed all the flyers for the productions herself, wrote the press releases that went to the local papers. Sometimes, she polished the windows, supervised and made the sets, called the roster of donors. Even before they'd pulled off their first production with Noelle at the helm, she was convinced she'd been right to move out here by herself, to let an apartment above a farmhouse several miles outside downtown. She spent her days in the theater, her nights drinking beers at home from a growler she filled every few days at one of the breweries in town. She fried fish and made chowder, started pickling the vegetables she bought each week at the farmers' market. She didn't want to spend money on a car, so she rode her bicycle everywhere. Her legs had grown wider, stronger, her arms freckled and tan. It was routine, and it was solitary, but it was different from the drudgery of Golden Brook. She wasn't waiting on anyone, not a husband, or a future, or a better version of herself. Her life was little, complete. And when the child came, she would fold him into the life she had already built. She could raise him in her flat, affix a little trailer to her bicycle, bring him with her to the theater, take him kayaking at the beach.

"You can do it on your own," Ruth said, although Noelle hadn't asked for the reassurance. "It's not as bad as people say. It isn't easy, but *hard* and *bad* aren't the same thing. You know Bailey is the love of my life."

Noelle nodded, although it hurt her to hear it. She had wanted Ruth to say that she was, too, but she knew she had no right to a wish like that.

"Seeing much of my mother these days?"

"I ran into her and Hank at the mall the other day. I was getting my hair done" — Ruth gestured to her new incandescent blond — "and there she was, shopping for a present for Alma and Diane. They just adopted a dog, she told me, and Lacey was shopping for a collar, a rhinestone collar for her. They named the dog Princess. Can you believe it? Your mother sure has come a long way."

"Maybe. I can never tell with her."

Since her surgery, Lacey May had taken to wearing a beautiful auburn wig around town. They were waiting to see if the tumor would grow back, and in the meantime, she had quit working at the store, declaring life was too short to spend it restocking shelves. She sometimes helped Diane at the camp, said she liked being with the dogs because they reminded her of Jenkins. Now, Alma came along to dinners at the house; Lacey May served them coffee and dessert.

"We all learn from our mistakes, Noelle. She won't do to Alma what she did to Nelson. Honestly, I'm impressed! Alma isn't just a woman — she's a different race, too."

"Sure, but it's not quite the same."

Ruth furrowed her eyebrows in confusion, and Noelle decided to push a little more. "It's not the same as being black."

Ruth smiled, disbelieving, and shook her head, as if what Noelle had said was absurd, but it wasn't worth arguing. She was willing to indulge her, her foolish notions. She tucked back into her crab cakes. Noelle figured this was bound to be her life if she stayed tethered to the people she had known since she was a girl. They'd be decent in some ways; they'd astonish her with how they seemed to keep up with the news, the shifting language around identity and race. Once, she'd even overheard Lacey May refer to Alma as *a person of color.* But they'd be incensed, too, by the encroachments they saw on their world — the stars cast in movie franchises they had formerly adored, the people who had the nerve to go to marches and complain and vote in elections. They would guard everything they had, however little, as if their lives were prizes they'd rightly won that others had no right to claim. They'd never admit how willingly they'd played their parts.

For all the years that Ruth had loved her, and called from time to time, and sent Christmas cards, she hadn't asked after Nelson much, requested he be put on the line so she could say hello. It was too easy for people to see their interests and disinterests as pure, functions of their desires and personalities. They just didn't like Nelson much; they just preferred that other candidate for mayor; something about that doctor just didn't sit right with them. She might not have believed it herself, if not for Nelson. Maybe that was proof she really was white — she had to love him in order to see.

"What about my father? Have you seen him around?"

"Your mother says he's fine. Goes to visit Diane sometimes, fixes little things for her around the house, and then asks for money."

"That sounds like him."

"But he's got a job for a moving company, so he does long hauls out of state. He's got an apartment somewhere on the east side. He's in a program."

"He's done programs before."

"It's a good thing, according to Lacey May."

"Those two are going to keep this up forever, aren't they?"

Ruth shrugged. "You're the one who wanted to know."

"You're right," Noelle said. "Enough about the Venturas and the Gibbses. You'll be back at the hospital tomorrow. We've got to squeeze out the most of your last day of vacation."

"Vacation?" Ruth rolled her eyes. "Bailey had me sticking my hand in beehives and pulling up weeds." She huffed and reached for the bill. Noelle didn't fuss and let her pay.

The Pirate Museum was along the boardwalk, and Ruth asked if Noelle would mind if she invited Bailey to join them. He'd been infatuated with Blackbeard as a boy and might get a kick out of the relics they'd salvaged from old ships.

"Wasn't he the one who killed all his wives?"

Ruth slapped her arm and laughed. "Of course not. You're thinking of Bluebeard." Ruth explained that when he was a boy, Bailey read storybooks about English pirates and marooned ships, the Graveyard of the Atlantic. He would dress up in her beaded necklaces and romp around the house, a miniature marauder. She relayed this history to Noelle all while beaming, as if the boy Bailey were in front of her now. It pleased Noelle to see how much contentment Ruth could still extract from her memories of her son as a boy. She relished it, longed to delight in a child the same way.

They waited for Bailey in front of the museum, and Noelle didn't recognize him when Ruth first started to wave. He was tall and sunburned, his face nearly all hair: a full beard and mustache, thick sideburns enclosing his cheeks. His dark hair curled beneath his ears. His eyes were blue, and Noelle couldn't help but remember lyrics from the song she'd listened to that morning. *Tus ojos azules, azul que tienen el cielo y el mar.* She'd never had a thing for blue eyes, but she couldn't help but be disquieted by his: they were the color of frozen water.

He kissed his mother before he awkwardly nodded at Noelle, folded her into a stiff hug. He smelled of wood chips, tobacco. He wore the same Clementine Farms T-shirt as his mother, brown work boots, and jeans. He had flecks of silver in his beard, lines at the corners of his eyes that swept up to his temples when he smiled. But he was younger, she remembered, around Margarita's age: thirty or close to it.

"You're all grown up," she said, unsure of how else to greet him.

Bailey smiled at her. "You too." He ushered his mother inside, away from the sun.

The museum was hokey and dim. Old wooden steering wheels were mounted on the walls, alongside replicas of the bronze mermaids that had adorned the prows of the ships. Nautical maps were displayed in glass cases; a long, battered sail drooped from the ceiling. Ruth pointed to the placards she thought Bailey would find most interesting. He and Noelle trudged behind her, studying each other more than they did the exhibits. When she caught him looking at her, he'd snatch his eyes away, look at his hands, then back up at her, as if for permission to go on staring. She smiled at him, and they ambled on together.

"How's your sister?" Bailey finally asked.

"Which one?"

"Margarita. The model."

"Oh, she's an actress now. She just landed a recurring part on a show for this season. She's a nurse on a hospital drama."

"Does my mother know? She'll get a kick out of that."

They wandered past a display of a typical sailors' lunch — a rubber fish, a bowl of cornmeal mush, a plastic goblet filled with plastic rum.

"I used to have a crush on her, you know. I thought she was so beautiful." Bailey stammered and corrected himself. "You all were."

Noelle smiled. "I don't remember that."

He asked her about the theater, and she told him, although he must have known much more about her than he let on. He didn't bring up Lacey May's cancer, or the divorce. She asked about his farm. He raised chickens and bees; eggs and honey and beeswax paid the bills. But he harvested grapes, too, and flowers, the garden vegetables he'd grown as a boy: tomatoes and bell peppers, cucumber and squash.

"Clementine is my ex-wife. When we separated, I bought her out. A buddy and I keep it up now."

"So, you're still gardening?" Noelle teased. She asked why they'd separated.

"We stayed together for a while after she got saved and became born-again, but it wasn't the same after that. She was always picking on me for something — smoking a cigar, drinking too much. And I'm not a drinker — believe me. Finally, she figured

445

divorce was bad but being yoked to an unbeliever was worse."

"You don't believe in God?"

"I'm mostly interested in this life," Bailey said. "It's enough for me."

Noelle stared at him, wondered what kind of man he was.

"We got married too fast. I was twenty-two, and just finishing up school. We liked surfing together. I thought she was the prettiest girl I'd ever seen. It was stupid."

"Prettier than Margarita?"

Bailey put his hand over his heart. "Oh, no. No one, in my book, is prettier than Margarita Ventura, age fourteen."

They left the museum before long, under-whelmed by the exhibits, but Ruth was electric, satisfied at seeing the two of them together. She flung an arm around each of them and suggested ice cream. Noelle showed them to a parlor, warned them it was mediocre, but they all ordered their cones, and Bailey paid.

"Agribusiness treating you well?" Noelle said, and realized she was flirting.

"You can get the next round," he said, and they all walked back toward the water.

They sat on a bench facing a strip of marshland where the horses grazed.

"Isn't this nice?" Ruth said. She seemed nervous, talking to fill the silence, as if she could sense what was between them now. They licked their cones, and eventually threw them away. The ice cream was too fatty, not sweet enough. Ruth muttered it was a pity. Wasted calories, she said. Soon it was time for her bus.

"Well, now you know where to find me," Noelle said. She pressed Ruth's body to hers and felt naked in her need for the woman. She admired her, longed for her. She was the mother Noelle had always wanted to have. Sometimes, she wondered whether she should say these things to Ruth, but she assumed she already knew.

"Next time I come and see Bailey, I'll stop by and see you, too. And you let me know when you're back in town. I hardly saw you last time. It was criminal."

"It was a bad time."

"I know," Ruth said. She took Noelle's face in her hands, kissed both her cheeks.

As she was boarding the bus, she pointed firmly at her son.

"Now, you drive Noelle home before you hit the road. I don't want her cycling back in the dark."

"I'll be fine, Ruth. I do it all the time."

Ruth shook her head, waved her index

447

finger in the air. "You let him drive you home."

They stood together in the street until the bus disappeared, turning toward the highway. It was dusk, the light over the water transforming to gold.

"It sure is pretty here," Bailey said. "You'll probably spend the whole summer in the water."

"I sure as hell won't. Don't you listen to the news? Every year, there's a shark attack somewhere new. Atlantic Beach, Wrightsville Beach. All up and down the coast, there's some kid whose lost an arm, a leg. And that's in the shallows. No thank you."

"Didn't you all go to the beach a lot when we were kids?"

"I'm not a kid anymore."

"I can see that," Bailey said, slitting his eyes against the setting sun. "Let me take you home."

They picked up Noelle's bicycle, and Bailey drove them along the sound toward her apartment. He kept looking over the wheel at her, and she felt herself go warm. There weren't very many single men her age in this town. They were married, or, if they weren't, there was a sour story as to why not. She didn't like picking up men in bars, and the ones she found online lived too far away. Noelle didn't know how else people met each other. She hadn't dated all of her adult life.

She felt herself growing larger under Bailey's attention. Her skin expanded, a gentle thrum in her throat, her limbs. She wasn't surprised when he pulled over, said, "Let's go for a swim."

"But I already told you about the sharks."

"Those are ocean beaches. This is a sound."

"It's too cold," Noelle said.

"We'll be fine."

They parked atop a small hill and crawled down through a thick brush of sea lavender. They found a strip of sandy beach, ringed by high grass that gave way to the water, placid and slate blue. Down the bank, a few boats were docked in front of large Gothic Revival houses, their peaks facing the sound. There was no clear entrance to the tiny beach, no one else around. A lone bench stood at the edge of the water.

Bailey stripped down to his underwear, and Noelle followed him. They waded in. It was cold, and Noelle let the water fill her mouth when she sank under. It had the sweet tang of fresh water mixed with salt.

"I didn't think you'd come in," Bailey

said. He was treading water, his hair slicked back. "My mother told me you've had a rough time. But we can't stop living. We've got to keep on doing things like this."

Noelle swam toward him. "And why is that?"

"The planet is dying. We've got to cherish it all."

"That's true," Noelle said, and she wondered why she didn't think of it more, the wreckage that was soon to come. She wanted children. She wanted them to live on the earth. Maybe this was another way that she was white: the ease with which she could ignore calamity, focus mainly on what she wanted.

She swam closer to Bailey. His shoulders were beaded with water. A band of fat clouds was blowing in toward the shore.

"You know, they say that's what gives life meaning. The fact that we're all going to die," he said. "I don't believe that at all. I don't need death to remind me how good life is. If I had an infinite amount of life, I'd be happy to go on living. Look at all this."

He swept his hand toward the endless water, the pale pink sky.

"It's beautiful," he said, and the plainness of his declaration, the truth of it, was so

450

great that Noelle didn't know how to answer except to say, "Yes, it is."

They were Onshore and Giddy, shaking their hands and feet to shuck off the water, the sand caked to their legs, when Noelle heard a chirp from her phone. She was shivering in her underwear as she clicked through her messages and saw one from Diane pronouncing she had better call her back right away. She thought first of her mother, then of her father, all the things that might have gone wrong.

Diane picked up quickly, and Noelle couldn't help herself. "Well, what is it?" she sputtered.

"I finally did it," Diane said. "I asked Alma to marry me."

Noelle felt relief, then the rush of excitement. "This is so wonderful. I'm happy for you."

"You better think about getting a car. I'm going to be needing lots of help from my maid of honor."

"What do you think Margarita will say?"

"Relax, I'm having two."

"Well played, sister."

"Look, I've got to go. The dog is chewing up some wires."

"I love you."

"Me too."

The sisters said their good-byes and hung up. It had gone unnoticed how plainly she had told her sister how she felt, how easily her sister had reciprocated. Noelle resolved that was how it should be. Love was regular; love was everyday.

"Should I take you home?" Bailey asked. He was dressed, watching her from the bench.

"My sister is getting married."

His face turned solemn. "Not Margarita, right?"

They laughed, and Noelle led the way back through the brush.

The farmhouse was at the end of a long, dusty driveway, a quarter of a mile long. They passed the pond with ducks, the tree swing that the owners' children must have used when they were young, and the shed where the mean old basset hounds that wandered the farm liked to lurk. They sprang out as soon as they heard Bailey's car rumbling by. Noelle lowered the window and shooed them away. They were slow moving and fat but still ferocious.

Her apartment was just two rooms. The kitchen and living room were one, already furnished with a wooden table, old plaid armchairs, a corduroy couch. In the bedroom, she kept a mattress on a box spring with no frame. There were taxidermy mallards, an egret hanging from the ceiling, a deer and his antlers poised over the doorway.

"The old farmer's a hunter," Noelle explained, pulling down towels from a closet. She handed one to Bailey and started making tea. He had a long drive back, nearly two hours, but neither of them mentioned that. She didn't have much in her refrigerator by way of dinner, so she smeared toast with butter and honey, set out a little pitcher of milk. He joined her at the table under the low glow of the overhead lamp. She used her phone to play a bolero on the speakers. It was all she listened to these days, although she couldn't say why. Maybe it was being divorced, wanting clichés about love lost. Maybe it was about wanting more Spanish as she prepared to adopt a baby. Or maybe the music brought romance into her life, without any of its accoutrements: a husband, a shared bank account, the problems of pleasing a man.

Bailey slurped at his tea. "How do you like the single life? It's lonely but easier, right?"

"At least now I know what to expect,"

Noelle said. "When you're married, you think you're going to spend your life with someone, but it isn't true. You can only ever spend your life with you."

"I think back to being married, and I don't know how Clem and I spent all that time. Probably making dinner, arguing about pointless things." He spooned more honey onto his toast. "My life is so wide open now."

Noelle was noncommittal. "I'm adopting a baby, so I'm going to be plumb out of time soon. But I don't mind. I've had my fair share of it."

"A baby? All by yourself?"

"Sure. You know something about that, don't you?"

"My mother is a queen. I couldn't have asked for a better one."

"I've always envied you. I've always wanted Ruth to think of me like a daughter."

"Well, she does, doesn't she?"

"I suppose."

"I can't say I ever thought of you as a sister though. Not even when you were living with us. If I had, it would make things too awkward now." Bailey leaned across the table. "You know, between me and Margarita."

454

"Come on," she said, and took him by the hand.

They undressed each other efficiently, their bodies still clammy and cold from the swim. They contemplated each other, and Bailey was every bit as fine as she'd expected, from the muscles in his arms to the span of his chest, the shape of his legs, his cock. The first thing he did was put his mouth on her. He kissed her face, her ears, her eyelids, her collarbone, her breasts. He laid her back on the bed, finally kissed her lips, then snaked his way down to the center of her. A shock went through Noelle's body. She rose to meet him. She was so pleased, she came before he was through. Her head was swimming. She was floating, grinning, serene. He asked if it would be all right to be inside her, and she said yes. He asked whether she had a condom.

She shook her head. "It's been just me for so long. You didn't bring one?"

"I was spending the day with my mother." He was naked, still kneeling over her body.

"I don't care if you don't care," Noelle said.

"All right."

He crawled forward to rest his elbows on either side of her head. He kissed her long

455

and slow, parted her legs with his, and lowered himself into her. She shuddered under the warmth and weight of his body. It was everything she'd been missing. He worked himself up, and Noelle panted along with him, although she knew she wouldn't come again. He unloaded himself with a gorgeous grunting in her ear. She kissed his shoulder over and over again, as if she loved him, as if she were offering him a benediction. She felt herself begin to weep.

"I'm sorry," she said. "I'm so sorry."

He rolled onto his side, knit his hand with hers. "Why are you apologizing?" He handed her the bundle of his T-shirt. She blew her nose on *Clementine Farms*.

"I just haven't felt that good in a long time."

"The pleasure was all mine. I'm tempted to write home about it."

Noelle laughed through her tears. "Don't you tell your mama."

"She'd be thrilled," he said. "But I won't."

They lay for a while, catching their breath, soaking in the scent of each other's skin and wetness, the water and silt from the sound. Noelle felt herself recovering from the onslaught of feeling: how she had wanted Bailey and missed Nelson at the same time, how deep she had been in her body and her mind all at once. Bailey leaned off the bed and rummaged in his jeans. He withdrew a slender brown cigarillo, pointed it at Noelle.

"Do you mind?"

"Those are bad for you."

"Get out of here. Are you serious? No one's ever told me that." He winked at her and lit up. He smoked silently, his free hand massaging her thigh. When he was done, he stamped out the butt and dozed off. Noelle figured she'd let him sleep, wake him up in a few hours for his drive. From what she knew, work started early on a farm, and he'd have to get back.

With his eyes closed, he looked like Ruth, his skin easily weathered, lined. It occurred to her that she should have slept with more men when she had the chance. She wouldn't be able to do all this when there was a child in the house.

It might have been the sex, or the news of Diane's wedding, but soon her mind turned to Nelson. She thought of him often, although he had gone out of focus for her, their life together blurred, as if by a merciful trick of memory. She remembered vaguely how it felt to argue with him, to miss him when he was away. She remembered how he'd tended to look at her, how his kisses tended to feel. It was all habitual.

The discrete moments she remembered most clearly were all from the end: the terrible phone call on Diane's porch, the morning she'd sent him away.

When she first arrived on the coast, they were still sending emails back and forth, settling what to do about the house, the furniture, the little fund in the bank. In the end, they'd sold everything, split it all down the middle. The only thing either of them wanted was cash. It was as amicable as divorces went. Noelle had given some of the money to Margarita to help her get a stable place in L.A., and she had saved the rest, decided to live meagerly because she could. She had nearly enough for the adoption, but she wanted enough for a down payment, too, a place they could move into when the child got older. She wanted a boy from Colombia; there were already too many women in her family. But she wasn't opposed to a girl, or a child from elsewhere in Latin America.

Nelson knew she planned to adopt, but they stuck to divorce business in their emails. They were cordial, passive, in their negotiations. *Sure, if you like,* they said, and *That's fine with me, whatever you need.* Eventually, they were done dividing, and the emails stopped. Then he wrote to her again.

He had landed somewhere else in Europe for a long residency. Noelle hadn't paid attention to the details of his new life. What was it, now, to her?

But he had written to her so baldly, so wholeheartedly, she had wondered if he hadn't meant to send the email at all. It was what she had been missing all the time she was his wife. She had read his email many times since it arrived. While Bailey slept beside her, she searched for it on her phone. She turned her blue screen away from him, read it again feverishly.

Noelle —
Every city in Europe seems to have a river running through it. I know it's a holdover from when there was trade along these waters, but it never stops seeming symbolic to me. There's this bank and that bank, an east side and a west, like every city in the world is the same.
Sometimes, I like to think we're still in the same city, and there's a river between us, but at any time, one or the other of us could cross over. Our lives are sepa-

rate but still close. I know that's not the case.

I should have told you about how losing the pregnancy affected me. I thought mostly about you, my duty to snap you out of it, to get us back to our life. I always felt like our life was something we could lose if we weren't careful. I couldn't see our life was everything all around us, the things we shared every day.

Maybe there's nothing I've ever held dearer than my own potential — the idea of it, the idea that I had to make good on all my luck, my life. But one day I'll be fifty or a hundred, and all the things I've done, or could have done, won't matter. No one will have anything to say about my potential, which doors are open to me, and which are closed. No one will remember me at all. I don't mean to sound like a nihilist.

It was hard to watch you lose your way. You were the one who kept us steady, who held it all together. Your strength was a fact of my life, and I passed it off as my own. I am sorry about that. Sometimes I think I'm still that little boy looking for proof I'm as good as everyone else. I'm that little boy waiting for the white people to come and kick me out. I'm that boy who can't remember his lines. But I can't let myself get too pessimistic either. I don't regret very much — it's all led me to this life I could never have imagined.

Anyway, I'm at this café, overlooking the river, and it's not like the States. You don't have to keep ordering things for them to let you stay. Just one little cup of coffee and they leave you alone for hours. Even me. And the waiters are rude to everybody, so you don't have to worry if it's just you.

I started writing to you because I was here, drinking my coffee, and I saw a man come in with his wife. He was black, and I couldn't tell with her — Egyptian, maybe. Who knows? But they had a little girl with them, green eyed and brown skinned. She had her hair in twists. They ordered cake for her. They had wine. And it was sweet because the little girl really occupied herself, taking the cherry off the cake, peering out at the water, chattering every once in a while to her parents, who were very quiet. They watched her, and they watched the water. They held hands under the table and, only once in a while, took sips of their wine. It was like they were in their own world, and the girl was a part of it, but, really, it was mostly the two of them. I thought of the girl growing up, passing in and out of their lives, as all children do when they're grown, but they'd still be at that table, holding hands, glancing over at each other from time to time. It was beautiful. It broke my heart.

Noelle closed her eyes and tried to imagine the child Nelson had described in the letter, but she saw only herself as a girl: spindly, long haired, and indignant, waiting for her father to show up and wrench them all away, to take them home. And she couldn't picture the child they'd lost: he had been a mound in her stomach, a thing with no life outside of her.

She checked to make sure Bailey was still asleep. He was. Noelle kissed his forehead, felt herself swell with gratitude. She slid a pillow under her hips, then another, tilting her pelvis toward the ceiling. She braced herself, turned back to her phone, and read the rest.

I guess what I'm trying to say is the only time I've never tried to prove anything was with you. I didn't worry about what other people would think or what it said about me. It was simple. I wanted you for myself.

16

DECEMBER 2002
THE PIEDMONT, NORTH CAROLINA

The parents were meeting in the back room of a restaurant just north of downtown, on Beard Street. One of the mothers knew the owner, and he had provided them all with pitchers of sweet tea and platters of lemon bars on the house. The committee members sat around a long table underneath a crystal chandelier and ordered lunch off the menu. Mrs. York would call them to order eventually, but Lacey May couldn't wait that long. She blew into the room, without looking anyone in the eye, and went directly to the chairwoman.

"Lacey May, you didn't RSVP," Mrs. York said. "I thought you weren't coming." She looked smart in her blue blazer, a ballpoint pen stuck behind her ear. Lacey May admired her, and she knew she had to say what she had come to say quickly, before she changed her mind.

"I wanted to tell you in person that I quit."

A dozen heads turned toward Lacey May, but she didn't let the attention deter her.

"The campaign is causing too much trouble with my family. I can't go on like this."

A few other members spoke up all at once, trying to talk her out of it. Her daughters would thank her in the long run; they were shifting gears. They needed Lacey May; why didn't she just sit down for a while and see?

Lacey May had never had many friends. She didn't tend to get along with other women, or they didn't tend to get along with her. She didn't go to church or participate in any neighborhood associations. This had been the first group she had belonged to since high school, and they had welcomed her. They had asked for her help finding the right words for their flyers; they had asked her to sign the op-ed in the paper. They had walked shoulder to shoulder with her to tack up posters that day in the hall. She hadn't told them much about her life, but it didn't matter. They had stood together, stood up for their children. Lacey May didn't want to leave them, but she knew Noelle wouldn't come back as long as she was involved in the campaign. There was no other way.

"Well, stay for the meeting at least," Mrs. York said. "We're talking about how to move on from that poster fiasco. It didn't move us one step closer to what we want. There's even talk of a reprimand from the mayor. It doesn't mean anything, but it's embarrassing. He says we were trespassing, vandalizing."

Mrs. Gray, a young mother with bobbed hair, chimed in. "Have you ever heard anything more ridiculous?" In the beginning, Lacey May hadn't been sure about her. She had a tiny diamond nose ring, a tattoo of starlings across her chest. But she had proven one of the most dedicated to the cause, and Lacey May liked her. She worked at a preschool downtown.

"We're changing our focus," Mrs. York went on. "There's a way we can win."

"I'm sorry," Lacey May said. "I can't be a part of it."

"We're getting organized before the next school board elections. We're going to run our own candidates, petition the ones who are against us."

"You're going to leave the students alone?"

Mrs. York and Mrs. Gray nodded at Lacey May.

"That's how we'll get what we want in the long run," Mrs. Gray said.

Lacey May stood, considering. Finally, she shook her head. As much as they might have needed her, her daughters needed her more.

"Good luck," she said, and left in a hurry. She didn't look back.

She was relieved when she surfaced on Beard Street. It was quiet, midday, the winter sun white, and the air cold. Not far from here, the garage where Robbie used to work was still open. Lacey May scanned across the street for it, and there it was, the large doors lifted. Just to see it flooded Lacey May with memories: the sight of Robbie in a work shirt and overalls, the smell of paint thinner on his skin. The street had changed over the years, slowly sprouting a half-dozen new businesses. Besides the restaurant, there was a brewery, a lunch window, a nightclub, and a sandwich shop. It had flowerboxes in the window, a neon COFFEE sign overhead.

There, beneath the blinking sign, she saw Robbie. He was shaking a paper cup at a passerby, a man in a suit who ignored him. Robbie strode away from the shop, following the man, murmuring something at him, then he stopped in front of the nightclub, its windows shuttered. He leaned against the building, sucked on a cigarette, and their eyes met from across the street.

Lacey May went to him, and he slipped the paper cup into his back pocket. As she neared him, she could see he looked beat-up, his hair standing up on his head, his button-up shirt too large. He was missing his gold chain. When he hugged her, he smelled of sweat, and something sickly sweet, maybe whiskey, although it wasn't his drink. The stench of smoke lingered on his hands.

"Oh, Robbie," she said. "What are you doing down here?"

Robbie shrugged. "I come here sometimes," he said, and then, "Would you believe that someone stole my car?"

"Really?" Lacey Macy paused, caught herself. "That's terrible."

Robbie nodded, looking off in the distance. "I reported it and everything. Called the police. They couldn't do nothing. Now I'm just waiting for my ride."

Lacey May didn't bother asking who was coming to get him. It was nobody, or it was someone she didn't want to know.

Robbie pointed across the street. "I left it in that lot, and when I came back, it was gone."

"How long did you leave it there?"

"Not long."

"Maybe it was towed."

"Somebody stole it," Robbie said firmly.

"That's terrible," Lacey May repeated.

They stood silently, letting Robbie's story settle between them. He asked about the girls.

"Oh, they're fine." Lacey May decided against telling him any more. What would be the point? What could he do? He had enough troubles of his own.

"Noelle is in this play," she said. "You should come."

"Yeah, great idea. I should come," he said.

Lacey May watched him smoke, his fingers trembling as he drew from the cigarette. Lacey May realized that if she didn't know him, she would have assumed he was homeless. His palms were stained orange, his neck scruffy and unshaven. He still managed to clean up, most of the time, before she saw him, before he saw the girls. They weren't too far from Central right now. There was Cedar's, that place the kids liked to go, a few streets away.

"Let me drive you home," she said.

"Sure, if you've got nothing better to do."

They were crossing the street, Robbie shuffling behind her, when Lacey May told him about Jenkins. Robbie stopped dead in his tracks.

"You checked the pound?"

"I've been calling every day, and nothing.

You know they don't keep dogs for very long."

"Maybe somebody picked him up and adopted him right away?"

"He's so old," Lacey May said. She saw Robbie's face and went on. "But maybe."

Robbie stood still in the street, his brow furrowed, his mouth hanging open.

"He was such a good dog," he said. Lacey May took him by the arm and pulled him out of the street.

In the car, his odor was even stronger. Lacey May rolled down the window.

"My poor girls," he said. "What are they going to do without their dog?"

Lacey May started the engine. "They'll get over it."

"No, Lacey."

His voice was urgent, and Lacey May saw his eyes were burning, bulging, as he stared at her.

"How could you say that? How could you say — ?"

Robbie slammed his hands against the dashboard. He bunched his fists and punched. *Goddamn it,* he screamed. The car rattled with the force of his blows.

When he was done, he was panting, seething, his cheeks red. He put his head in his hands and slumped over.

"It isn't fair," he said, and Lacey May rubbed him between the shoulders. There were things she had done, things she hadn't done, to spare him. What had she spared him at all?

"Take it easy," she said. "Maybe I was wrong. He might still turn up after all."

The morning of the first dress rehearsal, Gee woke up early to practice his big speech. It was from the beginning of the third act, when Claudio tries to convince his sister Isabella to trade her virginity to Angelo for his freedom. It was twisted, the biggest sign Claudio wasn't all good intentions. He was selfish, pleading, but Gee empathized with his feeling, his terror of death. *Ay, but to die, and go we know not where,* he said. *To lie in cold obstruction and to rot.* Those lines came readily to him. He tripped over the middle parts of the monologue, the *'tis,* the clauses so long they lost their meaning. He rushed until he got to the phrases that anchored him, reminded him of what he was trying to say. *The weariest and most loathed worldly life . . . is a paradise to what we fear of death.*

He did all right, and when he was through, he kissed his fingers, pressed them to the picture of Ray on the wall. He wished his

471

father could come and see him in the play. He went downstairs.

Linette was already dressed and frying eggs in the kitchen. She had agreed to drive him to the school. To his surprise, Jade was at the table, too, her eyes rimmed in black, an untouched cup of coffee in her hands. She was in her pajamas, but she didn't look as if she'd been sleeping at all. Gee wouldn't be surprised if she had slipped in that morning, changed into her pajamas, and come back down. She liked to pretend. He was sick of it.

"Linette told me where you're going."

"It's no big secret."

"You don't listen, Gee, do you? You don't listen at all."

"We already talked about this," he said, but Jade went on.

"You're playing with fire, and I'm trying to help you see that the wrong choice can ruin your life."

"Why don't you just say that having me ruined your life, if that's what you mean?"

"Gee!" Linette interjected. "Show your mother some respect."

"She should just come out and say it, instead of pretending I don't know what she means."

Jade sat calmly at the table, knitting and

unknitting her fingers. "My life isn't ruined," she said. "But believe me, I know things about that girl that you don't want to know."

"I wouldn't care."

"That's cause you're not thinking with your head."

Gee felt a rush of shame. He said nothing, stepped back onto the stairs as if he could turn and run for his room, shut the door.

"If you go on with this play, don't you expect me to come and see it."

Gee was struck dumb, silent. "You would do that?"

"If you want to act like a man, then I'll treat you like one. If you think you're grown, then you be grown."

"But all the other parents will be there."

"Don't expect me to sit there and cheer, like I'm proud, when I'm not."

Gee felt that his mother was testing him. She wanted to show him how weak he was, compared to her. She wanted him to give in. And she was right — he was weak. He wanted her to say she'd changed her mind, she didn't mean it. He waited, and she didn't.

"Linette, will you take me now?"

Linette had stopped working over the

stove. She leaned against the wall, biting her lip hard, and she looked as if she'd burst into tears. She nodded at him, turned off the burner, left the eggs in their oil in the skillet. She gathered her things in a hurry, and Gee slumped out to the courtyard. He heard Linette and Jade arguing. When Linette came out, she flung an arm around him, ferried him to the car, and headed for Central.

"I'm sure by now I've told you why I never wanted to have kids."

"Mm-hmm. You spent your whole life taking care of them, and you didn't want to anymore."

"And look at me. Will you look at life? I've been watching over you for ten years." Linette seemed to blink back tears. "Although you hardly need me now."

"Come on, Linette," he said, because he didn't know what else to say. Did he need her? He liked having her around. Did anybody really need anybody?

"It's been the great privilege of my life. Do you know why?"

"Cause you loved Daddy."

"No, sir. I'm no martyr. Even in my old age." She caressed his face, where he was tender. "I'm with you because I want to be."

Gee was unmoved; he was still thinking

about Jade.

"Right. She's the one who got stuck with me," he said.

"You've got to understand. If your father had lived longer, she might have become a different kind of person. He helped her. But this is the mother you got. And she's trying."

Gee didn't care. He was tired of everyone making excuses for grown-ups who didn't know how to act. He'd woken up feeling triumphant: he was going back to Central, claiming his role in the play. And she'd taken that from him. She saw no good in anything he did.

"I got beat up."

"I know, sweetheart."

"And she still has to have her way."

"I know."

They were off the freeway, rolling across the train tracks that crossed behind the old factories. Soon, they'd be at the school.

"Well, I know I'm not your mother, but you can count on me," she said.

"Linette, I'll be fine. Just watch the road."

"Are you kidding? I've been driving in this city since before you were born. I could get us there with my eyes closed. Now did you hear me? I said, I'll be there. Front row. Even if I won't understand a word —"

A tear loosened itself from Gee before he could stop. He was laughing. He felt lighter, although not completely. The weight Jade had put on him was still there. If he could forget her, he would. If he could erase her, he would.

"So what's this play about anyway?" Linette said. "Explain it to me now so I can follow along."

She listened, pinching her eyes to mime concentration. She looked silly and lovely, all her uncombed hair curling around her ears. He wished he could take a picture of her, the way she was right then.

He told her about Claudio being hauled to jail, how he meant well but wound up in trouble all the same. He had a big speech, a few other lines here and there, but besides that, all he did was pace in his cage, fight off despair while he waited to be released.

"Well, that's more than it sounds like," Linette said. "That's all I've been doing for going on fifteen years."

When Gee walked into the rehearsal, there was a riotous round of applause: whistles and hoots and stomping feet. He felt himself burn under the attention, but it felt good to see the faces of his friends cheering for him: Adira, Shawn, Rosa, the whole cast, except for Beckett, who wasn't there. Mr. Riley clapped his hands on Gee's shoulders, pulled him into their circle. Noelle stood before the stage in an oversized flannel shirt and leggings, her usual boots. Her face was pink and she was clapping fiercely, beaming at him. Gee could sense his morning, all those bad feelings, vaporize around him. He went and stood beside Noelle, and she wrapped an arm around him. Gee felt the ugly parts of him float away.

Eventually, Mr. Riley called them to business, and they all settled down. They would run the play from the top without stopping, but before that, he wanted to talk through the ending, the slurry of betrothals — Juliet to Claudio, the duke to Isabella, Mariana to Angelo. He explained there were many ways they could play the final scene. They could try to make it simple and joyous, but any audience member who was paying attention would see the cracks — all the marriages weren't meant to be equal. But to play it all as uneasy, absurd was a risk — the audience could think they'd botched the play. The audience would be quicker to assume the cast had gotten the ending wrong and acted it badly than to assume Shakespeare had written it to feel strange. Mr. Riley decided to let them vote on how they wanted it all to end.

Noelle was the first to speak up — let it be strange. The audience was bound to be confused anyway, and they shouldn't try to make it all so neat. Nothing in life was like that, anyway, even the good parts.

Adira and Rosa favored a festive end, and they said so. The cast was split down the middle.

Mr. Riley asked Gee to break the stalemate, and this time he didn't hate Mr. Riley for putting him on the spot. He knew exactly what he wanted to say.

"Let's do it like Noelle said," he answered. "Let's do it her way."

And so Gee had the final word, and they ran the play from the top.

After, the theater emptied out, and Noelle stayed behind to put away the props. Gee offered to help her, and Mr. Riley left them alone. He was being too lax, they knew, but neither of them protested. He told them to turn off the lights before they left.

They were hanging costumes back on a rack when Noelle touched his forehead, the cut over his eye, smeared in ointment.

"Does it hurt?"

Besides the cut, he still had a bruise on his cheek, his finger set in a splint, an achy tailbone.

"It's no big deal."

"Stop that," Noelle said. "You know it is."

"My mother wanted me to quit."

"So why'd you come back?"

"You know why," Gee said, and Noelle's cheeks turned a beautiful peach color.

"When'd you get so bold, Gee?" she asked, and he shrugged, his nerve running out on him.

"Come here," she said, and tugged him offstage into the empty rows of chairs. She wanted to ask him something. They sat beside each other as she fished in her book bag. She withdrew the program, simple black text on flimsy blue-green paper.

She pointed to his name, listed near the top, across from the role of Claudio. "Explain it to me," she said.

"Well, my father is the one who started calling me Gee. His last name was Gilbert, and I was Little Gee. It's the only thing I ever remember anyone calling me. But I wanted to use my real name in the program."

"How come?"

"I'm not a little kid anymore."

Noelle nodded solemnly. "Well, I like it. Nelson James Gilbert."

"Just Nelson is fine."

Noelle smiled at him, the program clutched in her hands. She looked down, almost bashfully. For once, she was waiting. Gee had been sure she would be the one to move first. After all, she was the one with experience, and he didn't know what he was doing. Still, he lunged forward and kissed her. She kissed him back. He closed his eyes, gave himself over to feeling.

It was different than he'd imagined. Sloppier, wetter, more exhilarating. He had thought he would be scared. He had thought he might feel guilty, dirty, the way he did when he watched his videos and was swallowed up by desire he knew he shouldn't have. What he felt instead was clear, sure. He felt himself liquefy. He hung his hands around her neck. She looped her arms around his chest. They were close, closer. He opened his mouth, and she opened hers, and Gee tried to transmit everything he had ever felt, everything he was feeling now, with his tongue, his mind. He sent her missives and hoped that she could hear. *You are beautiful,* he said, and *I want you. Forever,* he said. *I am yours.*

17

Alma wore a pink gown, a tiny veil that sliced across her eyes. Her hair gleamed even redder than usual in the glow of dusk, the barn doors flung open despite the cold, so the guests could see the golden sky over the fields of the farm.

Her shoulders were bare under a knit cape, her cheeks and lips bronze, and Diane waited for her at the front, with her sisters, and their dog Princess, who wore a pink bow tie for the occasion. The guests turned to watch Alma with an attention they hadn't for Diane, but Diane couldn't begrudge them. She felt glorious simply to be the one waiting for Alma, and she knew she looked good in a simple white dress, cut to her knees. She blended in with her sisters, also in white. Noelle wore a dress to her ankles, and she held Baby Agnes, outfitted in white lace, on one hip. Margarita wore a dress that looked like a white dressing robe, cut low in the front, barely covering her thighs, tied at the waist with an enormous sash. They had never looked so much alike, the three of them, and they had marveled at how kindred they looked as they posed for pictures before the ceremony, in front of the barn. They had never been the kind of sisters complimented for their similarities; some had even said they looked as if they'd been born of different parents. But in the light, in their white clothes, they were indisputably born of the same blood.

It had been the first great joy of the day — posing with her sisters — feeling gathered between them. She held her niece for a few of the pictures, Baby Agnes cupping her hands around the curls of her hair. Alma's grandmother was a hairdresser, and she had brought her entire kit with her from the Bronx. She had done all the sisters' hair, and Alma's too, that morning in their little house, while they all drank coffee and fretted about the time. Margarita had switched between recording them on her phone, doing makeup, and volunteering to lead the group in a collective breathing exercise.

The second, greater joy was now, watching Alma parade toward her, the tulips in her hand so violently pink they seemed to be aflame. It was a small wedding, no more than seventy people assembled in the barn, and they would all help to rearrange the chairs and set up the dance floor before the reception began.

Lacey May and Hank sat in the front row, Lacey May in a white skirt suit and her new auburn hair. Hank wore a blazer. When the pastor asked who gave Diane in marriage, it was the two of them who stood, and Diane could see Hank was crying. She blew him a kiss, and he waved his soggy handkerchief at her.

She and Alma held hands during the short sermon about faithfulness and trust, the need for mercy in every bond, especially marriage. *Forgive them, Father, for they know not what they do,* the pastor said. There was a reading of a poem that Alma loved, and then they exchanged rings and made their vows. They were promises the women had already made and kept for years, but to say it all out loud, in public, tipped Diane into rapture. She kissed Alma, drew her body close; the dog wedged its nose between their knees.

The party started, and they danced to nineties hip-hop and romantic salsa, "Wagon Wheel" for the North Carolinians. Alma and Diane fed each other slices of the vanilla-and-rose pink cake. They tossed their bouquets. Margarita and Noelle gave speeches, Hank spun a spindly Lacey May around the oak dance floor, and the dog barked whenever the music got too loud. Diane and Alma didn't bother dancing with anyone else, although Diane wasn't particularly good, especially not at the salsa. Alma steered her around the room. They nestled their heads together and cooed over Baby Agnes, the pretty lanterns hung from the beams of the ceiling. They didn't mention Robbie, how he'd never checked into the motel room they had reserved for him, hadn't called. For once, Diane didn't worry he was dead — he was simply elsewhere, himself.

The closest Diane came to mentioning his absence was when she whispered into Alma's ear, "Tonight is better than it has any right to be," and Alma had furrowed her eyebrows and said, "What are you talking about? We've got every right."

They hadn't created a seating plan, so Nelson sat himself with the staff of the doggie day care. They spent their time pummeling bourbon and saying things like *I always knew,* and *they look so natural together* about Alma and Diane. They asked Nelson how he knew the couple, and he was honest, explained that Noelle was his ex-wife. They glanced at Baby Agnes, her fair skin and inexplicable red hair, and pieced together that things had ended badly. They pretended to be interested in his work and asked him whether he ever shot weddings, and when he said he wasn't that kind of photographer, they turned their attention away. Nelson finished one glass of wine and then another, did his best to look preoccupied by his plate of shrimp and grits, instead of Noelle.

She had a soft paunch of a belly visible through the drape of her dress. Her skin was buffed from all her time at the shore, her hair even paler, teased into a high, stiff knot on the top of her head. The little girl made the rounds from her aunts' arms to Inéz, Noelle's old college best friend, who had accompanied her, it seemed, as a plus-one. She and Nelson had stood together in the food line, and she had been civil but cold. It was clear to him that they had lost any bond they once had; Inéz was solid in her fealty to Noelle. Although he'd never felt particularly strongly about her, he had known Inéz long enough that he'd assumed she'd be a fixture in his life: someone he'd see periodically at birthdays and holidays and, someday, funerals. It was disorienting to see she was a stranger to him now.

It was even stranger to be in the company of the Venturas and the Gibbses. They had been his family, however distantly, for so long. Despite all his disdain for Lacey May over the years, their bond had never been tenuous — it had been like Noelle's bond to her: unfortunate but fixed. Who was he to them now? Noelle flitted among her sisters, Alma and her relatives from New York, her mother and Hank. She was still anchored to them, no matter the years she'd spent away. She would never lose them, whereas he had been cut out swiftly, easily. He had no place.

She had hugged him, briefly, when he arrived. She was taking pictures with her sisters and she stole away to thank him for coming and then rushed back to join her fold. He hadn't seen the baby close up; she'd left the girl in the arms of Margarita, who seemed to be frowning at him, bare legged, menacing, her face a painted shield of color.

It was his first time at a wedding without her. Before, when they'd gone to weddings, he was the one with whom she left her drink, the one to whom she announced, *I'm going to the bathroom.* She was the one who reminded him to count his drinks, who dipped a finger in the frosting of his slice of cake without asking, without wondering whether she could. Now he drank one glass of wine after another, waiting for a chance to talk to her alone. She was surrounded constantly by well-wishers, her sisters, the child. He couldn't remember ever feeling so unmoored.

He was ignoring, or being ignored by, the Paws & Friends staff when he felt a tap on his shoulder. He turned and saw Adira, plump and beautiful in a crimson dress with bows at the shoulders.

"Oh, my God, Gee," she said, and embraced him.

"Senator Howard," he said.

She laughed. "It's just the General Assembly for now. I almost didn't recognize you — you look so different."

"It's the veneers," he said. "I didn't expect to see you here."

"Why not? Everyone likes having a dignitary at their wedding." Adira pulled up a chair. "Besides, I used to take my dog to Diane and Alma's camp before I moved to Raleigh."

"You with anyone?"

"If you mean, am I married, no. Not everybody finds their soul mate in high school."

He smiled at her, but she must have seen straight through to his sadness.

"What happened? You know Noelle announced the birth in the class notes, and I couldn't believe it when I saw the picture and there was no mention of you."

"Somehow you just knew that redheaded baby wasn't mine?"

Nelson's joke landed flat, and he decided he might as well tell her the truth.

"More than once?" Adira said. "That doesn't sound like you at all."

"I guess I was trying to blow up my life."

"Well, you did it."

Her voice was firm, but she placed a hand on his knee and squeezed. "You know, I really thought the two of you would make it. You were a big success story for Central. If we'd had brochures, you'd have been on the cover."

"I didn't see us that way."

"And then the fairy tale continued. You went to college together, you got married. You had your careers. The only thing missing was the baby."

"It wasn't ever a fairy tale. But I did love her."

Adira nodded sagely. "It was a lot to overcome."

"What do you mean?"

488

"It's just the two of you combined — your stories. The way you grew up. A marriage is hard enough. Sometimes, it's easier when at least one of you has had a simple life."

It stung to hear Adira speak that way about him and Noelle, as if they'd had no choice in the matter, and there was nothing they could have done. And yet, it felt true. He had often thought that the problem was him. He had never managed to bury the boy he had been.

Adira took away his wine, handed him a glass of water. "Go and talk to her. You're nearly out of time." She nodded at the bartender who was packing up the bar, the wedding planner handing out little bags of rice to send off the brides.

Nelson approached her table, and Noelle propped up the baby to greet him. She planted her feet on her lap, waved her little arm, and said, "Say hello to Mr. Nelson." It nearly ruined him.

He sat beside them, and the baby lurched toward him, unsteady on her feet. Noelle handled her deftly, both hands clutching her waist, and he knew he shouldn't be surprised by how at ease she seemed, how expert. He didn't want to hold the baby or touch her, but he bowed his face close to hers and tried to look friendly, pleased to meet her. She had chunky limbs and a face that was mostly forehead. She looked nothing like Noelle, or like he had imagined their child. He wondered if Noelle was thinking the same thing, but he answered his own question. Noelle beamed at her daughter, brushed her lips against her scalp. She had no reason to cling to the child that wasn't.

As far as he knew, Noelle hadn't disclosed the father to anyone. She hadn't said whether she'd used a donor or had a one-night stand with a man on the coast. If she was seeing someone, he hadn't accompanied her to the wedding.

She introduced him to everyone at the table: Inéz, and Ruth, whom he remembered, and her son, Bailey. Nelson recognized the contempt on his face when he saw it, and he figured Ruth had told him why their marriage had ended. Noelle and Ruth had always been close. He ignored the way Bailey was glaring at him, and asked Noelle to dance.

She handed the baby to Ruth and gave him her hand. On the dance floor, she curled into his body, her hands on his shoulders, as if they were old friends, as if it meant nothing to stand this close.

"How's your mother?"

"Remission," Noelle said. "She refuses to die."

They laughed.

"She says she wants to live long enough to see all her grandchildren born. I don't think Agnes will be enough for her. She's started dropping hints to Diane and Alma, asking Margarita if she's seeing anyone in L.A."

"Lacey May on a mission . . . God help you all."

"Even after everything, she still says the best thing she ever did was have kids and get married. I don't bother asking whether she means the first or second time."

"I don't remember her being such a big advocate for marriage when it was our turn."

"Me neither," Noelle said, and Nelson felt a relief they could still speak the truth to one another, that what they had lived together hadn't been erased.

"Your daughter came out light. Red hair?"

"I know. I spend my whole life frustrated by all the white people around me, and then I wind up with this red-haired baby. It's strange. Sometimes people don't even think I'm her mother."

"And you haven't told anyone about the father? Not even your sisters?"

"You and I aren't going to talk about it

for sure."

"I always knew that if you left me, it would be for some well-adjusted white boy."

"And I always knew I was never going to leave you. Here we are."

The music slowed, and they swayed in place. Nelson looked over Noelle's shoulder at the table where Agnes was with Bailey now, the baby pulling at his ear.

"She's beautiful," he said, and Noelle seemed to forgive him. They revolved around the room. The music was soft and soulful, and they held each other under the dimming lights. She asked him about Vienna, and he didn't want to pretend with her, to give a spiel about cafés and sprawling parks, immaculate trains and world-class museums.

"I've met a lot of former Nazis in bars. A woman spat at me on the street once. But, mostly, it's fine. I've got a flat overlooking the Danube."

"Are you still with that publicist? Jemima?"

There would be no good in telling Noelle about the women he picked up and left, or who picked up and left him. They meant little to him. He liked making coffee for someone in the morning, the scent of a woman on his sheets. Sex and companionship could be simple, amiable things. Jemima visited sometimes, and they both understood it would be their habit until it wasn't anymore.

"There's no one like you," Nelson said.

"How unfortunate you couldn't remember that when you decided to fuck her."

He said nothing. He deserved it. He felt her stiffen as if she might move away, leave him on the dance floor, but she stayed where she was. Underneath her makeup, she looked tired. He wanted to kiss the dark circles under her eyes.

"Is it what you thought it would be? Being a mother?"

"It's worse. I couldn't breastfeed. During the delivery, I tore right open. I still can't ride my bicycle. And community theater directors don't get maternity leave. I pay a babysitter a few days a week. I am so broke. But she's objectively perfect. Do you see her?"

Nelson nodded but didn't look toward the child. He had a vision of Noelle, the day they had started trying. He had been reading on the bed when she surged into the bedroom, already naked, brandishing a tiny blue-and-white strip. She was ovulating, she said. She was ready, she said. Nelson was the one who had been unsure; he didn't want anything to disrupt the equilibrium they had. But then he saw her climb onto the mattress on her knees, teetering toward him, her arms wide open, and there had been no question he would oblige.

He rested his face against hers. He wanted to kiss her.

"You know what I kept thinking about during the ceremony?" she said.

"Our wedding?"

"The play."

"Which one?"

Measure for Measure."

"Oh God," he said. "My debut and my denouement."

They both laughed.

"Something about the pageantry of it all — the marching down the aisle, the people clapping. It reminded me of opening night."

The first performance of the play had gone as smoothly as anyone could have imagined. The audience was smaller than Mr. Riley had hoped: just the cast members' parents and siblings, a few of the girls from Concerned Students for Justice. Even with the modest crowd, they were all nervous. Alex, who had been recast as the duke, threw up backstage. Adira, radiant in her nun's costume, had led them in prayer before the curtain went up. And Nelson, somehow, had felt surprisingly calm. He knew the play wasn't resting on his shoulders; it wasn't about him. He needed only to be a part of the organism, and together, they'd create the play, just as they had in the dress rehearsals. The feeling was magic.

Miraculously, everyone remembered their lines. Noelle made sure the curtains closed and opened when they were supposed to; she positioned them backstage, brushed lint off their costumes. And Nelson had projected his voice better than he had known he could, aided by the brightness of the lights, how little of the audience he could see.

And yet, despite their triumphs, the audience never quite laughed when they were supposed to; the emotions the actors meant to convey were never quite the ones that came through. Isabella's horror at Angelo's predation came across as mild annoyance; the duke's pomposity seemed to be rage; only Angelo's lust was clearly expressed, which made the parents fidget in their seats. The final slew of betrothals at the end left the crowd puzzled, and they clapped halfheartedly as they tried to sort out what had happened, whether all was well. No one was very good, and they knew it, but it didn't matter. For two brief hours, they melded

495

together, the kids who had been at Central before, and the ones who were new. At the end, they linked arms and bowed, and Mr. Riley handed out roses, two for Noelle. And Noelle and Nelson had climbed down from the stage to greet their families, Linette in the front row, Lacey May and Hank with the girls. Jade and Robbie were nowhere to be seen, and they held hands and presented themselves for the first time as a unit: *Nelson and Noelle.*

"I was lucky to have you love me then, despite all my problems."

"Please," Noelle said. "I was the one getting drunk and knocked up and running away."

"At least you knew who you were. I couldn't stand being me."

"You're fine, you know. You always have been. But you still can't see it, can you?"

She unglued her cheek from his, stared at him plainly. Nelson felt his skin thrum; he was desperate for her to say more.

"I'm sorry," she said, shaking her head, her eyes glistening. "I can't make you know. It isn't my job anymore."

She kissed the palm of his hand and then returned to her daughter. Nelson wanted to follow her, the urge so strong he nearly did. Alone on the dance floor, he finally felt himself drunk, his body listing, a searing pressure in his eyes and skull. Adira steadied him in her arms. She steered him beyond the barn, its hardwood floors. His shoes sank into the mud. They crested the pasture in the darkness, headed for the lot.

"Where can I drop you off?" she asked.

His hotel was near the airport, but he knew where he needed Adira to take him.

"I have to see her," he said. "Take me to see her."

The new house where Jade lived wasn't far from the main street. It was brick, two stories, the screened-in porch obscured by a massive rhododendron. The neighborhood was quiet, surreptitiously wealthy. An elementary school and its playground was on one side of the street, a stone Baptist church on the other, oaks and dogwoods in the front lawns, a large park at the end of the road, all hills and towering magnolias. It was the kind of neighborhood where the university professors bought their homes years ago, and where the new tech workers were just moving in. He had only ever driven through this part of the city before.

Adira parked neatly in front of the house, and he invited her in.

"No, thank you. I don't want to be a party

to that conversation. But before you go, Gee, please . . ." She handed him a tin of mints and waved a tiny can of air freshener. He worked the lid open and swallowed a handful while she sprayed him down.

He thanked Adira, hugged her hard. He watched her drive away, headed for Raleigh. He found himself trembling, terrified to see his own mother. It had been years.

Jade startled when she opened the door. He watched her face shift from disbelief to suspicion, then a smile that seemed wary, questioning. She wore a long black robe, her hair braided and twisted into a crown. León appeared behind her in the threshold in checkered pajama pants and a matching robe. It was almost too intimate to see them side by side, dressed for bed, but he shouldn't have expected anything different. Nelson looked down at his shoes, his vision blurry, and he wondered whether they could notice him wobbling on his feet.

He followed them into the house. The kitchen was all hardwood and blue tile, brightly colored paintings on the wall. A black cat weaved between their legs, leapt onto the windowsill. He hadn't known his mother had a cat; he'd never known her to care for animals.

León made tea and kept up the small talk.

He asked about the wedding once Nelson explained why he was in town. He asked about Vienna, his latest residency. He complained about his own work at the hospital, said Jade was the one really making a difference at the clinic. She'd been elected to the board of a statewide reproductive rights group. León filled the silence, and Nelson and Jade sipped their tea, avoided looking at one another.

Nelson wondered whether his mother was angry with him. He'd never visited her in this house, although he knew the address from the occasional mail, her Christmas cards. He called her every once in a while, whenever he had good news, and they'd gloss over the last several months of their lives in a few minutes. *We bought a house; I'm traveling to Paris; the book is coming out in hardcover.* He had told her about the divorce matter-of-factly, long after Noelle had served him with papers. He hadn't mentioned it again, and she hadn't asked.

But Jade's face betrayed nothing, not elation, or rage. He wanted to hear her say she was upset he'd traveled across the ocean for the Venturas and not for her. He wanted her to say he had been wrong to give his whole life to Noelle and then betray her. But she

499

went on sipping her tea, leaning close to her lover.

León mentioned that they'd gone to see Linette recently at the nursing home. She didn't recognize Jade anymore, but they still went to bring her flowers and take her for walks.

"You should see her if you've got the time. How long are you in town?" León said.

"It doesn't make sense to go now. You should have come sooner, when she was asking for you. She used to ask about you all the time."

Jade was staring at him finally. Something in her had turned. Through the fog of his drunkenness, he felt himself quake. Maybe she'd let him have it, and that would be right. Someone ought to punish him.

León seemed to sense the charge between them. He announced he had rounds in the morning and was off to bed. He clapped Nelson on the shoulder, kissed Jade, and climbed the stairs too swiftly for a man in his sixties.

Jade and Nelson were left alone, their bare feet on the cold tile.

"Was my old friend there at the wedding? Lacey May?"

"I didn't speak to her, but I saw her. She's doing fine."

Jade chuckled. "You know how they say the good die young? Well."

The cat was perched now on the counter, sniffing at a pile of dishes waiting to be washed. Nelson offered a hand tentatively to the cat, who cowered away, hid behind Jade.

"You mad at me over Linette?"

"That's my fault," Jade said. "I realized a long time ago that if you didn't understand you were supposed to come home, it was because I didn't teach you."

"You never asked me to come home either."

"Would you believe me if I said I didn't know any better?"

Her face was gaunt, minuscule wisps of gray curling out of her braids. Her fingers were still ornamented with gold rings, glittering black and white stones. He could see the residue of her dark eye makeup, partially scrubbed away. She seemed as invincible as ever. He knew he'd never be as remarkable as she was — the awareness snaked at the back of his mind every time he seemed to accomplish something: a fellowship abroad, a sleek redesign of his website. He'd been given so much more, and still he had disappointed her.

"I want to show you something," Jade

501

said, and she led him to the rear of the house.

The sunroom was three walls of glass looking out onto the dark. In one corner, there was a record player, a stereo, Jade's collection of albums. An upholstered rocking chair nuzzled a side table stacked high with books. Big potted palms were strewn around the room.

"This is my place in the house," Jade said. "León has a room in the attic that's just for him. It's where we each go when we want to be alone."

Nelson looked around the sunroom, tried to imagine all the hours his mother spent there. He pictured them on different continents, living in parallel, in solitary, airy rooms, nursing glasses of whiskey or tending to plants, looking out the window onto different stretches of earth.

"We've got chickens in the yard," Jade said. "I'll have León make you some eggs in the morning."

"I'll be moving on by then."

"All right."

Still, she was letting him go, and it plunged him into an old sinking feeling.

He spotted the shrine on his own. It was a pine hutch littered with plants, their vines hanging over the shelves. It was filled with knickknacks that he couldn't tell the meaning of — a postcard of a beach in Orlando, a folded red-and-pink plaid shirt, a half-dozen ceramic ramekins. There was the photograph of him and Ray, the one that had hung in the kitchen of their first apartment, then in his bedroom at Linette's. Nelson looked at their sunlit faces. Jade handed him a newspaper clipping in a gilded frame.

It was the article about the shop, Linette and Ray and his devil's food, the revival on Beard Street. The black-and-white photographs were too grainy for Nelson to see the pastries his father had made that day in the shop very well, but Jade had pasted a photograph of Ray onto the page. It was a faded snapshot of Ray smiling in his apron, his hands knotted behind his back. He looked earnest and dimpled, far younger than Nelson would ever have guessed. He looked at him now, and Nelson saw a man in his twenties, just beginning his life, too young for what would happen to him. He was older now than his father would ever be. He had been older than his father would ever be for nearly a decade.

"Since he missed getting his picture taken that day, I thought I'd put one in there," Jade said.

"León doesn't mind you keeping all this around?"

"Ray is a part of me. Where I go, he goes. León wouldn't expect me to hide him."

"Then why'd you take down his picture in the first place? Why'd it take you so long to put it back up?"

Jade sank into her armchair.

"I was so angry at what the world had put on you. I didn't want you to miss him too much, to carry that burden any more than you had to."

"He was my father."

"I wanted you to know you'd be fine on your own, the way I was."

"But we weren't alone."

"I see that now," Jade said, her eyes on him. Her gaze was tender, serious. "I miss him. Did I ever tell you that? I've never stopped missing him."

Nelson realized he was biting down on his cheek. Any harder and he'd taste his own blood. He unclamped his jaw and felt dizzy, sick. He sat on the floor across from his mother. He wanted to keep talking to her. He wanted to tell her everything.

"Noelle has a baby now. With someone else."

"That was quick."

"We were going to have one, too, but she

lost it. I didn't tell you. I wanted to pretend it never happened."

Jade attempted to shush him. She reached for him. He shook his head, pushed her away. He felt frightened, as if someone were watching them, as if an unseen danger — cyclonic, absolute — would swallow them up, if they weren't careful.

"She needed me, and I left. What kind of man is that? What kind of man am I?"

Jade fell out of her chair, cast her arms around her son. He tried to break free of her, but she wouldn't loosen her hold on him. He gave way to her arms. She held him to her breast, cradled him roughly.

"My boy," she said. "My sweet boy."

ACKNOWLEDGMENTS

Thank you to the inimitable Kristyn Keene Benton. You are the fiercest champion, and I am so grateful for all your sharp shooting and care for my writing and my career. Thank you also to Cat Shook for the early reads and encouragement, and for always being there.

Thank you to the marvelous team at Grand Central for ushering this book into the world, especially Seema Mahanian. Thank you for pushing me and helping this novel to grow. I am so proud of what we did together.

Thank you to my brilliant ninth-inning readers who swept in with notes, wisdom, and clarity at the final hour: Crystal Hana Kim, Meghan Flaherty, and Thomas Sun. Crystal, I am grateful for your candor and generosity, your friendship and frankness. Thomas, your mind for story inspires me, and it's useful that you're usually right.

Thank you for being honest, present, and such a dear friend. Meghan, you are my trusted companion in motherhood and in letters — no one knows how to work a sentence like you do. Thank you for encouraging me right up until the very end.

I wouldn't have been able to finish this book without those who held my baby and who held me as I became a mother. Gracias a mi querida suegra Miyerladi Pérez por ayudarme tantas veces y por su ternura y sus brazos abiertos. Gracias a mis tías Mayra Ureña y Ylonka Olivo por cuidar a mi niña y cuidarme a mí. No me siento sola porque las tengo a ustedes. Thank you to my dear friends who traveled to offer hands-on help for days at a time: Maddox Pennington, Madeline Johnson, and Frances Kelley. And special thanks to the mothers who went before me, especially Erin Branch and Meghan Flaherty, who shared in the journey so closely. Thank you to the many friends, unnamed here, who offered support and love.

Finally, thank you to my husband, Jonathan, for your unwavering belief in my writing, your ideas (solicited and otherwise), and your love. Thank you for whispering in my ear that I could do it. And thank you to my daughter, Esmeralda. You are amazing company, and I am so fortunate to be your mother. I love you so completely.

ABOUT THE AUTHOR

Naima Coster is the author of *Halsey Street,* and a finalist for the 2018 Kirkus Prize for fiction. In 2020, she received the National Book Foundation's "5 Under 35" honor. Naima's stories and essays have appeared in the *New York Times, Kweli,* the *Paris Review Daily, Catapult, The Rumpus,* and elsewhere. She holds an MFA in creative writing from Columbia University, as well as degrees from Fordham University and Yale. She has taught writing for over a decade in community settings, youth programs, and universities. She lives in Brooklyn with her family.

The employees of Thorndike Press hope you have enjoyed this Large Print book. All our Thorndike, Wheeler, and Kennebec Large Print titles are designed for easy reading, and all our books are made to last. Other Thorndike Press Large Print books are available at your library, through selected bookstores, or directly from us.

For information about titles, please call:
(800) 223-1244

or visit our website at:
gale.com/thorndike

To share your comments, please write:
Publisher
Thorndike Press
10 Water St., Suite 310
Waterville, ME 04901